# STARPLEX

# STARPLEX

## ROBERT J. SAWYER

ACE BOOKS, NEW YORK

This book is an Ace original edition,
and has never been previously published.

STARPLEX

An Ace Book / published by arrangement with
the author
This novel was serialized in the July through October 1996 issues
of *Analog Science Fiction and Fact* magazine.

ISBN: 0-441-00372-9

ACE®
Ace Books are published by The Berkley Publishing Group,
200 Madison Avenue, New York, NY 10016.
ACE and the "A" design are trademarks
belonging to Charter Communications, Inc.

PRINTED IN THE UNITED STATES OF AMERICA

# For Ariel Reich

Every SF writer should be lucky enough to have a good friend who is both a Ph.D. in physics *and* a lawyer specializing in intellectual property. Thanks, Ari, for helping me launch the *Argo* on its relativistic flight, work out the Lagrange points for the Quintaglio system, design a chemical structure for a new form of matter, and prosecute an extraterrestrial defendant.

# Acknowledgments

This novel coalesced from my primordial cloud of ideas with the help of editors Susan Allison at Ace and Dr. Stanley Schmidt at *Analog*; Richard Curtis; Dr. Ariel Reich; fellow writers J. Brian Clarke, James Alan Gardner, Mark A. Garland, and Jean-Louis Trudel; proofreader extraordinaire Howard Miller; and my usual incisive manuscript readers: Ted Bleaney, David Livingstone Clink, Terence M. Green, Edo van Belkom, Andrew Weiner, and, most of all, my lovely wife, Carolyn Clink.

# STARPLEX

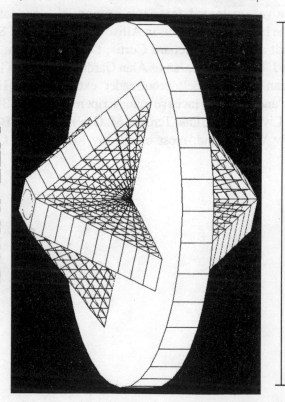

◄ Deck 1 sensor array

◄ Upper habitat modules (4)

210 meters tall

◄ Central disk (ocean deck, engineering torus, docking bays, cargo holds)

◄ Lower habitat modules (4)

◄ Deck 70 sensor array

290 meters diameter

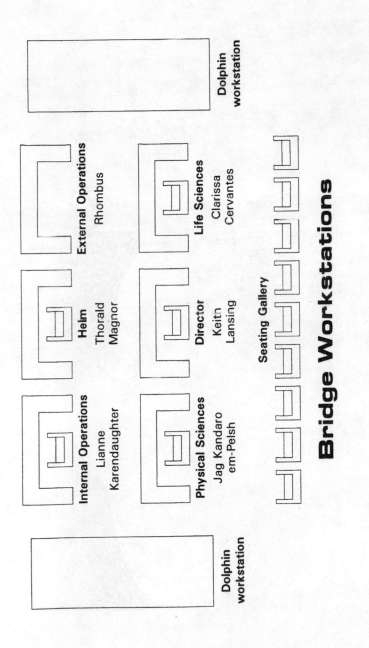

Dolphin
workstation

Internal Operations
Lianne
Karendaughter

Helm
Thorald
Magnor

External Operations
Rhombus

Physical Sciences
Jag Kandaro
em-Pelsh

Director
Keith
Lansing

Life Sciences
Clarissa
Cervantes

Seating Gallery

Dolphin
workstation

# Bridge Workstations

*Even though the arc of the moral universe is long, it bends toward justice.*

—Martin Luther King, Jr.

# ALPHA DRACONIS

*There would be hell to pay.*

*The gravity had already been bled off, and Keith Lansing was now floating in zero-g. Normally he found that experience calming, but not today. Today, he exhaled wearily and shook his head. The damage to Starplex would cost billions to repair. And how many Commonwealth citizens were dead? Well, that would come out in the eventual inquest—something he wasn't looking forward to one bit.*

*All the amazing things they had discovered, including first contact with the darmats, could still end up being overshadowed by politics—or even interstellar war.*

*Keith touched the green GO button on the console in front of him. There was a banging sound, conducted through the glassteel of the hull, as his travel pod disengaged from the access ring on the rear wall of the docking bay. The entire run was preprogrammed into the pod's computer: exiting Starplex's docks, flying over to the* shortcut, entering it, exiting at the periphery of the Tau Ceti system, and moving into one of the docking bays on Grand Central, the United Nations space station that controlled traffic through the shortcut closest to Earth.

And, because it was all preprogrammed, Keith had nothing to do during the journey but reflect on everything that had happened.

He didn't appreciate it at the time, but that, in itself, was a miracle. Traveling halfway across the galaxy in the blink of an eye had become routine. It was a far cry from the excitement of eighteen years ago, when Keith had been on hand for the discovery of the shortcut network—a vast array of apparently artificial gateways that permeated the galaxy, allowing instantaneous point-to-point transfer. Back then, Keith had called the whole thing magic. After all, it had taken all of Earth's resources twenty years earlier to establish the New Beijing colony on Tau Ceti IV, just 11.8 light-years from Sol, and New New York on Epsilon Indi III, only 11.2 light-years away. But now humans routinely popped from one side of the galaxy to the other.

And not just humans. Although the shortcut builders had never been found, there were other forms of intelligent life in the Milky Way, including the Waldahudin and the Ibs, who, together with Earth's humans and dolphins, had established the Commonwealth of Planets eleven years ago.

Keith's pod reached the edge of docking bay twelve and moved out into space. The pod was a transparent bubble, designed to keep one person alive for a couple of hours. Around its equator was a thick white band containing life-support equipment and maneuvering thrusters. Keith turned and looked back at the mothership he was leaving behind.

The docking bay was on the rim of Starplex's great central disk. As the pod pulled farther away, Keith could see the interlocking triangular habitat modules, four on top and four more on the bottom.

Christ, thought Keith as he looked at his ship. Jesus Christ.

The windows in the four lower habitat modules were all

*dark. The central disk was crisscrossed with hairline laser scorches. As his pod moved downward, he saw stars through the gaping circular hole in the disk where a cylinder ten decks thick had been carved out of it—*

*Hell to pay, thought Keith again. Bloody hell to pay.*

*He turned around and looked forward, out the curving bubble. He'd long ago given up scanning the heavens for any sign of a shortcut. They were invisible, infinitesimal points until something touched them, as—he glanced at his console—his pod was going to do in forty seconds. Then they swelled up to swallow whatever was coming through.*

*He'd be on Grand Central for perhaps eight hours, long enough to report to Premier Petra Kenyatta about the attack on Starplex. Then he'd pop back here. Hopefully by that time, Jag and Longbottle would have news about the other big problem they were facing.*

*The pod's maneuvering thrusters fired in a complex pattern. To exit the network back at Tau Ceti, he'd have to enter the local shortcut from above and behind. The stars moved as the pod modified its course to the proper angle, and then—*

*—and then it touched the point. Through the transparent hull, Keith saw the fiery purple discontinuity between the two sectors of space pass over the pod, mismatched starfields fore and aft. To the rear, the eerie green light of the region he was leaving, and up ahead, pink nebulosity—*

*Nebulosity? That can't be right. Not at Tau Ceti.*

*But as the pod completed its passage, there could be no doubt: he'd come out at the wrong place. A beautiful rose-colored nebula, like a splayed six-fingered hand, covered four degrees of sky. Keith wheeled around, looking out in all directions. He knew well the constellations visible from Tau Ceti—slightly skewed versions of the same ones seen from Earth, including Boötes, which contained bright Arcturus and Sol itself. But these were unfamiliar stars.*

*Keith felt adrenaline pumping. New sectors of space were being opened at a great rate, as new exits became valid choices on the shortcut network. Clearly, this was a shortcut that had only just come on-line, making more narrow the acceptable angles of approach to reach Tau Ceti.*

*No need to panic, thought Keith. He could get to his intended destination easily enough. He'd just have to reenter the shortcut on a slightly different path, making sure he didn't vary at all from the mathematical center of the cone of acceptable angles for Grand Central Station.*

*Still—another new sector! That made five in the last year. God, he thought, it was too bad they'd had to cannibalize half of* Starplex's *planned sister ship for parts; they could use another exploration mothership immediately if things kept on like this.*

*Keith checked his flight recorder, making sure he'd be able to return to this place. The instruments seemed to be operating perfectly. His first instinct was to explore, discovering whatever this new sector had to offer, but a travel pod was designed only for quick journeys through shortcuts. Besides, Keith had a meeting to get to and—he glanced at his watch implant —only forty-five minutes before it would begin. He looked down at his control panel and keyed in instructions for another pass through the shortcut network. He then checked the settings that had brought him here— and frowned. Why, he had come through at precisely the right angle for Tau Ceti. He'd never heard of a shortcut transfer going wrong before, but . . .*

*When he looked up, the starship was there.*

*It was shaped like a dragon, with a long, serpentine central hull and vast swept-back extensions that looked like wings. The entire thing consisted of curves and smooth edges, and there was no detailing on its robin's-egg-blue surface, no sign of seams or windows or vents, no obvious engines. The whole thing must have been glowing, since there were no stars nearby to illuminate it, and no shadows fell across any part of its surface. Keith had thought* Starplex *beautiful before its recent battle scars, but it had still always seemed manufactured and functional. This alien ship, though, was art.*

*The dragon ship was moving directly toward Keith's pod. The readout on his console said it was almost a kilometer* long. Keith grabbed the pod's joystick, wanting to get out of the approaching ship's path, but suddenly the dragon came to a dead stop relative to the pod, fifty meters ahead.

Keith's heart was pounding. Whenever a new shortcut came on-line, Starplex's first job was to look for any signs of whatever intelligence had activated the shortcut by passing through it for the first time. But here, in a one-person travel pod, he lacked the signaling equipment and computing power needed to even attempt communications.

Besides, there had been no sign of the ship when he'd surveyed the sky moments ago. Any vessel that could move that quickly then stop dead in space had to be the product of very advanced technology. Keith was in over his head. He needed if not all of Starplex, at least one of the diplomatic craft it carried in its docking bays. He tapped the key that should have started his pod back toward the shortcut.

But nothing happened. No—that wasn't quite right. Craning his neck, Keith could see his pod's maneuvering thrusters firing on the outside of the ring around the habitat bubble. And yet the pod wasn't moving at all; the background stars were rock steady. Something had to be holding him in place, but if it was a tractor beam, it was the gentlest one he'd ever encountered. A travel pod was fragile; a conventional tractor would have made its glassteel hull groan at the seams.

Keith looked again at the beautiful ship, and as he watched a—a docking bay, it must have been—appeared in its side, beneath one of the curving wings. There had been no sign of a space door moving away to reveal it. The opening simply wasn't there one instant, and the next instant, it was —a cube-shaped hollow in the belly of the dragon. Keith found his pod moving now in the opposite direction he was telling it to go, moving toward the alien vessel.

Despite himself, he was starting to panic. He was all in favor of first contact, but preferred it on more equal terms. Besides, he had a wife to get back to, a son away at university, a life he very much wanted to continue living.

*The pod floated into the bay, and Keith saw a wall wink into existence behind him, closing the cube off from space. The interior was lit from all six sides. The pod was presumably still being held by the tractor beam—no one would pull an object inside just to let it crash into the far wall under its own inertia. But nowhere could Keith see a beam emitter.*

*As the pod continued its journey, Keith tried to think rationally. He had entered the shortcut at the right angle to come out at Tau Ceti; no mistake had been made. And yet, somehow, he had been— been diverted here . . .*

*Which meant that whoever controlled this interstellar dragon knew more about the shortcuts than the Commonwealth races did.*

*And then it hit him.*

*The realization.*

*The horrible realization.*

Time to pay the toll.

I

It had been like a gift from the gods: the discovery that the Milky Way galaxy was permeated by a vast network of artificial shortcuts that allowed for instantaneous journeys between star systems. No one knew who had built the shortcuts, or what their exact purpose was. Whatever hugely advanced race created them had left no other trace of its existence.

Scans made by hyperspace telescopes suggested that there were four *billion* separate shortcut exits in our galaxy, or roughly one for every hundred stars. The shortcuts were easy to spot in hyperspace: each one was surrounded by a distinctive sphere of orbiting tachyons. But of all those shortcuts, only two dozen appeared to be active. The others clearly existed, but there seemed to be no way to move to them.

The closest shortcut to Earth was in the Oort cloud of Tau Ceti. Through it, ships could jump seventy thousand light-

years to Rehbollo, the Waldahud homeworld. Or they could
jump fifty-three thousand light-years to Flatland, home of
the bizarre Ib race. But the shortcut exit that existed near
Polaris, for instance, just eight hundred light-years away,
was inaccessible. It, like almost all the others, was dormant.

A particular shortcut would not work as an *exit* for ships
arriving from other shortcuts until it had first been used
locally as an *entrance*. Thus, the Tau Ceti shortcut had not
been a valid exit choice for other races until the UN sent a
probe through it, eighteen years ago, back in 2076. Three
weeks later, a Waldahud starship popped out of that same
shortcut—and suddenly humans and dolphins were not
alone.

Many speculated that this was how the shortcut network
had been designed to work: sectors of the galaxy were
quarantined until at least one race within them had reached
technological maturity. Given how few shortcuts were
active, some argued that Earth's two sentient species, *Homo
sapiens* and *Tursiops truncatus,* were therefore among the
first races in the galaxy to reach that level.

The next year, ships from the Ib homeworld popped
through at Tau Ceti and near Rehbollo—and soon the four
races agreed to an experimental alliance, dubbed the Commonwealth of Planets.

In order to expand the usable shortcut network, seventeen
years ago each homeworld launched thirty *boomerangs.*
Each of these probes flew at their maximum hyperdrive
velocity—twenty-two times the speed of light—toward
dormant shortcuts that had been detected by their tachyon
coronas. Upon arrival, each boomerang would dive through
and return home, thus activating the shortcut as a valid exit.

So far, boomerangs had reached twenty-one additional
shortcuts within a radius of 375 light-years from one or
another of the three homeworlds. Originally, these sectors
were explored by small ships. But the Commonwealth
had realized a more comprehensive solution was needed: a
giant mothership from which exploration surveys could be
launched, a ship that could serve not only as a research base
during the crucial initial exploration of a new sector, but

also could function as embassy for the Commonwealth, if need be. A vast starship capable of not just astronomical research, but of undertaking first-contact missions as well. And so, a year ago, in 2093, *Starplex* was launched. Funded by all three homeworlds and constructed at the Rehbollo orbital shipyards, it was the largest vessel ever built by any of the Commonwealth races: 290 meters at its widest point, seventy decks thick, a total enclosed volume of 3.1 million cubic meters, outfitted with a crew of a thousand beings and fifty-four small auxiliary ships of various designs.

*Starplex* was currently 368 light-years due galactic south of Flatland, exploring the vicinity of a recently activated short cut. The closest star was an F-class subgiant a quarter-light–year away. It was surrounded by four asteroid belts, but no planets. An uneventful mission so far—nothing remarkable astronomically, and no alien radio signals detected. *Starplex*'s staff was busy winding down its explorations. In seven days, another boomerang was due to reach its designated shortcut target, this one 376 light-years away from Rehbollo. *Starplex*'s next scheduled assignment was to investigate that sector.

Everything seemed so peaceful, until—

"Lansing, you will hear me out."

Keith Lansing stopped walking down the cold corridor, sighed, and rubbed his temples. Jag's untranslated voice sounded like a dog barking, with occasional hisses and snarls thrown in for good measure. His translated voice —rendered in an old-fashioned Brooklyn accent—wasn't much better: harsh, sharp, nasty.

"What is it, Jag?"

"The apportioning of resources aboard *Starplex*," barked the being, "is all wrong—and you are to blame for that. Before we move to the next shortcut, I demand you rectify this. You consistently shortchange the physics division and give preferential treatment to life sciences."

Jag was a Waldahud, a shaggy piglike creature with six limbs. After the last ice age ended on Rehbollo, the polar

caps had melted, flooding much of the land and crisscrossing what remained with rivers. The Waldahudin's ancestors
adapted to a semiaquatic lifestyle, their bodies becoming
well insulated with fat overlain by brown fur to keep out the
chill of the river waters they lived in. Keith took a deep
breath and looked at Jag. *He's an alien, remember. Different
ways, different manners.* He tried to keep his tone even. "I
don't think that's quite fair."

More dog barks. "You give special treatment to life
sciences because your spouse heads that division."

Keith forced a small laugh, although his heart was
pounding with repressed anger. "Rissa sometimes says the
opposite—that I don't give her enough resources, that I'm
bending over backward to appease you."

"She manipulates you, Lansing. She—what is the human
metaphor? She has you wrapped around her little finger."

Keith thought about showing Jag a different finger.
*They're all like this,* he thought. *An entire planet of
quarrelsome, bickering, argumentative pigs.* He tried not to
sound weary. "What exactly is it that you want, Jag?"

The Waldahud raised his upper left hand, and ticked off
stubby, hairy fingers with his upper right. "Two more
probeships assigned exclusively to physical-sciences missions. An additional Central Computer bank dedicated to
astrophysics. Twenty more staff members."

"The staff additions are impossible," said Keith. "We
don't have apartments to house them. I'll see what I can do
about your other requests, though." He paused for a second,
and then: "But in the future, Jag, I think you'll find that I'm
easier to convince when you don't bring my private life into
the discussion."

Jag barked harshly. "I knew it!" said the translated voice.
"You make your decisions based on personal feelings, not
on the merit of the argument. You are truly unfit to hold the
post of director."

Keith felt his anger about to boil over. He tried to calm
himself, and closed his eyes, hoping to summon a tranquil
image. He expected to see his wife's face, but the picture
that came to him was of an Asian beauty two decades

younger than Rissa—and that just made Keith madder at himself. He opened his eyes. "Look," he said, a quaver in his voice, "I don't give a damn whether you approve of the choice of me as *Starplex* director or not. The fact is that I *am* director, and will be for another three years. Even if you could somehow get me replaced before my term is over, the agreed-to rotation calls for a human to hold this post at this time. If you get rid of me—or if I quit because I'm fed the hell up with you—you're still going to be reporting to a human. And some of us don't like you"—he stopped himself before he said "you pigs"—"at all."

"Your posturing does you no credit, Lansing. The resources I am demanding are for the good of our mission."

Keith sighed again. He was getting too old for this. "I'm not going to argue anymore, Jag. You've made your request; I'll give it all the consideration it is due."

The Waldahud's four square nostrils flared. "I am amazed," said Jag, "that Queen Trath ever thought we could work with humans." He rotated on his black hooves, and headed down the corridor without another word. Keith stood there for two minutes, doing calming breathing exercises, then headed along the chilly corridor toward the elevator station.

Keith Lansing and his wife, Rissa Cervantes, shared a standard human apartment aboard *Starplex:* L-shaped living room, a bedroom, a small office with two desks, one bathroom with human fixtures, and a second with multispecies fixtures. There was no kitchen, but Keith, who liked to cook, had rigged up a small oven so that he could indulge his hobby.

The main door to the apartment slid open, and Keith stormed in. Rissa must have arrived a few minutes earlier; she came out of the bedroom naked, obviously preparing for her midday shower.

"Hi, Chesterton," she said, smiling. But the smile faded away, and Keith imagined that she could see the tension in his face, his forehead creased, his mouth downturned. "What's wrong?"

Keith flopped himself onto the couch. From this angle, he was facing the dartboard Rissa had mounted on one wall. The three darts were clustered in the tiny sixty-point part of the triple-scoring band—Rissa was shipboard champion. "Another run-in with Jag," said Keith.

Rissa nodded. "It's his way," she said. "It's their way."

"I know. I know. But, Christ, it's hard to take sometimes."

They had a large real window on one wall, showing the starfield outside the ship, dominated by the bright F-class star nearby. Two other walls were capable of displaying holograms. Keith was from Calgary, Alberta; Rissa had been born in Spain. One wall showed glacier-fed Lake Louise, with the glorious Canadian Rockies rising up behind it; the other a long view of downtown Madrid, with its appealing mixture of sixteenth- and twenty-first-century architecture.

"I thought you'd show up here around now," said Rissa.

"I was waiting to shower with you." Keith was pleasantly surprised. They'd showered together a lot when they'd first gotten married, almost twenty years ago, but had gotten out of the habit as the years wore on. The necessity of showering twice a day to minimize the human body odor Waldahudin found so offensive had turned the cleansing ritual into an irritating bore, but maybe their impending anniversary had Rissa feeling more romantic than usual.

Keith smiled at her and began to undress. Rissa headed into the main bathroom and began running the water. *Starplex* was such a contrast to the ships of Keith's youth, like the *Lester B. Pearson* he'd traveled on back when first contact with the Waldahudin had been made. In those days, he'd had to be content with sonic showers. There was something to be said for carrying a miniature ocean around as part of your ship.

He followed her into the bathroom. She was already in the shower, soaking down her long, black hair. Once she'd moved out from under the shower head, Keith jockeyed into position, enjoying the sensation of her wet body sliding past his. He'd lost half his hair over the years, and what was left he kept short. Still, he massaged his scalp vigorously, trying to work out his anger with Jag in doing so.

He scrubbed Rissa's back for her, and she scrubbed his in turn. They rinsed, then he turned off the water. If he hadn't been so angry, perhaps they'd have made love, but . . .

Dammit. He began to towel off.

"I hate this," Keith said.

Rissa nodded. "I know."

"It's not that I hate Jag—not really. I hate . . . hate myself. Hate feeling like a bigot." He ran the towel up and down his back. "I mean, I know the Waldahudin have different ways. I *know* that, and I try to accept it. But— Christ, I hate myself for even thinking this—they're all the same. Obnoxious, argumentative, pushy. I've never met one who wasn't." He sprayed deodorant under each arm. "The whole idea of thinking I know all about somebody just because I know what race they belong to is abhorrent—it's everything I was brought up to fight against. And now I find myself doing it day in and day out." He sighed. "Waldahud. Pig. The terms are interchangeable in my mind."

Rissa had finished drying herself. She pulled on a beige long-sleeve shirt and fresh panties. "They think the same way about us, you know. All humans are weak, indecisive. They don't have any *korbaydin*."

Keith managed a small laugh at the use of the Waldahudar word. "I do too," he said pointing down. "Of course, I only have two instead of four, but they do the job." He got a fresh pair of boxer shorts and a pair of brown denim pants out of the closet, and put them on. The pants constricted to fit around his waist. "Still," he said, "the fact that they also generalize doesn't make it any better." He sighed. "It wasn't like this with the dolphins."

"Dolphins are different," said Rissa, pulling on a pair of red pants. "In fact, maybe that's the key. They're so different from us that we can bask in those differences. The biggest problem with the Waldahudin is that we have too much in common with them."

She moved over to her dresser. She didn't put on any makeup; the natural look was the current style for both men and women. But she did insert two diamond earrings, each the size of a small grape. Cheap diamond imports from Rehbollo had destroyed any remaining value natural gemstones had, but their innate beauty was unsurpassed.

Keith had finished dressing, too. He'd put on a synthetic shirt with a dark brown herringbone pattern, and a beige cardigan sweater. Thankfully, as humanity moved out into the universe, one of the first bits of needless mass to be ejected had been the jacket and tie for men; even formal wear did not demand them anymore. With the advent of the four-day, and then the three-day, workweek on Earth, the distinction between office clothes and leisure clothes had disappeared.

He looked over at Rissa. She *was* beautiful—at forty-four, she was still beautiful. Maybe they *should* make love. So what if they just got dressed? Besides, these crazy thoughts about—

*Bleep.* "Karendaughter to Lansing."

Speak of the devil. Keith lifted his head, spoke into the air. "Open. Yes?"

Lianne Karendaughter's rich voice came out of the wall speaker. "Keith—fantastic news! A watson just came through from CHAT with word that a new shortcut has come on-line!"

Keith raised his eyebrows. "Did the boomerang reach Rehbollo 376A ahead of schedule?" That sometimes happened; judging interstellar distances was a tricky game.

"No. This is a *different* shortcut, and it came on-line because something—or, if we're lucky, *someone*— moved through it locally."

"Has anything unexpected come through any of the homeworld shortcuts?"

"Not yet," said Lianne, her voice still bubbling with excitement. "We only discovered this one was now on-line because a cargo module accidentally got misdirected to it."

Keith was on his feet at once. "Recall all probeships," he said. "Summon Jag to the bridge, and alert all stations for a possible first-contact situation." He hurried out the apartment door, Rissa right behind him.

# BETA DRACONIS

*Keith Lansing looked around the docking bay aboard the strange alien craft. Like the ship's exterior, this part, too, was featureless. No seams, no equipment, nothing marring the six glowing cube faces.*

*When the shortcuts were discovered, the press had delighted in bandying around a century-old saying, attributed to the Sri Lankan writer Arthur C. Clarke: "Any sufficiently advanced technology is indistinguishable from magic."*

*The shortcuts were magic.*

*And so was this strange, beautiful starship, this starship that moved in apparent defiance of Newton's laws . . .*

*Keith took a deep breath. He knew what was about to happen, knew it in his bones. He was about to meet the makers of the shortcuts.*

*The pod's course across the bay curved gently downward and soon it came to rest on the flat lower face of the bay.*

*Keith felt weight returning. It continued to grow slowly, and he settled to the floor. The gravity kept increasing, more and more, until it had reached Starplex's shipboard standard. But still it grew, and Keith fought a wave of panic, fearing he would be crushed to jelly.*

*Finally, though, it stopped—and Keith realized that it was at just about the level he kept it at in his cabin aboard ship, nine percent higher than the Commonwealth standard but equal to Earth's sea-level surface gravity.*

*And then, suddenly—*

*Everything around him was . . . was familiar.*

*Was Earth.*

*The edge of a mixed forest, maple trees and spruces rising to a sky the shade of blue no other planet he'd ever seen had. Sunlight precisely the color of Sol's—matching the antihomesickness lamps he and Rissa had in their apartment aboard Starplex. To his right, a lake covered with lily pads, bulrushes rising from its edge. Overhead, a V-shaped flock of —no mistake—of Canada geese, and— yup, just to dispel any final doubt, a daytime gibbous moon, showing the Sea of Tranquility and the O-shaped Sea of Crises to its right.*

*An illusion, of course. Virtual reality. Make him feel at home. Perhaps they could read his mind, or perhaps they'd already contacted other travelers from Earth.*

*The travel pod had no elaborate sensors. There was air in the bay, though. He could hear—God, he could hear crickets, and bullfrogs, and, yes, the haunting call of a loon, all transmitted through the hull of the ship from the air outside. No way to test a sample, but they couldn't have gotten all the other details right and screwed up on something as simple as the gas mixture for human-breathable air.*

*And yet, he hesitated. The trip to Tau Ceti was supposed to be a simple run; Keith hadn't even bothered to see if there was a spacesuit in the pod's emergency locker before departure.*

*But it was clearly an invitation—an invitation to first contact. And first contact was what Starplex was all about.*

*Keith touched a series of controls, overriding the safety interlocks that kept the pod's rear door from opening when it wasn't connected to an access ring. The glassteel panel slid up into the roof.*

*Keith took a tentative breath—*

*And sneezed.*

*Jesus Christ, he thought. Ragweed pollen. These guys* were *good.*

*He sniffed again, and could smell all the things he'd have smelled if he really were back on Earth. Wildflowers and grass and damp wood and a thousand other things, subtly mixed. He stepped out.*

*They'd thought of everything—a perfect re-creation. Why, he even left footprints in the soft earth, something most virtual-reality simulations tripped up on. Indeed, he could feel the texture of the ground through the soles of his shoes, feel it give with each step, feel the springiness of grass compressing beneath his feet, the sharp jab of a stone. It was perfect . . .*

*And then it hit him. Maybe he* was *back on Earth. The shortcut makers knew how to cut across space in the twinkling of an eye. Maybe this was the real thing, maybe he was home—*

*But there had been no second shortcut inside the docking bay, no flash of purple Soderstrom radiation. And besides, if this was Earth, where had they found such unspoiled wilderness? He looked again at the sky, searching for an airplane or shuttle contrail.*

*Still—his sneezing meant they'd actually manufactured allergen molecules, or were manipulating his mind on a very sophisticated level. Suddenly Keith felt his throat constricting. A zoo! A goddamned zoo, and he was a specimen in it. He was trapped, a prisoner. He turned around, about to rush back to his pod, and saw the glass man.*

*"Hello, Keith," said the man. His whole body was transparent, made of perfect crystal that flowed as he moved. There was only the faintest hint of color to the transparent form, a touch of cool aquamarine.*

Keith said nothing for several seconds. The pounding of his heart was drowning out the wilderness sounds. "You know who I am?" he said at last.

"Sort of," said the glass man. His voice was masculine, deep. His body, although humanoid, was stylized, like a mannequin in a trendy store. His head was a featureless egg shape, with the point forming the chin. Although the arms and legs seemed well proportioned, they were smooth, without any apparent musculature. The belly and chest were flat, and the transparent sex organ between the legs was simplified, rocket-shaped.

Keith stared at the glass man, wondering what to do next. Finally, desperate to know his status, he said: "I want to leave."

"You may," said the glass man, spreading his transparent arms. "Anytime you wish. Your pod stands waiting for you." There was no sign of a speaking orifice on the simple ovoid head, but Keith's ears told him the sound was indeed emanating from it.

"This—this isn't a zoo?" asked Keith.

There was a sound like wind chimes—glassy laughter? "No."

"And I'm not a prisoner?"

The wind chimes again. "No. You are—is 'guest' the right word? You are my guest."

"How can you speak English?"

"I don't, actually, of course. My reckoner is translating the words for you."

"Did you make the shortcuts?"

"The what?"

"The shortcuts. The interstellar gateways, the stargates— whatever you want to call them."

" 'Shortcuts,' " said the glass man, nodding. "A good name for them. Yes, we created them."

Keith's pulse was racing. "What do you want from me?"

The wind chimes once more. "You seem defensive, Keith. Isn't there some standard speech you're supposed to make in a first-contact situation? Or is it too early for that?"

Too early? "Well, yes." Keith swallowed. "I, G. K.

*Lansing, Director of* Starplex, *bring you friendly greetings from the Commonwealth of Planets, a peaceful association of four sentient races from three different homeworlds."*

"Ah, now that's better. Thank you."

Keith was struggling to take it all in: the transparent humanoid, the forest re-creation, the beautiful starship, the diverting of his pod. *"I'd still like to know what you want from me,"* he said at last.

The glass man tipped his featureless head at Keith. "Well, at the risk of sounding melodramatic, the fate of the universe is in question."

Keith blinked.

"But, more than that," said the glass man, "I need to ask you some questions. For you see, Keith Lansing, you hold not only the key to the future, but also to the past."

# II

A new sector of space—and one that had opened unexpectedly. Keith and Rissa hurried to the bridge, entering through the port-side door . . . which meant that Keith had to pass right by Lianne Karendaughter. Brilliant (a master's in electrical engineering from MIT), beautiful (luscious Asian features, mounds of platinum hair pinned up by gold clips), and young, Lianne had joined *Starplex* just six weeks ago, after a distinguished term as chief engineer on a large commercial hyperliner. She smiled at Keith as he passed— a radiant smile, a supernova smile. Keith felt his stomach flutter.

*Starplex's* bridge appeared to have no walls, floor, or ceiling. Instead, it was enveloped by a spherical hologram of the ship's surroundings, its workstations seemingly floating amongst the stars. The actual room was rectangular, with a doorway built into each wall, but the doors were invisible, lost within the spacescape. When they split down the middle and slid aside, it was as though space were opening up, revealing the corridors beyond. Apparently suspended in midair—but really attached to the invisible walls just above the doors—were trios of glowing clocks in each homeworld's timekeeping system.

Keith and Rissa hurried to their workstations, looking as though they were running in space.

The bridge workstations were laid out in two rows of three, with the director's position in the middle of the back row. The front row was constantly occupied. The rear stations were only used when necessary; Jag, Keith, and Rissa all had separate offices where they did most of their work. By default, one of Keith's monitors showed a chart of who was currently authorized to use each bridge station. It was the standard alpha-shift team in the front row:

| Internal Operations | Helm | External Operations |
|---|---|---|
| Lianne Karendaughter | Thorald Magnor | Rhombus |
| **Physical Sciences** | **Director** | **Life Sciences** |
| Jag Kandaro em-Pelsh | Keith Lansing | Clarissa Cervantes |

The InOps manager was responsible for all onboard activities, including engineering. On the opposite side of the room was her opposite number, the ExOps manager, who supervised the docking bays and missions conducted by the fifty-four assorted ships stored there. To Keith's left was the station for Jag, head of physical sciences. To his right, again an opposite number: Rissa, head of life sciences.

Since most physics research was conducted aboard ship, it made sense that InOps was in front of the physics station. Lianne could swivel her chair around, or rotate the work-station on its turntable base, for face-to-face consultations with Jag. Likewise, most life-sciences work was done away from the mothership; Rhombus at ExOps could easily consult with Rissa (although being an Ib, Rhombus had 360-degree vision; he didn't have to turn around to see her).

To make communication even easier, ten-centimeter-high real-time holograms of Lianne and Thor's heads, plus a full body shot of Rhombus, normally floated above the rim of Jag, Keith, and Rissa's consoles; those in the front row had holos of the back-row heads floating above their stations.

On each side of the room was a large pool covered by an antisplash forcefield; any of the workstations could have its functions transferred to a dolphin in either pool. Behind the workstations was a row of nine polychairs for observers.

Keith watched as Jag entered through the starboard door. The Waldahud moved across the starfield, squat bow legs carrying him in short steps, four arms stiff at his sides. Jag wore a couple of functional pieces of clothing, including a belt with storage pouches depending from it, and a band with a pocket on it around his upper left arm. The damned thing was practically naked except for his thick fur while Keith was freezing to death. The ship's common areas were kept at fifteen degrees Celsius, equivalent to a hot summer's noon on Rehbollo. Keith half expected to see his breath whenever he left his apartment.

As Jag sat down, the Waldahud's monitor screens configured themselves to be twice as tall as they were wide. Jag could watch two of them simultaneously, one with his vertically stacked left pair of eyes, the other with his vertically stacked right pair. Like humans, Waldahudin had two-sided brains, but each of their hemispheres could process a separate stereoscopic image.

There was no flicker of expression on Jag's face—not that Keith was good at decoding such things, anyway. Their altercation in the corridor an hour ago merited no comment, apparently. Of course not, thought Keith. Just business as usual for one of them.

He shook his head, and turned away. Thorald Magnor, at the helm station, was a giant human of about fifty, with a fiery red beard. At ExOps, the polychair had been retracted beneath the floor, and the console lowered on its slim legs to accommodate its current user. Rhombus, like all Ibs, resembled a stone wheelchair with a watermelon in the seat.

One of Keith's monitors was already showing the report from CHAT—the Commonwealth Hyperspace Astrophysics Telescope—about the newly activated shortcut. The exit

was in the Perseus Arm, some ninety thousand light-years
from their current location. And that was all that was known
about it, except that something had recently gone through
this shortcut, activating it. What that something was, and
where it had gone through the network, was anyone's guess.

"All right, everyone," said Keith. "We'll start with a
standard alpha-class probe. Thor, move us to within twenty
klicks of the shortcut."

"Give me two seconds, boss," said Thor. Keith could
simultaneously see Thor's face in the miniature hologram,
and the back of his real head at the station in front of his. His
face was large and rough, his beard and hair long and wild.
Keith had seen a Viking helmet on a shelf in Thor's
shipboard apartment once; it would have suited him. "We've
got a probeship in the process of docking."

A moment later, lights flashed on Rhombus's sensor web.
"I announce with pleasure that the *Marc Garneau* is secured
in docking bay eight," said a voice with a British accent in
Keith's ear. By convention, Waldahud voices were translated into English with old-fashioned New York accents,
while the Ibs were assigned British ones—it made it easier
to sort out who was speaking, since the translated voices all
came from the same source, the listener's cochlear implant.

"Okay, boss," said Thor. "Here we go." In front of him,
Keith could see Thor's large hands manipulating controls.
The starfield surrounding the bridge began to shift. About
five minutes later, the stars stopped moving again. "As
requested, boss," said Thor. "Twenty thousand meters from
the shortcut, on the button."

"Thank you," said Keith. "Rhombus, please launch the
probe."

Rhombus's ropelike tentacles snapped across his console
as if he were whipping it into submission. His sensor web
flashed. "A pleasure to do so."

A schematic of the probe appeared on one of Keith's
monitors: a silver cylinder, four meters long by one in
diameter, its surface studded with scanners, sensors, camera
lenses, and CCD plates. The probe had only thruster power
and four clusters of conical attitude-control jets; a hyper-

drive engine was far too expensive to risk, given that the probe might never come back.

The probe accelerated through a mass-driver tube in one of *Starplex's* upper-habitat modules. As soon as the probe was out in space, the bridge staff could see the glow of its thrusters in the holographic sphere surrounding them. The probe rotated along its axis so that each of its instruments would be exposed to the entire panorama of the sky.

There was no visible target for the probe—at least, not yet. But its course had been computed so that it would enter the shortcut at the exact angle specified by CHAT. When it did so, the probe seemed to disappear, a tiny ring of violet fire swallowing it up.

"In friendship I observe that passage through the shortcut was normal," reported Rhombus in his rich Oxford tones.

And now the waiting began. Each person showed tension in a different way. Lianne at InOps drummed her painted fingernails on the edge of her console. The lights on Rhombus's web flashed randomly—not a coherent pictogram, but just a sign of mental agitation. Jag picked at his fur and slid his translucent dental plates across each other, making a faint chalk-on-slate sound. Keith got up and paced. Rissa busied herself organizing files on her computer. Only the unflappable Thorald Magnor seemed calm, swinging his giant feet onto his console, and leaning back in his chair, hands interlaced behind his orange mane.

But despite Thor's appearance, there was reason for concern. Ten years ago, a boomerang launched from Tau Ceti had reached its target, a dormant shortcut near the M3-class star Tejat Posterior in the constellation Gemini. That boomerang never returned to Tau Ceti. Instead, at about the time it was supposed to come home, a smooth ball of metal shot out of the Rehbollo shortcut. Analysis determined that the ball was the remains of the probe after some process had briefly broken all molecular bonds in its construction.

The word "process" had been deliberately chosen for the public reports, but many believed that no natural activity could have done that, not even if the Tejat Posterior shortcut

exit had been inside a star's core. The hypothetical beings
responsible were dubbed "Slammers," because they'd apparently slammed the interstellar doorway in the Commonwealth's collective face.

Additional hyperspace probes with heavy shielding had
been sent toward Tejat Posterior (from launch points well
away from any of the Commonwealth homeworlds), but it
would still be another two years before they arrived there.
Until they did, the mystery of the Slammers remained
unresolved—but there was always a fear that they might be
lurking behind other shortcuts.

"With relief, I report a tachyon pulse," announced Rhombus.

Keith let out his breath; he hadn't been aware that he'd
been holding it until then. The pulse meant something was
coming through the shortcut; the probe was returning. They
watched as the shortcut grew from an infinitesimal point to
a meter in diameter, with a violet periphery. The cylindrical
object popped through. Keith nodded slightly: the probe
appeared undamaged. It maneuvered back toward *Starplex*
under its own power, meaning its internal electronics were
still intact, and slid down the launching tube into its berth.
Umbilicals were attached to it, and its store of data was
uploaded into PHANTOM, *Starplex*'s central computer.

"Let's see it," Keith said, and Rhombus complied, replacing the spherical hologram of space outside *Starplex* with
what the probe had seen on the other side of the shortcut. At
first, it just seemed to be more space, different constellations
enveloping them. There were murmurs of disappointment.
One always hoped that a spacecraft would be visible—
a ship from whatever race had brought the shortcut on-line.

Jag got out of his chair, and walked around to stand in
front of the two rows of workstations. He rotated on his
hooves, looking at various parts of the hologram, then began
interpreting what was visible for the rest of them. "Well,"
said a translated Brooklyn accent overtop of his dog barks,
"it looks like normal interstellar space. Just what you'd
expect for the Perseus Arm—lots of blue stars, not too

densely packed." He stopped and pointed. "See that band of light? We're on the inner edge of the Perseus Arm, looking back toward the Orion Arm. Neither Galath nor Hotspot would be visible from here, but we might be able to find Sol in a telescope."

He began a circumnavigation of the bridge, his black hooves ticking against the invisible floor. "The only thing that looks bright enough to be a nearby main-sequence star is that one there." He indicated a blue-white point that was indeed brighter than all the others. "Still, it shows no sign of a visible disk, so at a minimum we are several billion kilometers from it. Of course, we can use a couple of probes to do some long-base-line parallax tests to see how close it is as soon as we go through the shortcut; I don't normally favor A-class stars for having habitable planets, but it seems as good a place as any to start looking for whoever activated this exit."

"So you think it's safe for us to go on through?" Keith asked.

The Waldahud turned to face him, and his left pair of eyes blinked. "There doesn't appear to be any immediate danger," he said. "I'll want to review the rest of the probe's data, but it looks just like, well, space."

"Okay. In that case, let's try—"

"Just a second," said Jag, apparently catching sight of a part of the hologram over Keith's shoulder. He walked toward the director, then continued on, past the seating gallery behind his station. "Just a second," he said again. "Rhombus, how much real-time hologram is left?"

"I abase myself to admit we exhausted the real-time playback two minutes ago," said the Ib at the ExOps console. "I've been looping the playback since then."

Jag walked over to the bridge wall—which was something like taking a few steps toward a distant mountain in hopes that doing so would improve one's view of it. He peered into the darkness. "That area there," he said, circling his upper left arm to indicate a large portion of the starfield. "There is something unusual . . . Rhombus, speed up the playback. Ten times normal rate, and loop it continuously."

"Done without rancor," said Rhombus, ropes snapping.

"That can't be," said Thor, who had turned around to look as well. He half rose from his chair at the helm console.

"But it is," said Jag.

"What is it?" asked Keith.

"You see it," said Jag. "Look."

"All I see is a bunch of stars twinkling."

Jag lifted his upper shoulders, the Waldahud equivalent of a nod of assent. "Exactly. Just like a clear winter's night back on your wondrous Earth, no doubt. Except," he said, "that stars do not twinkle when seen from space."

# GAMMA DRACONIS

You hold, *the glass man had said,* not only the key to the
future, but also to the past. *The glass man's words echoed in
Keith's mind. He looked around at trees, the lake, the blue
sky. All right, all right—Glass had said it was not a cage,
not a zoo, that he could leave at any time. Still, his head was
reeling. Maybe it was because all this was too much to take
in at once, despite Glass's attempt to provide familiar
surroundings. Or maybe the sensation was an aftereffect of
Glass's mind-probe—Keith still suspected something like
that was at work here. Either way, he found himself feeling
dizzy, and decided to lower his body down to the grass. At
first he knelt, but then he moved into a more comfortable
position, with his legs sticking out to one side. He was
astonished to see he'd gotten a grass stain on the knee of his
pants.*

*The glass man flowed into a lotus position about two*

*meters away from Keith. "You introduced yourself as G. K. Lansing."*

*Keith nodded.*

*"What does the G stand for?"*

*"Gilbert."*

*"Gilbert," said Glass, nodding his head as if this was significant.*

*Keith was perplexed. "Actually, I go by my middle name, Keith." A self-deprecating chuckle. "You would, too, if your first name was Gilbert."*

*"How old are you?" asked Glass.*

*"Forty-six."*

*"Forty-six? Just forty-six?" The being's tone was strange— wistful or perplexed.*

*"Um, yes. Forty-six Earth years, that is."*

*"So young," Glass said.*

*Keith lifted his eyebrows, thought about his bald spot.*

*"Tell me about your mate," asked Glass.*

*Keith's eyes narrowed. "Why would you possibly be interested in that?"*

*Wind-chime laughter. "I am interested in everything."*

*"But questions about my mate—surely there are more important things to explore?"*

*"Are there more important things to you?"*

*Keith thought for a second. "Well—no. No, I suppose there aren't."*

*"Then tell me about—about her, I presume."*

*"Yes, her."*

*"Tell me."*

*Keith shrugged. "Well, her name is Rissa. That's short for Clarissa. Clarissa Maria Cervantes." Keith smiled. "Her last name always makes me think of Don Quixote."*

*"Who?"*

*"Don Quixote. The Man of La Mancha. Hero of a novel by a writer named Cervantes." Keith paused. "You'd like Cervantes—he once wrote a book about a glass man. Anyway, Quixote was a knight-errant, caught up in the romance of noble deeds and the pursuit of unattainable goals. But . . ."*

*"But what?"*

*"Well, the funny thing is that it was Rissa who used to call me quixotic."*

Glass tipped his head in puzzlement, and Keith realized that he couldn't discern the connection between the unknown and apparently unrelated words kwik-sah-tik and kee-hoe-te. *" 'Quixotic' means similar to Don Quixote,"* said Keith. *"Visionary, romantic, impractical—an idealist bent on righting wrongs."* He laughed. *"Of course, I wasn't content to love Rissa pure and chaste from afar, but I suppose I do have a tendency to take on battles other people let pass, or aren't even aware of, and, well . . ."*

The egg-shaped transparent head tilted slightly. *"Yes?"*

*"Well,"* said Keith, spreading his arms, encompassing not just the forest simulation but everything beyond, *"we did reach the unreachable stars, didn't we?"* He grew silent, feeling a little embarrassed. *"Anyway, you were asking about Rissa. We have been married—permanently pair-bonded—for almost twenty years now. She's a biologist—an exobiologist, to be precise; her specialty is life that is not indigenous to Earth."*

*"And you love her?"*

*"Very much indeed."*

*"You have children."* Keith assumed it was a question, but Glass's voice did not rise at the end of the sentence.

*"One. His name is Saul."*

*"Sol? After your home star?"*

*"No, Saul. S-A-U-L. After the man who had been my best friend before he died, Saul Ben-Abraham."*

*"So your son's name was—what? Not Saul Lansing-Cervantes?"*

Keith was surprised that Glass grasped human naming conventions. *"Yes, that's right."*

*"Saul Lansing-Cervantes,"* repeated Glass, his head tilted as if lost in thought. He looked up. *"Sorry. It's, ah, quite a musical name."*

*"Which you'd say is funny, if you knew him,"* said Keith. *"I love my son, but I've never met anyone with less musical talent. He's nineteen now, and is away at university. He's*

*studying physics; that's something he* does *have an aptitude for, and I suspect someday he'll make quite a name for himself in that field."*

"Saul Lansing-Cervantes . . . your son," said Glass. "Fascinating. Anyway, we keep getting *off the topic of Rissa."*

Keith looked at him for a moment, puzzled. But then he shrugged. "She's a wonderful woman. Intelligent. Warm, funny. Beautiful."

"And you say you are pair-bonded with her?"

"That's right."

"And that means . . . monogamy, correct? You couple with no one else?"

"Yes."

"Without exception?"

"Without exception, that's right." A pause. "So far."

"So far? You are contemplating a change in this relationship?"

Keith looked away. *Christ, this is crazy. What could this alien possibly know about human marriage?* "Move along," said Keith.

"Pardon?" asked Glass.

"Move along, move along. Another topic."

"Do you feel guilty, Keith?"

"What are you—my bloody conscience?"

"I am just someone who is interested, that's all."

"Become interested in something else."

"I'm sorry," said Glass. "Where did you and Rissa first meet?"

"La Belle Aurore. *The Germans wore gray; she wore blue.*"

"Pardon?"

"Sorry. Another knight-errant hero of mine said that. We met at a party on New Beijing—that's the Earth colony on Tau Ceti IV. She was working in the same lab there as someone I had gone to school with."

"Was it—what is the saying? Was it love at first sight?"

"No. Yes. I don't know."

*"And you have been married for twenty years?"* asked Glass.

*"Just about. Our anniversary is next week."*

*"Twenty years,"* said Glass. *"A blink of an eye."*

Keith frowned. *"Actually, it's considered quite an achievement to make it work that long."*

*"Apologies for my comment,"* said Glass. *"Congratulations."* A pause. *"What do you like most about Rissa?"*

Keith shrugged. *"I don't know. Several things. I like that she is content with who she is. Me, I've got to put on airs—to sometimes pretend I've accomplished more, or am more sophisticated, than I really am. In fact, it's common among humans who have attained a significant position to suffer from what's called 'the impostor syndrome'—the fear that others are going to discover that they don't deserve what they've got. I admit to having a touch of that, but Rissa is immune to it. She never pretends to be anything she's not."*

Glass nodded.

*"And I like her equanimity, her evenness of temper. If something goes wrong, I tend to swear and get upset by it. She just smiles and does whatever needs to be done to set things right. Or if they can't be set right, she accepts it."* Keith paused. *"In many ways, she's a better person than I."*

Glass seemed to consider this for a moment. *"She sounds like someone you should hold on to, Keith."*

Keith looked at the transparent man, perplexed.

# III

A child's blocks. That's the image that had come to Keith Lansing's mind two years ago, while watching *Starplex*'s components being assembled at the Rehbollo orbital shipyards. The giant ship was made up of just nine pieces, eight of which looked identical.

The largest piece was the central disk/shaft combination. The disk was 290 meters in diameter and 30 meters thick. The square shaft extended up and down from the center of the disk 90 meters in each direction, making *Starplex* a total of 210 meters tall. A parabolic radio/hyperspace-telescope dish was set into each of the shaft's end caps.

The central disk actually consisted of three wide rings surrounding the shaft. First, stretching out to a radius of 95 meters was the vast space that would be filled with 686,000 cubic meters of salt water, forming the ocean deck. Second, twenty meters wide and ten decks thick, was the engineering torus. The final ring consisted of *Starplex*'s eight mammoth cargo holds and twenty docking bays, their space doors arrayed along the disk's curving edge.

The other building blocks were the eight habitat modules. Each was a right-triangular prism, ninety meters tall, ninety meters wide at its base, and thirty meters thick. One module was attached to each of the four sides of the shaft that stuck out above the disk. These were mirrored by four more mated to the portion that protruded below. In profile the assembled ship resembled a diamond with a bar through it; seen from above, it was a circle with the interlocking habitats forming a cross in its center.

Each habitat module was divided into thirty decks. Any of the modules could be replaced to accommodate a new race or special equipment, or one could be left behind as a separate base for long-term explorations in a new sector.

In the year since the ship had been launched, *Starplex*'s missions had been uneventful. But now, at last, a real first-contact situation was at hand. Now, at last, all that the great ship had to offer would be put to the test.

A second, more sophisticated probe was sent through to the newly opened sector. It, too, detected the twinkling stars, and its hyperspace telescopes indicated a solar system's worth of mass was present in the vicinity; to get more resolution of exactly how the mass was deployed would require much larger 'scopes, such as those that were set into either end of *Starplex*'s central shaft.

Keith next ordered a probeship with a human and an Ib from Jag's staff to fly through to the other side and do a more complete reconnaissance. They didn't actually travel into the source of the twinkling stars. There was no way to communicate in real time through a shortcut, so if they got in trouble it might be too late to help before *Starplex* realized it. But they did do full-spectrum EM scans, a complete-sky search for artificial radio signals, and so on. They returned to *Starplex*, reporting that there was no apparent danger on the other side, although the cause of the twinkling starscape remained as elusive as ever.

Keith waited until all data from the two probes and the

crewed reconnaissance had been reviewed by each department. Finally, satisfied that it would represent a low risk, he ordered Thor to take *Starplex* itself through the shortcut into the newly opened sector of space.

People occasionally used the terms "wormhole" or "tunnel" as synonyms for shortcut, but that wasn't correct. There was no intervening space between the shortcut entrance and the exit. They were like doors between rooms in a house with paper-thin walls: as you walked through, you were partly in one room and partly in another. As simple as that—except that the rooms were separated by many light-years.

The Commonwealth had slowly worked out how to navigate the shortcut network. In normal space, a dormant shortcut is a point. But in hyperspace, that point is surrounded by a rotating sphere of tachyons. The tachyons move along millions of polar orbital lines, all of which are equally spaced, except that one is missing on one side, its tachyon looping back in a hemispherical path. That narrow tachyon-free gap is known as "the zero meridian," and it means you can treat the sphere of tachyons just like a planetary globe, with a coordinate system of longitude and latitude.

To travel through a shortcut, you set a straight-line path toward the point at the center of the sphere. As you approach that point, you pass through the sphere at a specific latitude and longitude. Those coordinates determine which other shortcut you will exit from: where in the galaxy you come out depends on the direction from which you approached the local shortcut.

Of course, to get the ball rolling, there had to be one shortcut on-line at the outset that was not associated with any race—otherwise there'd be no location for the first emerging civilization to travel to with their shortcut. The initial shortcut—Shortcut Prime—was clearly a freebie, given by the shortcut makers. It was located in the heart of the Milky Way galaxy, within sight of the central black hole. Earth's initial explorations of that sector had found no native life there, of course; the galactic core was far too radioactive for that.

At the beginning of the Commonwealth, there were only four active shortcuts—Tau Ceti, Rehbollo, Flatland, and Shortcut Prime. As more shortcuts were activated, the acceptable approach angles for each possible exit became smaller. After a dozen shortcuts were on-line, it became clear that to return to the Tau Ceti shortcut, one had to pierce the tachyon sphere surrounding another shortcut at about 115 degrees east longitude and 40 degrees north latitude. On Earth, that's close to Beijing, which gave rise to the "New Beijing" nickname for the colony on Silvanus, Tau Ceti's fourth planet.

When a ship touches the shortcut, the shortcut point expands—but only in two dimensions. It forms a hole in space perpendicular to the direction of the ship's travel. The hole's shape is the same as the cross-sectional profile of whatever part of the ship is passing through it. The opening is outlined in a violet ring of Soderstrom radiation, caused by tachyons spilling out around the edges and spontaneously translating into slower-than-light particles.

An observer looking at the shortcut from the front would see the ship disappearing into the violet-limned entrance. Looking from the back, he or she would only see a black void blocking the background stars; the void would have the same silhouette as the disappearing object.

Once the ship is all the way through, the shortcut loses its height and width, collapsing back down to nothingness—awaiting the next galactic traveler . . .

Thor sounded the pretransfer alarm, five successively louder electronic drumbeats. Keith touched keys, and his number-two monitor switched to a split-screen mode. One side displayed normal space, in which the shortcut was invisible; the other, a computer simulation based on hyperspace scans, showing the shortcut as a bright white point on a green background surrounded by a glowing orange sphere of field lines.

"All right," said Keith. "Let's do it."

Thor operated controls. "As you say, boss."

Starplex closed the twenty kilometers between itself and the shortcut, and then it touched the point. The shortcut expanded to accommodate the ship's diamond-shaped profile, fiery purple lips matching the giant mothership's shape. As *Starplex* passed through, the holographic bubble surrounding the bridge showed the two mismatched starfields, and the stormy discontinuity between them that moved from bow to stern as they completed their passage. As soon as the ship was all the way through, the shortcut shrank back down to nothingness.

And there they were, in the Perseus Arm—two thirds of the way across the galaxy, and tens of thousands of light-years from any of the homeworlds.

"Shortcut passage was normal," said Thor. The tiny hologram of his face floating above the rim of Keith's workstation was lined up with the back of Thor's actual head, and the holographic mass of red hair blended into the real mane beyond, making his ax-blade features seem lost in a vast orange sea.

"Good work," said Keith. "Let's drop a marker buoy."

Thor nodded and pushed some keys. Although the shortcut stood out in hyperspace, if *Starplex*'s hyper-radio equipment broke down, they'd have trouble finding it again. The buoy, broadcasting on normal EM frequencies and containing its own hyperscope, would be their beacon home in that case.

Jag got up and pointed out the twinkling stars again; they were quite easy to see. Thor rotated the holographic bubble so that they appeared front and center, instead of off behind the observation gallery.

Lianne Karendaughter was leaning forward at her workstation, a delicate hand supporting her chin. "So what's causing the twinkling?" she said.

Behind her, Jag lifted all four shoulders in a Waldahud shrug. "It can't be atmospheric disturbances, of course," he said. "Spectrographs confirm that we're in a space-normal vacuum. But something is in between our ship and the background stars—something that is at least partially opaque and shifting."

"Perhaps a nonluminous nebula," said Thor.

"Or, if I may be allowed a suggestion, perhaps just a tract of dust," said Rhombus.

"I'd like to know how far away it is before I hazard a guess," said Jag.

Keith nodded. "Thor, shoot a comm laser at—at whatever it is."

Thor's broad shoulders moved as he worked controls on either side of his workstation. "Firing."

Three digital counters appeared floating in the holographic display. Each one incremented at a different rate, in the smallest standard units of each of the three homeworld's timekeeping systems. Keith watched the one counting seconds climb higher and higher.

"Reflected light received at seventy-two seconds," said Thor. "Whatever is out there is pretty damn close—about eleven million klicks away."

Jag was consulting his monitors. "Hyperspace telescope readings show that the obstructing material consists of a large amount of mass—a sixteen-multiple or more times the combined mass of all the planets in a typical solar system."

"So it's not spaceships," said Rissa, disappointed.

Jag lifted his lower shoulders. "Probably not. There's a small chance that we're seeing a large number of vessels—a vast fleet of craft, whose individual movements are eclipsing background stars, and whose artificial gravity generators are making big dents in spacetime. But I doubt that."

"Let's close the distance by half, Thor," said Keith. "Bring us in to about six million klicks from the periphery of the phenomenon. See if we can make out more detail."

The little face and the big head behind it nodded in unison. "As you say, boss."

As he brought the ship closer, Thor also rotated *Starplex* so that deck one was facing forward into its direction of movement. The ship's thrusters could move the vessel in any direction, regardless of its orientation, but one of the

twin radio telescopes was mounted in the center of that
square deck, and four optical telescopes were mounted at
the corners.

As they got closer, it became apparent that whatever was
obscuring the background stars was reasonably solid and
large. Stars were being eclipsed now with only a short
period of fading out as they disappeared. But there wasn't
enough light to see clearly. The nearby A-class star was just
too far away. So far, all that they could make out was a
series of maddeningly vague shadows.

"Any radio signals?" asked Keith. As had become his
habit, he'd shut off the hologram of Lianne's head that by
default hovered above the rim of his console. In the past,
he'd found himself staring at it, and that was awkward with
Rissa sitting right next to him.

"Nothing major," she said. "Just wisps of milliwatt noise
now and again near the twenty-one-centimeter line, but it's
all but lost against the cosmic microwave background."

Keith looked to Jag, seated on his left. "Ideas?"

The Waldahud was growing frustrated as they got closer—
his fur was standing up in tufts. "Well, an asteroid belt seems
unlikely, especially this far from the nearest star. I suppose it
could be material in the A's Oort, but it seems much too dense
for that."

*Starplex* continued to move in. "Spectroscopy?" asked
Keith.

"Whatever those objects are," barked Jag, "they're nonluminous. As for absorption of starlight from behind as it
passes through the less opaque parts, the spectra I'm seeing
is typical of interstellar dust, but there's much less absorption going on than I'd expect." He turned to face Keith.
"There's simply not enough light out here to see what's
going on. We should send up a fusion flare."

"What if they *are* ships?" asked Keith. "Their crews
might misconstrue it—think we're launching an attack."

"They are almost certainly not ships," said Jag, curtly.
"They are planet-sized bodies."

Keith looked at Rissa, at the holographic Thor and
Rhombus, and at the back of Lianne's head, to see if any of

them had any objections. "All right," he said. "Let's do it."

Jag got up and walked over to stand beside Rhombus at the external-operations station. Keith found it funny watching them talk: Jag barking like an angry dog, and Rhombus replying in shimmering lights. Since they were just conversing among themselves, PHANTOM didn't bother to translate their words for Keith, but Keith tried to listen in, just for the practice. Waldahudar was a difficult language for English speakers to follow, and it required a different grammatical mood depending on the gender of the speaker and the person being spoken to (males could only address females in a conditional/subjunctive way, for instance). On the other hand, specific nouns were avoided as much as possible in polite Waldahudar, lest disagreements over terminology ensue. Throughout the conversation, Jag leaned on Rhombus's workstation for support; his medial limbs could be used for locomotion or manipulation, but Waldahudin didn't like dropping down onto their rear four in the company of humans.

Finally, Jag and Rhombus had agreed on what characteristics the flare should have. Lianne at InOps issued an order that all windows on decks one through thirty be covered or turned opaque. She also drew the protective covers over sensitive external cameras and sensors.

When that was done, Rhombus launched the flare—a ball about two meters in diameter—out through a horizontal mass-driver tube that exited on the outer rim of the central disk. He let the flare get about twenty thousand klicks above the ship and then ignited it. The flare burned with the light of a miniature sun for eight seconds.

Of course, it took the light from that flare almost twenty seconds to reach the beginning of the phenomenon that was obscuring the background stars. It turned out that the phenomenon was roughly spherical, measuring some seven million kilometers in diameter, so it took twenty-four seconds—or three times the length of the light pulse—for the illumination to pass through it in a circular band. When it was done, Rhombus summed the various illuminated parts of the image to give a view of the whole thing as if it had been lit up simultaneously. In the all-encompassing holo-gram, the bridge crew could finally see what was out there.

There were dozens of gray-and-black spheres, each one so dark that the illuminated side was hardly much brighter than the unilluminated one.

"Each of the spheres is roughly the size of the planet Jupiter," said Thor, his head bent down, consulting a readout. "The smallest is 110,000 klicks wide; the largest, about 170,000. They're clustered into a spherical volume seven million klicks wide, or about five times the diameter of Sol."

The individual orbs looked a lot like black-and-white photographs of Jupiter, except that they didn't have neat latitudinal bands of cloud. Rather, the clouds—or whatever it was that formed the visible surface markings—seemed to swirl in simple convection cells from equator to pole, the kind of pattern one might expect if the spheres had next to no rotation. In the intervening space between the world-sized spheres was a diaphanous fog of gas or particles that formed a translucent haze; doubtless this fog had been responsible for most of the twinkling effect they'd observed. The whole thing—spheres and surrounding fog—looked like assorted steel ball bearings rolling around in a pile of black silk stockings.

"How do they—" barked Jag, and Keith immediately knew what he was going to say. How could world-sized objects be packed so closely together? There were perhaps ten diameters between the closest of the objects, and fifteen or so between the ones that were least tightly packed. Keith couldn't imagine any pattern of stable orbits that would keep them from collapsing together under their own gravi-tational attraction. If this was a natural grouping, it seemed unlikely that it could be an old one. Throwing some light on the subject had only made the mystery deeper.

# IV

On Earth, cells contain mitochondria for converting food to energy, undulopodia (thrashing tails including those that propel sperm), and, in plants, plastids for storing chlorophyll. The ancestors of these organelles were originally independent free-swimming creatures. They came together in symbiosis with a host being whose DNA is now walled off in the nucleus; to this day, some organelles still contain vestigial DNA of their own.

On Flatland, diverse ancestors also learned to work together, but on a much grander scale. An Ib was actually a combination of seven large life-forms—indeed, "Ib" is short for "integrated bioentity."

The seven parts are the *pod,* the watermelon-shaped creature containing the supersaturated solution in which the crystals of the principal brain grow; the *pump,* the digestive/respiratory structure that surrounds the pod like a blue sweatshirt tied around a green pot belly, with tubular arms hanging down for feeding and excreting; the twin *wheels*, fleshy hoops coated with quartz; the *frame*, a saddle-shaped gray construct that provides axles for the wheels and anchor points for the other elements; the *bundle*, sixteen copper-colored ropes that normally form a heap in front of the pump but can snake out as needed; and the *web*, a sensor net that covers the pump, pod, and upper frame.

The web has an eye and a bioluminescent dot wherever two or more of its strands intersect. Although they have no speech organs, Ibs hear as well as terrestrial dogs do, and they accept with good humor spoken names bestowed by members of other races. *Starplex*'s ExOps manager was Rhombus; Snowflake was senior geologist; Vendi (short for Venn Diagram) was a hyperdrive engineer; and Boxcar—well, Boxcar was the biochemist with whom Rissa was collaborating on the most important project in history.

In 1972, Earth's Club of Rome began preaching the limits of growth. But with all of space now at humanity's fingertips, there were no more constraints. To hell with the textbook 2.3 children. If you wanted $2 \times 10^3$ kids, there was room enough for all of them—and for you, too. The argument that individuals *had* to die in order to allow the race to advance no longer applied.

Boxcar and Rissa were trying to increase the lifespans of the Commonwealth races. The problem was daunting; so much of how life worked still remained mysterious. Rissa doubted that the riddle of aging would be solved in her lifetime, although within a century someone would likely find the key. The irony was not lost on her: Clarissa Cervantes, senescence researcher, probably belonged to the final human generation that would know death.

The average human lifespan was a hundred Earth years; Waldahudin lived to be about forty-five (the fact that they were self-sufficient after only six years didn't quite compensate for the shortness of their span; some humans thought the knowledge that they were the shortest-lived of the Commonwealth sentients was what made them so disagreeable); dolphins were good for eighty years with proper health care; and, barring accidents, an Ib would live for precisely 641 Earth years.

Rissa and Boxcar thought they knew why Ibs lived so much longer than the other races. Human, dolphin, and Waldahud cells all have a Hayflick limit: they properly reproduce only a finite number of times. Ironically, Waldahud cells had the highest limit—about ninety-three times—but their cells, like the creatures composed of them, had the shortest life cycle. Human and dolphin cells could divide about fifty times. But the organelle clusters—there was no overall membrane to make them a single cell—that made up the body of an Ib could reproduce indefinitely. What eventually kills most Ibs is a mental short circuit: when the crystals of the central brain, which form matrices at a constant rate, reach their maximum information capacity, the overflow causes the basic routines governing respiration and digestion to become garbled.

Since she didn't seem to be needed on the bridge, Rissa had gone down to her lab to join Boxcar. She was sitting in a chair; Boxcar was positioned next to her. They watched the data scrolling up the monitor plate rising from the desk in front of them. The Hayflick limit had to be governed by cellular timers of some sort. Since it was observed in cells from both Earth and Rehbollo, they'd hoped comparison genome mapping would help. Attempts to correlate across genetic platforms the mechanisms for timing body growth, puberty, and sexual functions had all been successful. But, maddeningly, the cause of the Hayflick limit remained elusive.

Maybe this latest test—maybe this statistical analysis of inverted telomerase RNA codons—maybe—

Lights winked on Boxcar's sensor web. "It saddens me to note that the answer is not there," said the translated voice, British, as all Ib voices were, and female, as half of them were arbitrarily assigned.

Rissa let out a heavy sigh. Boxcar was right; another dead end.

"I intend no offense with this comment," said Boxcar, "but I'm sure you know that my race has never believed in gods. And yet when I encounter a problem like this—a problem that seems, well, *designed* to thwart solution—it does make one think that the information is being deliberately withheld from us, that our creator does not want us to live forever."

Rissa made a small laugh. "You may be right. A common theme among human religions is the belief that gods jealously guard their powers. And yet why build an infinite universe, but put life on only a handful of worlds?"

"Begging your generous pardon for pointing out the obvious," said Boxcar, "but the universe is only infinite in that it has no borders. It does however contain a finite amount of matter. Still, what is it that your god is said to have commanded? Be fruitful and multiply?"

Rissa laughed. "Filling the universe would take an awful lot of multiplying."

"I thought that was an activity you humans enjoyed."

She grunted, thinking of her husband. "Some more than others."

"Forgive me if I'm being intrusive," said Boxcar, "but PHANTOM prefaced the translation of your last sentence with a glyph indicating that you spoke it ironically. It is doubtless me who is to blame, but I seem to be missing a layer of your meaning."

Rissa looked at the Ib—a faceless, six-hundred-kilogram wheelchair. Pointless to discuss such matters with her— with *it,* a sexless gestalt that knew nothing of love or marriage, a creature to whom an entire human lifespan was a brief interlude. How could it understand the stages a marriage went through—the stages a *man* went through?

And yet—

She could not talk about it with her female friends aboard ship. Her husband was *Starplex*'s director—the . . . the *captain* they would have called it in the old days. She couldn't chance gossip getting around, couldn't risk diminishing him in the eyes of the staff.

Rissa's friend Sabrina had a husband named Gary. Gary was going through the same thing—but Gary was just a meteorologist. Not someone to whom everyone looked up, not someone who had to endure the gaze of a thousand people.

I'm a biologist, thought Rissa, and Keith's a sociologist. How did I ever end up a politician's wife, with him, me, and our marriage under the microscope?

She opened her mouth, about to tell Boxcar that it was nothing, nothing at all, that PHANTOM had mistaken fatigue or perhaps disappointment in the latest experiment's results for irony.

But then she thought, why the hell not? Why not discuss it with the Ib? Gossiping was a failing of *individual* life-forms, not of gestalt beings. And it would feel good—oh so very good—to get it off her chest, to be able to share it with someone.

"Well," she said—an articulated pause, giving herself one last chance to rein in her words. But then she pressed on: "Keith is getting old."

A slight ripple of lights on Boxcar's web.

"Oh, I know," said Rissa, lifting a hand. "He's young by Ibese standards, but, well, he is becoming middle-aged for a human. When that happens to a human female, we undergo chemical changes associated with the end of our childbearing years. Menopause, it's called."

Lights playing up the web; an Ibese nod.

"But for male humans, it isn't so cut-and-dried. As they feel their youth slipping away, they begin to question themselves, their accomplishments, their status in life, their career choices, and . . . well, whether they are still attractive to the opposite sex."

"And is Keith still attractive to you?"

Rissa was surprised by the question. "Well, I didn't marry him for his looks." That hadn't come out the way she'd intended. "Yes, yes, he's still attractive to me."

"It is doubtless wrong for me to remark upon this, and for that I apologize, but he is losing his hair."

Rissa laughed. "I'm surprised you would notice something like that."

"Without intending offense, please know that telling one human from another is difficult for us, especially when they are standing close by and so are visible to only part of our webs. We're attentive to individual details. We know how upsetting it is to humans to not be recognized by someone they think *should* know them. I have noticed both his loss of hair and its change of color. I have learned that such changes can signal a reduction in attractiveness."

"I suppose they can, for some women," said Rissa. But then she thought, this is silly. Dissembling to an alien. "Yes, I liked his looks better when he had a full head of hair. But it's such a minor point, really."

"But if Keith is still attractive to you, then—forgive my boundless ignorance—I don't see what the problem is."

"The problem is that he doesn't care if he's still attractive to *me*. Appealing to one's mate is taken as a given. I suppose that's why men in the past often put on weight after they'd gotten married. No, the question running through Keith's mind these days, I'm sure, is whether he's attractive to *other* women."

"And is he?"

Rissa was about to respond with a reflex "of course," but then paused to really consider the question—something she hadn't done before. "Yes, I suppose he is. Power, they say, is the ultimate aphrodisiac, and Keith is the most powerful man in—in our space-going community."

"Then, begging forgiveness, what is the difficulty? It sounds as though he should have the answer to his question."

"The difficulty is that he may have to prove it to himself—prove that he's still attractive."

"He could conduct a poll. I know how much you humans rely on such information."

Rissa laughed. "Keith is more of . . . more of an *empiricist*," she said. Her tone sobered. "He may wish to conduct experiments."

Two lights winking. "Oh?"

Rissa looked at a point high up on the wall. "Whenever we're in a social situation with other humans, he spends too much time with the other women present."

"How much is too much?"

Rissa frowned, then said, "More than he spends with me. And often, he's off talking to women who are half his age—half *my* age."

"And this bothers you."

"I guess so."

Boxcar considered for a moment, then: "But is this not all natural? Something all men go through?"

"I suppose."

"One cannot fight nature, Rissa."

She gestured at the monitor, with the negative results of the last Hayflick-limit study still displayed on it. "So I'm beginning to find out."

# V

"Get me a sample of the material those spheres are made of," barked Jag, standing up at his bridge station and looking at the director. Keith gritted his teeth, and thought, as he often did, of asking PHANTOM to translate Jag's words less directly, inserting the human niceties of "please" and "thank you."

"Should we send a probe?" Keith asked, looking at the Waldahud's four-eyed face. "Or do you want to go out yourself?" If the latter, thought Keith, I'd be glad to show you the airlock door.

"A standard atmospheric-sampling probe," said Jag. "The gravitational interplay between that many large bodies so close together must be complex. Whatever we send out might end up crashing into one of them."

All the more reason to send Jag, thought Keith. But what he said was, "A probe it is." He turned and looked at the workstation positioned at two o'clock to his own. "Rhombus, please take care of that."

The Ib's web rippled assent.

"A delta-class probe would be most appropriate," said Jag, slipping back into his chair and speaking now into a little hologram of Rhombus above the rim of his console.

Keith tapped a key and joined the conference as well; a miniature Waldahud head popped up in front of him next to the full body shot of the Ib. "How many spheres are there in total?" asked Keith.

Rhombus's ropes operated controls. "Two hundred and seventeen," he said. "But they all look pretty much the same, except for some variation in size."

"Well, then, for an initial test, it doesn't make any difference which sphere we sample," said Jag. "Choose the one that presents the fewest navigational difficulties. First, scoop up some of that material that's between the spheres. Then buzz into one of the spheres and get me a sample of the gas, or whatever it is that they're made of. Take some from the top of the clouds, and another sample from about two hundred meters down into the clouds, if the probe can stand the pressure. As you fill them, heat and pressurize the sample compartments to match the ambient at the collection points; I want to minimize chemical changes in the material."

Lights moved up Rhombus's sensor web, and a few moments later he was launching the probe. He switched the control-room spherical display to the view from the probe's cameras. The stars that were behind the haze between the spheres still seemed to be twinkling; the spheres themselves were just circles of black against a backdrop that consisted of a starfield and some faint blue nebulosity beyond.

"What do you think the spheres are?" asked Rhombus, while the probe closed toward its target.

Jag moved all four of his shoulders in a Waldahud shrug. "Might be the remnants of a brown dwarf star that recently blew apart. Any fluid will take on a spherical shape in zero-g, of course. The material in between will presumably eventually be swept up by the larger bodies."

The probe was getting close to the material between the spheres. "The fog seems to consist of gas studded with solid particles averaging about seven millimeters in diameter," said Rhombus, whose sensor web had partially crawled onto the console in front of him so that he could read the instruments more easily.

"What kind of gas?" Keith asked.

"Its apparent molecular weight suggests a reasonably heavy or complex compound," replied Jag, now looking at one of his monitors. "However, the absorption spectrum is that of normal space dust—carbon grains, and so on." A pause. "There's no discernible magnetic field around the spheres. That's surprising; I had supposed the gas particles might have been held in place by such fields."

"Will the probe be damaged by impact with the particles?" asked Keith.

"It pleases me to respond in the negative," said Rhombus. "I'm slowing the probe down to avoid that."

Part of the hologram was obscured as the hatch that covered the atmospheric scoop opened up—bad design, that. "Now collecting samples of the material between the spheres," said Rhombus. A few moments later the view cleared as the hatch closed. "Sample bay one full," the Ib reported. "Changing course for atmospheric skim."

The starfield wheeled around as the probe altered its trajectory. One of the circles of blackness was soon in the center of its view. The ebony sphere grew larger and larger until it dominated everything. The probe had headlights, which Rhombus had turned on. They made two murky shafts that penetrated a few meters into the dark, swirling material. A different part of the view was obscured as another sample hatch opened.

"Taking upper-atmosphere samples," reported the Ib, and then, a moment later, "Sample container full."

"Adequate," said Jag. "Now dive down two hundred meters—or however far you can go safely—and get some more sphere material."

"Doing so, in harmonious peace," said Rhombus's clipped tones.

Everything was pitch-black, except for the twin pools of light from the headlight beams. They were now only penetrating a meter or so. For one brief moment, something solid seemed to be in the probe's path—an ovoid shape the size of a dirigible—but it was gone from view almost at once.

"Depth now ninety-one meters," said Rhombus. "Surprising. External pressure is very light—far less than I'd have expected."

"Keep going down, then," said Jag.

The probe continued to descend. Rhombus's web flashed in consternation. "The pressure sensor must have been damaged—maybe an impact with a piece of gravel. I'm still reading almost no atmospheric pressure."

Jag lifted his upper shoulders. "All right. Fill a compartment here, then bring it all home."

The third hatch did not obscure the camera at all, although its opening probably shook the craft enough that had they been able to see anything the view would have jiggled a bit.

"The internal-pressure gauge inside the sample compartment shows the same almost-zero pressure the external gauge is indicating," said Rhombus. "Of course, they run through the same microprocessor. Anyway, the compartment should have filled instantly, given that it was a vacuum before the hatch opened."

Rhombus left the hatch open for a few more seconds, just to be sure, then closed it, and turned the probe around, bringing it back to *Starplex*.

Once the probe was back in its launching tube, its sample compartments were disengaged and moved by robot arms onto conveyors, which took them down to Jag's lab. Jag, meanwhile, took an elevator there himself.

The containers plugged into jacks on the walls of the lab. They didn't have to be opened; sensors and cameras could look inside through the jacks.

Jag sat down in his chair—a real handcrafted Waldahud seat, not a polychair—and activated the tall, thin monitors in front of him. He then keyed in a sequence of commands that selected a standard barrage of tests, and watched with growing amazement as the results appeared on his screens.

Spectroscopy: negative findings.

Electromagnetic sweep: negative findings.

Beta decay: none.

Gamma-ray emissions: none.

Screen after screen lit up: negative findings; none; negative findings; none.

He tapped a key, and the scale beneath the testing bay read off the mass of the sample container: 12.782 kilograms.

"Central Computer," called Jag into the air. "Check the spec sheet for this sample container. How much does it mass when empty?"

"The container's mass is 12.782 kilograms," barked PHANTOM in Waldahudar.

Jag swore. "The *fardint* thing is empty."

"Correct," said PHANTOM.

Jag tapped a key, and a hologram of Rhombus appeared. "Teklarg," said Jag, calling the Ib by his name in Waldahudar, "that probe you sent out was defective. All of the sample material from its number-two container leaked out on the way back."

"Sincere apologies, good Jag," said Rhombus. "I submit to punishment for wasting your time, and will dispatch a replacement at once."

"Do so," said Jag, and he stabbed the button that cut off communications. He turned his attention to the number-one sample container . . . and was shocked to discover that it, too, had leaked out its contents on the way back. "Shoddy human engineering," he grumbled to himself.

But he was grumbling even more once the second probe's sample containers had been conveyed to his lab. The readings were the same—including the anomalously low air-pressure readings after it had dived into the large sphere.

Once again, Jag summoned up a hologram of Rhombus.

"I say with all peaceful good wishes, dear Jag, that there does not appear to be anything wrong with either probe. The container seals are perfect. Nothing should have been able to leak out."

"Regardless, whatever samples we are collecting *are* getting out," said Jag. "Which means . . . well, which means that whatever the samples are made of must be unusual stuff indeed."

Lights moved up Rhombus's web. "A fair assumption."

Jag slid his dental plates together. "There must be a way to bring some of that material aboard for study."

"Doubtless you have already thought of this," said Rhombus, "and I waste both our time by mentioning the idea, but we could use a force box. You know, like the kind they use in labs for handling antimatter."

Jag lifted his upper shoulders. "Acceptable. But don't use an EM forcefield; instead, use artificial-gravity fields to hold the contents away from the box's walls, regardless of what acceleration we use."

"Will do, with obeisance," said Rhombus.

The force box was manipulated by tractor beams. It consisted of eight antigrav generators arranged as the corners of a perfect cube, with wide, paddlelike handles sticking off each face's midpoint to give the tractors something to hold on to. The box was pushed into one of the large gray spheres, and opened there. A second box was manipulated into the swarm of gravel between two of the spheres and activated there. The two boxes were then quickly hauled back in to *Starplex*.

Finally, the sample containers were maneuvered into separate isolation chambers in Jag's lab. The antigrav trick had been a success: one box did indeed contain samples of the gas that constituted the sphere, and the other held several pieces of translucent gravel plus one partially transparent rock the size of a hen's egg. Now, at last, Jag would find out what they were dealing with.

# VI

Keith ran a hand over his pate, and leaned back in his chair, looking out at the starscape hologram enveloping the bridge. There wasn't much else to do, until Jag reported back. Rissa was still off working with Boxcar, and alpha shift was coming to an end. Keith exhaled—probably too noisily. Rhombus had rolled up to the director's workstation to discuss something or other. Lights flashed across the Ib's mantle. "Irritated?" said his translated voice.

Keith nodded.

"Jag?" asked the Ib.

Keith nodded again.

"In politeness, I observe that he's not that bad," said Rhombus. "As Waldahudin go, he's positively genteel."

Keith gestured toward the part of the starfield that hid the door Jag had gone through. "He's so . . . competitive. Combative."

"They're all like that," said Rhombus. "All the males, anyway. Have you spent much time on Rehbollo?"

"No. Although I was in on the first contact between humans and Waldahudin, I always thought that it was best for me to stay away from Rehbollo. I—I've still got a lot of anger over the death of Saul Ben-Abraham, I guess."

Rhombus was quiet for a few moments, perhaps digesting this. Then his web rippled with light again. "Our shift is over, friend Keith. Will you grant me nine minutes of your time?"

Keith shrugged and got to his feet. He addressed the room. "Good work, everyone. Thank you."

Lianne turned around, her platinum hair bouncing as she did so, and smiled at Keith. Rhombus and Keith headed out into the chilly corridor, the Ib rolling beside the human.

A couple of slim robots were moving down the corridor as well. One was carrying a lunch tray for someone; another was running a vacuum cleaner along the floor. Keith still privately thought of such robots as PHARTs—PHANTOM ambulatory remote toilers—but the Waldahudin had started throwing things when it was suggested that *Starplex* terminology contained acronyms nested within acronyms.

Through a window in the corridor wall, Keith could see one of the vertical dolphin-access tubes, consisting of meter-thick disks of water separated by ten centimeters of air held in place by forcefields. The air gaps prevented the water pressure from increasing over the tube's height. As he watched, a bottle-nosed dolphin passed by, swimming up.

Keith looked at Rhombus. Lights were flashing in unison on his web. "What's so funny?" Keith asked.

"Nothing," said the Ib.

"No, come on. What is it?"

"I was just thinking of a joke Thor told today. How many Waldahudin does it take to change a lightbulb? Answer: five—and each one has to get credit."

Keith frowned. "Lianne told you that same joke weeks ago."

"I know," said Rhombus. "I laughed then, too."

Keith shook his head. "I'll never understand how you Ibs can find the same thing funny over and over again."

"I'd shrug if I could," said Rhombus. "The same painting is pretty each time you look at it. The same dish is tasty each time you eat it. Why shouldn't the same joke be funny each time you hear it?"

"I don't know," said Keith. "I'm just glad I got you to stop telling me that stupid 'that's not my axle—it's my feeding tube' joke every time we met. That was irritating as hell."

"Sorry."

They continued down the corridor in silence for a while, then: "You know, good Keith, it's a lot easier to understand the Waldahudin if you've spent time on their world."

"Oh?"

"You and Clarissa have always been happy together, if you'll permit me to say so. We Ibs don't have such intimacy with other individuals; we shuffle our own genetic material amongst our component parts, rather than bonding with a mate. Oh, I take comfort from my other components—my wheels, for instance, are not sentient, but they have intelligence comparable to that of a terrestrial dog. I have a relationship with them that gives me great joy. But I perceive that the relationship you enjoy with Clarissa is something much, much more. I only dimly understand it, but I'm sure Jag appreciates it. Waldahudin, like humans, have two sexes, after all."

Keith couldn't see where this was going, and, on the whole, thought Rhombus was presuming on their friendship. "Yes?"

"Waldahudin have two sexes, but they do not have equal numbers of each sex," said the Ib. "There are, in fact, five males for every female. Yet, despite this, they are a monogamous race, forming lifetime pairbonds."

"So I've heard."

"But have you contemplated the ramifications of that?" asked the Ib. "It means that four out of every five males end up without a mate—end up being excluded from the gene pool. Perhaps you had to fend off some other suitors in your pursuit of Clarissa—or maybe she had to fend off others who were pursuing you; forgive me, but I've no idea how these things work. But I imagine in such contests it was a comfort to all the participants to know that for each male there was a female, and vice versa. Oh, the pairings might not end up as one might wish, but the chances were good that each man would find a woman, and vice versa—or a mate of their own gender, if that was their preference."

Keith moved his shoulders. "I suppose."

"But for Jag's people, that is not the case. Females have absolute power in their society. Every single one of them is—courted, I believe is the word—by five males, and the female, when she reaches estrus at thirty years of age, will pick her one mate from the five who have spent the last twenty-five years vying for her attentions. You know Jag's full name?"

Keith thought for a moment. "Jag Kandaro em-Pelsh, isn't it?"

"That's right. Do you know its derivation?"

He shook his head.

"Kandaro is a regional designation," said Rhombus. "It refers to the province Jag traces lineage to. And Pelsh is the name of the female of whose entourage he is a member. She's quite a significant power on Rehbollo, actually. Not only is she a famous mathematician, she's also a niece of Queen Trath. I met Pelsh once, while attending a conference. She's charming, intelligent—and about twice Jag's size, as are all adult Waldahud females."

Keith contemplated a mental picture, but said nothing.

"Do you see?" asked Rhombus. "Jag has to make his mark. He has to distinguish himself from the other four males in her entourage if he is to be chosen. Everything a premating Waldahud male does is geared toward making him stand out. Jag came aboard *Starplex* looking for glory enough to earn him Pelsh's affection . . . and he's going to find that glory, no matter how hard he has to push."

That night, lying in bed, Keith rolled onto his back.

All his life, he'd had trouble sleeping—despite the

advice people had given him over the years. He never drank caffeinated beverages after 1800. He had PHANTOM play white noise through the bedroom speakers, drowning out the sound of Rissa's occasional snoring. And although there was a digital-clock display built into his night table, he'd covered its readout with a little square of plasticard slipped into a join between the pieces of wood composing the table. Staring at a clock, worrying about how late it was, about how little sleep he was going to get before morning came, was counterproductive. Oh, he could see the clock face when standing in the bedroom, and he could always reach over and bend down the plasticard to look at it in bed if he was really curious, but it helped.

Sometimes, that is.

But not tonight.

Tonight, he tossed and turned.

Tonight, he relived the encounter in the corridor with Jag.

*Jag.* Perfect name for the bastard.

Keith rolled onto his left side.

Jag was currently running a series of professional-development seminars for those *Starplex* staff members who wanted to know more physics; Rissa was running a similar series for those who wanted to learn some more biology.

Keith had always been fascinated by physics. Indeed, while taking a range of sciences in his first year at university, he'd thought seriously about becoming a physicist. So much neat stuff—like the anthropic principle, which said that the universe *had* to give rise to intelligent life. And Schrödinger's cat, a thought experiment that demonstrated that it was the act of observing that actually shaped reality. And all the wonderful twists and turns to Einstein's special and general theories of relativity.

Keith loved Einstein—loved him for his fusion of humanity and intellect, for his wild hair, for his own knight-errant quest to try to put the nuclear genie he'd made possible back into the bottle. Even after choosing sociology as his major, Keith had still kept a poster of the grand old man of physics on his dorm wall. He would enjoy taking some physics seminars . . . but not with Jag. Life was too short for that.

He thought about what Rhombus had said about Waldahud family life—and that turned his mind to his older sister Rosalind and younger brother Brian.

In a way, Roz and Brian had shaped him as much as his genetic makeup had. Because they existed, he was a middle child. Middle children were the bridge-builders, always trying to make connections, to bring groups together. It had always fallen to Keith to organize family events, such as parties for their parents' milestone anniversaries and birthdays, or Christmas gatherings of the clan. And he'd organized his high-school class's twentieth reunion, thrown receptions in his home for colleagues visiting from out of town, supported multicultural and ecumenical groups. Hell, he had spent most of his professional life working to get the Commonwealth off the ground, the ultimate exercise in bridge-building.

Roz and Brian didn't worry about who liked them and who didn't, about whether there was peace between all parties, about networking, about whether people were getting along.

Roz and Brian probably slept well at nights.

Keith switched back to lying on his spine, an arm behind his head.

Maybe it *was* impossible. Maybe humans and Waldahudin could never get along. Maybe they were too different. Or too similar. Or . . .

Christ, thought Keith. Let it go. Let it go.

He reached over, bent down the piece of plasticard, and looked at the glowing, mocking red digits.

*Damn.*

Now that they had collected samples of the strange material, it fell to Jag and Rissa, as the two science-division heads, to come up with a research plan. Of course, the next step depended on the nature of the samples. If it turned out to be nothing special, then *Starplex* would continue its quest for whoever activated this shortcut—a life-sciences priority mission. But if the strange material was out of the ordinary, Jag would argue that *Starplex* should stay here to study it, and Rissa's team should take one of *Starplex*'s two diplomatic vessels—either the *Nelson Mandela* or the *Kof Dagrelo em-Stalsh*—to continue the search.

The next morning Jag used the intercom to contact Rissa, who was up in her lab, saying he wanted to see her. That could mean only one thing: Jag was intending a preemptive strike to set mission priorities. She took a deep breath, preparing for a fight, and headed for the elevator.

Jag's office had the same floor plan as Rissa's, but he'd decorated it—if that was the word—in Waldahud mud-art. He had three different models of polychairs in front of the desk. Waldahudin disliked anything that was mass-produced; by having different models he could at least give the appearance that each was one of a kind. Rissa sat in the polychair in the middle and looked across Jag's wide, painfully neat desk at him. "So," she said. "You've presumably analyzed the samples we collected yesterday. What are the spheres made of?"

The Waldahud shrugged all four shoulders. "I don't know. A small percentage of the sample material is just the regular flotsam of space— carbon grains, hydrogen atoms, and so on. But the principal material is eluding all standard tests. It doesn't combust in oxygen or any other gas, for instance, and as far as I can tell it has no electrical charge at all. Regardless of what I try, I can't knock electrons off it to get positively charged nuclei. Delacorte up in the chemistry lab is having a look at a sample now."

"And what about the gravel from between the spheres?" Rissa asked.

Jag's bark had an unusual quality. "I'll show you," he said. They left his office, went down a corridor, and entered an isolation room. "Those are the samples," he said, gesturing with a medial arm at a glass-fronted cubic chamber measuring a meter on a side.

Rissa looked through the window and frowned. "That big one—does it have a flat bottom?"

Jag peered through the window. "Gods—"

The large egg-shaped piece of material had sunk about halfway into the bottom of the chamber, so that only a domelike part stuck up. Peering more closely, Jag could see that some of the smaller gravel pieces were sinking, too. He pointed with his upper-left first finger as he counted the fragments. Six were gone, presumably sunk beneath the surface of the chamber's bottom. But no holes had been left in their wake.

"It's dropping right through the floor," said Jag. He looked at the ceiling. "Central Computer!"

"Yes?" said PHANTOM.

"I want zero-g inside that sample chamber now!"

"Doing so."

"Good—no, wait. Change that! I want five standard gees in there, but I want them coming from the chamber's ceiling, not its floor. Got that? I want gravity in there to pull objects up toward the roof."

"Doing so," said PHANTOM.

Rissa and Jag watched, fascinated, as the egg-shaped piece of material started to rise out of the bottom of the chamber. Before it was all the way out, pieces of gravel welled up from beneath the solid floor and fell up toward the ceiling, hitting it not with the ricochet bounce one would expect but more like pebbles falling into tar and beginning to sink.

"Computer, oscillate the gravity until all the objects are free from the floor and ceiling, then shift to zero-g, with the objects floating in the chamber."

"Doing so."

"My word, that's incredible," said Rissa. "The stuff can pass right through other matter."

Jag grunted. "The original samples we tried to collect must have leaked through the probes' walls, pushed out by the force of their acceleration toward *Starplex*."

By bouncing the apparent source of gravity inside the chamber between the top and the bottom, PHANTOM eventually got all the gravel pieces to float freely. But Jag's fur danced when he saw the results of two pieces moving together. He'd expected to see them hit, then bounce off. Instead, when they got to just a few millimeters apart they deflected away from each other.

"Magnetic," said Rissa.

Jag moved his lower shoulders. "No, there's no magnetism at work here —there are no charges present."

There were four articulated arms ending in tractor-beam emitters inside the chamber, and Jag operated all of them in unison, controlling one with each hand. He used one beam to lock onto a piece of translucent gravel a centimeter in diameter, and used a second beam to grab another piece of equal size. He then operated the controls to move the two pieces together. Everything went fine until the chunks were within a very short distance of each other, but then no matter how much power he fed into the tractor beams, he was unable to bring them any closer. "Amazing," said Jag. "There's some sort of force repelling them—a nonmagnetic repulsive force. I've never seen anything like it."

"That must be what keeps the haze of gravel from coalescing," said Rissa.

Jag lifted his upper shoulders. "I suppose. The net effect is that the material in the haze between the spheres is bound together gravitationally, but it won't ever coalesce more than it already has."

"But then what keeps these pebbles together? Why doesn't that repulsive force blast them apart?"

"They must be locked chemically. I suspect they were originally formed under great pressure—pressure that defeated the repulsion we're observing. Now that their constituent atoms are bonded, they stay together, but it would take great effort to combine the pebbles into bigger groupings."

"Oh, hell," said Rissa. "You know what I'm thinking . . ."

Jag's four eyes went wide. "The Slammers! We've only ever seen what their weapon did to one of our probes. Perhaps if they turned it on a world, this might be the result. Quite the doomsday device: not only does it destroy the planet, but it also imparts a force to the rubble to prevent it from ever collecting back together to form another world."

"And now there's an open shortcut leading from here to the Commonwealth worlds. If they were to come through—"

At that moment, Jag's wall beeped, and the elderly face of Cynthia Delacorte appeared on it. "Jag, it's—oh, hi, Rissa. Listen, thanks for sending up those samples. Do you know that this stuff sinks into normal matter?"

Jag lifted his upper shoulders. "Incredible, isn't it?"

Delacorte nodded. "I'll say. It's not normal baryonic matter. It's not antimatter, of course. We'd have been blown out of the skies if it were. But where normal protons and neutrons consist of combinations of down quarks and up quarks, this stuff is made of matte quarks and glossy quarks."

Jag's fur danced excitedly. "Really?"

"I've never heard of those kinds of quarks," said Rissa.

Jag made a sound like she was a fool, but Delacorte nodded. "Since the twentieth century, humans have known of six flavors of quarks—up, down, top, bottom, strange, and charmed. In fact, six was the maximum number allowed for under the old Standard Model of physics, so we'd pretty much given up looking for more, which turned out to be a big mistake." She looked pointedly at Jag. "The Waldahudin had only found the same six flavors, too. But when we met the Ibs, they were aware of two more, which we refer to by opposing lusters, glossy and matte. There's no way you can get them by breaking down normal matter, but the Ibs had done unique work pulling matter out of quantum fluctuations. In their experiments, luster quarks were sometimes produced, but only at very, very high temperatures. What we've got here are the first-known naturally occurring luster quarks."

"Incredible," said Jag. "You've noticed the *fardint* things carry no charge? What explains that?"

Delacorte nodded, then looked at Rissa. "Electrons have a charge of negative one unit, up quarks have a positive two-thirds charge, and down quarks have a negative one-third charge. Each neutron is made of two downs quarks and an up, which means the net charge is zip. Meanwhile, each proton consists of one down and two ups, which gives a charge of positive one. Since atoms have equal numbers of protons and electrons, they have an overall neutral charge."

Rissa understood that the explanation had been for her benefit. She nodded at the wall monitor for Delacorte to go on.

"Well, this luster-quark matter consists of what I'm calling para-neutrons and para-protons. Para-neutrons consist of two glossy quarks and one matte, and para-protons consist of a pair of mattes plus a glossy. But neither glossies nor mattes carry any charge whatsoever—so regardless of how you combine them, there's no charge on the nucleus. And without a positive nucleus, there's nothing to attract negatively charged electrons, so a luster-quark atom is *solely* a nucleus; it has no electron orbital shells. The bottom line is that luster matter isn't just electrically neutral. Rather, it's *non*electrical; it's immune to electromagnetic interactions."

"Gods," said Jag. "That would explain why it can sink into solid objects. It would probably pass through completely unhindered if it weren't for drag caused by the regular-matter carbon grains and hydrogen polluting it, and—of course! That explains why we can see it, too. If it were purely luster quarks, it would be invisible, since the reflection and absorption of light depend on vibrating charges. We're just seeing the interstellar dust that's caught gravitationally inside the luster matter, like sand in jelly." He looked at the wall screen. "All right—it doesn't interact electromagnetically. What about the nuclear forces?"

"It *is* affected by both the strong and the weak nuclear force," said Delacorte. "But those forces are so short-range, I doubt we'd get any interaction through them with regular matter except at incredibly high pressures and temperatures."

Jag was quiet for a moment, considering. When he next spoke, his barking was subdued. "It's incredible," he said. "We knew the Slammer weapon could break chemical bonds, but changing regular matter into luster matter is —"

"Slammer weapon?" said Delacorte, her gray eyebrows arching. "Is that what you think produced this stuff? No, I doubt that. It'd take thousands of years for that much dust to be swept up by the spheres. My guess is that we're seeing a natural phenomenon."

"Natural . . . " said Jag, repeating the bark his translation implant had provided. "Fascinating. What about gravitational effects?"

"Well, luster quarks each mass about seven hundred and sixteen times what an electron does; that's about eighteen percent more than an up or a down quark. So a luster atom has a little more mass, and therefore produces a little more gravity, than does a normal atom with a comparable number of nucleons. Damned if I know how these luster quarks interact chemically with each other, though."

Jag was pacing back and forth. "All right," he said. "All right—how about this? Let's propose two more fundamental forces on top of the traditional four. Ever since the old Standard Model broke down, we've been looking for additional forces anyway. Say one force is long-range and repulsive—Cervantes and I have already observed that one at work while trying to push pieces of the gravel together with tractor beams. The other force would be medium-range and attractive."

"What does that do for us?" asked Delacorte.

"Well," said Jag, "normal chemistry is the result of orbital overlap of electrons surrounding charged nuclei; there's none of that going on here. But if the medium-range attractive force was stronger than the weak nuclear force, then it could act almost as a 'meta-charge,' making possible a kind of 'meta-chemistry.' It could bind atoms without relying on electromagnetism to do so. Meanwhile, the long-range repulsive force would repel luster quarks from each other. It would only be overwhelmed by the quarks' own gravity when enough mass density was present to force them together. It's similar to gravity forcing electrons and protons together to make a neutron star despite the degeneracy pressure wanting to keep electrons out of each other's orbitals." He looked at Rissa. "That means we've got 'meta-chemistry' that can conduct possibly quite complex reactions at the molecular level, but at the macro level luster matter can only clump together in world-sized masses whose own gravity is enough to overpower the repulsive force."

Delacorte looked impressed. "If you can work out the mechanics of all that, you'll win the Nobel of Kayf-Dukt for sure. It really is incredible—a whole different kind of matter that only interacts slightly with baryonic—"

"*Pastark!*" barked Jag. "By all the gods, do you know what this is?" His fur was whipping about like wheat in a high wind.

"Tell us," Rissa said at last, irritated.

"We shouldn't be calling it 'luster matter,'" Jag said. "The stuff already has a perfectly good common name." His two right eyes looked at Delacorte's image and his two left at Rissa. "Dark matter!"

"Good God!" said Delacorte. "Good God, I think you're right." She shook her head in wonder. "Dark matter."

"That it is," howled Jag. "It makes up the vast bulk of our universe, and until now we've never known what it was. This is the find of the century!" His four eyes closed, picturing the glory.

# DELTA DRACONIS

*"What was Saul Ben-Abraham like?" asked Glass.*

*Keith looked around the forest simulation, thinking of all the ways he could describe the man who had been his best friend. Tall. Boisterous. A guffaw that could be heard a kilometer away. A guy who could identify any song in three notes. A man who could drink more beer than anyone Keith had ever met—he must have had a bladder the size of Iceland. Finally, Keith settled on, "Hairy."*

*"I beg your pardon?" said Glass.*

*"Saul had a great beard," said Keith. "Covered most of his face. And he had this one giant eyebrow, like a chimp had laid its forearm across his head. The first time I ever saw him in shorts, I was amazed. The guy looked like sasquatch."*

*"Sasquatch?"*

*"A mythical primate from my part of Earth. I still remember seeing him in shorts for the first time and saying, gee, Saul, you've got hairy legs. He let out that great laugh of his and said, 'Yes—like a man!' I said it was more like* ten *men." Keith*

*paused. "God, how I miss him. Friends like that, who mean that much to you, come along perhaps once in a lifetime."*

*Glass was quiet for several seconds. "Yes," he said at last. "I suppose that's true."*

*"Of course," said Keith, "there was more to Saul than just a thick coat of fur. He was brilliant. The only person I've ever met who I thought might be brighter than him is Rissa. Saul was an astronomer. He's the person who discovered the Tau Ceti shortcut, from its footprint in hyperspace. The guy should have won a Nobel prize for that . . . but they don't like to award them posthumously."*

*"I appreciate your loss," said Glass. "It's as if—oh, excuse me. My reckoner says I've got an incoming thought package. Will you excuse me for a little while?"*

*Keith nodded, and Glass took an odd step, sort of sideways, and disappeared. Doubtless he'd gone through a door hidden by the forest simulation filling the docking bay—the only direct visual evidence Keith had had that he wasn't actually back on Earth. Well, if there was a door, Keith wanted to find it. He patted the air in the spot that Glass had disappeared from, but there was nothing.*

*There had to be a wall somewhere around, though. The bay wasn't that big. Keith began to walk, figuring he was bound to hit a wall eventually. He continued on for perhaps five hundred meters without encountering any obstruction. Of course, if his—he started to think the word "captor," again, but fought it down and substituted "host" instead—if his host were being clever, he could have manipulated the images to make Keith think he was walking in a straight line when he was really going in a circle.*

*Keith decided to rest. As much as he tried to find time to work out in Starplex's Earth gym, which had gravity set to a full standard gee, he'd lost some muscle tone because of all the time he spent in the lighter Wald-standard gravity used in the ship's common elements. He really should take Thor Magnor up on his offer of playing handball; Keith and Saul had played the game regularly, but he'd given it up when Saul had died.*

*Keith lowered himself to the ground again, which, at this spot, was covered with clover. Keith found it quite comfort-*

*able to sit on. He ran his hand through the clover, enjoying the feel of it against his skin, and looked around. It was a remarkable simulation, he thought. So relaxing, so beautiful. He watched some birds moving high overhead, but they were too far away for him to identify the species.*

*Keith plucked a piece of clover and brought it up to look at. Maybe this was his lucky day; maybe he'd find a four-leaf clover . . .*

*What luck! He did!*

*He plucked a few more pieces, and his jaw dropped.*

*He pressed his face to the ground, and examined plant after plant.*

*They were all four-leaf clovers.*

*He brought one up to his face, held between thumb and index finger, and scrutinized it. It seemed like normal clover in almost every way. It even bled a little green plant juice from its severed stem. But each of these clovers had four leaves. Keith remembered from undergraduate botany that the genus name for clover was* Trifolium— *three leaves. By definition, clover had three leaves, except in the odd mutant individual. But these plants* all *had four distinct oval leaves.*

*Keith looked at the white and pink flowers growing from some of the plants. Definitely clover—but four-leaf clover. He shook his head. How could Glass have gotten all the other details right, but have made a mistake such as this? It didn't make any sense.*

*He looked around again, searching for any other discrepancies. Most of the deciduous trees did indeed seem to be maple—sugar maple, in fact, if he wasn't mistaken. And those conifers were jack pine, and the big one a little farther along was a blue spruce. And—*

*And what kind of bird was that? Sitting in that blue spruce? Surely not a cardinal or a jay. Oh, it had the tufted head crest, but it was emerald green, and its bill was flat and spatulate, unlike that of most songbirds.*

*It was Earth; no doubt about it. That was Earth's moon, still sitting high in the daytime sky. And yet, it wasn't quite Earth—some of the details weren't right.*

*Keith chewed at his lower lip, puzzled . . .*

# VII

Jag and Rissa took an elevator up to the bridge, and soon the Waldahud was standing in front of the two rows of workstations, telling his colleagues of the fantastic discovery. "There's a metaphor that's been carried by the current for years," he barked, "that visible matter is just froth on an inky ocean of dark matter. We knew the dark matter was there because of its gravitational effects, but we've never seen it—until now. Those spheres out there, and the gravel fog between them, are made out of dark matter."

Lianne let out a low whistle. Keith raised an eyebrow. He knew a bit about dark matter, of course. CalTech astronomer Fritz Zwicky had deduced its existence back in 1933, through observations of the galaxies in the Virgo Cluster. Those galaxies were rotating around each other so quickly that if the visible stars were the only major source of mass present, the whole thing should have flung apart long ago. Subsequent studies showed that almost every large structure in the universe—including our Milky Way galaxy—behaved as if there were far more mass present than could be accounted for by the suns and any reasonable number of attendant planets. Some previously undetected matter, dubbed "dark matter" because it was apparently neither luminous nor highly reflective, accounted for over 90 percent of the gravity in the universe.

As usual, Thorald Magnor had his large feet up on his console, and his thick fingers interlaced behind his head, buried in his red hair. "I thought we'd already discovered what dark matter was," he said.

"Only part of it," said Jag, lifting two of his four hands. "We've long known that baryonic matter—matter made up of protons and neutrons—accounts for less than ten percent of the mass of the universe. In 2037, we discovered that the ubiquitous tau neutrino has a very slight mass—about seven electron volts' worth. And we found that the muon neutrino also has a trifling mass, about three one-thousandths of an electron volt. Since these two types of neutrinos are so abundant, in total they account for about three or four times more mass than all the baryons do. But that still left us with as much as two thirds of the universe's mass unaccounted for—until now."

"What makes you think the stuff out there is dark matter?" Keith asked.

"Well," said Jag, "it isn't normal matter; that much is certain." Although he was trying to hide it, Jag was holding on to the beveled edge of Thor's console with one hand so that he wouldn't drop down onto four legs. *Starplex* operated on a four-shift cycle as a concession to the Waldahudin, who came from a world with a short day, but Jag had been working overtime. "In early dark-matter studies, there were two candidates for the material composing it, named WIMPs and MACHOs by human astronomers— all of whom should have to swim in a river of urine, by the way. WIMPs are 'weakly interacting massive particles'—you see the gibberish foisted upon us in search of these silly acronyms? Anyway, the tau and muon neutrinos turned out to be WIMPs."

"And MACHOs?" asked Keith.

"'Massive compact halo objects,'" said Jag. "The 'halo' is the sphere of dark matter that has a galaxy at its center. The 'massive compact objects' were thought to be billions of Jupiter-sized bodies not associated with any particular star—a fog of gaseous worlds through which the luminous material of the galaxy moves."

Lianne was leaning forward, chin resting on her hand. "But if the universe really were permeated with—with MACHOs," she asked, "wouldn't we have detected them by now?"

Jag turned to her. "Even Jupiter-sized objects are puny on the cosmic scale. And since they're nonluminous, the only way we would see them is if one wandered in front of a star we happened to be observing. Still, the effect would be minor: just a slight gravitational lensing of the star's light, causing a temporary brightening. Such events have occasionally been seen; the oldest recorded observation of one was made by human astronomers in 1993. But even if space were lousy with MACHOs—enough so that they made up two thirds of all the mass in the universe—only one out of every five million stars you could observe at any given moment would likely be undergoing gravitational lensing due to one passing by." He gestured toward the twinkling part of the starfield. "We only see gross effects here because we're so close to the field of dark matter, and because the dark matter itself is transparent. We're actually just seeing regular space dust, sprinkled throughout the dark-matter objects."

Keith looked at Rissa, his eyebrows raised. She made no objection. "Well," said the director, "this certainly seems to be a major discovery, worthy of further—"

"Forgive the interruption," said Rhombus, "but I'm detecting a tachyon pulse." Rhombus rotated the starfield hologram surrounding the bridge to bring the shortcut front and center; the effect on Keith's stomach was similar to what he experienced in a planetarium when the operator was trying to demonstrate that learning could be fun. Jag quickly took his seat on Keith's left. The shortcut was a pinprick of green—the color of whatever was coming through it— surrounded by the usual ring of violet Soderstrom radiation.

"Is it a Commonwealth ship?" Keith asked.

"No," said Rhombus. "There's no transponder signal of any kind." The green spot continued to grow. "Incredulous: that is bright"—PHANTOM's stilted translation of the words that were flashing over Rhombus's mantle. But the Ib was right. The shortcut was the brightest object in the sky, exceeding even the A-class star Jag had spotted earlier.

"Let's give it lots of room, whatever it is," said Keith. "Thor, start backing us away."

"Doing so."

Keith looked to his left. "Jag, spectral analysis."

The Waldahud read from one of his monitors. "Scanning. Hydrogen, helium, carbon, nitrogen, oxygen, neon, magnesium, silicon, iron . . ."

"It looks pure green," said Keith. "Could it be a laser?"

Jag turned his two right eyes to look at the director, while keeping his other two focused on his instruments. "No. There's nothing coherent about that light."

The fiery green pinprick was growing wider; it had become a fiercely bright circle several meters in diameter.

"How about a fusion exhaust?" asked Lianne. "Could it be a ship coming out of the shortcut tail first, as if it were decelerating?"

Jag consulted more readouts. "It certainly *is* a fusion signature," he said. "But it would have to be a *very* powerful engine."

Keith left his console and walked over to stand just behind Rhombus. "Any chance of contacting that ship?"

One of Rhombus's manipulatory ropes whipped out to touch a control. "Forgive me, but not on conventional radio. The thing is putting out an enormous amount of EMI. A hyperspace radio link might work, but there's no way of knowing which quantized level they use for communication."

"Start at the lowest and work your way up," Keith said. "Standard prime-number sequences."

Another flick of a rope. "Transmitting. But it would literally take forever to try every level."

Keith turned around and faced Rissa. "Looks like you might get your first-contact opportunity after all." He turned back to look at the shortcut. "Christ, that's bright." Every object on the bridge that wasn't swathed in the hologram was bathed in green light now. Although no shadows fell on the invisible floor, the staff members were all casting harsh ones on the seating gallery behind the workstations.

"It's even brighter than it looks," said Jag. "The camera is filtering most of it."

"What the hell could it be?" Keith asked, looking at Jag.

"Whatever it is," said Jag, "it's streaming out a lot of charged particles—could be a particle-beam weapon." The green circle continued to expand. "Diameter is now one hundred and ten meters," said Jag. "One fifty." His barking grew softer, incredulous. "Two fifty. Five hundred. A full kilometer. *Two kilometers.*"

Keith turned back to the flaring image in the hologram. "Jesus," he said, bringing an arm up to shield his eyes.

Slapping of ropes from Rhombus—an Ibese scream. "Profuse apologies," he said a moment later as the display darkened somewhat. "The object is brighter than the automatic compensators are designed to deal with. I shall henceforth monitor the display directly."

The green circle kept expanding at a great rate. Its edges were coruscating with violet Soderstrom discharges—a pyrotechnical halo around the vast green center. The central area still seemed to be a flat circle.

"Temperature is about twelve thousand Kelvin," said Jag.

"That's *hot,*" said Rissa. "What in God's name is it?"

An alarm started sounding, warbling high and low. "Radiation warning!" shouted Lianne. She wheeled to face Keith. "Recommended action: move *Starplex.*"

"Right," Keith said, sprinting back to his command station. "Thor, pick up the pace. Put us another fifty thousand klicks from the shortcut." He glanced at his astrogation readout. "Course two hundred and ten degrees by forty-five degrees. Use thrusters only; I don't want to drop into hyperspace until we know what that thing is."

"As you say, boss," said Thor, hands flying over his instruments.

The apparent growth of the green circle slowed, but it was

still getting larger; its expansion rate was exceeding *Starplex*'s maneuvering speed.

"I didn't know a shortcut could open that wide," said Rhombus. "Jag, just what exactly is coming through it?"

Both sets of Jag's shoulders rose and fell. "Unknown. The spectral analysis is unusual—lots of heavy-element Fraunhofer absorption lines. It matches nothing in our database." He paused. "If it *is* a fusion exhaust, the ship must be gigantic."

"It looks perfectly flat," said Rissa. "How can it keep expanding as a circle?"

"The apparent expansion is caused by the opening up of the shortcut aperture," said Jag. "They open at a finite speed, and, when touched by a flat surface, an aperture will take on a circular shape until the edges are reached." He used his left eyes to glance at a readout. "The rate at which the aperture is opening is increasing, although at an uneven rate."

The halo of violet, representing the edges of the portal, was just the faintest border around the vast circle, like a matte line around a spaceship model in an old-fashioned SF movie.

"How big is it now?" Keith asked.

Jag was evidently getting tired of answering that question. He touched keys on his console and a trio of color-coded rulers demarcated in different units formed a glowing three-quarters frame around the green circle. It now measured 450 kilometers in diameter.

"Radiation levels are increasing rapidly," said Lianne.

"Thor, double our retreat speed," Keith said. "Can our force screens handle this?"

Lianne was consulting a set of readouts. She shook her head. "Not if it gets much bigger."

The warbling sound was continuing in the background. "Turn that damned alarm off," Keith said. He looked at the Waldahud. "Jag?"

"It's flat," Jag said. "Like a wall of flame. Diameter is now over a thousand kilometers. Thirteen hundred . . . Seventeen hundred . . ."

The emerald light dominated the sky. The humans brought up hands to shield their eyes again.

Suddenly, a streamer of green fire shot out of the wall,

like a neon whiplash against the night. It continued to stretch out until it had extended over fifty thousand kilometers from the shortcut.

"My God . . ." said Rissa.

"Tell me that's *not* a weapon," said Jag, rising to his feet, and standing with both sets of arms crossed behind his back. "We would have been incinerated if we hadn't moved the ship."

"Could it—could it be the Slammers?" asked Lianne.

The green streamer was now falling back toward the vast luminescent circle of the shortcut. As it did so, it broke up into fiery segments, each thousands of kilometers long.

"Thor, prepare to go into hyperdrive on my order," Keith said.

"All stations, secure for hyperdrive," said Lianne's voice over the loudspeakers.

"Is it a forcefield of some kind?" asked Rissa.

"Unlikely," said Jag.

"If that *is* a ship's exhaust," Keith said, "it must have the biggest goddamn ramscoop in history attached to the other end."

"Diameter is eight thousand kilometers," said Jag. He had already recalibrated the units on the scale bars twice. "Ten thousand . . ."

"Thor, thirty seconds to hyperdrive!"

"All stations, alert," said Lianne. "Hyperdrive in twenty-five seconds, mark."

Another tongue of green flame shot out of the widening circle. "Hyperdrive in fifteen seconds, mark," said Lianne.

"Sweet Jesus, it's huge," Rissa said, under her breath.

"Hyperdrive in five sec—hyperdrive initialization canceled! Automatic override!"

"What? Why?" Keith looked at the pair of computer eyes mounted on his workstation. "PHANTOM, what's happening?"

"Gravity well is too steep for safe hyperspatial insertion," replied the computer.

"*Gravity well?* We're in open space!"

"Oh, Gods," said Jag. "*It's big enough to curve space-*

*time.* " He moved out from behind his console and jogged in front of the cluster of workstations. "Reduce display brightness by half."

Rhombus's ropes flicked. The view of the giant green circle dimmed, but it was still flaring, overexposed.

"Halve it again," snapped Jag.

The view grew dimmer. Jag was trying to look at it, but it was still too bright for eyes that had evolved under a dim red sun. "Once more," he said.

The view darkened further—and suddenly there was detail visible on the green surface: a granularity of lighter and darker shades . . .

"That's not a ship," said Jag, his own voice, audible beneath PHANTOM's translation, the staccato barking of Waldahud astonishment. "It's a *star.*"

"A *green* star?" said Rissa, amazed. "There's no such thing."

"Thor," Keith snapped, "full thruster power—perpendicular course away from the shortcut. Move!"

The alarm began to warble again. "Level-two radiation warning!" shouted Lianne overtop of it.

"Force screens to maximum," Keith snapped.

"Can't do both, boss," shouted Thor. "Full thrusters can't be combined with maximum screens."

"Priority to thrusters, then! Get us out of here!"

"If that's a star," said Rissa, "we're *way* too close, aren't we?" She looked at Jag, who said nothing. "Aren't we?" she asked again.

Jag lifted his upper shoulders. "Way, way too close," he said softly.

"If the radiation doesn't fry us," said Rissa, "the heat will."

"Thor, can't you get any more speed?" Keith said.

"No can do, boss. The local gravity well is steepening rapidly."

"Would we do better to abandon the mothership?" asked Lianne. "Perhaps our smaller ships could escape more easily?"

"Forgive me, but no," said Rhombus. "Beside the fact that we don't have enough auxiliary vessels to evacuate everyone, only a few of them are outfitted with shielding for close approaches to stars."

Lianne had her head tilted to one side; listening to private communications over her ear implant. "Director, we have panicked messages coming in from all over the ship."

"Standard radiation precautions," snapped Keith.

"Those will be inadequate," said Jag softly as he moved back to his workstation.

Keith looked over at Rissa. One of her monitors was displaying plans for *Starplex*, showing the two mutually perpendicular diamonds intersecting the wide central disk. "What happens," she said, turning to him, "if we rotate *Starplex* so that the ocean deck is at a right angle to our line of travel?"

"What difference will that make?" asked Keith.

"We could use the seawater as radiation shielding. The ocean is filled to a depth of twenty-five meters. That's a lot of insulation."

Lights on Rhombus's web winked on and off. "It would certainly help—everyone who isn't on or below the ocean deck, that is."

Lianne spoke up. "We'll *all* be fried unless we do something."

Keith nodded. "Thor, rotate *Starplex* as described."

"ACS jets firing."

"Lianne, devise a plan to evacuate all personnel from decks thirty-one through seventy."

She nodded.

"PHANTOM, intercom now!"

"Intercom on," said PHANTOM.

"Everyone—quickly. This is Director Lansing. Following instructions from Internal-Ops Manager Karendaughter, evacuate decks thirty-one through seventy. Get out of the engineering torus, out of the docking bays, out of the cargo holds, and out of all four lower-habitat modules. Everyone move into the upper-habitat modules. All dolphins—either get out of the ocean deck altogether, or swim up to the surface of the ocean and stay there. Everyone, move in an orderly fashion—but move! PHANTOM, end, translate, and loop."

In the holo display, the surface of the star was bulging out of the circular shortcut opening. "The shortcut-aperture expansion rate is increasing rapidly," said Jag. "It seemed to take a while to get going, probably because the star was essentially flat at first, but now that the surface is showing curvature, the thing is opening more quickly. Diameter is now one hundred and ten thousand kilometers."

"Radiation is increasing rapidly as more of the surface comes through," said Lianne. "And if it shoots another prominence in our direction, we'll be cinderized."

"Evacuation status," snapped Keith.

Lianne pushed buttons and twenty-four square images appeared, replacing part of the starscape bubble. Each showed a different view through PHANTOM's eyes, and the scenes kept shifting, cycling through the computer's various cameras.

A corridor—level fifty-eight, according to the superimposed status line: six Ibs rapidly rolling forward.

An intersection: three human women in track suits hurrying toward the camera from one direction, and two Waldahudin and a human male rushing in from the other direction.

The zero-g part of the central shaft: people using the handholds to shoot themselves upward.

A vertical water tube, with three dolphins swimming up it.

An elevator car, with a Waldahud holding the door open with one arm and urging passengers in with the other three.

Another elevator car, containing an Ib surrounded by a dozen humans.

"Even with everyone above the ocean deck," said Lianne, "I don't think we're going to have enough radiation shielding."

"Wait!" said Thor. "What about going behind the shortcut?"

"Eh?" said Rhombus—or, at least, that's the sound PHANTOM gave to the little ripple of lights that passed over his mantle.

"The shortcut's a circular hole," said Thor, looking over his shoulder at Keith. "The star is emerging from it. The rear part of the shortcut is a flat, empty circle—a black void in the shape of whatever's passing through it. If we're behind the shortcut, we'll be protected—at least for a while."

Jag slapped all four of his hands against his console. "He's right!"

Keith nodded. "Do it, Thor. Alter course to put us in the lee of the shortcut, keeping the bottom of the ocean deck facing the emerging star."

"Executing," said Thor. "But it'll take a while to get there." In the spherical holo display encompassing the bridge, the brilliant circular profile of the star slowly became a green dome as Thor maneuvered the ship.

"Talldorsal to Lansing!" A high-pitched dolphin voice over the intercom, with splashing in the background.

"Open. Lansing here."

"Thor's not moving in a line straight the ship. We're getting *tides* on the ocean deck."

"Lianne?" Keith said, and the twenty-four views of the evacuation all changed to different angles on the ocean. Seawater was sloshing up to the holographic ceiling on the port side, real waves touching fake clouds, forcing all the dolphins to the starboard so that they could breathe.

"Damn," said Thor. "Hadn't thought about that. I'll rotate the ship around its axis as we move. With luck, I should be able to keep all the forces balanced. Sorry!"

As *Starplex* continued to move, the bulging dome of the green star became progressively eclipsed by the featureless black circular backside of the shortcut. And then, at last, the green disappeared; *Starplex* was in the shortcut's lee. The only evidence for the emerging star was the emerald cast on the dark-matter field beyond it. Even the ring of Soderstrom radiation was invisible back here; it, after all, was caused by tachyons spilling out of the shortcut, heading in the opposite direction. The black circle continued to grow, though, blotting out more and more background stars. Its diameter was now 800,000 kilometers.

"Can you extrapolate how big the star is going to get, based on the curvature we observed on the other side?" Keith asked Jag.

"It's not yet halfway through," Jag replied, "and it's

oblate from high-speed rotation. Best guess? One-point-five million kilometers."

"Thor, any chance of the hyperdrive?" Keith asked.

Thor spoke into the hologram of Keith floating above his console rim. "Not yet. We'd have to be at least seventy million klicks from the star's center before space would be flat enough to engage it. I estimate we'll reach that distance in eleven hours."

"*Hours!* How long till the star's equator passes through the shortcut?"

"Perhaps five minutes," said Jag.

"Evacuation status?"

"One hundred and ninety people are still below the ocean deck," said Lianne.

"Will we make it?" Keith asked her.

"I'm not—"

"Red light on thruster number six," shouted Thor. "It's overheating."

"*Great,*" Keith said. "Do you need to take it off-line?"

"Not yet," said Thor. "I'm injecting repair nanotechs into its intercoolers; they may be able to correct the problem."

"The green star's equator is about to pass through the shortcut," said Jag.

A portion of the holographic display changed to a schematic representation of what was happening. At the left was the bulging hemisphere of the part of the star that had already protruded from the shortcut. The shortcut itself was seen from the side as a vertical line. Behind that, and receding away from it, was the diamond-shaped profile of *Starplex*. As the equator passed out of the shortcut, the hole the shortcut made in space started shrinking, and photons and charged particles from the star began spilling backward. The edges of the radiation backwash were like the hands of a clock starting at noon and six and converging toward three o'clock.

Thor pushed *Starplex* as hard as he could. Keith could see constellations of yellow warning indicators lighting up on the pilot's panel. The ship continued to climb out of the star's gravity well, its escape tunnel narrowing as the shortcut shrank in size.

"Lansing!" shouted Jag. "The dark-matter field is *moving*—moving away from the star."

"Could it be because of that repulsive force you mentioned?"

Jag moved both sets of shoulders. "It's not the kind of effect I'd predict, but—"

"Lower-deck evacuation now complete," said Lianne, swinging around to face the director.

"Even so," said Thor, "we're going to take one hell of a lot radiation kick when that backwash hits us."

Finally, the star finished emerging, and the shortcut disappeared. At that point, Thor switched all power from the engines to the force screens, trying to deflect as much of the incoming radiation as possible. *Starplex* continued to travel under momentum. The radiation alarm began to warble again.

"Are we far enough away?" Keith asked. Thor was too busy with the controls to answer. "Are we far enough away?" he asked again.

Jag did some calculations. "I think so," he said, "but only because we're using the ocean deck as shielding. Otherwise, we would all have taken a lethal dose."

"All right," Keith said. "Let's continue on until we're at a safe distance. Lianne, draw up a new duty roster that makes minimal use of cetaceans, and put any nonessential dolphins into medical hibernation until we can replace the water on the ocean deck. At the rate the star is receding from the shortcut, it'll be days before we can approach the portal safely." He paused, then: "Good work, everyone. Rhombus, what's the status of our docking bays?"

"They should still be usable. Their walls are heavily shielded against radiation leakage, in case a ship crashes or explodes in them."

"Good," said Keith. "Thor, let me know when we're an acceptable distance from that star." He turned to the Waldahud. "Jag, you should go have a close look at it. I want to know exactly where it came from and why it's here."

# VIII

It had taken a long time for humans to decipher dolphin speech. When they finally did so, delphinese names turned out to be sonargrams of individual dolphins, with their most unusual physical characteristics exaggerated. It was no surprise, then, that the only form of human art dolphins really enjoyed was political cartooning.

One of *Starplexs'* best probeship pilots was a dolphin whose English name was Longbottle—a poor substitute for the song of trills and clicks that painted a caricature of him for his kinfolk, emphasizing his mighty snout.

Longbottle's favorite probeship was the *Rum Runner,* a bronze wedge twenty meters long and ten wide. A water tank ran down the ship's axis. To the left and right were separate air-filled habitats that joined at the rear in a U-shape with an airlock between them. The port side was normally kept to human standards; the starboard was set to cooler Waldahud conditions.

To pilot the vessel, Longbottle let small free-floating sensor drones clamp onto his flukes and pectoral fins. The ship had hundreds of attitude-control jets that allowed it to move in direct approximation of the dolphin's own movements in his tank. Such a technique was extraordinarily wasteful of fuel—so much so that the Waldahudin had refused to bid on the contract to build these vessels—but it provided incredible maneuverability and, according to Longbottle, was an absolute joy to fly.

Although the *Rum Runner* could operate away from *Starplex* for weeks at a time, on this mission it would be gone for less than a day, and the crew would consist of just Longbottle and Jag.

The *Rum Runner* was normally stored in docking bay seven, one of five that had locks leading through the engineering torus to the ocean deck. The ship was clamped to the deck's wall, and three access tubes at shallow angles entered its rooftop hatches.

Once Longbottle and Jag were aboard, the segmented docking-bay door moved up into the roof. Longbottle was famous for his theatrical launches. He zoomed the ship out of the bay, then rolled and arched in his tank, taking the *Rum Runner* on a breathtaking warm-up flight past all the docking-bay doors, swinging in a great circle around the central disk. He then rolled to one side in his tank, and the ship made a wide arc—looking for all the world as though it were banking in the vacuum of space.

Jag was getting impatient, but Longbottle, like all dolphins, was oblivious to that. He did a series of turns and flips in his tank, and the ship responded in kind. The gravity plates under Jag's compartment compensated completely for the movements, but in his water-filled tube, Longbottle could feel the ship as if it were an extension of his own body.

Finally, when he'd had enough fun, Longbottle set off on a wildly curving path—again, wasteful of energy, but so much more interesting than the straight lines and precise arcs of normal celestial mechanics.

The green star dominated the sky, even though its surface

was now thirty million kilometers distant. The *Rum Runner* had much better force screens and physical shielding than did *Starplex* itself; it could make a very close passage. Under Longbottle's fanciful guidance, the ship dived in, skimming the vast orb from just 100,000 kilometers above its photosphere. Scoops on the ship's leading edge sucked in samples of stellar atmosphere.

"Greenness of this star a bafflement to me," said Longbottle, through the hydrophone in his tank. Like most dolphins, Longbottle could approximate the sounds of both English and Waldahudar (although with mangled syntax— there was no such thing as appropriate word order in cetacean grammar). The computer simply processed those sounds to make them intelligible; it would only switch over to translation mode if a dolphin was actually speaking in delphinese.

Jag grunted. "I'm puzzled, too. Its surface temperature is twelve thousand degrees. The *fardint* thing should be blue or white, not green. The spectral analysis doesn't make any sense either. I've never seen such high concentrations of heavy elements in a star."

"Damaged perhaps by passage through shortcut?" asked Longbottle, twisting in his tank so that the ship would roll slowly around its axis. Even with extra shielding, it wasn't safe to keep the same side facing the star.

Jag grunted again. "I suppose that's possible. Most of the star's chromosphere and corona were probably scraped off during passage through the shortcut. The shortcut's lips clamped down on the photosphere, stripping away the rarefied gas above. Still, all previous tests have shown zero structural change in objects passing through a shortcut. Of course, nothing this big has ever gone through one before."

The *Rum Runner's* viewscreens were filled to the edges with flaming green; the physical windows had all turned opaque. "Take us in once around the star's equator," said Jag, "then do a polar loop. It's possible that the star's structure isn't uniform. Before I get too worked up over these absorption lines, I want to be sure the spectra are the same all over."

It took almost five hours at one one-thousandth of
lightspeed to complete the five-million-kilometer sweep
around the equator, and another five to do the loop from
pole to pole. Longbottle kept the *Rum Runner* corkscrewing
all the while. Jag's eyes were glued to his scanning
equipment, watching the dark vertical absorption lines. He
kept muttering to himself, "Silt in the water, silt in the
water"—the truth remained hidden.

Jag had no trouble measuring the star's mass from its
footprint in hyperspace; it was somewhat heavier than he'd
expected. Except for the color, the star's surface was fairly
typical, consisting of tightly packed beads of light and dark
caused by convection cells in the photosphere. It even had
sunspots, but unlike those of other stars, these were all
connected in dumbbell shapes. It was, without doubt, a
star—but it was also unlike any star Jag had ever seen
before.

Finally, the flybys were complete. "Ready home to go?"
asked Longbottle.

Jag lifted all four arms in a gesture of resignation. "Yes."

"Mystery solved?"

"No. A star like this should simply not exist."

The *Rum Runner* swept back toward *Starplex*, Jag muttering over his data for the entire journey.

Keith lay in bed next to his wife, unable to sleep. He looked
over at Rissa's form in the darkness, watched the thin sheet
covering her rise and fall in time with her breathing.

She deserved better, he thought. He exhaled, trying to
force the worries out of himself with the escaping breath,
and conjured up images of happier times.

Rissa had dark eyes that turned into upward-arching
crescents when she smiled. Her mouth was small, but her
lips were full—half as tall as they were wide. Her mother
had been Italian; her father, Spanish. She had inherited her
lustrous dark hair and his fiery eyes. In his forty-six years of
life, Keith Lansing had never met anyone who looked more
appealing by candlelight than Rissa.

When they'd first met, in 2070, he'd been twenty-two and

she'd been twenty, with a wonderfully curvy figure. Of course, her body shape was changing in natural ways as she aged; she was still in fine condition, but the proportions had shifted. Back then, Keith couldn't have imagined finding a woman of forty-four attractive, but to his infinite surprise, his tastes had altered as the years passed, and although two decades of marriage had doubtless dulled his immediate reaction to her, when he saw Rissa in an unusual way—in a new suit, or stretching to reach something on a top shelf, or with her hair swept in a different manner—she could still take his breath away.

And yet . . .

And yet, Keith was aware that time was taking its toll on him. His hair was departing. Oh, there were "cures" for that—imagine suggesting that something as natural as male-pattern baldness required a cure!—but to employ them seemed vain and foolish. Besides, middle-aged scientists were supposed to be bald. It was in the rule book somewhere.

Keith's father had had a full head of dark hair up until he'd been killed at age fifty-five; Keith wondered now whether he'd used a hair restorer. But for Keith to do something like that would be silly.

He remembered Mandy Lee, a holovid star he'd been infatuated with as a twelve-year-old boy. Back then, nothing had been more exciting to him than large breasts on a woman, probably because none of the girls in his class yet had them; they were a symbol of the forbidden, alien world of adult sexuality. Well, Mandy—dubbed "the binary star system" by some wag at *HV Guide*—was famous for her physique. But Keith had lost all interest in her when he'd found out that her breasts were fake; he couldn't look at her without imagining the implants beneath the swelling alabaster skin and the surgical scars (even though he knew, of course, the anabolizing laser scalpels would have left no marks at all). Well, he'd be damned if he'd turn his head into a fake; he'd be damned if he'd let people looking at him think, hey, the guy's really bald, you know . . .

And so there they were, Rissa Cervantes and Keith

Lansing: still in love, if not in the passionate way of their youth, in what was ultimately a more satisfying, more relaxing fashion.

And yet—

And yet, dammit, he'd just turned forty-six. He was aging, balding, graying, and hadn't been with another woman since his three—such a small number!—awkward encounters in high school and at university. Three, plus Rissa—a total of four. An average of less than one a decade. Christ, he thought, even a Waldahud could count my partners on the fingers of one hand.

Keith knew he shouldn't think about such things, knew that what he and Clarissa had was something most people never really achieved: a love affair that grew and evolved as they aged, a relationship that was solid and secure and warm.

And yet—

And yet there was Lianne Karendaughter. Like Mandy Lee, the very symbol of beauty in his youth, Lianne had exquisite Asian features; something about Asian women had always appealed to Keith. He didn't know how old Lianne was, but there was no doubt that she was younger than Rissa. Of course, as ship's director, Keith could easily access Lianne's personnel records, but he was afraid to do so. For God's sake, she might be as young as thirty. Lianne had come aboard the last time *Starplex* had passed by Tau Ceti, and now, as Internal Operations manager, she and Keith often spent hours together on the bridge. And yet, to his surprise, no matter how much time he spent with her, he always wished it were more.

He hadn't done anything foolish yet. Indeed, he thought he had everything under control. Still, he'd always been an introspective sort; he wasn't blind to what was going on. Midlife crisis, the fear that he was no longer virile. And what better way to dispel that notion than by bedding a beautiful, young woman?

Idle fantasies. Of course, of course.

He rolled onto his side, facing away from Rissa, tucking himself into a semifetal position. He didn't want to do anything that would hurt Rissa. But if she never learned about it—

*Christ, man, get a grip.* She'd find out for sure. How would he face her after that? And their son Saul? How would he face him? He'd seen his son beam at him with pride, yell at him in fury, but he'd never seen him look at him with disgust.

If only he could get some sleep. If only he could stop tormenting himself.

He stared into the darkness, eyes wide open.

Once the *Rum Runner* had docked, Longbottle went off to eat, and Jag returned to the bridge. The Waldahud was now keeping erect by use of an intricately carved cane—still better than reverting to four legs. Keith, Rissa, Thor, and Lianne had all had a night's sleep, and Rhombus—well, Ibs didn't sleep, a fact that made their long lifespans seem doubly unfair. Jag usually stood in front of the six workstations to give reports, but this time he walked back to the seating gallery and collapsed into the center chair, letting the others rotate their stations to face him.

Keith looked at the Waldahud expectantly. "Well?"

Jag marshaled his thoughts a moment, then began to bark. "As some of you know, stars are divided into three broad age categories. First-generation stars are the oldest in the universe, and consist almost entirely of hydrogen and helium, the two original elements. Less than 0.02 percent of their composition is heavier atoms, and those, of course, were produced internally through the stars' own fusion processes. When first-gens go nova or supernova, the interstellar dust clouds are enriched with these heavier elements. Since second-generation stars coalesced from such clouds, a full percent or a bit more of a second-gen's mass comes from metals—'metals' in this context meaning elements heavier than helium. Third-generation stars are even more recent; the suns of all the Commonwealth homeworlds are third-gens, as are all stars being born today, although, of course, some first-gens and a lot of second-gens are still around, too. Third-gens consist of about two percent metals."

Jag paused for a moment, and looked from face to face in the room. "Well," he said, "that star"—he gestured with one of his medial arms at the green orb in the holo sphere—"has about *eight* percent of its mass as metals, four times as much as even a typical third-gen. The thing has enough iron in it that you could actually *mine* it."

"What about the green color?" asked Keith.

"It's not really green, of course, any more than a so-called red star is actually red. Almost all stars are white, with just a hint of color." He gestured with his medial limbs at the starfield around them. "PHANTOM routinely colorizes the stars in our holo bubble, assigning them colors based on their Hertzsprung-Russell categories. The star out there just has a greenish tinge. The absorption-line blanketing due to its metal content is stronger than the backwarming, and that weakens the star's output in the blue and ultraviolet. The result is more of the star's light coming out in the green region of the spectrum." His fur danced. "I would have said a star with so much metal content would be impossible in our universe at its present age if I hadn't seen one with my own four eyes. It must have formed under very peculiar local conditions, and—"

"Forgive the interruption, good Jag," said Rhombus, "but I'm detecting a tachyon pulse."

Keith swiveled in his chair, facing the shortcut.

"Gods," said Jag, rising to his feet. "Most stars are part of *multiple* star systems—"

"We can't take another close passage," said Lianne. "We'll—"

But the shortcut had already stopped expanding. A small object had popped through. The gateway had grown to only seventy centimeters in diameter before collapsing down to an invisible point.

"It's a watson," announced Rhombus. An automated communications buoy. "Its transponder says it's from Grand Central Station."

"Trigger playback," Keith said.

"The message is in Russian," said Rhombus.

"PHANTOM, translate."

The central computer's voice filled the room. "Valentina Ilianov, Provost, New Beijing Colony, to Keith Lansing, commander, *Starplex*. An M-class red-dwarf star has erupted from the Tau Ceti shortcut. Fortunately, it emerged heading away from Tau Ceti, rather than toward it. So far, no real damage has been done, although we had trouble piloting this watson past the star and into the portal. This is our third attempt to reach you. We did manage to contact the astrophysics center on Rehbollo for advice, and they had the incredible news that a star has popped out of the shortcut near them as well—a blue B-class star, in their case. I am now contacting all other active shortcuts to find out just how widespread this phenomenon is. End of message."

Keith looked around the bridge, bathed in green starlight. "Christ Jesus," he said.

# IX

"I say we're under attack," announced Thorald Magnor, getting up from the helm position, and walking over to the seating gallery to sit a few chairs to the right of Jag. "We've apparently been lucky so far, but dropping a star into a system could destroy all life there."

Jag moved his lower two arms in a Waldahud gesture of negation. "Most shortcuts are in interstellar space," he said. "Even the one you call 'the Tau Ceti shortcut' is still thirty-seven billion kilometers from that star, more than six times as far as Pluto is from Sol. I would say that in fifteen out of sixteen cases, the arrival of additional stars would have minor effects on the closest systems, and, since inhabited worlds are few and far between, the chances of actually doing short-term damage to a planet with life on it are quite small."

"But could these stars be, well, bombs?" asked Lianne. "You said that the green star is very unusual. Could it be about to explode?"

"My studies of it have only begun," said Jag, "but I would say that our new arrival has at least a two billion years of life left. And singleton M-class dwarfs, like the one that popped out near Tau Ceti, don't go nova."

"Still," said Rissa, "couldn't they disturb the Oort clouds of star systems they pass close to, sending showers of comets in toward the inner planets? I remember an old theory that a brown dwarf dubbed—Nemesis, I think it was—might have passed close to Sol, causing an onslaught of comets at the end of the Cretaceous."

"Well, Nemesis turned out not to exist," said Jag, "but even if it did, today each of the Commonwealth races has the technology to deal with any reasonable number of cometary bodies—which, after all, would take decades or even centuries to fall into the inner part of a system. It is not an immediate concern."

"But why, then?" asked Thor. "Why are stars being moved around? And should we try to stop it?"

"Stop it?" Keith laughed. "How?"

"By destroying the shortcuts," said Thor, simply.

Keith blinked. "I'm not sure they can be destroyed," he said. "Jag?"

The Waldahud's fur danced pensively for a moment, and when he spoke, his bark was subdued. "Yes, theoretically, there is a way." He looked up, but neither of his eye pairs met Keith's gaze. "When first contact with humans was not going well, our astrophysicists were charged with finding a way to close the Tau Ceti shortcut, if need be."

"That's outrageous!" said Lianne.

Jag looked at the human. "No, that is good government. One must prepare for contingencies."

"But to destroy our shortcut!" said Lianne, anger bringing unfamiliar lines to her face.

"We did not do it," said Jag.

"To contemplate it, though! If you didn't want us to have access to Rehbollo, you should have destroyed your own shortcut, not ours."

Keith turned around to look at the young woman. "Lianne," he said softly. She faced him, and he mouthed the words "cool it" at her. He turned back to Jag. "Did you find a way to do it? To destroy a shortcut?"

Jag lifted his upper shoulders in assent. "Gaf Kandaro em-Weel, my sire, was head of the project. The shortcuts are hyperspatial constructs that extrude a nexus point into normal space. An absolute coordinate system exists in hyperspace. That's why Einsteinian speed restrictions don't apply there; it is not a relativistic medium. But normal space *is* relativistic, and the exit—the thing we call the shortcut portal—has to be anchored *relative* to something in normal space. If one could disorient the anchor point, so that it no longer could extrude through from hyperspace, the point should evaporate in a puff of Cerenkov radiation."

"And how would you disorient the anchor?" Keith asked, his tone betraying his skepticism.

"Well, the key is that the shortcut is indeed a point, until it swells up to accommodate something passing through it. A spherical array of artificial-gravity generators assembled around the dormant shortcut could be designed to compensate for the local curvature of spacetime. Even though most shortcuts are in interstellar space, they are still within the dent made by our galaxy. But if you remove that dent, the anchor would have nothing to hold on to, and—*poof!*—it should disappear. Since the shortcut is so small when dormant, an array only a meter or two across should be able to do the trick, so long as it is fed enough power."

"Could *Starplex* provide the power required?" asked Rhombus.

"Easily."

"That's incredible," Keith said.

"It isn't, really," said Jag. "Gravity is the force that dents spacetime; artificial gravity is all about modifying those dents. In my home system, we have used gravitation buoys in emergency situations to flatten spacetime locally so that hyperdrives could be engaged while still close to our sun."

"How come none of this has ever appeared on the Commonwealth Astrophysics Network?" asked Lianne, her tone sharp.

"Um, because no one ever asked us?" said Jag weakly.

"Why didn't you suggest we do that, then, to enable us to go to hyperdrive when the green star first appeared?" demanded Keith.

"You can't do it to yourself; it has to be done to you, by an external power source. Believe me, we've tried to develop ways for ships to do it on their own, but it doesn't work. To use the human metaphor, it would be like trying to pull yourself up by your own bootstraps. It can't be done."

"But if we were to do this right here and now—cause this shortcut to evaporate—we wouldn't be able to get back home," Keith said.

"True," said Jag. "But we could set up the antigrav buoys to converge on the shortcut after we had gone through it."

"But stars are apparently popping out of lots of shortcuts," said Rissa. "If we were to evaporate the Tau Ceti and Rehbollo and Flatland shortcuts, we'd be destroying the Commonwealth, cutting each of our worlds off from the other."

"To protect the individual worlds of the Commonwealth, yes," said Thor.

"Christ," said Keith. "Surely we don't want to end the Commonwealth."

"There is one other possibility," said Thor.

"Oh?"

"Transplant the Commonwealth races to adjacent star systems far distant from any shortcut. We could find three or four systems close together, with the right sorts of worlds, terraform them into habitable conditions, and move everyone there. We would still be able to have an interstellar community via normal hyperdrive."

Keith's eyes were wide. "You're talking about moving—what?—thirty *billion* individuals?"

"Give or take," said Thor.

"The Ibs will not leave Flatland," said Rhombus, with uncharacteristic bluntness.

"This is crazy," Keith said. "We can't shut down the shortcuts."

"If our homeworlds are in jeopardy," said Thor, "we can—and we should."

"There's no proof that the arriving stars represent any

threat," Keith said. "I can't believe that beings advanced enough to move stars around are malevolent."

"They may not be," said Thor, "any more than construction workers who destroy anthills are malevolent. We might simply be in their way."

There was nothing Keith could do about the arriving stars until more information was available, and so, at 1200 hours, he and Rissa went off to find something to eat.

There were eight restaurants aboard *Starplex*. The terminology was deliberate. Humans kept wanting to refer to *Starplex*'s components in naval terms: mess halls, sickbays, and quarters, instead of restaurants, hospitals, and apartments. But of the four Commonwealth species, only humans and Waldahudin had martial traditions, and the other two races were nervous enough about that without being reminded of it in casual conversation.

Each of the restaurants was unique, both in ambience and fare. *Starplex*'s designers had taken great pains to make sure that shipboard life was not monotonous. Keith and Rissa decided to have lunch in Kog Tahn, the Waldahud restaurant on deck twenty-six. Through the restaurant's fake windows, holograms of Rehbollo's surface were visible: wide, flat flood plains of purple-gray mud, crisscrossed by rivers and streams. Clumps of *stargin* were scattered about— Rehbollo's counterpart of trees, looking like three- or four-meter-tall blue tumbleweeds. The moist mud didn't offer any firm purchase, but it was rich with dissolved minerals and decaying organic material. Each *starg* had thousands of tangled shoots that could serve either as roots, or, unfurling themselves, as photosynthesis organs, depending on whether they ended up on top or on the bottom. The giant plants blew across the plains, rotating end over end, or floated down the streams, until they found fertile mud. When they did so, they settled in, sinking until about a third of their height was embedded in the ooze.

The holographic sky was greenish gray, and the star overhead was fat and red. Keith found the color scheme dreary, but there was no denying that the food here was excellent. Waldahudin were mainly vegetarians, and the plants they enjoyed were succulent and delicious. Keith found himself craving *starg* shoots three or four times a month.

Of course, all eight restaurants were open to every species, and that meant offering a range of meal items that met the various races' metabolic requirements. Keith ordered a grilled cheese sandwich and a couple of pickled gherkins to go with his *starg* salad. Waldahudin, whose females, like terrestrial mammals, secreted a nutritive liquid for their offspring, found it disgusting that humans drank the milk of other animals, but they pretended not to know what cheese was made of.

Rissa was sitting opposite Keith. Actually, the table was shaped in the Waldahud standard, like a human kidney, and made of a polished plant material that wasn't wood, but did have lovely bands of light and dark in it. Rissa was in the indentation in the table. The Waldahud custom was that a female always sat in this honored position; on their home-world a dame would be positioned here, with her male entourage seated around the curving form.

Rissa's tastes were more adventurous than Keith's. She was eating *gaz torad*—"blood mussels," Waldahud bi-valves that lived in the slurry layer at the bottom of many lakes. Keith found the bright purple-red color disgusting—as did most Waldahudin, for that matter, since it was a precise match for the hue of their own blood. But Rissa had mastered the trick of bringing the shell to her mouth, popping it open, and slurping out the morsel within, all without letting the soft mass be seen either by herself or anyone sitting across from her.

Keith and Rissa ate in silence, and Keith wondered if that was good or bad. They'd run out of idle chitchat ages ago. Oh, if there was something on either of their minds, they'd talk at length, but it seemed that they just enjoyed being in each other's company, even if they said barely a word. At least that's the way Keith felt, and he hoped Rissa shared that feeling.

Keith was using a *katook* (Waldahud cutlery, like duck-billed pliers) to bring some *starg* to his mouth when a comm panel popped up from the table's surface, showing the face of Hek, the Waldahud alien-communications specialist.

"Rissa," he barked in a voice somewhat more Brooklynish than Jag's; from the way the comm panel was angled, the Waldahud couldn't see Keith. "I have been analyzing the radio noise we've been detecting near the twenty-one-centimeter band. You won't believe what I've found. Come to my office at once."

Keith put down his eating utensil, and looked across the table at his wife. "I'll join you," he said, and stood up to leave. As they made their way across the room, he realized it was the only thing he'd said to her during the entire meal.

Keith and Rissa got into an elevator. As always, a monitor on the cab's wall showed the current deck number and floor plan: "26," and a cross shape with long arms. As they rode up, and the deck numbers counted down, the arms of the cross grew shorter and shorter. By the time they reached deck one, the arms had almost completely retracted. The two humans got out and entered the radio-astronomy listening room. Hek, a small Waldahud with a hide much redder in color than Jag's, was leaning against a desk. "Rissa, your presence is welcome"—the standard deference shown females. A tilt of the head: "Lansing." The rude indifference reserved for males, even if they were your boss.

"Hek," said Keith, nodding in greeting.

The Waldahud looked at Rissa. "You know the radio noise we've been picking up?" His barking echoed in the tiny room.

Rissa nodded.

"Well, my initial analysis showed no repetition in it." He swiveled a pair of eyes to look at Keith. "When a signal is a deliberate beacon, it usually has a repeating pattern over a course of several minutes or hours. There's nothing like that at work here. Indeed, I've found no evidence of any overall pattern. But when I started analyzing the noise more minutely, patterns of one-second duration or less kept cropping up. So far, I've cataloged six thousand and seventeen sequences. Some have only been repeated once or twice, but others have been repeated many times. Over ten thousand times, for a few of them."

"My God," said Rissa.

"What?" said Keith.

She turned to him. "It means that there might be information in the noise—it might be radio communications."

Hek lifted his upper shoulders. "Exactly. Each of the patterns could be a separate word. Those that occur most frequently could be common terms, maybe the equivalent of pronouns or prepositions."

"And where are these transmissions coming from?" asked Keith.

"Somewhere in or just behind the dark-matter field," said Hek.

"And you're sure they're intelligent signals?" asked Keith, his heart pounding.

Hek's lower shoulders moved this time. "No, I'm not sure. For one thing, the transmissions are very weak. They wouldn't be discernible from background noise over any great distance. But if I'm right that they're words, then there *does* appear to be some discernible syntax. No word is ever doubled. Certain words only appear at the beginning or end of transmissions. Some words only appear after certain other words. The former are possibly adjectives and adverbs, and the latter the nouns or verbs they are modifying, or vice versa." Hek paused. "Of course, I haven't analyzed all the signals, although I am recording them for future study. It's a constant bombardment, on over two hundred frequencies that are very close to each other." He paused, letting this sink in. "I'd say there's a good possibility that there's a fleet of craft hiding inside or just past the dark-matter field."

Keith was about to speak again when Hek's desk intercom bleeped. "Keith, Lianne here."

"Open. Yes?"

"I think you'll want to come to the bridge. A watson has arrived with word that the boomerang has returned from shortcut Rehbollo 376A."

"On my way. Summon Jag, too, please. Close." He looked at Hek. "Good work. See if you can narrow down the source of the signals further. I'll have Thor take *Starplex* in a circular path around the dark-matter field, scanning for tachyon emissions, radiation, thruster glow, or any other signs of alien ships."

Keith strode onto the bridge, Rissa right behind him. They moved to their workstations. "Trigger watson playback," said Keith.

Lianne pushed a button, and a full-motion video message appeared in a framed-off section of the holographic bubble. The image was of a Waldahud male with a silvery-gray hide. PHANTOM replaced the sound of the creature's barking with English words for the playback into Keith's ear implant, although, of course, they didn't fit the movements of the Waldahud's mouth.

"Greetings, *Starplex*." The status line at the bottom of the screen identified the speaker as Kayd Pelendo em-Hooth of the Rehbollo Center for Astrophysics. "The boomerang sent to the shortcut designated Rehbollo 376A has returned. I suspect you'll want to stay where you are, investigating the shortcut you're at now, since its appearance on the network is unexplained. However, we thought Jag and others would be interested in seeing the recordings made by the boomerang just before returning home. They are appended to this message. I think you will find them . . . interesting."

"Okay, Rhombus," said Keith. "Use the data from the boomerang to create a spherical holo display around us. Show us what it saw."

"A pleasure to serve," said Rhombus. "Downloading now; the display will be ready in two minutes, forty seconds."

Lianne rubbed her hands together. "It never rains but it pours," she said, turning around and grinning at Keith. "Yet another new sector of space opened up for exploration!"

Keith nodded. "It never ceases to amaze me." He got up from his chair, and paced a little, waiting for the hologram to be prepared. "You know," he said absently, "my great-great-grandfather kept a diary. Just before he died, he wrote about all the great advancements he'd seen in his lifetime:

radio, the automobile, powered flight, spaceflight, lasers, computers, the discovery of DNA, and on and on." Lianne seemed rapt, although Keith was aware that he might be boring everyone else. To hell with them; rank hath its privileges, chief among them the right to ramble on. "When I read that as a teenager, I figured I'd have nothing to write about for my own descendant when my life came to a close. But then we invented hyperdrive and AI, and discovered the shortcut network, and extraterrestrial life, and learned to talk to dolphins, and I realized that—"

"Excuse me," said Rhombus, his lights flashing in the strobing pattern his species used to signal an interruption. "The hologram is ready."

"Proceed," Keith said.

The bridge darkened as the image of *Starplex*'s current surroundings was shut off, shrouding the room in featureless black. Then a new picture built up from left to right, scan line by scan line, washing over the bridge, until it seemed once again to be floating in space—the space of the newest sector to become accessible to the Commonwealth races.

Thor let out a long, low whistle.

Jag clicked his dental plates in disbelief.

Dominating the view, receding slowly, was another fiery green star, perhaps ten million kilometers from the shortcut point.

"I thought you said our green star was a freak," said Keith to Jag.

"That's the least of our worries," said Thor. He swung his feet off his console and turned to face Keith. "Our boomerang didn't activate that shortcut until it dived into it."

Keith looked at him blankly.

"And these pictures were taken *before* it did that."

Jag rose to his feet. "*Ka-darg!* That means—"

"It means," said Keith, suddenly getting it, too, "that stars can emerge from *dormant* shortcuts. Christ, they could be popping out of all four billion portals throughout the Milky Way!"

# X

That night, Keith was eating dinner alone. He loved to cook, but he also loved to have someone to cook for—and Rissa was working late this evening. She and Boxcar had finally had a breakthrough in their Hayflick-limit studies, or, at least, so it appeared. But they were having trouble replicating the results, and so she'd just had sandwiches sent up to her lab.

Keith sometimes wondered how he'd gotten the job as *Starplex*'s head honcho. Oh, it made sense, of course. A sociologist was assumed to be good both at managing the miniature society aboard the ship and at dealing with any new civilizations they might encounter.

But right now, despite all that was going on, there was little for him to do beyond the administrative. Jag would continue his dark-matter studies, as well as trying to make sense of the onslaught of stars; Hek would try to further decode the potentially alien radio signals; Rissa would pursue her life-prolongation project. And Keith? Keith kept hoping a windmill somewhere would start tilting at him— kept hoping for something important to do.

He'd decided to dine in one of the Ib restaurants. Not for the atmosphere, of course. With its almost billiard-ball-smooth surface, Flatland's landscapes, as depicted in the restaurant's holographic windows, were even less visually interesting than Rehbollo's; there was no doubt that when it came to interesting geography, Earth was the most beautiful of the homeworlds. But Ibese food was based on right-handed amino acids; it was completely indigestible by the other three races. This restaurant, though, offered a wide range of human fare—including a chicken stir-fry, which was exactly what Keith had been craving.

The restaurant was inordinately crowded; the four eating establishments in the lower-habitat modules were still uninhabitable. But one of the other privileges of rank was always getting a table without a wait. A sleek, silver robot showed Keith to a booth in the back. A large gestalt plant arched over it, orange octagonal leaves roaming its body freely.

Keith told the server what he wanted, and then he spoke to the desktop viewer, asking for the latest issue of the *New Yorker* to be displayed. The server returned with a glass of white wine, then rolled away. Keith was settling into the lead fiction piece in the magazine when—

*Bleep.* "Karendaughter to Lansing."

"Open. Yes, Lianne?"

"I've finished the engineering study on what to do about the irradiated lower decks. Can we get together so that I can give you my report?"

Keith swallowed once. Of course the report had to be dealt with right away; they needed to solve the overcrowding problem quickly. But where to meet Lianne? Gamma shift would be on the bridge now; no need to disturb them. Keith's office would be the natural place, but . . . but . . . did he really trust himself to be alone with her?

Christ, this is stupid. "I'm in the Drive-Through, having dinner. Can you bring the report here?"

"Sure thing. On my way. Close."

Keith had a sip of wine. Maybe this was a mistake. Maybe people would misconstrue, tell Rissa that he'd had a rendezvous in a booth with Lianne. Maybe—

Lianne came in, escorted to his table by a robot. She sat down opposite him and smiled. Geez, she'd arrived quickly—almost as if she'd known where he was before calling, almost as if she'd planned to catch him alone at dinner . . .

Keith shook his head. *Get real.* "Hi, Lianne," he said. "You've got a report for me?"

"That's right." She was dressed in a cyan suit, crisp and professional. But on her head, crowing her lustrous platinum hair, she was wearing a smart replica of an old-style railway engineer's cap. Keith had seen her wearing it before, whimsical and stylish and sexy all at once. "There are techniques," she said, "for cleaning up radiation damage. But they're all time-consuming, and—"

The server arrived, bringing Keith's dinner.

"Stir-fry," said Lianne, smiling. "I make a mean one of those. You should let me do it for you sometime."

Keith reached for his wine, thought better of it, picked up his napkin, and, in so doing, sent his fork tumbling onto the rubberized floor. He bent down to retrieve it—and saw Lianne's shapely legs beneath the table.

"Um, thank you," he said, straightening back up. "That'd be nice." He indicated the steaming platter between them. "Did you—did you want some?"

"Oh, no," she said, patting her flat stomach, causing the fabric of her suit to pull tight across her breasts as she did so. "I'll have a salad later. I've got to watch my figure."

No need for that, thought Keith. I'll be glad to watch it for you. "About the radiation?" he said.

She nodded. "Right. Well, as I said, we can clean it up—but not quickly, and not without putting into drydock for several weeks."

"Weeks!" said Keith. "We can't afford that kind of time."

"Exactly. Which brings me to my suggested solution."

Keith waited for her to go on. "Which is?"

"*Starplex 2.*"

Keith frowned. *Starplex* had been built at the Rehbollo orbital shipyards, and its sister ship—currently carrying the prosaic name of *Starplex 2,* although something else would likely end up being the official name—had been under construction now for close to a year. It was being built at Flatland; two such prime contracts couldn't go to the same homeworld, naturally. "What about her?"

"Well, she's not yet ready for launch, or I'd say simply commandeer the whole thing. But she's being built from identical blueprints to *Starplex 1*—and five of her eight habitat modules are already completed, according to the last report I received. We could pop through the shortcut to the Flatland shipyards, dump our lower-four habitat modules there, and replace them with four of the completed ones for *Starplex 2.* The modules that we leave off could then be cleaned up at leisure. *Starplex 2*'s central disk won't be ready for another five months; the four hyperdrive generators have to be extensively tested before the engineering torus can be built around them. That should give plenty of time for the cleanup. When the time comes, our four old modules could be incorporated into the new ship. Of course, all the individual furnishings and equipment we had in our lower four will need to be cleaned up, too, but at least we'll have quarters and lab space for everyone right away."

Keith nodded, impressed. "That's brilliant. How long would that take?"

"The specs for habitat-module power-grid deconnection and reconnection call for three days, but I've devised an improved method that doesn't require powering down the couplings. I could do it in fifteen hours if we didn't need to wear radiation suits in the lower modules; in this case, eighteen hours should do the trick."

"Excellent. What about the lower part of our main shaft and our central disk?"

"Well, the shaft is three quarters fixed up already. We can't clean it easily, but I've had nanotechs laying down extra shielding on its inner surface. As for the central disk, we'll have to completely replace the water in the ocean deck, of course. And not just with plain water, either. It has to be a full seawater formulation, with dissolved salt and other minerals, plus, if possible, plankton and fish stocks. Also, I'd like to replace all the shipboard air, just to be on the safe side. The docking bays are no problem—they're heavily shielded. Same thing for the engineering torus; its shielding kept it from getting too much of a hit of radiation, as well."

Keith nodded. "How long till we can safely maneuver through the shortcut?"

"Tomorrow afternoon, maybe earlier. The gap between the shortcut and the green star is opening rapidly. And as long as you're willing to risk losing half a dozen watsons in trying, we should be able to get word of our intentions through to the Flatland shipyards right away so that the Ibs can start preparing for our arrival."

"Good work, Lianne." He looked at her, and she smiled again, a beautiful, warm, *intelligent* smile. Keith mentally kicked himself for sometimes forgetting that there *was* a reason she was aboard *Starplex*. Lianne Karendaughter was the best starship engineer in the business.

Thor piloted *Starplex* through the shortcut, and it popped out at the periphery of the Flatland system. From here, the Magellanic Clouds dominated the sky. Flatland's sun, Hotspot, was a white F-class star, and Flatland itself was a featureless ball, shrouded in white clouds.

Ibs were incapable of working in zero-g. Keith watched from a window as thousands of them swarmed around *Starplex* in hockey-puck-shaped solo travel units, transparent except for the opaque artificial-gravity plates that made up their bottoms. Since the work was being done by Ibs, not a second was being wasted. The new habitat modules were locked into place, giving *Starplex* all-new decks forty-one through seventy. Keith could just make out the bubble-shaped travel pod from which Lianne was orchestrating the entire operation. The only problem during the whole refit occurred when the hose draining off the ocean deck ruptured, and salt water sprayed into space, freezing into tiny ice particles that sparkled like diamonds in the white glare from Hotspot.

When it was all done, *Starplex*—now a hybrid of *Starplexes 1* and 2—headed back through the shortcut.

Keith was delighted with the repairs—and even more delighted that everyone would no longer have to crowd into the upper half of the ship. Arguments had been breaking out among members of all the races. Perhaps now that they had plenty of room again, peace would once more reign aboard *Starplex*.

While at the Rehbollo shipyards, five new researchers were brought aboard—one Ib and two Waldahud darkmatter specialists, and a dolphin and a human who were experts in stellar evolution. All of them had dropped everything at receipt of *Starplex*'s reports, and immediately headed through the shortcut network to rendezvous with the ship at Flatland.

As she had promised, Lianne finished the refit in less than eighteen hours. Thor piloted the ship back through the shortcut, and they reemerged in the vicinity of the darkmatter field and the enigmatic green star.

# XI

*Starplex*'s designers had planned to put the director's office adjacent to the bridge, but Keith had insisted that be changed. The director, he felt, should be seen all over his ship, not just in one isolated area. He had ended up with a large square room, almost four meters on a side, located on deck fourteen, halfway along one of the triangular faces of habitat module two. Through the window that covered one wall, he could see module three, perpendicular to the one he was in, as well as a ninety-degree slice of the copper-colored circular roof of *Starplex*'s central disk sixteen floors below. That particular part of the roof was marked with *Starplex*'s name in wedge-shaped Waldahudar lettering.

Keith sat behind a long rectangular desk, made of real mahogany. On it were framed holos of his wife Rissa, looking exotic in an old-fashioned Spanish dancing dress, and their son Saul, wearing a Harvard sweatshirt and sporting that strange goatee that was the current fashion among young men. Next to the holos was a 1:600 scale model of *Starplex*. Behind his desk was a credenza with globes of Earth, Rehbollo, and Flatland on it, as well as a traditional go board with playing pieces of polished white shell and slate. Above the credenza was a framed print of an Emily Carr painting, depicting a Haida totem pole in a forest on one of the Queen Charlotte Islands. Flanking the credenza on either side were large potted plants. A long couch, three polychairs, and a coffee table were also in the room.

Keith had his shoes off, and had swung his feet up on his desk. He never emulated Thor while on the bridge, but when alone he often adopted this posture. He was leaning back in his black chair, reading a report on the signals Hek had been detecting, when the door buzzer sounded.

"Jag Kandaro em-Pelsh is here," announced PHANTOM.

Keith sighed, sat up straight, and made a let-him-in motion with his hand. The door slid aside, and Jag walked in. After a moment, the Waldahud's nostrils started flaring, and Keith thought perhaps Jag could smell his feet. "What can I do for you, Jag?"

The Waldahud touched the back of one of the polychairs, which configured itself to accommodate his frame. He sat down and began to bark. The translated voice said, "Few of your Earth literary characters appeal to me, but one who does is Sherlock Holmes."

Keith lifted an eyebrow. Rude, arrogant—yes, he could see why Jag might like the guy.

"In particular," continued Jag, "I like his ability to encapsulate mental processes into maxims. One of my favorite sayings of his is, 'The truth is the residue, lacking in likelihood though it may be, that is left behind when those things that cannot be are omitted from consideration.'"

That, at least, brought a smile to Keith's face. What Conan Doyle had actually written was, "Eliminate the impossible, and whatever remains, however improbable, must be the truth," but considering that the words had been translated into Waldahudar then back into English, Jag's version wasn't half-bad.

"Yes?" said Keith.

"Well, my original analysis, that the fourth-generation star that appeared here was a one-of-a-kind anomaly, must now be amended, since we've seen a second such star at Rehbollo 376A. By applying Holmes's dictum, I believe I now know where these two green stars, and presumably the other rogue stars as well, have come from." Jag fell silent, waiting for Keith to prod him further.

"And that is?" Keith said, irritated.

"The future."

Keith laughed—but then, he had a barking laugh; perhaps it didn't sound derisive to Waldahud ears. "The future?"

"It is the best explanation. Green stars could not have evolved in a universe that is as young as ours is. A single such star could have been a freak, but multiple ones are highly unlikely."

Keith shook his head. "But perhaps they come from—I don't know—some unusual region of space. Maybe they had been companions of a black hole, and the gravitational stresses had caused fusion reactions to proceed more quickly."

"I thought of such things," said Jag. "That is, I thought of probable alternative scenarios, of which that is not one. But none of them fits the facts. I have now done radiometric dating, based on isotope proportionalities, of the material Longbottle and I scooped from the atmosphere of the green star near us. The heavy-metal atoms in that star are twenty-two billion years old. The star itself is not that old, of course, but many of the atoms it is composed of are."

"I thought all matter was the same age," said Keith.

Jag lifted his lower shoulders. "It's true that, excepting the small amount of matter constantly being created out of energy, and excepting that in certain reactions neutrons can essentially turn into proton-electron pairs, and vice versa, all fundamental particles in the universe were created shortly after the big bang. But the atoms made up of those particles can be formed or destroyed at any time, through fission or fusion."

"Right," said Keith, embarrassed. "Sorry. So you're saying the heavy-metal atoms in the star formed longer ago than the universe is old."

"That's correct. And the only way that could happen is if the star came to us from the future."

"But—but you said the green stars are billions of years older than any current star could be. You're trying to tell me that these stars have traveled back in time *billions* of years? That seems incredible."

Jag preceded his barking reply with a snort. "The intellectual leap should be in the acceptance of time travel, not the length of time an object is cast back. If time travel can exist at all, then the distance traveled back surely is only a function of appropriate technology and sufficient energy. I submit that any race that has the power to move stars around has both in abundance."

"But I thought time travel was impossible."

Jag lifted all four shoulders. "Until the shortcuts were discovered, instantaneous transportation was impossible. Until the hyperdrive was discovered, faster-than-light travel was impossible. I cannot begin to suggest how time travel might be made to happen, but apparently it *is* happening."

"There are no other explanations?" asked Keith.

"Well, as I said, I *have* considered other possibilities— such as that the shortcuts are now acting as gateways to parallel universes, and that the green stars come from there rather than from our future. But except for their age, they are what one would expect of matter formed in this specific universe, from our specific big bang, under the very specific physical laws that operate here."

"Very well," said Keith, holding up a hand. "But why send stars from the future back to the past?"

"That," said Jag, "is the first good question you have asked."

Keith spoke through clenched teeth. "And the answer is?"

Jag lifted all four shoulders again. "I have no idea."

As he moved down the dim, cold corridor, Keith accepted that each of the races aboard *Starplex* managed to piss the others off in different ways. One of the things humans did that he knew bugged the hell out of everyone else was spending endless time trying to come up with cute words made from the initial letters of phrases. All the races called such things "acronyms" now, since only the Terran languages had a word for them. Early on in planning *Starplex,* some human came up with the term CAGE for "Common Access General Environment," referring to the shipboard conditions in those areas that had to be shared by all four races.

Well, it felt like a goddamned cage, thought Keith. Like a dungeon.

All the races could exist in nitrogen-oxygen atmospheres, although Ibs required a much higher concentration of carbon dioxide to trigger their breathing reflex than humans did. Common-area gravity ended up being set at .82 of Earth's—normal for a Waldahud, light for a human or dolphin, and only half of what an Ib was used to. Humidity was kept high, too: Waldahud sinuses seized if the air was too dry. Common-area lighting was redder than humans liked—similar to a bright terrestrial sunset. Further, all lighting had to be indirect. The Ib homeworld was perpetually shrouded in cloud, and the thousands of photosensors in their webs could be damaged by bright lighting.

Even so, there were still problems. Keith moved to one side of the corridor to let an Ib roll by, and as it passed, one of the two dangling blue tubes coming off the creature's pump pushed out a hard gray pellet, which fell to the corridor floor. The pod's brain had no conscious control over this function; for Ibs, toilet training was a biological impossibility. On Flatland, the pellets were scooped up by scavengers that reprocessed them for the nutrients the Ib had been unable to use. Aboard *Starplex,* little PHARTs the size of human shoes served the same function. One such came zipping along the corridor as Keith watched. It sucked up the dropping and rolled upon its way.

Keith had finally gotten used to the Ibs defecating everywhere; thank God their feces had no discernible odor. But he didn't think he'd ever get used to the cold, or the damp, or any of the other things forced upon them by the Waldahudin—

Keith stopped dead in his tracks. He was coming to a T-intersection in the corridor, and could hear raised voices up ahead: a human male shouting in—Japanese, it sounded like—and the angry barking of a Waldahud.

"PHANTOM," Keith said softly, "translate those voices for me."

A New York accent: "You are weak, Teshima. Very weak. You don't deserve a mate."

"Have sex with yourself!" Keith frowned, suspecting the computer wasn't doing justice to the original Japanese.

The New York accent again: "On my world, you would be the least significant member of the entourage of the ugliest, puniest female—"

"Identify the speakers," Keith whispered.

"The human is Hiroyuki Teshima, a biochemist," said PHANTOM through Keith's implant. "The Waldahud is Gart Daygaro em-Holf, a member of the engineering staff."

Keith stood there, wondering what to do. They were both adults, and although they reported to him, they could hardly be said to be under his command. And yet—

*Middle child.* Keith stepped around the corridor. "Guys," he said evenly, "you want to cool it?"

All four of the Waldahud's fists were clenched. Teshima's round face was flushed with anger. "Stay out of this, Lansing," said the human, in English.

Keith looked at them. What could he do? There was no brig to throw them into, no particular reason why they had to listen to his orders about their personal affairs.

"Maybe I could buy you a drink, Hiroyuki," said Keith. "And, Gart, perhaps you'd enjoy an extra leisure period this cycle?"

"What I would enjoy," barked the Waldahud, "is seeing Teshima fired through a mass driver into a black hole."

"Come on, guys," said Keith, stepping closer. "We've all got to live and work together."

"I said stay out of this, Lansing," snapped Teshima. "It's none of your damned business."

Keith felt his cheeks flushing. He couldn't order them apart, and yet he couldn't have people brawling in the corridors of his ship, either. He looked at the two of them—a short, middle-aged human, with hair the color of lead, and a fat, wide Waldahud, with fur the shade of oak wood. Keith didn't know either of them well, didn't know

what it would take to placate them. Hell, he didn't even
know what they were fighting about. He opened his mouth
to say—to say *something,* anything—when a door slid
open a few meters away, and a young woman—Cheryl
Rosenberg, it was—appeared, wearing pajamas. "For Pete's
sake, will you keep it down out here?" she said. "It's
nighttime for some of us."

Teshima looked at the woman, bowed his head slightly,
and began to walk away. And Gart, who likewise by nature
was deferential to females, nodded curtly and moved in the
other direction. Cheryl yawned, stepped back inside, and the
door slid shut behind her.

Keith was left standing there, watching the Waldahud's
back recede down the corridor, angry with himself for not
being able to deal with the situation. He rubbed his temples.
We're all prisoners of biology, he thought. Teshima unable
to turn down the request of a pretty woman; Gart unable to
disobey a female's orders.

Once Gart had disappeared from sight, Keith headed
down the cold, damp hallway. Sometimes, Keith thought,
he'd give anything to be an alpha male.

Rissa was sitting at her desk, doing the part of her job she
hated—the administrative duties, the burden still called paperwork even though almost none of it was ever printed out.

The door buzzer sounded, and PHANTOM said, "Boxcar
is here."

Rissa put down her input stylus and straightened her hair.
Funny that, she thought—worrying about whether her hair
was messy when the only one going to see it isn't even
human. "Let her in."

The Ib rolled in; PHANTOM slid the polychairs to one
side to make room for her. "Please forgive my disturbing
you, good Rissa," said the beautiful British voice.

Rissa laughed. "Oh, you're not disturbing me, believe
me. Any break is welcome."

Boxcar's sensor web arched up like a ship's sail so that
she could see onto Rissa's desktop. "Paperwork," she said.
"It does look boring."

Rissa smiled. "That it is. So, what can I do for you?"

There was a long pause—unusual from an Ib. Then, finally, "I've come to give notice."

Rissa looked at her blankly. "Notice?"

Lights danced on her web. "Profound apologies, if that is not the correct phrase. I mean to say that, with regret, I will no longer be able to work here, effective five days from now."

Rissa felt her eyebrows lifting. "You're quitting? Resigning?"

Lights played up the web. "Yes."

"Why? I thought you were enjoying the senescence research. If you wish to be assigned to something else—"

"It is not that, good Rissa. The research is fascinating and valuable, and you have honored me by letting me be a part of it. But in five days other priorities must take precedence."

"What other priorities?"

"Repaying a debt."

"To whom?"

"To other integrated bioentities. In five days, I must go."

"Go where?"

"No, not go. *Go*."

Rissa exhaled, and looked at the ceiling. "PHANTOM, are you sure you're translating Boxcar's words correctly?"

"I believe so, ma'am," said PHANTOM into her implant.

"Boxcar, I don't understand the distinction you're making between 'go' and 'go,'" said Rissa.

"I am not going someplace in the physical sense," said Boxcar. "I am going in the sense of exiting. I am going to die."

"My God!" said Rissa. "Are you ill?"

"No."

"But you're not old enough to die. You've told me enough times that Ibs live to be exactly six hundred and forty-one. You're only a little over six hundred."

Boxcar's sensor web changed to a salmon color, but whatever emotion that conveyed apparently had no terrestrial analog, since PHANTOM didn't preface the translation of her next words with a parenthetical comment. "I am six hundred and five, measured in Earth years. My span is about to be fifteen-sixteenths completed."

Rissa looked at her. "Yes?"

"For offenses committed in my youth, I have been assessed a penalty of one-sixteenth of my lifespan. I am to be ended next week."

Rissa looked at her, unsure what to say. Finally, she settled for simply repeating the word "ended," as if perhaps it, too, had been mistranslated.

"That is correct, good Rissa."

She was quiet again for a moment. "What crime did you commit?"

"It shames me to discuss it," said Boxcar.

Rissa said nothing, waiting to see if the Ib would go on. She did not.

"I've shared a lot of intimate information about myself and my marriage with you," said Rissa lightly. "I'm your friend, Boxcar."

More silence; perhaps the Ib was wrestling with her own feelings. And then: "When I was a tertiary novice—a position somewhat similar to what you call a graduate student—I reported incorrectly the results of an experiment I was conducting."

Rissa's eyebrows rose again. "We all make mistakes, Boxcar. I can't believe they'd punish you this severely for that."

Boxcar's lights rippled in random patterns. Apparently, they were just signs of consternation; again, PHANTOM provided no verbal translation. Then: "The results were not accidentally misreported." The Ib's mantle was dark for several seconds. "I deliberately falsified the data."

Rissa tried to keep her expression neutral. "Oh."

"I did not think the experiment was of great significance, and I knew—*thought* I knew, anyway—what the results should be. In retrospect, I realize I only knew what I wanted them to be." Darkness; a pause. "In any event, other researchers relied upon my results. Much time was wasted."

"And for this they're going to execute you?"

All the lights on Boxcar's web came on at once—an expression of absolute shock. "It is *not* a summary execution, Rissa. There are only two capital crimes on Flatland:

pod murder and forming a gestalt with more than seven components. My lifespan has simply been shortened."

"But—but if you're six hundred and five now, how long ago did you commit this crime?"

"I did it when I was twenty-four."

"PHANTOM, what Earth year would that have been?"

"A.D. 1513, ma'am."

"Good God!" said Rissa. "Boxcar, surely they can't punish you for a minor offense committed that long ago."

"The passage of time has not changed the impact of what I did."

"But so long as you're aboard *Starplex,* you're protected by the Commonwealth Charter. You could claim asylum here. We could get you a lawyer."

"Rissa, your concern touches me. But I am prepared to pay my debt."

"But it was so long ago. Maybe they've forgotten."

"Ibs cannot forget; you know that. Because matrices form in our pod brains at a constant rate, we all have eidetic memories. But even if my compatriots could forget, it would not matter. I am honor bound in this."

"Why didn't you say anything about this earlier?"

"My punishment did not require public acknowledgment; I was allowed to live without constant shame. But the terms under which I work here require me to give you five days' notice if I intend to leave. And so now, for the first time in five hundred and eighty-one years, I am telling someone of my crime." The Ib paused. "If it is acceptable, I will use the remaining days of my life putting our research in order so that you and others may continue it without difficulty."

Rissa's head was swimming. "Um, yes," she said at last. "Yes, that would be fine."

"Thank you," said Boxcar. She turned and started to roll toward the door, but then her web flashed once more. "You have been a good friend, Rissa."

And then the door slid open, Boxcar rolled away, and Rissa slumped back in her chair, dumbfounded.

# XII

Rissa came to the bridge, wanting to talk to Keith about Boxcar's announcement. But just as she was striding toward his workstation, Rhombus spoke up. "Keith, Jag, Rissa," he said, in his crisp, cool translated voice, "innumerable apologies for the interruption, but I think you should see this."

"What is it?" said Keith.

Rissa took a seat as Rhombus's ropes tickled his console. A section of the holo bubble became framed off in blue. "I wasn't paying enough attention to the real-time scans, I'm afraid," said the Ib, "but I've been reviewing the data we've been recording, and—well, watch this. This is a playback speeded up one thousand times. What you're going to see in the next six minutes took almost all of the time we've been here to occur."

In the framed-off area was a dark-matter sphere, seen from almost directly above its equator. Actually, it wasn't anywhere near a perfect sphere: this one was flattened at the poles. Light and dark latitudinal cloud bands crossed its face. According to the scale bars, this was one of the largest spheres they'd found, measuring 172,000 kilometers in diameter.

"Wait a minute," said Keith. "It's got cloud bands, yet it doesn't seem to be spinning at all."

Rhombus's web twinkled. "I hope the truth does not prove embarrassing, good Keith, but in fact, it's spinning faster than any other sphere we've yet observed. At this point, it's rotating on its axis once every two hours and sixteen minutes—almost five times as fast as Jupiter revolves. The speed is so great that any normal turbulence in the clouds has been smoothed out. And in this speeded-up playback, the image you're seeing is rotating every eight seconds." Rhombus snaked out a rope and flicked a control. "Here, let me have the computer put a reference mark on the equator. See that orange dot? It's at an arbitrary zero degrees of longitude."

The orange spot whipped across the equator, disappeared around back, reappeared four seconds later, and traversed the visible face again. After a few cycles, Jag barked out, "Are you increasing the playback speed?"

"No, good Jag," said Rhombus. "Speed is constant."

Jag gestured at the digital clocks. "But that dot of yours took only seven seconds to go around that time."

"Indeed," said Rhombus. "The sphere's actual rate of rotation is increasing."

"How can that be?" asked Keith. "Are other bodies interacting with it?"

"Well, yes, the other spheres are all having an effect on it—but that's not the cause of what we're seeing," said Rhombus. "The increased rotation is *internally* generated."

Jag's head was bent down to his console, running quickie computer models. "You can't get increased spin unless you pump energy into the system. There must be some complex reactions going on inside the sphere, ultimately fueled by some outside source, and—" He looked up, and let out a high-pitched bark, which PHANTOM translated as "Expression of astonishment."

In the blue framed-off area, the dark-matter object had

started to pinch in at its equator. The northern and southern halves were no longer perfect hemispheres, but rather they curved in a little before they joined each other. The orange reference dot was now whipping around the smaller waist even faster than before.

As the sphere continued to rotate with increasing speed, the pinching-off became more and more pronounced. Soon the profile of the object had taken on a figure-eight shape.

Rissa rose to her feet, and stood staring, mouth agape. The equator was now so narrow that the orange dot covered almost a quarter of its width. Rhombus touched some keys and the dot disappeared, replaced by separate orange dots on the equators of each of the two joined spheres.

The view in the frame went dark. "Please forgive this," said Rhombus. "Another dark-matter sphere moved into our line of sight, obscuring the view. At this playback speed, we lose the picture for about fourteen seconds. Let me jump past that."

Ropes touched the ExOps console. When the image reappeared, the two spheres were joined by only about a tenth of the original globe's diameter. Everyone watched, rapt, silence broken only by the gentle whir of the air-conditioning equipment, as the process reached its inevitable conclusion. The two spheres broke free from each other. One immediately started curving toward the bottom of the frame; the other, toward the top. As they distanced themselves from each other, the orange reference dots on each of their equators began to take longer and longer to complete their paths—the rotation was slowing down.

Rissa turned to face Keith, her eyes wide. "It's like a cell," she said. "A cell undergoing mitosis."

"Exactly," said Rhombus. "Except that in this case, the mother cell is some hundred and seventy thousand kilometers in diameter. Or, at least it was before this started happening."

Keith cleared his throat. "Excuse me," he said. "Are you trying to tell me that those things out there are *alive*? That they're living cells?"

"I finally saw the recordings Jag's atmospheric probe had made," said Rissa. "Remember that blimplike object it saw as it went into the atmosphere? I'd idly thought that it might be an individual life-form—a gasbag creature, floating in the clouds. Earth scientists in the 1960s proposed just such life-forms for Jupiter. But such blimps could just as easily be organelles—discrete components within a larger cell."

"Living beings," said Keith, incredulous. "Living beings almost two hundred thousand kilometers in size?"

Rissa's voice was still full of awe. "Perhaps. In which case, we've just seen one of them reproduce."

"Incredible," said Keith, shaking his head. "I mean, we aren't just talking about giant creatures. And we aren't just talking about life-forms living freely in open space. We're talking about living beings made of *dark matter*." He turned to his left. "Jag, is that even possible?"

"Possible that dark matter—or some portion of it—is alive?" The Waldahud shrugged all four shoulders. "Much of our science and philosophy tell us that the universe should be teeming with life. And yet, so far, we've only found three worlds on which life has arisen. Perhaps we've just been looking in the wrong places. Neither Dr. Delacorte nor I has yet figured out much about dark-matter meta-chemistry, but there *are* lots of complex compounds in those spheres."

Keith spread his arms in an appeal for basic common sense, and looked around the bridge, trying to find someone else as lost by all this as he was.

And then an even bigger thought hit him, and he leaned back in his chair for a moment. Then he touched his comm control panel, selecting a general channel. "Lansing to Hek," he said.

A hologram of Hek's head appeared in a second framed-off part of the starscape. "Hek here."

"Any luck pinpointing the sources of those radio trans-missions?"

Keith imagined the Waldahud's lower shoulders moving outside the camera's field of view. "Not yet."

"You said there were over two hundred separate frequencies upon which you were finding apparently intelligent signals."

"That's right."

"How many? Exactly how many?"

Hek's face turned to a profile view, showing his projecting snout, as he consulted a monitor. "Two hundred and seventeen," he said. "Although some are much more active than others."

Keith heard Jag, on his left, repeat the same bark of astonishment he'd made earlier.

"There are," said Keith slowly, "precisely two hundred and seventeen separate Jupiter-sized objects out there." He paused, backtracking away from his own conclusion. "Of course, gas-giant worlds like Jupiter are often sources of radio emissions."

"But these are spheres of dark matter," said Lianne. "They're electrically neutral."

"They are not pure dark matter," said Jag. "They're permeated with bits of regular matter. The dark matter could interact with protons in the regular matter through the strong nuclear force, thereby generating EM signals."

Hek lifted his upper shoulders. "That might work," he said. "But each sphere is broadcasting on its own separate frequency, almost like . . ." The Brooklyn-accented voice trailed off.

Keith looked at Rissa, and could see that she was thinking the same thing. He lifted his eyebrows. "Almost like separate voices," he said at last, finishing the thought.

"But there aren't two hundred and seventeen objects anymore," said Thor, turning around. "There are two hundred and eighteen now."

Keith nodded. "Hek, do another inventory of signals. See if there's new activity at a frequency just above or just below the block of frequencies you've identified as being active."

Hek tilted his head as he worked his controls up on deck one. "Just a second," he said. "Just a second." Then: "Gods of the mud and the moons, yes! Yes, there is!"

Keith turned to Rissa, grinning. "I wonder what baby's first words were?"

# EPSILON DRACONIS

Keith hadn't seen Glass reenter the docking bay, but when he looked up, there he was, coming closer, transparent legs carrying him over the fields of grass and four-leaf clover. His walking was fluid, beautiful, giving the appearance of being in slow motion even though he was moving at normal speed. The hint of aquamarine—the only color in his clear body—was eye-catching.

Keith thought about rising to his feet but instead simply looked up at the transparent man, sun glinting off the latter's body and egg-shaped head.

"Welcome back," said Keith.

Glass nodded. "I know, I know. You're frightened. You hide it well, but you're wondering how much longer I will keep you here. It won't be long, I promise. But there is something else I want to explore with you before you go."

Keith lifted his eyebrows, and Glass sat down, leaning his back against a nearby tree. Whatever his body was made of

*wasn't glass. His tubular torso didn't magnify the patterns
of the bark on the other side of it. Rather, they were seen
with only slight distortion.*

"*You are angry,*" *said Glass, simply.*

*Keith shook his head.* "*No, I'm not. You've treated me
well so far.*"

*The wind-chime laughter.* "*No, no. I don't mean you're
angry with me. Rather, you're angry in general. There's
something inside you, something down deep, that has
hardened your heart.*"

*Keith looked away.*

"*I'm right, aren't I?*" *said Glass.* "*Something that has
upset you greatly.*"

*Silence.*

"*Please,*" *said Glass.* "*Share it with me.*"

"*It was a long time ago,*" *said Keith.* "*I—I should be
over it, I know, but . . .*"

"*But it festers still, doesn't it? What is it? What changed
you so?*"

*Keith sighed, and looked around. Everything was so
beautiful, so peaceful. He couldn't remember the last time
he'd sat outside among the grass and trees, and just enjoyed
the surroundings, just—just relaxed.*

"*It has to do with Saul Ben-Abraham's death,*" *said
Keith.*

"*Death,*" *repeated Glass, as if Keith had used another
unknown word like* "*quixotic.*" *He shook his see-through
head.* "*How old was he when he died?*"

"*It was eighteen years ago now. He would have been
twenty-seven.*"

"*A heartbeat,*" *said Glass.*

*There was silence between them for a moment, Keith
recalling his reaction when Glass had dismissed his two
decades of marriage in a similar fashion. But Glass was
right this time. Keith nodded.*

"*How did Saul die?*" *asked Glass.*

"*It—it was an accident. At least, that's what the HuGo
decided. But, well, I always thought it was swept under the
rug. You know: deliberately suppressed. Saul and I were*

*living on Tau Ceti IV. He was an astronomer; I was a sociologist, doing a postdoctoral fellowship studying the colonists there. He and I had been friends since our undergrad days; we'd been roommates at UBC. And we had a lot in common—both liked to play handball and go, both acted in student theater, both had the same tastes in music. Anyway, Saul discovered the Tau Ceti shortcut, and we sent a small probe through it to Shortcut Prime. New Beijing was a mostly agricultural colony back then, not the thriving place it is now. Of course, it hadn't yet acquired the New Beijing nickname. It was just 'the Silvanus colony' then; Silvanus is the name of Tau Ceti's fourth planet. Anyway, they didn't have many sociologists there, so I ended up in charge of trying to figure out what effect the discovery of the shortcut network would have on human culture. And then the Waldahud starship popped through. A first-contact team had to be hastily assembled; even under hyperdrive, it would take six months for people to arrive from Earth. Saul and I ended up being part of the party that went up to meet the ship, and . . ." Keith* trailed off, closed his eyes, shook his head ever so slightly.

"Yes?" said Glass.

*"They said it was an accident. Said they'd misinterpreted. When we came face-to-face with the Waldahudin for the first time, Saul was carrying a holographic camera unit. He didn't aim it at the pigs, of course—no one could be that stupid. He was just holding it at his side, and then, with a flick of his thumb, he turned it on." Keith* sighed, long and loud. *"They said it looked like a traditional Waldahud hand weapon—same basic shape. They thought Saul was readying a weapon to fire on them. One of the pigs was carrying a sidearm, and he shot Saul. Right in the face. His head exploded next to me. I—I got splattered with . . . with . . ." Keith* looked away, and was quiet for a long moment. "They killed him. The best friend I ever had, they killed him." He stared at the ground, plucked a few four-leaf clovers, looked at them for a moment, then threw them away.

They were quiet for several moments. Crickets chirped,

and birds sang. Finally, Glass said, "That must be difficult to carry around with you."

Keith said nothing.

"Does Rissa know?"

"She does, yes. We were already married at that point; she'd come to Silvanus to try to fathom why it didn't have any native life, despite apparently having conditions that should have given rise to it, according to our evolutionary models. But I rarely talk about what happened with Saul— not with her, or with anyone else. I don't believe in burdening those around me with my suffering. Everyone has their own stuff to deal with."

"So you keep it inside."

Keith shrugged. "I try for a certain stoicism—a certain emotional restraint."

"Commendable," said Glass.

Keith was surprised. "You think so?"

"It's the way I feel, too. I know it's unusual, though. Most people live, if you'll pardon me my humor, transparent lives." Glass gestured at his own see-through body. "Their private self is their public self. Why are you different?"

Keith shrugged. "I don't know. I've always been this way." He paused again, thinking for a long time. Then: "When I was about nine or so, there was a bully in my neighborhood. Some big oaf, probably thirteen or fourteen. He used to pick up kids and drop them into this thornbush in the park. Well, everyone would kick and scream and cry while he was doing this, and he seemed to feed off that. One day, he came after me—grabbed me when I was playing catch, or something like that. He picked me up, carried me over to the bush, and dumped me in. I didn't struggle. There was no point; he was twice as big as me, and there was no way I could get away. And I didn't scream or cry, either. He dumped me in, and I simply got myself out. I had a few scrapes and cuts from it, but I didn't say anything. He just looked at me for about ten seconds, then said, 'Lansing, you've got balls.' And he never touched me again."

"So this internalizing is a survival mechanism?" asked Glass.

*Keith shrugged. "It's enduring what you have to endure."*

*"But you don't know where it came from?"*

*"No," said Keith. Then, a moment later, "Well, actually, yes. I suppose I do. My parents were both quite argumentative, and had short fuses. You'd never know when one of them was going to blow up over something. Publicly, privately, it didn't make any difference. You couldn't even make polite conversation without risking an explosion from one of them. We'd have family dinners together every night, but I always was silent, hoping we could just get through it, just once, without it being unpleasant, without one of them storming away from the table, or yelling, or saying something nasty."*

*Keith paused again. "In fairness, there were other issues in my parents' relationship that I didn't understand when I was a child. They'd started as a two-career family, but automation kept eliminating more and more jobs as the years went by—this was back before they outlawed true artificial intelligence. The Canadian government changed the tax laws so that second income earners in a family were taxed at a hundred-and-ten-percent rate. It was a move designed to spread out what work there was amongst the most families. Dad had been making less than Mom, so he was the one who stopped working. I'm sure that had a lot to do with his anger. But all I knew was that my parents were taking out their anger and frustration on everyone around them, and even as a kid, I vowed never to do that."*

*Glass was rapt. "Amazing," he said. "It all makes sense."*

*"What does?" asked Keith.*

*"You."*

# XIII

Keith's mind was reeling. So many discoveries, so much happening. He drummed his fingers on his bridge workstation for a moment, thinking. And then: "Okay, people, what now?"

The front row of workstations all rotated around on their individual pedestals so that they faced the back row: Lianne was facing Jag, Thor was facing Keith, and Rhombus was facing Rissa. Keith looked at each member of his bridge staff in turn. "We've got almost an embarrassment of riches here," he said. "First, there's the mystery of the stars erupting from the shortcuts—stars that Jag thinks come from the future. As if that's not a big enough puzzle to try to figure out, we've also stumbled upon life—*life!*—made out of dark matter." Keith looked from face to face. "Given the complexity of the radio signals Hek's been picking up, there's a chance—a small one, I grant you—that we're even looking at first contact with intelligent life. Rissa, it would have been crazy to say this yesterday, but let's make the dark-matter investigations the province of the life-sciences division."

She nodded.

Keith turned to Jag. "The stars coming out of the shortcuts, on the other hand, may pose a threat to the Commonwealth. If you're right, Jag, and they *are* coming from the future, then we've got to find out why they're coming back. Is it by deliberate design? If so, is it for a malevolent purpose? Or is it just an accident? A globular cluster, say, colliding with a shortcut billions of years from now, and overloading it somehow so that its constituent stars are spewed back to here?"

"Well," barked Jag, "a globular cluster wouldn't pass through a shortcut. Only one of its member stars would."

"Unless," said Thor, sounding a bit feisty, "that globular cluster was enclosed in a sort of super Dyson sphere—a shell around the entire assembly of stars. Imagine something like that touching a shortcut billions of years from now. The shell could break apart while traversing the gate, and send the component stars scattering out of different exit points."

"Ridiculous," said Jag. "You humans always reinforce each other in even your wildest fantasies. Take your religions, for instance—"

"Enough!" snapped Keith, bringing his open palm down loudly on the edge of his workstation. "Enough. We're not going to get anywhere squabbling." He looked at the Waldahud. "If you don't like Thor's suggestion, then make one of your own. Why are the stars coming back here from the future?"

Jag was facing the director, but only his right eyes were looking at Keith; the left pair was scanning the surroundings, an instinctual precursor to a fight. "I don't know," he said at last.

"We need an answer," said Keith, his voice still edged.

"Interrupting in all politeness," said Rhombus. "Offense not intended and hopefully not taken."

Keith turned to face the Ib. "What is it?"

"Perhaps you are asking the wrong person. No slight is

intended of good Jag, of course. But if you want to know why the stars are being sent back in time, then the person to ask is the person who is sending them back."

"You mean ask some person in the future?" Keith said. "How can we possibly do that?"

The Ib's mantle twinkled. "Now that *is* a question for good Jag," he said. "If material from the future can exit the shortcut in the past, can we then send something from the past into the future?"

Jag was quiet for a second, thinking. But then he moved his lower shoulders. "Not as far as I can tell. Every computer simulation I've done shows that any object entering the shortcut in the present gets shunted to another present-day shortcut. Assuming the rogue stars are being sent back by conscious design, I don't know how whoever is controlling the shortcuts is doing it, and I have no idea how to send something forward."

"Ah, good Jag," said Rhombus, "forgive me, but there is of course one way to send something forward."

"And what's that?" Keith asked.

"A time capsule," said the Ib. "You know: just make something that will last. Eventually, without our doing anything special, it will end up in the future through the natural passage of time."

Jag and Keith looked at each other. "But—but Jag says the stars are coming from *billions* of years in the future," Keith said.

"In fact," said the Waldahud, "if I had to guess, I would say they come from something like ten billion years from now."

Keith nodded, turning back to face Rhombus. "That's double the current age of any of the Commonwealth homeworlds."

"True," said the Ib. "But, forgive me, despite what you Humans think, neither Earth nor the other homeworlds were created by deliberate design. Our time capsule would be."

"A time capsule that would last ten billion years . . ." said Jag, clearly intrigued. "Perhaps . . . perhaps if it were made out of extremely hard material, like . . . like diamond, but without the cleavage planes. But even if we made such a thing, there is no guarantee that anyone would ever find it. And, besides, this part of the galaxy will rotate around the core forty-odd times before then. How do we possibly keep the object from drifting away from during all that time?"

Lights danced on Rhombus's sensor web. "Well, assume that this particular shortcut will continue to exist for the next ten billion years; that's a fair assumption, since it's here now, and must also still exist at the time the star was pushed through it. So, make our time capsule self-repairing—the nanotech lab should be able to come up with something— and have it hold position near this shortcut."

"And then just hope that someone will notice it when they come by here in the future to use the shortcut?" asked Keith.

"It may be more than that, good Keith," said Rhombus. "It may be that they come by here to *build* the shortcut. The shortcuts may have been created in the future, and had their exit points extruded into the past. If their real purpose is to shunt stars back here, then that's a likely scenario."

Keith turned to Jag. "Objections?"

The Waldahud lifted all four shoulders. "None."

He turned back to Rhombus. "And you think this will work?"

A tiny flash of light on the Ib's sensor web. "Why not?"

Keith thought about it. "I suppose it's worth a try. But ten billion years—all of the Commonwealth races might be extinct by then. Hell, they'll *probably* be extinct by then."

Lights moved up Rhombus's web; a nod of assent. "So we'll have to contrive our message in symbolic or mathematical language. Ask our good friend Hek to devise something. As a radio astronomer involved with searching for alien intelligence, he's an expert in designing symbolic communication. To use an expression that both your people and mine share, this project will be right up his alley."

The bridge was bustling with activity, and there was plenty of work to be done. But Jag and Hek were visibly flagging. Although they didn't do the theatrical yawns humans were

famous for, their nostrils were dilating rhythmically, a
physiological response that amounted to the same thing.

Keith thought for a moment that he could pull an
all-nighter. Hell, he'd done that often enough at university.
But university had been a quarter century ago, and he had to
admit that he, too, was exhausted.

"Let's call it a night," he said, rising from his workstation.
The indicators on it went dark as he did so.

Rissa nodded and rose as well. The two of them headed
toward one of the bridge's hologram-shrouded walls. The
door opened, exposing the corridor beyond. They headed
down toward the elevator station. A car was waiting for
them—PHANTOM had routed one there as soon as they
had started down the corridor. Keith got in, followed by
Rissa. "Deck eleven," he said, and PHANTOM chirped an
acknowledgement. They turned around, just in time to catch
sight of Lianne Karendaughter jogging down the corridor
toward them. PHANTOM saw her, too, of course, and held
the elevator door open until she arrived. Lianne smiled at
Keith as she got in, then called out her floor number. Rissa
affixed her gaze on the wall monitor that showed the current
level's deck plan.

Keith had been married to Rissa too long not to be
sensitive to her body language. She didn't like Lianne—
didn't like her standing this close to Keith, didn't like being
in a confined space with her.

The elevator began to move. On the monitor, the arms of
the floor plan began to contract. Keith breathed deeply—
and realized, perhaps for the first time, that he missed the
subtle smell of perfume. Another concession to the damn
pigs, and their hypersensitive noses. Perfume, cologne,
scented aftershave—all were banned aboard *Starplex*.

Keith could see the reflection of Rissa's face in the
monitor screen, see the tight lines at the corners of her
mouth, see the tension, the hurt.

And Keith could also see Lianne. She was shorter than he
was, and her lustrous blond hair half shielded her exotic,
young face. If they'd been alone, Keith might have chatted
with her, told her a joke, smiled, laughed, maybe even

touched her arm lightly as he made a comment. She was so—so *alive;* talking to her was invigorating.

Instead, he said nothing. The deck-number indicator continued to count down. Finally, the car hummed to a stop on the floor containing Lianne's apartment.

"Good night, Keith," said Lianne, smiling up at him. "Good night, Rissa."

"Good night," replied Keith. Rissa nodded curtly.

Keith was able to watch her walk down the corridor for a few seconds before the door closed behind her. He'd never been to her apartment. He wondered how she had it decorated.

The elevator continued to ascend briefly and then it stopped again. The door opened, and Keith and Rissa walked the short distance to their apartment.

Once they were inside, Rissa spoke—and Keith could hear in her voice that said she was speaking against her better judgment. "You're quite fond of her, aren't you?"

Keith weighed all the possible answers. He had too much respect for Rissa's intelligence to try to get away with saying, "Who?" After a moment's hesitation, he decided simple honesty was the best policy. "She's bright, charming, beautiful, and good at her job. What's not to like?"

"She's twenty-seven," said Rissa, as if that were an indictable offense.

*Twenty-seven!* thought Keith. Well, there it was. A concrete number. But—twenty-seven. Jesus Christ . . . He took off his shoes and socks, and lay down on the couch, letting his feet air out.

Rissa sat down opposite him. Her face was a study in thought, as if she were deciding whether to pursue the topic further. Evidently she chose not to, and instead changed the subject. "Boxcar came to see me today."

Keith wriggled his toes. "Oh?"

"She's quitting."

"Really? Got a better offer somewhere else?"

Rissa shook her head. "She's going to discorporate next week. She was assessed a penalty of one sixteenth of her lifespan because she wasted some people's time almost six hundred years ago."

Keith was quiet for a few moments. "Oh."

"You don't sound surprised," said Rissa.

"Well, I've heard of the procedure. Never quite made sense to me, the way Ibs are so obsessive about wasted time. I mean, they live for centuries."

"To them, it's just a normal lifespan. They don't think of it as inordinately long, of course." A pause. "You can't let her go through with it."

Keith spread his arms. "I don't know that I have any choice."

"Dammit, Keith. The execution is to take place here, aboard *Starplex*. Surely you have jurisdiction."

"Over ship's business, sure. Over this, well . . ." He looked up at the ceiling. "PHANTOM, what powers do I have in this area?"

"Under the Articles of Commonwealth Jurisprudence, you are obliged to recognize all sentences imposed by the individual member governments," said PHANTOM. "The Ib practice of exacting penalties equal to a portion of the standard lifespan is specifically excluded from the section of the articles that deals with cruel and unusual punishment. Given that, you have no power to interfere."

Keith spread his arms, and looked at Rissa. "Sorry."

"But what she did was so minor, so insignificant."

"You said she fudged some data?"

"That's right, when she was a student. A stupid thing to do, granted, but—"

"You know how the Ibs feel about wasted time, Rissa. I imagine others relied on her results, right?"

"Yes, but—"

"Look, the Ibs come from a planet that's perpetually shrouded in cloud. You can't see the stars or their moons from the surface, and their sun is only a bright smudge behind the clouds. Despite that, by studying tides in those shallow puddles that pass for oceans there, they managed to work out the existence of their moons. They even managed to deduce the existence of other stars and planets, all before any of them had ever traveled above their atmosphere. The things they've figured out would have been impossible for humans, I bet. It's only because they live for such a long time that they were able to puzzle them through; a shorter-lived race on such a world would probably never have realized that there was a universe out there. But to accomplish what they have, they have to be able to trust each other's observations and results. It all falls apart if someone is monkeying with the data."

"But no one could possibly still care about what she did after all this time. And—and I need her. She's an important part of my staff. And she's my friend."

Keith spread his arms. "What would you have me do?"

"Talk to her. Tell her she doesn't have to go through with this."

Keith scratched his left ear. "All right," he said, at last. "All right."

Rissa smiled at him. "Thank you. I'm sure she'll—"

The intercom chimed. "Colorosso to Lansing," said a woman's voice. Franca Colorosso was the delta-shift InOps officer.

Keith tipped his head up. "Open. Keith here. What is it, Franca?"

"A watson has come through from Tau Ceti, with a news report I think you should see. It's old news, in a way—sent from Sol to Tau Ceti by hyperspace radio sixteen days ago. As soon as Grand Central received it, they relayed it to us."

"Thanks. Pipe it down to my wall monitor, please."

"Doing so. Close."

Keith and Rissa both turned to face the wall. It was the BBC World Service, being read by an East Indian man with steel-gray hair. "Tensions," he said, "continue between two of the Commonwealth governments. On one side: the United Nations of Sol, Epsilon Indi, and Tau Ceti. On the other, the Royal Government of Rehbollo. Rumors of further deterioration in the situation were fueled today by the terse announcement that Rehbollo is closing three more embassies—New York, Paris, and Tokyo. Coupled with the four other closings a week ago, this leaves only the Ottawa and Brussels embassies open in all of Sol system. The consular staffs from the embassies closed today have already departed on Waldahud starships for the Tau Ceti shortcut."

The view cut to a beefy Waldahud face. The super at the bottom of the screen identified him as Plenipotentiary Daht Lasko em-Wooth. He spoke in English, without aid of a translator—a rare feat for a member of his race. "It's with great regret that economic necessity has forced us into this move. As you know, the economies of all the Commonwealth races have been thrown into disarray by the unexpected development of interstellar commerce. Reducing the number of our embassies on Earth simply represents an adjustment to the times."

The screen changed to show a middle-aged African woman, identified as Rita Negesh, Earth-Wald Political Scientist, Leeds University. "I don't buy that—not for a minute," she said. "If you ask me, Rehbollo is recalling its ambassadors."

"As a prelude to what?" asked an off-camera male voice.

Negesh spread her arms. "Look, when humanity first moved out into space, all the pundits said the universe is so big and so bountiful, there was no possibility of material conflict between separate worlds. But the shortcut network changed all that; it forced us up close with other races, perhaps before we or they were ready."

"And so?" said the unseen questioner again.

"And so," said Negesh, "if we are moving toward an . . . an incident, it may not just be over economic issues. It may be something more basic—the simple fact that humans and Waldahudin get on each others' nerves."

The wall monitor changed back to the hologram of Lake Louise. Keith looked at Rissa, and let out a long sigh. "An 'incident,'" he said, repeating the word. "Well, at least we're both too old to be drafted."

Rissa looked at him for a long moment. "I think that makes no difference," she said, at last. "I think we're already at the front lines."

# XIV

Keith always enjoyed taking an elevator to the docking bays. The car dropped down to deck thirty-one, the uppermost of the ten decks that made up the central disk. It then began a horizontal journey along one of the four spokes that radiated out from there to the outer edge of the disk. But the spokes were transparent, as were the elevator cab's walls and floors, and so the passengers were treated to a view looking down on the vast circular ocean. Keith could see the dorsal fins of three dolphins swimming along just below the surface. Agitators in the ocean walls and central shaft produced respectable half-meter waves; dolphins preferred that to a calm sea. The radius of the ocean deck was ninety-five meters; Keith was always staggered by the amount of water contained there. The roof was a real-time hologram of Earth's sky, with towering white clouds moving against a background of that special shade of blue that always tugged at Keith's heart.

The elevator finally reached the edge of the ocean and passed through into the prosaic tunnels of the engineering torus. Once it came to the outer edge of the torus, it descended the nine levels to the floor of the docking bays. Keith disembarked, and walked the short distance to the entrance to bay nine. As soon as he entered, he saw Hek, the symbolic-communications specialist, and a slim human named Shahinshah Azmi, the head of the material-sciences department. Between them was a black cube measuring a meter on a side. The cube was resting on a pedestal that brought it up to eye level. Keith walked over to them.

"Good day, sir," said the ever-polite Azmi, in a flat voice. Keith knew from old movies how musical Indian accents used to be; he missed the rich variety that human voices had had before instantaneous communications had smoothed out all the differences. Azmi gestured at the cube. "We've built the time capsule out of graphite composite with a few radioactives added. It's solid except for the self-repairing hyperspatial sensor, which will lock onto the shortcut, and the starlight-powered ACS system for helping the cube hold position relative to it."

"And what about the message for the future?" asked Keith.

Hek pointed to one of the cube's sides. "We've incised it into the cube's faces," he said, his barking echoing in the bay. "It begins on this side. As you can see, it consists of a series of boxed examples. Two dots plus two dots equals four dots; a question with its answer. The second box, here, has two dots plus two dots, and a symbol. Since any arbitrary symbol would do, we just used the English question mark, but without the separate dot underneath; that might confuse one into thinking it was two symbols rather than one. Anyway, that gives us a question and a symbolic representation of the fact that the answer is missing. The third box shows the question symbol, the symbol I've established for 'equals,' and four dots, the answer. So that box says, 'The answer to the question is four.' Do you see?"

Keith nodded.

"Now," continued Hek, "having established a vocabulary

for our dialogue, we can ask our real question." He waddled around to the opposite side of the cube, which was also incised with markings.

"As you can see," said Hek, "we have two similar boxes here. The first one has a graphic representation of the shortcut, with a star emerging from it. See that scale mark showing the width of the star, and the series of horizontal and vertical lines beneath? That's a binary representation of the star's diameter in units of the box's width, in case there's any confusion about what the image represents. And then there's the equals symbol, and the question symbol. So it says, 'shortcut with star emerging from it equals what?' And beneath it is the question symbol, the equals symbol, and a large blank space: 'The answer to the above question is . . .' and a space implying that we want a reply."

Keith nodded slowly. "Clever. Good work, gentlemen."

Azmi pointed to one of the cube's other faces. "On this face, we've incised information about the periods and relative positions of fourteen different pulsars. If the shortcut makers in the future—or whoever it is who finds this—have records going back this far in time, they'll be able to identify the specific year in which the cube was created from that information."

"Beyond that," said Hek, "they might also assume, quite reasonably, that the cube had been created shortly after the green star emerged from this shortcut—and presumably they'll know what date they sent that star back to, as well. In other words, they've got two independent ways of determining when to send any reply back to."

"And this will work?" Keith asked.

"Oh, probably not," said Azmi, smiling. "It's just a bottle in the ocean. I don't seriously expect any results, but I suppose it's worth a try. Still, as Dr. Magnor has told me, if we don't get a good explanation, and if we decided the stars are a threat, we can use the Waldahud space-flattening technique to evaporate the shortcuts. Granted, stars may be popping out of thousands of exit points, so we probably can't do much to stop them. But if they know we have the capability to interfere to some degree, perhaps they'll provide an explanation rather than have us do that."

"Very good," said Keith. "But what will make the cube conspicuous? How can you be sure someone will find it?"

"That's the hardest part of all," barked Hek. "There are only a few ways to get something to stand out. One is to make it reflective. But no matter what we make this box out of, it will have to endure perhaps ten billion years of scouring by interstellar dust. Granted, that's only a few microscopic impacts per century, but the net effect over that much time would be to dull any reflective surface.

"The second possibility we'd considered was to make the time capsule big—so that it's eye-catching; or heavy—so that it warps spacetime. But the bigger you make it, the more likely it is to be destroyed by a meteor collision.

"The final possibility was to make it loud—you know, by broadcasting a radio signal. But that requires a power source. Of course, right now the green star is close by, and we can use simple solar cells to generate electricity from it, but the star has a respectable proper motion relative to the shortcut. In just a few thousand years, it'll be a full light-year from here, much too far away to provide significant power. And any internal power source we use would exhaust its fuel, or have most of its radioactives decay to lead, long before the target date."

Keith nodded. "But you said you were using starlight converted to electricity to power the attitude-control system?"

"Yes. But there's almost no spare power for a beacon of any sort. We're just going to have to assume that whoever built the shortcuts will have detectors that will find the cube regardless."

"And if they don't?"

Hek moved all four shoulders up and down in a shrug. "If they don't—well, we've hardly lost much by trying."

"All right," said Keith. "It looks good to me. Is this a prototype, or the actual time capsule?"

"We'd intended it as just a prototype, but everything

came together perfectly," said Azmi. "I say we might as well go ahead and use this one."

Keith turned to Hek. "What about you?"

The Waldahud barked once. "I concur."

"Very well," said Keith. "How do you propose to launch it?"

"Well, it has nothing but ACS jets," said Azmi. "And I don't dare put it out there on its own with those dark-matter creatures swarming around; it would probably get sucked into their gravity. But we've already seen that the dark-matter beings have some mobility, so I'm assuming they won't be in this exact spot forever. I've programmed a standard payload carrier to take the cube away from here, but come back in a hundred years and dump it about twenty klicks from the shortcut. After that, the time capsule's own ACS jets should be able to hold it in place relative to the exit point."

"Excellent," said Keith. "Is the launcher ready, too?"

Azmi nodded.

"Can you launch it from down here?"

"Of course."

"Let's do so, then."

The three of them exited the bay, and took a lift up to the docking control room, which had angled windows that overlooked the interior of the cavernous hangar. Azmi took a seat in front of a console and began operating controls. Under his command, a motorized flatbed rolled into the bay, carrying a cylindrical payload carrier. Mechanical arms mated the cube to the clamps on the front of the carrier.

"Depressurizing the bay," said Azmi.

Shimmering forcefield sheets started to close in from three of the four walls and the floor and ceiling, forcing the air in the bay out through vents in the rear wall. When all the air had been swept up and compressed into tanks, the forcefield sheets collapsed, leaving an interior vacuum.

"Opening space door," Azmi said, operating another control. The segmented curving outer wall began to slide up into the ceiling. Blackness became visible, but the glare of the bay's internal lighting washed out the stars.

Azmi touched some more buttons. "Activating time-capsule electronics." He then tapped a key, initiating a preprogrammed sequence for the tractor-beam emitter mounted on the rear bay wall. The payload carrier lifted off the flatbed, flew over the floor plates, passed the spindly form of a repair skiff that was parked inside the bay, and headed out into space.

"Powering up carrier," said Azmi. The cylinder's end lit up with the glow of thrusters, and the contraption rapidly receded from view.

"And that," said Azmi, "is that."

"Now what?" asked Keith.

Azmi shrugged. "Now just forget about it. Either this will work, or it won't—probably won't."

Keith nodded. "Excellent work, guys. Thank you. It's—"

"Rissa to Lansing," said a voice over the speakers.

Keith looked up. "Open. Hi, Rissa."

"Hi, hon. We're ready to take our first whack at communicating with the dark-matter creatures."

"I'm on my way. Close." He smiled at Azmi and Hek. "Sometimes, you know, my staff is almost *too* efficient."

Keith rode up to the bridge and took his seat in the center of the back row. The holographic bubble was filled not with the normal space view but rather with red circles against a pale white background, a plot of the locations of the dark-matter spheres.

"Okay," said Rissa. "We're going to try communicating with the dark-matter beings using radio and visual signals. We've deployed a special probe that will do the actual signaling. It's located about eight light-seconds off the starboard side of the ship; I'm going to operate it by comm laser. Of course, the dark-matter beings may already have detected our presence, but, then again, they may not have. And just in case the dark-matter beings turn out to be the Slammers, or something equally nasty, it seems prudent to have their attention drawn to an expendable probe rather than *Starplex* itself."

" 'Dark-matter beings,' " repeated Keith. "That's a bit of a mouthful, no? Surely we can come up with a better name for them."

"How about 'darkies'?" said Rhombus, helpfully.

Keith cringed. "That's not a good idea." He thought for a second, then looked up, grinning. "What about MACHO men?"

Jag rolled all four eyes and made a disgusted bark.

"How does 'darmats' sound?" asked Thor.

Rissa nodded. "Darmats it is." She addressed everyone in the room. "Well, as you all know, Hek has been cataloging the signal groups he's picked up from the darmats. On the assumption that each group is a word, we've identified the single most commonly used one. For the first message, I'm going to send a looping repeat of that word. We assume it's innocuous—the darmat equivalent of 'the,' or some such. Granted, the repetition will convey no meaningful information, but with luck the darmats will recognize it as an attempt to communicate." She turned to Keith. "Permission to proceed, Director?"

Keith smiled. "Be my guest."

Rissa touched a control. "Transmitting now."

Lights flashed on Rhombus's web. "Well, that certainly did something," he said. "The conversation level has increased dramatically. All of them talking at once."

Rissa nodded. "We're hoping they'll triangulate on the probe as the source."

"I'd say they've figured it out," said Thor, a moment later, pointing at the display. Five of the world-sized creatures had begun to move toward the probe.

"Now the tricky part begins," said Rissa. "We've got their attention, but can we communicate with them?"

Keith knew that if anyone could pull it off, it would be his wife, who had been part of the team that had first communicated with the Ibs. That effort had started with a simple exchange of nouns—this pattern of lights meant "table," that one meant "ground," and so on. Even then, there had been difficulties. The Ib body was so different from the bipedal human design that for many concepts they had no terms: stand up, run, sit down, chair, clothing, male, female. And because they'd always lived under cloud cover, for countless other ideas—day, night, month, year, constellation—there were no common Ibese words. Meanwhile, the Ibs had been trying to convey concepts that were central to their lives: biological gestalt, all-encompassing vision, and the many metaphorical meanings for roll ahead and roll back.

But that exercise had been a piece of cake compared with communicating with world-sized beings. Indeed, the Ibs had had no trouble understanding that particular metaphor— enjoyable, nonnutritive food being equated with ease—just as humans had no difficulty with the Ibese expression for the same sentiment, "downward slope." Communicating with aliens as big as Jupiter who might or might not be intelligent, might or might not be able to see, might or might not understand any principle of physics or mathematics, could prove impossible.

"The babble on all two hundred frequencies is continuing," said Rhombus.

Rissa nodded. "But no way to tell if it's chatter amongst the spheres, or responses aimed at us." She touched another button. "I'm going to try again with a loop of a different, almost-as-common darmat word."

This time, the radio cacophony was halted by one darmat who was apparently shushing the others. And then that darmat repeated a simple, three-word sentence over and over again.

"Time to play a hunch," said Rissa.

"How so?" asked Keith.

"Well, the first question we would ask in a circumstance such as this would be 'Who are you?' Hek and I had PHANTOM sample all the darmat words, and devise a signal that followed the apparent rules for valid word construction but had not, as far as we've been able to detect, been used by the darmats. We hope they'll take this signal to be *Starplex*'s name."

Rissa broadcast the made-up word several times—and, at last, the first breakthrough: the same sphere that had shushed the others repeated the term back at the probe.

"The rain in Spain," said Rissa, grinning, "falls mainly on the plain."

"A thousand pardons," said Rhombus. "My translator must be broken."

Rissa was still grinning. "It's not broken. It's just that I think she's got it—I think we've made contact."

Keith gestured at the display. "Which one is talking to us?"

Ropes danced on Rhombus's console. "That one," he said as a blue halo appeared around one of the red circles. He operated his console some more. "Here, let me give you a better picture. Now that we've got the green star for light, I can get good views of the individual darmats." The red circle disappeared, replaced with a gray-on-black rendering of the sphere.

"Can you increase the contrast?" asked Keith.

"A pleasure to do so." The parts of the sphere that had been gray or smoky now showed in a much wider range of intensities, all the way through to pure white.

Keith regarded it. With the enhanced contrast, a pair of vertical white convection lines were visible going from pole to pole, flaring out at the equator. "A cat's eye," he said.

Rissa nodded. "It does look like one, doesn't it?" She touched some controls. "Okay, Cat's Eye, let's see how intelligent you are." A horizontal black bar appeared floating in the holo bubble, about a meter long and fifteen centimeters tall. "That bar represents a series of fusion lamps on the probe," said Rissa. "The lamps have been turned off since the probe was deployed. Now, watch." She tapped a key on her console. The black bar turned electric pink for three seconds, went black again for three seconds, turned pink twice in rapid succession, blacked out for another three seconds, then blinked on three times. "When the bar is pink, I've got all the fusion lamps on," said Rissa. "The probe is also broadcasting white radio noise when the lights are on, and silence when they're off. I've set the bridge speakers to the frequency used by Cat's Eye."

The speakers were silent, but Keith could see indicators

blinking on Rhombus's panel, showing chatter on some of the other frequencies.

Rissa waited about half a minute, then touched a key. The whole sequence—one blink, two blinks, three blinks—repeated itself.

This time there was an immediate response: three darmat words, which PHANTOM translated over the speakers as three distinctive patterns of bleeps and bloops.

"Well," said Lianne, "if we're lucky, that's darmat talk for one, two, three."

"Unless," said Thor, "it's darmat for 'what the hell—?'"

Rissa smiled, and pushed the same key. The probe winked out one, two, three again, and Cat's Eye responded with the same three words. "Okay," said Rissa. "Now for the real test." She pressed another key, and everyone watched as the indicator bar winked in reverse sequence: three, two, one.

The darmat responded with three words. Keith couldn't quite tell for sure, but—

"Got it!" crowed Rissa. "Those were the same three words Cat's Eye said before, but in the opposite order. He understands what we're saying—and therefore has at least a rudimentary intelligence." Rissa ran the sequence again, and this time PHANTOM substituted the English words "three, two, one," in a synthesized male voice with an old-fashioned French accent—apparently that was to be the standard for darmats.

The bridge staff was rapt as Rissa pressed on, learning the Darmat words for the numerals four through one hundred. Neither she nor PHANTOM could detect any kind of repeating pattern in the word construction that would allow one to deduce the base the darmats used for counting; it seemed that each numeral was represented by a word unrelated to all the others. She stopped at one hundred, afraid the darmat would get bored by the game and cease communicating with her at all.

Next came exercises in simple math: two blinks, a six-second pause—double the normal length—two more blinks, another six-second pause, and then four blinks.

Cat's Eye dutifully provided the words two, two, and four each of the first five times Rissa repeated the sequence, but on the sixth, it finally caught the intended meaning of the prolonged gaps: a six-second gap meant a word was missing in the middle. PHANTOM didn't wait for Rissa's confirmation; when Cat's Eye next spoke, it translated the darmat sentence as "two plus two equals four"—adding the terms for the two operators to the translation database. In short order, Rissa also elicited the darmat words for "minus," "multiplied by," "divided by," "greater than," and "less than."

"I think," said Rissa, grinning from ear to ear, "that there's no doubt that we're dealing with highly intelligent beings."

Keith shook his head in wonder as Rissa continued to use mathematics to work out more vocabulary. She soon had the darmat terms for "correct" and "incorrect" (or "yes" and "no")—which she hoped would also be their terms for "right" and "wrong" in other areas. She then had Rhombus move the probe in specific ways (carefully avoiding splashing the darmat with hot ACS exhaust), and that led to the darmat words for "up," "down," "left," "right," "in front," "behind," "receding," "approaching," "turning," "tumbling," "circling," "fast," "slow," and more.

By moving the probe in a path right around Cat's Eye, Rissa was able to get the darmat word for "orbit," and soon had picked up the words for "star," "planet," and "moon," as well.

By using colored filters on the probe's fusion lamps, Rissa then elicited the darmat words for various hues. She next broadcast her first simple original sentence, beginning with the arbitrary sign they'd originally assigned to the probe that was *Starplex*'s mouthpiece: "*Starplex* moves toward green star." Rissa then had Rhombus make the probe do precisely that.

Cat's Eye understood at once, responding with the word for "correct." He then sent his own sentence: "Cat's Eye moves away from *Starplex*," then turned word into deed. Rissa replied with "correct."

When alpha shift was over, Keith went back to his apartment to shower and eat, but Rissa kept on long into ship's night, building up a bigger and bigger vocabulary. Never once did Cat's Eye show the slightest sign of impatience or fatigue. By the time gamma shift was coming on duty, Rissa herself was exhausted, and she turned the translation duties over to Hek. They worked for four days—sixteen shifts—slowly building up a darmat vocabulary. Cat's Eye never let his attention falter. Finally, Rissa said, they could engage in a simple conversation. Keith, as director, would vet the questions, but Rissa would actually pose them.

"Ask him how long he's been here," said Keith.

Rissa leaned into the microphone stalk emerging from her console. "How long have you been here?"

The answer came quickly: "Since the time we started talking, times one hundred times one hundred times one hundred times one hundred times one hundred times one hundred."

PHANTOM's voice came on, interpolating: "That is approximately four trillion days, or roughly ten billion years."

"Of course," said Rissa, "he could be speaking figuratively—just meaning to convey a very long time."

"Ten billion years," said Jag, "is, however, a rough approximation of the age of the universe."

"Well, if you were ten billion years old, I suppose you'd have a lot of patience, too," said Thor, chuckling.

"Maybe ask him a different way," suggested Lianne.

"Is that how long all of you have been here?" said Rissa into the mike.

"This group that duration," said the translated voice. "This one, duration since the time we started talking, times one hundred times one hundred times one hundred times fifty."

"That translates to approximately five hundred thousand years," said PHANTOM.

"Perhaps he's saying this group of darmats is ten billion years old," said Rissa, "but he's only half a million himself."

"'Only,'" said Lianne.

"Now tell him how old we are," said Keith.

"You mean *Starplex*'s age?" asked Rissa. "Or the age of the Commonwealth? Or the age of our species?"

"We're comparing civilizations, I guess," said Keith. "So the comparisons would be the oldest Commonwealth race." He looked at his little hologram of Rhombus. "That's the Ibs, who have existed in their current species form for about a million years, right?"

Rhombus's web rippled in agreement.

Rissa nodded and keyed her mike. "We duration since the time we started talking times one hundred times one hundred times one hundred times one hundred. This one duration since the time we started talking times one hundred *plus* one hundred." She touched the off switch. "I told him that as a civilization, we're a million years old, but *Starplex* itself is just two years old."

Cat's Eye replied by reiterating the number for its own personal age, followed by the word for minus, then repeating the equation for *Starplex*'s tiny age, adding the word for "equals," and then reiterating the same sequence it had used to express its own age. "Very loosely," said Rissa, "I think he's saying that our age is nothing compared to his."

"Well, he's right about that," said Keith, laughing. "I wonder what it would feel like to be that old?"

# XV

Keith rarely entered any of the ship's Ibese areas. Gravity was kept at 1.41 times Earth normal there (and 1.72 times ship's standard); Keith felt as though he weighed 115 kilograms, instead of his usual 82. He could stand it for short periods of time, but it wasn't pleasant.

The corridors here were much wider than elsewhere aboard *Starplex,* and the interdeck areas were thicker, making for lower ceilings. Keith didn't have to stoop, but he found himself doing so anyway. The air was warm and dry.

Keith came to the room he was looking for, its door marked with a matrix of yellow lights forming a rectangular shape with a small circle just below the rectangle's base at each end. Keith had never seen a train with wheels, except in a museum, but the pictogram did indeed look like a boxcar.

Keith spoke into the air. "Let her know I'm here, please, PHANTOM."

PHANTOM chirped acknowledgment, and a moment later, presumably having received Boxcar's permission, the door slid aside.

Ib living quarters were unusual by human standards. At first, they seemed luxuriously big—the room Keith had entered measured eight by ten meters. But then one realized that they were actually the same size as every other apartment aboard ship, but weren't divided into separate sleeping, living, and bathing areas. There were no chairs or couches, of course. Nor was there any carpeting; the floor was covered with a hard rubber material. On their home-world, in preindustrial times, Ibs built mounds of earth just wide enough so that they would fit between their wheels—so that the frame and the other components could be supported when the wheels temporarily separated from the body. Boxcar had the manufactured equivalent of such a mound in one corner of her room, but that was its only furnishing.

Keith found the art on the walls strange and disconcert-ing: peanut-shaped images consisting of multiple, often distorted, views of the same object from different angles superimposed one atop the other. He couldn't make out what the ones on the far wall showed, but he was startled to realize that the series of them nearest to him were studies of severely premature human and Waldahud babies, with stubby limbs, and strange, translucent heads. Boxcar was a biologist, after all, and alien life was probably fascinating to her, but the choice of subject matter was unsettling to say the least.

Boxcar rolled toward Keith from the far side of the room. It was nerve-racking to have an Ib approach from a good distance. They liked to accelerate to high speed and then stop with a jerk only a meter or two away. Keith had never heard of a human getting steamrollered by one, but he was always afraid he'd be the first.

The Ib's lights flashed. "Dr. Lansing," she said. "An unexpected pleasure. Please, please—I have no seat to offer you, but I know the gravity is too high. Feel free to rest on my comfort mound." A rope flicked in the direction of the wedge-shaped construct at the side of the room.

Keith's first thought was to reject the offer, but, dammit, it was unpleasant standing under this gravity. He walked over to the mound and rested his rear on it. "Thank you," he said. He didn't know how to begin, but he knew he would offend the Ib if he wasted time coming to the point. "Rissa asked me to come to see you. She says you are going to discorporate soon."

"Dear, sweet Rissa," said Boxcar. "Her concern is touching."

Keith looked around the room, thinking. "I want you to know," he said at last, "that you don't have to go through with the discorporation—at least so long as you are aboard *Starplex*. All staff aboard this ship are considered de facto embassy personnel; I can try to arrange immunity for you." He looked at the being; he wished it had a face—wished it had normal eyes, eyes that he could try to read. "Your service has been exemplary; there's no reason why you couldn't continue to serve aboard *Starplex* for the rest of your natural life."

"You are kind, Dr. Lansing. Very kind. But I must be true to myself. Understand that though I have not mentioned my impending discorporation to anyone, I have been preparing mentally and physically for it for centuries now. I have timed the events of my life to conclude now; I wouldn't know what to do with the extra fifty years."

"You could continue your research. Who knows? With another half century of work on the senescence problem, you might lick it. You might *never* have to die."

"An eternity of shame, Dr. Lansing? An eternity of guilt? No, thank you. I am unalterably committed to my stated course of action."

Keith was quiet for a moment, thinking. Arguments and counterarguments ran through his head; new tacks, new approaches. But he dismissed them all. It wasn't his business, wasn't his place. Finally, he nodded. "Is there anything I can do to make it easier for you? Any special facilities or equipment you need?"

"There is a ceremony. Normally, most Ibs would not attend; to do so would be to have the guilty party end up wasting even more of their time. I imagine that only my closest Ib friends will come. So, on that basis, I have no need for a large venue. But, since you have offered, I would request, if possible, that I be allowed to use one of the docking bays for the ceremony—and that once the ceremony is completed, my component parts be ejected into space."

"If that is what you'd like, then of course you have my permission."

"Thank you, Dr. Lansing. Thank you very much."

Keith nodded, and headed for the door. He made his way down the warm corridor, back into the CAGE conditions of the central shaft. Normally, when he exited an Ibese area into the lower gravity of the rest of the ship, he felt buoyant, light as a feather.

But not this time.

"Tachyon pulse!" announced Rhombus from the ExOps station. "Something coming through the shortcut. Small object, only about a meter in diameter."

Most likely a watson, Keith thought. "Let's have a look at it, Rhombus." Part of the spherical hologram was set off by a blue border, and inside the border was a telescopic view of the object that had popped out of the shortcut.

"Welcome home!" said Thor Magnor, grinning broadly.

"Somebody better get Hek and Shanu Azmi down here," said Keith.

"Will do," said Lianne, then a moment later, "They're on their way."

The port starfield split and the Waldahud alien-communications specialist waddled onto the bridge. Almost simultaneously, the door behind the seating gallery opened up, and Shahinshah Azmi came in. He was wearing tennis shorts and holding a racket. Keith gestured at the magnified image. "Look what's come back," he said.

All four of Hek's eyes went wide. "That's . . . that's wonderful!"

"Rhombus," Keith said, "scan it for anything untoward. If it's clean, use a tractor beam to haul it into docking bay six."

"Scanning . . . no obvious problems. Locking on tractor beam."

"Keep it isolated inside a forcefield once you get it aboard."

"Will do, with respect."

"I wish it had arrived last week," said Azmi.

"Why?" Rissa asked.

"It would have saved us all the work of building it."

Rissa laughed.

"Shanu, Hek, shall we repair to bay six?" Keith said.

"I'd like to have a look, too," said Rissa.

Keith smiled. "By all means."

The four made their way to the docking bay. There, they stood behind a forcefield curtain, Hek about two meters to Keith's right, Azmi just behind him, and Rissa so close to her husband's left side that their elbows lightly touched. The cube was maneuvered into the bay by a series of invisible beams. Once it was set down, a force bubble was erected around it, and the space door slid down from the ceiling. They waited until the bay was pressurized, then went out to look at the cube.

It had weathered the eons well. Its surface looked like it had been scoured with steel wool, but all the incised markings showing the sample questions on top were quite legible. It turned out that Rhombus had maneuvered the cube in so that the face with the answer was the one the cube was sitting on.

"PHANTOM," Keith said, "flip the cube a quarter turn so that the bottom face is visible."

Tractor beams manipulated the time capsule. In the space that had been left for the answer, black symbols stood out against a white background that had somehow been fused to the cube's surface.

"Gods," said Hek.

Rissa's jaw dropped.

Keith stood immobile.

At the top of the answer space was a string of Arabic numerals:

$$10\text{-}646\text{-}397\text{-}281$$

And beneath it, in English, was: "Pushing back the stars is necessary, and not a threat. It will benefit us all. Don't be afraid." Underneath all that, in somewhat smaller type, it said, "Keith Lansing."

"I don't believe this," Keith said.

"Hey, look at this," barked Hek, leaning closer. "That isn't how one makes that character, is it?"

Keith peered at it. The serif on each lowercase $u$ was on the left side of the letter instead of the right. "And the apostrophe in 'don't' is backward, too," said Keith.

"And what's that series of numbers at the top?" asked Rissa.

"It looks like a citizenship number," Keith said.

"No—a mathematical expression," said Hek. "It is—it is—Central Computer?"

"Negative one thousand three hundred and fourteen," said PHANTOM's voice.

"No, it's not that," said Rissa, shaking her head slowly. "When humans write a letter, that's where they put the date."

"So what's the format?" asked Hek. "Hour, then day, then month, then year? That doesn't work. How about the other way around? The tenth year, the six hundred and forty-sixth day. That makes no sense either, since they're only four hundred or so days in a Terran year."

"No," said Rissa. "No, it's not that. It's the year—the whole thing is the year. Ten billion, six hundred and forty-six million, three hundred and ninety-seven thousand, two hundred and eighty-one."

"The year?" said Hek.

"The year," said Rissa. "The Earth year. Anno Domini—after the birth of Christ, a prophet."

"But I've seen lots of human numbering before," said Hek. "Yes, you separate big numbers into thousands groups—my people do it into ten thousands. But I thought you used—what do you call them?—those subscripted curlicues?"

"Commas," said Rissa. "We do use commas, or spaces." She seemed to be having trouble keeping her balance; she moved over to the docking-bay wall and leaned against it. "But . . . but imagine a time so far in the future that English isn't used anymore . . . a time in which it's been millions or billions of years since—" she pointed at Keith— "since anyone has used English. They might indeed misremember the convention for writing big numbers, or how to make an apostrophe, or where the little extra doodad on a *u* went."

"It's got to be a fake," Keith said, shaking his head.

"If it is, it's a perfect one," said Azmi, waving a hand scanner. "We built some very long half-life radioactives into the cube's construction. The cube is now ten billion Earth years old plus or minus nine hundred million. The only way to fake that kind of dating would be to manufacture a counterfeit cube using the correct ratio of isotopes to give that apparent age. But even to the smallest detail this one matches our original—except for the radioactive decay and the surface scouring."

"But to have it signed with my name," said Keith. "Surely that's a mistake?"

"Perhaps somehow your name has come to be associated with *Starplex*," said Hek. "You are its first director, after all, and, frankly, we Waldahudin always thought you took too much of the credit. Maybe that was not a signature. Maybe it was the address, or the salutation, or—"

"No," said Rissa, eyes growing wide. Her voice was shaking with excitement. "No—it's from you."

"But . . . but that's crazy," Keith said. "There's no way I'm going to be alive ten billion years from now."

"Unless it's a relativistic effect," said Hek, "or perhaps suspended animation."

"Or . . ." said Rissa, her voice still shaking.

Keith looked at her. "Yes?"

She started jogging out of the bay.

"Where are you going?" barked Hek.

"To find Boxcar," she shouted. "I want to tell her that our life-prolongation experiments are going to succeed beyond our wildest dreams."

# ZETA DRACONIS

Glass rose from the clover-covered ground. "Perhaps you need some time to rest," he said. "I'll be back in a little while."

"Wait," said Keith. "I want to know who you are. Who you really are."

Glass said nothing, his head inclined to one side.

Keith got to his feet as well. "I've got a right to know. I've answered every one of your questions. Now, please, answer this one of mine."

"Very well, Keith." Glass spread his arms. "I'm you—Gilbert Keith Lansing—but you of the future. You don't know how long I'd been racking my brain trying to remember what the bloody G stood for."

Keith's jaw had dropped. "That—that can't be right. You can't be me."

"Oh, yes I am," said Glass. "Of course, I'm a little bit older." He touched the side of his smooth, transparent head, *then made the wind-chime laughter sound. "See? I've lost all my hair."*

Keith narrowed his eyes. *"How far in the future are you from?"*

*"Well,"* said Glass, gently, *"actually, you've got it backward. We are in* my *present. The appropriate question is, how far from the past are you from?"*

Keith felt himself losing his balance. *"You mean—you mean this isn't 2094?"*

*"Twenty-ninety-four what?"*

*"The Earth year 2094—2094 A.D. Two thousand and ninety-four years after the birth of Christ."*

*"Who? Oh, wait—my reckoner just reminded me. Let me work it out; I know the current year in absolute counting from the creation of the universe, but . . . ah, okay. In your system, this is the year ten billion, six hundred and forty-six million, three hundred and ninety-seven thousand, two hundred and eighty-one."*

Keith staggered back a half pace. *"You sent back our time capsule."*

*"That's right."*

*"How—how did I get here?"*

*"When your pod passed through the shortcut, I locked you into stasis. Time passed in the universe, but not for you. When it got to be this year, I unlocked you. Don't worry, though. I intend to put you back where you came from."* A pause. *"Remember that pink nebula you saw as you came out of the gate? That's what's left of what used to be Sol."*

Keith's eyes went wide.

*"Don't be concerned,"* said Glass. *"No one was injured when Sol went nova. It was all carefully engineered. See, that type of star doesn't naturally go nova; it just decays to a white dwarf. But we like to recycle. We blew it up so that its metals would enrich the interstellar medium."*

Keith felt dizzy. *"And how—how are you going to return me to my time?"*

*"Through the shortcut, of course. Time travel to the past works well; we just can't do it to the future—that's why we had to let you come forward in stasis through ten billion*

*years. Ironically, it turns out that it's forward time travel, not backward travel, that results in unsolvable paradoxes, making it impossible. We'll send you back to the moment you left. You don't have to worry about your friends missing you; no matter how many hours you generously stay with us, we'll get you to Tau Ceti at the time you're expected."*

*"This is incredible."*

*Glass shrugged. "It's science."*

*"It's magic," said Keith.*

*Glass shrugged again. "Same thing."*

*"But—but—if you're really me, if you're really from Earth, then why did you screw up on the simulation?"*

*"Pardon?"*

*"The Earth simulation. It has errors in it. Fields full of four-leaf clover, something only ever found as the occasional mutant, and birds that I've never seen before."*

*"Oh." The wind-chime sound. "My mistake. I took the simulation from some ancient recordings we had, but I was probably a bit sloppy. Let me just check with my reckoner . . . yup, my fault. It is a perfect simulation of Earth, but of Earth about one-point-two million years after you were born. The things that were out of place were species that hadn't yet evolved in your time. Come to think of it, you wouldn't have recognized the constellations, either, if I'd ever let it become nighttime."*

*"My God," said Keith. "I hadn't even begun to think about evolution. If you're ten billion years older than me, then—then you're older than any form of life on Earth in my time."*

*Glass nodded. "By your time, life had been evolving on Earth for four billion years. But there are Earth-descended life-forms in this time that are products of fourteen billion years of evolution. You'll never believe what daisies evolved into—or sea anemones, or the bacteria that caused whooping cough. In fact, I had lunch a few days ago with someone who evolved from whooping-cough bacteria."*

*"You're kidding."*

*"No, I'm not."*

*"But it's incredible . . ."*

*"No. It's just time. Lots and lots of time."*

*"What about humans? Did humans continue to breed, to have children? Or did that stop when—when life prolongation was discovered?"*

*"No, humanity continues to evolve and change. New humans—those who've been evolving for the last ten billion years—don't mix much with old humans like me. They're . . . quite different."*

*"But if you're me, how did you change? I mean, your body is see-through."*

Gluss shrugged. *"Technology. Flesh and blood tends to wear out; this is better. In fact, I can reconfigure myself any way I want. Transparent is in style right now, but I think the hint of aquamarine is quite classy, don't you?"*

# XVI

Rissa, Hek, and the rest of the alien-communications team continued to exchange messages with the darmat they'd dubbed Cat's Eye. The conversation became increasingly fluid as new words were added to the translation database, or old words had their meanings refined. When Keith next came onto the bridge, Rissa was in the middle of an apparently philosophic conversation with the giant being. The usual alpha-shift crew was on duty, except that the ExOps station was vacant: Rhombus was off doing something else, and his position had been slaved to a dolphin floating in the open pool on the starboard side of the bridge.

"We have been unaware of your existence," Rissa said into the microphone stalk rising from her console. "We knew a large amount of invisible matter was out there, because of the gravitational effects, but we didn't know it was alive."

"Two types of substance," replied the darmat in that French accent PHANTOM had assigned to him.

"Yes," said Rissa. She looked up and waved a greeting at Keith as he took his seat next to her.

"Not react sharply," said the Cat's Eye. "Only gravity the same."

"That's correct," said Rissa. The all-encompassing hologram showed an enhanced view of Cat's Eye in front of the cluster of workstations.

"Most like us," said the darmat.

"The vast majority of all matter is like you, yes," replied Rissa.

"Ignore you."

"You've ignored us?"

"Insignificant."

"Were you aware that part of our type of substance was alive?"

"No. Not occur to look for life *on* planets. So small you are."

"We wish to have a relationship with you," said Rissa.

"Relationship?"

"For mutual benefit. One plus one equals two. You plus us equals more than two."

"Understand. More than the sum of the parts."

Rissa smiled. "Exactly."

"Relationship sensible."

"Do you have a word for those with whom you have mutually beneficial relationships?"

"Friends," said the darmat, PHANTOM translating the word the first time it had been received. "We call them friends."

"We are friends," said Rissa.

"Yes."

"The kind of material you're made out of—the material we call dark matter—is all of it alive?"

"No. Only tiny fraction."

"But you say there has been living dark matter for a very long time?"

"Since the beginning."

"Beginning of what?"

"Of—all the stars combined."

"Of the totality of everything? We call that the universe."

"Since the beginning of the universe."

"That's an interesting point right there," said Jag, sitting on Keith's left. "The idea that the universe had a beginning—it did, of course, but how does it know that? Ask it about that."

"What was the universe like in the beginning?" said Rissa into the mike.

"Compressed," said the darmat. "Small beyond small. One place, no time."

"The primordial atom," said Jag. "Fascinating. It's right, but I wonder how such a creature would deduce that?"

"They communicate by radio," said Lianne, turning around at InOps to face Jag. "They probably reasoned it out the same way we did: from the cosmic microwave background and the redshifting of radio noise from distant galaxies."

Jag grunted.

Rissa continued her dialogue: "You have told us that neither you personally, Cat's Eye, nor this group of darmats is anywhere near that old. How do you know that darmat life existed all the way back to the beginning."

"Had to," replied the darmat.

Jag barked dismissively. "Philosophy," he said. "Not science. They just want to believe that."

"We have not existed nearly that long," said Rissa into the microphone stalk. "We have not found any evidence for life of any type made out of our kind of matter that is more than four billion years old." PHANTOM converted the time expression into something the darmat could understand.

"As said earlier, you are insignificant."

Jag barked at PHANTOM. "Query: How was the translation for 'insignificant' derived?"

"Mathematically," said the computer in the appropriate language into each individual's earpiece. "We established that the difference between 3.7 and 4.0 was 'significant,' but that the difference between 3.99 and 4.00 was 'insignificant.'"

Jag looked at Rissa. "So in this context the word might convey a different sense. It might mean something metaphorical—a 'late arrival' could be equated with insignificance, for instance."

Thor looked over his shoulder at the Waldahud and grinned. "Don't like the idea of being dismissed out of hand, eh?"

"Don't be abrasive, human. It's simply that we have to be careful when generalizing the use of alien words. And besides, perhaps he's referring to the signaling probe. At less than five meters in length, it could indeed be termed insignificant."

Rissa nodded and spoke into the mike. "When you say we are insignificant, are you referring to our size?"

"Not size of speaking part. Not size of part that ejected speaking part."

"So much for outsmarting him," said Thor, grinning. "He knows that the signaling probe came from this ship."

Rissa covered the mike with her hand; the gesture was as good a signal as any to PHANTOM to temporarily halt transmission. "It doesn't matter, I guess." She removed her hand and spoke again to Cat's Eye. "Are we insignificant because we haven't been around as long as you have?"

"Not a question of time length; a question of time absolute. We here from beginning; you not. By definition, we significant, you not. Obviously so."

"I don't know about that," said Keith, good-naturedly. "The good guys are never first, only better."

Rissa covered the mike and looked at him. "Regardless, I think we should steer clear of philosophy until we're more comfortable with each other. I don't want to accidentally give offense and cause him to clam up."

Keith nodded.

Rissa spoke into the mike again. "Presumably there are other communities of darmats."

"Billions of communities."

"Do you interact with them?"

"Yes."

"Your radio signals are not powerful, and are close to the frequency of the microwave background radiation. They would not be perceptible over a great distance."

"True."

"Then how do you interact with other darmat communities?"

"Radio-one only for local talk. Radio-two for communication between communities."

Lianne turned to Rissa. "Is he saying what I think he's saying? That the darmats are natural transmitters of hyperspace radio?"

"Let's find out," said Rissa. She faced the mike again. "Radio-one travels at the same speed as light, correct?"

"Yes."

"Radio-two travels faster than light, correct?"

"Yes."

"Jesus," said Keith. "If they use hyperspace radio, how come we've never encountered their signals before?"

"There are an infinite number of quantized hyperspace levels," said Lianne. "None of the Commonwealth races has had hyperspace radio for more than fifty years, and the whole Commonwealth uses only about eight thousand quantized levels; it's quite possible that we've never happened to key into one of the ones the darmats use." She turned her gaze to Rissa. "The way we do hyperspace radio requires an enormous amount of energy. It would be well worth pursuing this topic. They may have a method of doing it that takes a lot less power."

Rissa nodded. "We use a kind of radio-two, as well. Will you tell us more about how yours works?"

"Tell all," replied Cat's Eye. "But little to tell. We think one way, thought is private. We think another way, thought is transmitted on radio-one. We think a third, harder way, and thought is transmitted on radio-two."

Keith laughed. "It's like asking a human to explain how speech works. We just do it, that's all. It's—"

"Forgive me for interrupting, Dr. Lansing," said PHAN-

TOM, "but you asked me to remind you and Dr. Cervantes of your 14:00 appointment."

Keith's face fell.

"Damn," he said. "Damn." He turned to Rissa. "It's time."

She nodded. "PHANTOM, please get Hek down here to continue the dialogue with Cat's Eye."

As soon as Hek had arrived, they both rose from their chairs and left the room.

Keith and Rissa exited from the elevator and walked the short distance to the oversized black door with the giant fluorescent orange "20" painted on it. The locking bolts pulled aside. The noise they made had always been faintly familiar to Keith, but this time he finally placed it: it was just like the sound of a rifle being cocked in an old-time western movie.

Most doors aboard ship split down the middle with the two panels moving into pockets on either side, but this heavy one slid as one piece to the left—safety demanded there be no seams or weak points in the seal.

Rissa gasped. Keith felt his jaw go slack.

There were well over a hundred Ibs in the docking bay, lined up in neat rows—like a parking lot filled with wheelchairs. "PHANTOM, how many are there?" Keith said softly.

"Two hundred and nine, sir," replied the computer. "The entire ship's complement of Integrated Bioentities."

Rissa shook her head slightly. "She said only her closest friends would attend."

"Well," said Keith, stepping into the room, "Boxcar is very personable. I guess all the Ibs aboard consider her a close friend."

There were six other humans present, all members of Rissa's life-sciences staff. There was also one lone Waldahud, whom Keith couldn't quite place. Keith glanced at his watch: 13:59:47. No doubt whatever was going to happen would begin on time.

"Thank you all for coming," said Boxcar's voice, over

Keith's implant. It was easy to spot her: hers was the only web flashing. It was eerie, in a way. PHANTOM's translation was piped into his left acoustic nerve; the other ear heard nothing—even a room this size full of raucous Ibs would be dead silent.

Boxcar was fifteen meters from where Keith and Rissa were standing. In front of the plated space door, PHANTOM was projecting a giant hologram of Boxcar, so that all the Ibs could see her flashing web. Something strange, there: The strands of her web were bright green. Keith had never seen any Ib's web that color before.

He turned to Rissa, but she must have guessed his question. "It represents a deeply emotional state," she said. "Boxcar is choked up over the show of support from her people."

Boxcar's web flashed again. The translation said, "The whole and the parts—of one, and of them all. The gestalt has resonances on the macro scale and the micro. It binds."

Obviously, Boxcar was addressing her fellow Ibs. Keith thought he got the gist of what she was saying—something about being part of the Ib community having meant as much to her as being a community of parts herself. Keith prided himself on his acceptance of aliens, his run-ins with Jag notwithstanding. But this was all a little too surreal for him; he knew he was about to watch someone die, but the emotions he should be feeling hadn't yet come to the surface. Rissa, on the other hand, had that look she got when trying not to cry. She and Boxcar had been closer than he'd known, Keith realized.

"The road is clear," concluded Boxcar. She rolled several dozen meters away from the others, out into the center of the bay.

"Why's she doing that?" whispered Keith.

Rissa shrugged her shoulders, but PHANTOM replied into both of their implants: "During discorporation, components—especially wheels—may panic, and seek to bond with any other Ib in the area. It is customary to move far enough away so that if such a thing is attempted, there's plenty of time to react."

Keith nodded slightly.

And then it began. In the middle of the bay was a standard Ib comfort mound. Boxcar rolled over it so that the hump supported her frame from underneath. Her web—visible in PHANTOM's giant hologram—turned an almost electric purple, another color Keith had never seen before. The light points at the web's countless intersections grew brighter and brighter, a dense constellation map with every star a nova. Then, one by one, the lights winked out. It took perhaps two minutes for them all to go dark.

Boxcar's frame tipped forward, and her web slid off to the bay floor, landing in a loose pile. Keith had thought the web was already dead, but it arched up sharply, as if a fist were pushing it up from underneath. The strands had now lost all their color; they looked like thick nylon fishing line.

After a moment, though, the web finally did expire, collapsing into a heap. Boxcar was now blind and deaf (she had once had a magnetic sense, too, but that had been neutralized through nanosurgery when she'd left her home-world; it caused severe disorientation aboard spaceships).

Next, Boxcar's wheels disengaged from the axles on the frame. Wheel disengaging wasn't unusual in and of itself. The system that allowed nutrients to pass from the axle into each wheel didn't provide enough food for the wheels, and in their native environment they would periodically separate from the rest of the gestalt for feeding. Thick tendrils, similar to the Ib's bundle of manipulatory ropes, popped out of the sides of the wheels, preventing them from falling over (or righting them if they did).

Almost immediately after it separated, the left wheel tried to rejoin the frame. Just as PHANTOM said it might, it panicked when it realized that little bumps had risen up all around the axle's circumference, preventing it from recon-necting. It rolled around the bay, the grabbing projections around its rim extending and retracting at a great rate. The wheel had a few vision sensors of its own, and as soon as it caught sight of the huge collection of Ibs, it made a beeline for the closest. That Ib spun away, avoiding the wheel. One of the others—Butterfly, Keith assumed, the one Ib doctor on board—surged forward, a manipulatory rope extended, a silver-and-black medical stunner held at its tip. The stunner touched the wheel, and it stopped moving. It stood for several seconds, then the rootlike appendages coming out of its sides seemed to go soft, and the wheel toppled onto its side.

Keith turned his attention back to the center of the bay. Boxcar's bundle of ropes had slid to the floor, near the discarded sensor web. They were reaching up to the frame and disengaging the blue pump from the central green pod, and gently lifting the pump to the floor. Keith could see the pump's large central breathing orifice cycling through its usual four-step sequence of open, stretch, compress, and close. After about forty seconds, though, the sequence started to get distorted as the pump seemed to lose track of what it was doing. The orifice movements became jumbled—opening, then immediately compressing; trying to stretch wide after closing. There was a small gasping sound—the only sound in the entire bay. Finally the pump stopped moving.

All that was left was the pod, sitting on the saddle-shaped frame.

Keith whispered to Rissa: "How long can the pod survive without the pump?"

Rissa turned to him, her eyes wet. She blinked several times, dislodging tears. "A minute," she said at last. "Perhaps two."

Keith reached over and squeezed her hand.

Everything was still for about three minutes. The pod expired quietly, without movement or sound—although somehow, apparently, the Ibs knew when it was gone, and, as one, they began to roll out of the bay. All their webs were dark; not a word was passing between them. Keith and Rissa were the last to leave. Butterfly would return shortly, Keith knew, to take care of jettisoning Boxcar's remains into space.

As they walked out of the bay, Keith thought about his own future. He was going to live a long, long time, apparently. He wondered whether billions of years from now he'd be able to escape the mistakes of his own past.

They couldn't sleep that night, of course. Boxcar's death had upset Rissa, and Keith was wrestling with his own demons. They lay side by side in their bed, wide-awake, Rissa staring at the dark ceiling, Keith looking at the faint red spot on the wall made by the light seeping around the plasticard he used to cover his clock face.

Rissa spoke—just one word. "If . . ."

Keith rolled onto his back. "Pardon?"

She was quiet for a time. Keith was about to prod her again, when she said, very softly, "If you don't remember how to make a *u* or an apostrophe, will you remember me—remember us?" She rolled over, looked at him. "You're going to live another ten billion years. I can't begin to comprehend that."

"It's . . . mind-numbing," said Keith, shaking his head against the pillow. He, too, was quiet for a time. Then: "People always fantasize about living forever. Somehow, 'forever' seems less daunting than putting a specific date on it. I could deal with immortality, but contemplating the specific notion of being alive ten billion years from now . . . I just can't make sense of it."

"Ten billion years," said Rissa again, shaking her head. "Earth's sun will long be dead, Earth will be dead." A beat. "I will be dead."

"Maybe. Maybe not. If it *is* life prolongation, then surely it's because of your studies here on *Starplex*. After all, why else would I have ended up as one of the recipients of the process? Maybe we're both alive ten billion years from now."

More silence.

"And together?" said Rissa, at last.

Keith exhaled noisily. "I don't know. I can't imagine any of it." He sensed he was saying the wrong thing. "But . . . but if I'm to face that much of a future, I would want it to be with you."

"Would you?" said Rissa, at once. "Would we have

anything left to explore, to learn about each other, after all that time?"

"Maybe . . . maybe it's not corporeal existence," said Keith. "Maybe my consciousness is transferred into a machine. Wasn't there a cult on New New York that wanted to do that—copy human brains into computers? Or maybe . . . maybe all of humanity becomes one giant mind, but the individual psyches can still be tapped. That would be—"

"Would be less frightening that the concept of personally living another ten billion years. In case you haven't done the math yet, that would mean that so far, you've only lived one two-hundred-millionth of the age you're going to become." She paused and sighed.

"What?" asked Keith.

"Nothing."

"No, you're upset about something."

Rissa was quiet for about ten seconds. "Well, it's just that your current midlife crisis has been hard enough to live with. I'd hate to see what kind of stunts you're going to pull when you turn five billion."

Keith didn't know what to say. Finally, he settled on a laugh. It sounded hollow to him, forced.

Quiet again—long enough that he thought perhaps she'd at last fallen asleep. But he couldn't sleep himself. Not yet, not with these thoughts going through his head.

"Dulcinea?" he whispered softly—so softly that if she were already asleep he hopefully wouldn't wake her.

"Hmm?"

Keith swallowed. Maybe he should leave the issue alone, but . . . "Our anniversary is coming up."

"Next week," said the voice in the darkness.

"Yes," said Keith. "It'll be twenty years, and—"

"Twenty *wonderful* years, honey. You're always supposed to include the adjective."

Another forced laugh. "Sorry, you're right. Twenty wonderful years." He paused. "I know that we're planning to renew our wedding vows that day."

A small edge to Rissa's voice. "Yes?"

"Nothing. No, forget I said anything. It *has* been a wonderful twenty years, hasn't it?"

Keith could just make out her face in the darkness. She nodded, then looked at him, meeting his eyes, trying to see beyond them, see the truth, see what was bothering him. And then it came to her, and she rolled onto her side, facing away from him. "It's okay," she said at last.

"What is?"

And she spoke the final words that passed between them that night. "It's okay," she said, "if you don't want to say, 'for as long as we both shall live.'"

Keith sat at his workstation on the bridge. Holograms of three humans and a dolphin hovered above the station's rim. In his peripheral vision, he was aware of one of the bridge doors opening and Jag waddling in. The Waldahud didn't go to his own workstation, though. Instead he stood in front of Keith's and waited, in what seemed a state of some agitation, while Keith finished the conference he was conducting with the holographic heads. When they'd logged off, Keith looked up at Jag.

"As you know, the darmats have been moving," said Jag. "I'm frankly surprised at their agility. They seem to work together, each sphere playing off its own gravitational and repulsive forces against the others to move the whole community cooperatively. Anyway, in doing so, they've completely reconfigured themselves, so that individual darmats that we couldn't clearly observe before are now at the periphery of the assemblage. I've made some predictions about which darmat might next reproduce, and I'd like to test my theory. For that, I want you to move *Starplex* to the far side of the dark-matter field."

"PHANTOM, schematic local space," said Keith.

A holographic representation appeared in midair between Keith and Jag. The darmats had moved around to the opposite side of the green star, so that *Starplex,* the shortcut, the star, and the darmat community were pretty much arranged in a straight line.

"If we move to the far side of the darmat field, we'll be

out of view of the shortcut," said Keith. "We might miss seeing a watson come through. Can't you just put a probe there?"

"My prediction is based on very minute mass concentrations. I need to use either our deck-one or deck-seventy hyperscope to make my observations."

Keith considered. "All right." He tapped a key on his console and the usual holograms of Thor and Rhombus popped into being. "Rhombus, please check with everyone who is currently doing external scanning. Find out when the soonest we can move the ship without interrupting their work will be. Thor, at that time take us to the opposite side of the dark-matter field, positioning us at coordinates Jag will supply you with."

"Serving is the greatest pleasure," said Rhombus.

"Bob's your uncle," said Thor.

Jag moved his head up and down, imitating the human gesture. Waldahudin never said thank you, but Keith thought the pig looked inordinately pleased.

# XVII

The bridge was calm, the six workstations floating serenely against the holographic night. It was 0500 ship's time; delta shift was in the final hour of its watch.

In the director's position was an Ib named Wineglass; other Ibs were at the Internal-Ops and Helm stations. Physical sciences was slaved to a dolphin named Melondent, a Waldahud was at life sciences, and a human named Denna Van Hausen was at External Ops.

A grid of force screens radiated down from the invisible ceiling, creating millimeter-wide vacuum gaps between each workstation, preventing transmission of noise between them. The Ib at Internal Ops was engaged in a holographic conference with three miniature floating Ibs and three disembodied Waldahud heads. The human at External was reading a novel on one of her monitor screens.

Suddenly, the silencing forcefields snapped off and an alarm began to sound. "Unidentified ship approaching," announced PHANTOM.

"There!" said Van Hausen, pointing to the image of the nearby star. "It's just passing from behind the photosphere." PHANTOM was showing the unknown ship as a small red triangle; the actual vessel was far too small to be visible at this distance.

"Any chance that it's just a watson?" asked Wineglass, his British accent carrying a hint of Cockney.

"None," said Van Hausen. "It's at least as big as one of our probeships."

Lights moved across Wineglass's web. "Let's get a look at it," he said. The Ib at the helm station rotated the ship slightly so that the deck-seventy optical array was aimed at the intruder. A square frame appeared around part of the star, and within it a magnified view appeared. The approaching ship was illuminated on one side by the green star. The other side was a black silhouette, visible only because it eclipsed the background stars.

Wineglass spoke to Kreet, the Waldahud on his right. "That looks like a Waldahud design. The central engine pod, no?"

Waldahudin believed each ship—or building or vehicle—should be unique; they did not mass-produce from the same design. Kreet lifted all four of his shoulders. "Maybe," he said.

"Any transponder signal, Denna?" asked Wineglass.

"If there is one," the human said, "it's lost in the noise from the star."

"Please try to contact the ship."

"Transmitting," said Denna. "But they're still over fifty million klicks away; it'll take almost six minutes for any reply, and—God!"

A second ship was coming around the limb of the green star. It was similar in size to the first, but had a different, more blocky design. Still, the trademark Waldahud central engine pod was visible.

"Better get Keith down here," said Wineglass.

Lights rippled across the Ib at InOps. "Director Lansing to the bridge!"

"Try to contact the second ship, too," Wineglass said.

"Doing so," said Van Hausen. "And—Jesus, I'll try to contact that third one, as well." Another ship, half emerald fire glinting off polished metal, half black nothingness, was emerging from behind the star. A moment later a fourth and then a fifth appeared.

"It's a bloody armada," said Van Hausen.

"They Waldahud ships clearly are," said Melondent from his open pool to the left of the physics workstation. "Thruster exhaust signatures most characteristic."

"But what would five—six, *eight*—eight Waldahud craft want here?" asked Wineglass. "Denna, where are they heading?"

"They're doing parabolic paths around the star," the human woman said. "Hard to say exactly where they're planning to end up, but *Starplex*'s current position is within eight degrees of the most likely projected course."

"They after us are coming," said Melondent. "We should—"

A door appeared in the hologram. Keith Lansing strode onto the bridge, unshaven, hair matted down from sleep.

"Sorry to wake you early," said Wineglass, rolling away from the director's workstation, "but we have company."

Keith nodded at the Ib, and waited for a polychair to emerge from the trapdoor in front of his console. It was already morphing into human configuration as it rose up from the floor. Keith seated himself. "You've tried contacting them?"

"Yes," said Denna. "Earliest possible response is in forty-eight seconds, though."

"They're Waldahud ships, aren't they?" said Keith, his workstation rising to the height he preferred.

"Very likely so," said Wineglass, "although, of course, Waldahud ships are sold all over the Commonwealth. They could be crewed by somebody else."

Keith rubbed sleep from his eyes. "How did so many ships arrive without our knowing it?"

"They must have emerged one at a time from the shortcut while it was shielded from our view by the green star," Wineglass said.

"Christ, of course," said Keith. He consulted the readout of who was operating which station. "Double-Dot, get Jag down here."

The Ib at Internal Ops slapped his control panel with ropes, then, a moment later, said, "Jag has his communications routed to a voice mailbox. It's his normal sleep period."

"Override," said Keith. "Get him down here right now. Denna, any reply to our messages?"

"Nothing."

Keith glanced up at the glowing digital clocks floating against the starfield. "It's almost shift change anyway," he said. "Let's get the full alpha-shift staff down here."

"Alpha shift, report immediately to the bridge," said Double-Dot. "Lianne Karendaughter, Thorald Magnor, Rhombus, Jag, and Clarissa Cervantes to the bridge, please."

"Thank you," said Keith. "Denna, open a channel to all the approaching ships."

"Open."

"This is G. K. Lansing, Director of the Commonwealth research vessel *Starplex*. State your business, please."

"Transmitting," said Denna. "They've closed the distance between us and them considerably. If they care to respond to your latest message, we should have an answer in under three minutes."

A door opened up in the part of the hologram displaying the framed close-up of the approaching craft. Jag walked through, his fur not yet brushed. "What's wrong?" he said.

"Maybe nothing," said Keith "but eight Waldahud ships are approaching *Starplex*. Do you know why?"

All four shoulders moved up and down. "I have no idea."

"They are refusing to respond to hails, and—"

"I said I have no idea." Jag turned around and faced the hologram where the door had been. All his eyes began tracking independently, each one watching a different approaching ship.

"What kind of ships are those?" asked Keith. "Scouts?"

"They are the right size for that," said Jag.

"How many crew members aboard each?"

"Starships are not my field," said Jag.

Keith looked at the Waldahud at life sciences. "You, there—Kreet, is it? How many people aboard such a ship?"

"Perhaps six," said Kreet. "No more than that."

Two of the four bridge doors opened simultaneously. Thorald Magnor walked in through one, and Rissa Cervantes came in through the other. The Ib and the Waldahud vacated the helm and life-sciences stations to make room for them.

"Eight ships are approaching *Starplex*," said Keith, to Rissa and Thor.

Rissa nodded. "PHANTOM briefed us en route. But no additional ships should have come through the shortcut until we gave the okay." She stood by her console, waiting for the chair to configure itself.

"Maybe they're here by accident," said Thor, tapping some keys on his console while his chair rose from beneath the deck. "When a new shortcut comes on-line, the acceptable approach angles to select a desired destination grow narrower. They could have been sloppy in their calculations. Maybe they meant to go somewhere else."

"One pilot might make a mistake," said Keith. "But eight?"

"The communications-lag time is up," said Denna. "If they'd wanted to reply to your latest message, they could have done so by now." Rhombus had entered a moment earlier, but was content to wheel up to a position next to the ExOps workstation without getting Denna to vacate.

"Thor, if I give the order to get out of here," asked Keith, "can we escape those ships?"

Thor shrugged. "I doubt it. They're blocking the shortcut, so we can't go that way. And see those medial rings around their engine pods? Those are associated with Waldahud *Gatob*-class hyperdrives. Of course, no one can use a hyperdrive this close to the green star, but if we tried to get away, eventually we would be out in space that was flat enough for hyperdrives to be engaged, and then they'd be on us in a second."

Keith frowned.

"The ships are fanning out," said Thor. "I'd call it an attack formation."

"*Attack?*" said Rhombus, lights strobing incredulously.

"Incoming message," said Denna.

Another part of the sky hologram was blocked off by a glowing border. Inside it a Waldahud face appeared, framed by brown fur streaked with copper. "Lansing commanding *Starplex*," said the translated voice, "I am Gawst. Mark that name well: Gawst." Keith nodded; to a Waldahud male, credit was everything. "We have come to escort *Starplex* back through the shortcut. You will surrender—"

"How long for a reply to reach them?" asked Keith.

"—your ship to us."

Denna consulted a readout. "Forty-three seconds."

"Cooperate," continued Gawst, "and no harm will come to your vessel or crew."

"Thor, can we dive toward the shortcut apparently on one trajectory, but at the last moment change direction so that we'll exit somewhere other than where they'd expect?"

The helm officer shook his head. "Those little scouts might pull it off, but *Starplex*'s volume is three million cubic meters. I can't make it tap-dance."

"How long until those ships reach us?"

"They're moving at point-one-*c*," said Thor. "They'll be on us in less than twenty minutes."

"Lansing to Gawst: *Starplex* is Commonwealth property. Request denied. Off. Rhombus, let me know when they've received that message." Lianne Karendaughter strode onto the bridge. "I want some options, folks," said Keith.

"Option number one," said Lianne, taking her seat. "Retreat. The farther we are from the shortcut, the less likely they will be able to coerce us through it."

"Right. Thor, let's—"

"Forgive the interruption, Keith," said Rhombus. "Your message has been received."

"Good. Thor, let's get out of here. Full thruster power."

"I'll take us away at an angle," said Thor. "We don't want to move into the dark-matter field. It's an obstacle course, and small ships will be better able to handle it than we will."

"Fine," said Keith. "Rhombus, see if you can get a watson with today's mission logs through to Tau Ceti. I want to alert Premier Kenyatta."

"Doing so. But it will take over an hour to reach the shortcut from here, and—excuse me: incoming message from Gawst."

"Lansing," said Gawst, "*Starplex* was built at the Rehbollo shipyards and is of Rehbollo registry, and therefore is Waldahud property. Let us avoid as much unpleasantness as possible. Once the ship is returned to Rehbollo, we will release all crew members for immediate repatriation to their home systems."

"Reply," snapped Lansing. "*Starplex*'s construction was funded by all the Commonwealth worlds, and its registration is just a formality; all ships require a homeworld of record. Your claim is rejected. If necessary, this ship will defend itself against unlawful seizure. Off."

"Defend itself?" said Thor, shaking his head. "Keith, this ship has no armament."

"I'm well aware of that," snapped Keith. "Lianne, give me a full inventory of all shipboard equipment that can be used as weapons. If anything aboard can discharge an energy beam, or throw an object, or can be made to blow up, I want to know about it."

"Working on it," said Lianne, hands dancing over her console.

"*Starplex* wasn't designed for fancy flying," said Thor, speaking to a Keith hologram above the rim of his console. "We'll wallow like a hippopotamus in heat compared to small fighters."

"Then we'll fight them on their terms," said Keith. "We'll defend *Starplex* with our probeships." He glanced at the list Lianne was feeding through to his number-three monitor: geological digging lasers, mining explosives, mass drivers used for launching probes. "Lianne, coordinate with Rhombus on getting as much of that equipment as possible loaded into our five fastest probeships. I want everything aboard in fifteen minutes; I don't care what you have to rip apart to accomplish that."

Denna Van Hausen finally moved away from the ExOps console and Rhombus rolled into place. Manipulator ropes darted across the controls, and Rhombus's sensor web flowed half onto the panel to better interface with the equipment.

"Even with a slapped-together armament," said Thor, "our probeships aren't going to be able to outgun real fighting craft."

"I'm not planning to outgun them," said Keith. "*Starplex* may be of Waldahud construction, but our probeships aren't."

"Granted they may be reluctant to fire on Ibese craft," said Thor, "but—"

"That's not what I'm thinking," said Keith. "Unlike the approaching craft, our probeships weren't designed by Waldahud engineers."

"Ah—and we have dolphins to pilot them!" crowed Thor.

"Precisely," said Keith. "PHANTOM, intercom with direct holo links: Longbottle, Thinfin, Nickedfluke, Squint, Sidestripe, respond."

Drawn-out dolphin heads began to pop into existence above Keith's console.

"Here."

"What happening is?"

"Thinfin, acknowledging."

"Yes, Keith?"

"Hello."

"We are about to be attacked by Waldahud craft," said Keith. "Our probeships are more maneuverable—if dolphins pilot them. It will be dangerous, but so will staying here and doing nothing. Are you willing to—"

"Ship is home ocean now—we protect!"

"If necessary, help will I."

"Ready to assist."

"Okay."

"I—yes, will do it."

"Excellent," said Keith. "Proceed to launch bays. Rhombus will give you your ship assignments."

Thor looked at his Keith hologram. "There's no doubt that our ships are more responsive—but dolphins have no experience with weapons. They should each have someone else on board to act as gunner."

Rhombus's web flashed. "Sentients will die if weapons are used."

"We can't stand by and not defend ourselves," declared Thor.

"To surrender our ship is better," said Rhombus.

"No," said Keith. "I refuse to do that."

"But to kill—"

"No one need be killed," said Keith. "We can shoot for the engine units, try to disable the Waldahud ships without breaching their habitats. As for gunners—we're all just scientists and diplomats." He considered for a moment. "PHANTOM, consult personnel records. Who would make the five most proficient gunners?"

"Calculating. Done: Wong, Wai-Jeng. Smith-Tate, Helena. Leed Jelisko em-Layth. Cervantes, Clarissa. Dask Honibo em-Kalch."

"Rissa . . . ?" said Keith under his breath.

"If the object is to fire geological lasers," said Thor, "then why not use Snowflake? She's senior geologist."

"We Ibs have lousy aim," replied Rhombus. "Targeting works better when you have a single point of view."

"PHANTOM," said Keith, "find replacements from other species for the two Waldahudin, and set up an immediate intercom between all of them and me."

"Done. Intercom open."

"This is Director Lansing. PHANTOM has determined that each of you has the training and skill to best operate makeshift weapon systems aboard our five dolphin-piloted probeships. I can't order you, but we need volunteers. Are you up for it?"

A second row of holographic heads appeared above the dolphin faces. "Good God, I—yes, I'll do it."

"Count me in."

"I'm not sure that I'm the right person, but . . . yes, okay."

"On my way."

Rissa had moved over to stand next to her husband. "I'll do what I can," she said.

Keith looked at her. "Rissa . . ."

"Don't worry, honey. I gotta make sure you get to live all those billions of years."

Keith touched her arm. "Rhombus, assign each of them to a ship. PHANTOM, convey them there as fast as possible."

"Doing so."

"Good work, everyone," said Keith, leaning forward in his chair, fingers steepled in front of his face.

"Jesus!" shouted Thor. A tiny explosion was blossoming in the display. "They've shot our watson out of the sky."

"Jag, analyze the weapon used," said Keith. "At least we can figure out what their armament is."

Jag glanced at a square monitor screen. "Standard Waldahud police lasers," he said. But then he rose from his station and gestured toward Melondent, who had been serving as physics officer during delta shift. Jag touched a few keys. "Transferring physical sciences to dolphin station one," he said. He turned to Keith. "Perhaps . . . perhaps it would be best if I did not further participate. Gawst did not invoke the name of Queen Trath, so I assume that he and his associates are acting without royal approval—an attempt to garner considerable glory. Still, they are Waldahudin. Perhaps I should return to my apartment."

"Not so bloody fast, Jag," Keith said, rising to his feet. He glanced at Lianne. "Time to launch?"

"Ten, maybe eleven minutes."

Keith turned back to Jag. "You had me move *Starplex* so that we wouldn't be able to see the Waldahud forces massing on the green star's far side."

"I deny that," said Jag, both sets of arms crossed behind his back.

"Your loyalties don't lie with the Waldahudin?"

"My loyalty is to Queen Trath, but there is no evidence that she authorized the attempt to seize this ship."

"Lianne, how many watsons did Jag receive in the last two days?"

"Checking. Three. Two were from CHAT—"

"Which is located just outside the Waldahud home system—" said Keith.

"And the third was a commercial unit from a telecommunications utility on Rehbollo."

"It contained personal news," said Jag, "related to an illness in my family."

"Examine those watsons, Lianne," said Keith. "I want to check the messages that they carried."

"Once I had downloaded the data that I wanted," said Jag, "I released the watsons for reuse—wiping the data first, of course."

"We should be able to recover something," Keith said. "Lianne?"

"Checking," she said, then a moment later: "Okay, the watsons that came for Jag are still on board. We carry over a hundred of them, and those three are still in the queue for reuse." She pressed some keys. "I've interfaced with all three; they're blank."

"Nothing at all to unerase?"

"No. The data area has been wiped, then filled with a random pattern. There's nothing left."

"I routinely use a level-seven wipe," said Jag.

"That's two levels above Earth military standards," said Keith.

"It leaves things more tidy," said Jag. "You have often remarked on my predilection for neatness."

"This is all crap," said Keith. "I don't believe that it was coincidence that you asked me to move the ship; the Waldahudin couldn't have attacked en masse if we'd been there to see them popping out of the shortcut one by one."

"I tell you, it *is* coincidence," said Jag.

Keith turned to face the InOps station. "Lianne, immediately delist all command authorities for Jag Kandaro em-Pelsh. And terminate all jobs he has running."

Bleeps as keys were touched. "Doing so," said Lianne.

"You do not have the authority to do this," said Jag.

"So sue me," said Keith. He looked at the Waldahud. "I was one of those who argued against basing any part of *Starplex* on human military structures, but if we had done so, at least we'd have a brig to throw you in." He faced a set of glowing camera eyes floating above the seating gallery behind the workstations. "PHANTOM, record new protocol. Name: 'house arrest.' Authorizing authority, Lansing, G. K. Parameters: Individuals under house arrest are denied access to all work areas; PHANTOM will not open doors for them to such areas. They are also forbidden to use external communication equipment and to give PHANTOM commands above level-four housekeeping. Understand?"

"Yes. Protocol established."

"Record the following: As of this moment—0752 hours—

and effective until terminated personally by me, Jag Kandaro em-Pelsh is under house arrest."

"Acknowledged."

Keith's voice was controlled. "Now you may leave the bridge."

Jag folded both sets of arms behind his back again. "I don't believe you have the right to bar me from this room."

"A moment ago, you wanted to leave," said Keith. "Of course, that was back when you had the authority to launch a shuttle, and escape to the armada."

Rhombus had left the External-Ops station and had rolled near to the director's console. Lights played over his sensor web, and the web's strands had turned yellow, the color of rage. "I support Keith," said the cool British voice. "You have undermined everything we have worked for. Leave the bridge voluntarily, Jag, or I will eject you."

"You can't do that. It is against the operating code to assault a fellow sentient."

Rhombus began rolling toward Jag, a living steamroller. "Just watch me," he said.

Jag stood defiant a moment longer. Rhombus closed more of the distance between them, his quartz-rimmed wheels glinting in the starlight of the all-encompassing hologram. The Ib's ropelike tentacles were lifted from their usual bundle, darting in the air like angry snakes. Jag finally turned on his heel. The starfield in front of him split open, and he marched out. The door closed.

Keith nodded thanks to Rhombus, then: "Thor, status of the Waldahud ships?"

Thorald Magnor looked over his shoulder at Keith. "Assuming they've got nothing better than standard police lasers, they will be within effective firing range in three minutes."

"How long until our own ships are ready for launch?"

Rhombus's lights blinked out a reply as he rolled back to his workstation. "Two are ready to go now; the other three—grant me another four minutes."

"I want to launch all five at once. Everything goes out the door in two hundred and forty seconds."

"Will do."

"We'll still be outnumbered, eight to five," said Thor.

Keith frowned. "I know that, but it's only our five fastest ships that are set up for dolphin pilots. Rhombus, as soon as our ships are clear of our docking bays, I want full power to our force screens. Cut the engines; divert everything to the screens."

"Will do."

"Lianne," said Keith, "I want to put a message for Tau Ceti in another watson. Shoot this one out a mass-driver tube. Send it on a transfer orbit that'll take it to the shortcut under momentum only; I want it to fly all the way there without using power."

"It'll take a watson three days to get to the shortcut that way," Lianne said.

"I'm aware of that. Calculate the trajectory. How long do I have until our ships launch?"

"Two-point-five minutes," said Rhombus.

Keith nodded, and touched the privacy button that erected four double force-screen walls around his workstation, creating a sound-killing vacuum gap.

"PHANTOM," he said, "search all computer records for research done by Gaf Kandaro em-Weel and his associates, especially for material that's never been translated from Waldahudar."

"Searching. Found."

"Display titles and abstracts in English."

Keith scanned the screen in front of him. "Download into a watson articles two, nineteen, and—let's see, better add twenty-one, as well. Encrypt everything under the password 'Kassabian': K-A-S-S-A-B-I-A-N. Record the following, and add it to the watson as an unencrypted message:

"Keith Lansing to Valentina Ilianov, Provost, New Beijing. Val, we're under attack by Waldahud ships, and I wouldn't be surprised if you're under attack soon, too. I have learned that there is a theoretical way to destroy a shortcut, by flattening spacetime around it, preventing it from anchoring in normal space. If a Waldahud invasion force seems likely to overwhelm your fleet, perhaps you will want to consider destroying your shortcut exit. Doing so will, of course, effectively isolate Sol/Epsilon Indi/Tau Ceti from the rest of the galaxy, and give the Waldahudin forces no way to retreat. Think long and hard before you do this, old friend. The procedure can be gleaned from the articles appended to this message. I've encrypted them. The key is the last name of that woman we both fancied on New New York all those years ago. End."

"Done," said PHANTOM.

Keith tapped a key. The privacy force screens vanished. "Launch the watson, Lianne," he said.

"Doing so."

Keith watched the tiny canister drift away from *Starplex*. His heart was pounding. If Val decided to use the technique, there was one other consequence that Keith hadn't spelled out: he and Rissa and the rest of those from Earth aboard *Starplex* would never see home again.

"Here we go," said Rhombus. "Five. Four. Three. Two. One. Launching *PDQ*. Three. Two. One. Launching *Rum Runner*. Three. Two. One. Launching *Marc Garneau*. Three. Two. One. Launching *Dakterth*. Three. Two. One. Launching *Long March*."

The fusion flares of ten twin engines lit up the holographic sky as the five probeships shot away from *Starplex*'s central disk. The approaching Waldahud ships were now close enough that they could be seen directly, rather than as colored triangles.

"Force screens to maximum," said Rhombus.

"Open windows in the force screens and send the following via scrambled comm laser direct to each of our ships," said Keith. "No one is to fire unless the Waldahudin shoot at us first. Maybe a show of strength will be enough to get them to back down."

"They already creamed one of our watsons," said Thor.

Keith nodded. "But if shots are going to be taken at sentient beings, the Waldahudin are going to have to start it."

"Incoming message," said Lianne.

"Let's see it."

Gawst's face appeared. "Last chance, Lansing. Surrender *Starplex*."

"No reply," said Keith. He glanced at one of his monitors.

*Starplex* was still oriented with its lower telescope array facing the green star, and toward the approaching fighters.

"Gawst's ship is coming toward us fast," said Thor. "The other seven are holding position about nine thousand klicks away."

"Steady, everyone," said Keith. "Steady."

"He's firing!" said Thor. "Direct hit on our force screens. No damage."

"How long can we keep deflecting his lasers?" asked Keith.

"Four, maybe five more shots," said Lianne.

"The other Waldahud ships are moving in, trying to surround us," said Thor.

"Do you want our probeships to engage them?" asked Rhombus. Keith said nothing. "Director, do you want our probeships to engage them?"

"I—I didn't think Gawst would really fire," said Keith.

"They're taking up equidistant geodesic positions around us," said Thor. "If all eight ships shoot at us simultaneously and at the same wavelength, it will overload our shields. There will be nowhere to shunt the energy."

Holograms of the dolphin pilots and their gunners were floating above Keith's console. "Let me take out the ship nearest us," said Rissa, flying with Longbottle aboard the *Rum Runner*.

Keith closed his eyes for a second. When he opened them, he had found his resolve. "Do it."

"Shooting for the engine pod," said Rissa.

PHANTOM drew a red line in the holo sphere to represent the invisible output of the geological laser, lancing from the bow of the *Rum Runner* to the Waldahud craft. The beam sliced along the length of the engine pod, and a plasma tongue shot away from the ship.

"Hey," said Rissa, with a triumphant smile. "Guess all that time playing darts was good for something after all."

"Gawst is firing on *Starplex* again," said Thor. "And one of the other ships is going after the *Rum Runner*."

"Get out of there, Longbottle," said Keith. The *Rum Runner* did an arcing maneuver, exactly like a dolphin doing a backflip. It completed the move with its laser firing in the direction of the incoming ship, which swerved to avoid contact with the beam.

"Gawst's ship has two lasers, one port and one starboard," said Thor. "He's firing them both at our lower radio telescope—man, he's good. He's letting our antenna's parabolic dish focus his beams onto the instrument cluster."

"Rock *Starplex*," said Keith. "Lose him."

The stars in holographic display danced left and right.

"He's still on us," said Thor. "I bet—yup, he's done it. Even with full shields, enough of his laser leaked through, and the dish antenna focused it. He's taken out the deck-seventy sensor array, and—"

*Starplex* shook. Keith was startled; he had *never* felt the ship shake before. "The seven remaining Waldahud craft are firing on us in sequence," said Thor.

"Keith to probeships: engage the Waldahudin. Get them to stop their attack on us."

"They'll overload our shields in sixteen seconds," said Lianne.

In the holo display, Keith could see the *PDQ* and the *Long March* firing on two of the Waldahud ships. The Waldahudin were trying to keep a single force screen to their attackers while continuing to fire on *Starplex*, but the probeships were maneuvering wildly, making it hard for the Waldahudin to keep the screen positioned. Glancing blows were making it through.

An alarm started sounding. "Force-screen failure imminent," said PHANTOM's voice.

Suddenly one of the Waldahudin ships exploded silently; the *Marc Garneau* had wheeled from firing on one ship to firing on the same one that the *PDQ* had engaged. The target ship had had no force screens deployed along its bow. Keith lowered his head. The first casualties of the battle—and, with hand-aimed lasers, no one would ever know if gunner Helena Smith-Tate had aimed for the habitat, or had simply missed when shooting at the engine pod.

"Two down, six to go," said Thor.

"Force-screen failure," announced Lianne.

The five dolphin-piloted ships began swooping wildly,

their weapons firing at random. The holographic display was crisscrossed with animated laser beams, red for the Commonwealth forces, blue for the attackers.

Suddenly Gawst's vessel began revolving around its bow-stern axis, spinning like a corkscrew. "What the hell's he doing?" asked Keith.

It became apparent as PHANTOM drew in the two beams from Gawst's twin laser canons. With the ship rotating, the beams were forming a cylinder of coherent light—turning twin pinpoint weapons into effectively a wide-beam device. Gawst was aiming up, toward the underside of *Starplex*'s central disk, beneath one of the ship's four main generators.

"If he does it right," said Thor, impressed despite himself, "he'll be able to carve out the number-two generator, like a geologist taking a core sample."

"Move the ship!" snapped Keith.

The starfield wheeled. "Doing so—but he's got a tractor beam locked on us. We—"

The ship rocked again, and a new alarm started wailing. Lianne swung around to face Keith. "There's an internal hull breach on deck forty, where the bottom of the ocean deck joins the central shaft. Water is pouring down the shaft into the lower decks."

"Christ!" said Keith. "Did the Ibs screw up when they installed the replacement lower habitats?"

Rhombus's web turned yellow with rage again, and the dots on it flared brightly. "Excuse me?" he said sharply.

Keith raised his hands. "It's just that—"

"The work was done *perfectly*," said Rhombus, "but this ship's designers never thought we would be in a battle."

"Sorry," said Keith. "Lianne, what's the procedure in a situation like this?"

"There is no procedure," said Lianne. "The ocean deck was considered unbreachable."

"Can the water be contained with forcefields?" asked Keith.

"Not for long," said Lianne. "The forcefields we use in the docking bays have enough strength to hold air at normal pressure against vacuum. But each cubic meter of water masses a full ton; nothing short of the ship's external forcefield emitters could hold back that much pressure, and even if Gawst hadn't overloaded those, there's no way to aim them inside the ship."

"If you turn off the artificial gravity in the central disk and on all decks below it, at least the water won't flow down," said Thor.

"Good idea," said Keith. "Lianne, do that."

"Security override," said PHANTOM's voice. "Command disallowed."

Keith shot a look at the PHANTOM camera pair on his console. "What the — ?"

"It's because of the Ibs," said Rhombus. "Our circulatory system is based on a gravity feed; we'll die if you turn off the gravity."

"Damn! Lianne, how long to move all Ibs from decks forty-one through seventy to the upper decks?"

"Thirty-four minutes."

"Begin doing that. And get all dolphins out of the ocean deck—but tell them to stand by with breathing apparatus, in case we have to send them below into the flooded areas."

"If you evacuate starting from deck seventy," said Thor, "you can turn off the gravity there first, and work your way up."

"That won't make any difference," said Lianne. "By the time the water has fallen that far, it'll have enough momentum to continue on downward even if gravity is no longer pulling it."

"What about electrical shorting?" asked Keith.

"I've already shut off the electrical systems in flooded areas," said Lianne.

"If the ocean deck were to drain completely, how much of the lower decks would it fill?" asked Thor.

"One hundred percent," said Lianne.

"Really?" said Keith. "Christ."

"The ocean deck contains six hundred and eighty-six thousand cubic meters of water," said Lianne, consulting a monitor screen. "Even including all sealed interdeck areas, the entire enclosed volume of the ship below the central disk is only five hundred and sixty-seven thousand cubic meters."

"Excuse me, but I think the *PDQ* is in trouble," said Rhombus, gesturing with one of his ropes toward part of the holographic bubble. Two Waldahud ships were converging on the *Starplex* probeship, lasers crisscrossing.

Keith's eyes darted between the holo display and the monitor on his console showing the progress of the flooding.

"Wait," said Rhombus, "the *Dakterth* is coming up on the stern of the two ships attacking the *PDQ*. It should be able to draw their fire."

"How are the evacuations coming?" asked Keith.

"On schedule," said Lianne.

"Are we leaking any water into space?"

"No; it's just an internal breach."

"How watertight are our interior doors?"

"Well," said Lianne, "the sliding doors between rooms seal when closed, but they aren't strong. After all, the door panels are designed so that anyone can kick them free of their rails for emergency escape in case of fire. The weight of the water will burst them open."

"What genius thought of that?" asked Thor.

"I think he helped design the *Titanic*," muttered Keith.

The ship rocked again, heaving back and forth. In the holo display, a cylinder carved out of *Starplex*'s central disk, ten decks thick, was tumbling against the night. "Gawst has cut out our number-two generator," reported Lianne. "I'd evacuated that part of the engineering torus as soon as he started carving into it, so there were no casualties. But if he can get one more of our generators, this ship won't be able to enter hyperdrive, even if we could get far enough from the star to make that possible."

A burst of light caught Keith's eye. The *Dakterth* had severed the engine pod from one of the Waldahud ships that had been firing on the *PDQ*. The pod pinwheeled away. It looked as though it was going to crash into the cylindrical core that had been cut from *Starplex,* but that was only a trick of perspective.

"What if we vent the water out into space?" asked Rhombus.

"We'd have to cut our own hole into the ocean deck to do that," said Lianne.

"Where would be the easiest spot?" asked Keith.

Lianne consulted a schematic. "The rear wall of docking bay sixteen. Behind it is the engineering torus, of course. But right at that location, the torus contains a filtration station for the ocean deck. In other words, it's already filled with water right up to the back wall of the docking bay, so you'd only have to carve a hole in the bay's wall to get water to pour in."

Keith thought for a moment. And then it hit him. "Okay," he said. "Get someone with a geological laser down to bay sixteen right away." He turned to Rhombus. "I know the Ibs need gravity, but what if we cut the artificial gravity, and spin the ship instead?"

"Centrifugal force?" said Lianne. "People would be standing on the walls."

"Yes. So?"

"Well, and each deck is cross-shaped, so the apparent force of gravity would increase as you went farther out into each arm."

"But it would also keep the water from flowing down the central shaft," said Keith. "Instead, it would be trying to press against the outer walls of the ocean deck. Thor, could you set up such a spin using our ACS thrusters?"

"Can do."

Keith looked at Rhombus. "How much gravity do you Ibs need for your circulatory systems to work?"

Rhombus lifted his ropes. "Tests have suggested that at least one eighth of a standard-g is required."

"Below deck fifty-five," said Lianne, "even at the ends of the arms, we won't get that much apparent gravity at any reasonable rotation rate."

"But that's only fifteen floors that have to have their Ibs evacuated instead of forty," said Keith. "Lianne, inform everyone of what we're doing. Thor, as soon as no Ib is left below deck fifty-five, start spinning the ship. Bleed off the artificial gravity as we come up to speed."

"Will do."

"People should probably vacate the rooms at the ends of each arm, because of the windows," said Lianne.

"Why?" asked Keith. "They're transparent carbon composite; they won't break even if people are standing on them."

"Of course not," said Lianne. "But the windows are angled at forty-five degrees there, because the edges of the habitat modules slope at that angle. It'll be difficult to stand on them once the apparent gravity shifts so that those sloping windows become slanted floors."

Keith nodded. "Good point. Pass on that advisory as well."

"Will do."

The holographic head of Longbottle aboard the *Rum Runner* spoke up. "Polluted waters we are in. Engines overheating."

Keith nodded at the hologram. "Do what you can; if necessary, head away from us. Maybe no one will follow you."

*Starplex* rocked again. "Gawst has started carving into the central disk beneath our number-three generator," said Rhombus. "And a second one of his ships is carving in from the top of the disk, right above generator one."

"Start spinning the ship, Thor."

The starfield hologram began to rotate. The ship reeled again. "That took Gawst by surprise," said Thor. "His lasers are skittering across the entire undersurface of the central disk."

Lianne spoke up. "Jessica Fong is in position inside docking bay sixteen, Keith."

"Show me."

A frame appeared around part of the starfield hologram—now spinning at dizzying speed. Inside the frame, a picture of the interior of the docking bay appeared, with a space-suited woman floating in midair. She was tethered to the rear wall—the one that was shared with the engineering torus—and the tether was pulled taut as the ship's rotation flung her outward toward the inside of the curving space door. The bay's floor, crisscrossed with landing reference markers, was more than a dozen meters below her feet, and its roof, covered with lighting panels and housings for winches, was a dozen meters above her head.

"Open channel," said Keith, then: "Okay, Jessica. Behind the bay's rear wall, inside the engineering torus, is a water-filled ocean-deck filtering station. That station opens on to the ocean on the other side. Drill open a big hole in the docking bay's rear wall. Be careful, though: when you do that, water is going to hammer through at you."

"I understand," said Jessica. She reached to her waist and let out more tether. Keith watched breathlessly as she moved through the air across the bay. She wasn't wasting any time; meters of additional tether appeared each second. She finally reached the far side of the bay, slamming against the curving surface of the space door. For a horrible moment, Keith thought she'd been knocked unconscious by the impact, but she soon recovered from the blow and fought to bring the heavy geological laser into position. She was having trouble holding the unit steady. When she fired, her first shot crossed her own tether line, severing it at its midpoint. Fifteen meters of nylon line came crashing down at her; the other fifteen meters whipped around far over her head like a narrow yellow snake. She was now pinned against the center of the space door by the ship's spinning.

Fong's second shot went equally wild, taking out a junction box for the in-bay lighting system. Everything was plunged into darkness.

"Jessica!"

"I'm still here, Keith. God, this is awkward."

In the frame, all that was visible was black—black, and then a pinprick of ruby, as the laser found the rear wall. Keith watched as the metal began to glow, soften, ripple— —and then—

The sound of water rushing through, like a high-pressure fire hose. Jessica continued to shoot the laser, perforating a giant square along the rear wall. A hole here, move the laser a centimeter, another hole, shoot again, over and over—

The emergency lights came on, bathing the entire bay in red. Seawater erupted from the rear wall. The perforated square of bulkhead metal peeled back, then tore free, flinging across the bay, propelled by a geyser of water behind it.

Keith cringed. It looked as though the metal wall fragment was going to slap against Jessica, who was already being pummeled by wild fists of water, but she, too, must have seen it coming. There was an explosion of flame behind her, scorching the wall. She'd been smart enough to put on a suit with a thruster pack, and had fired herself up and away just in time. The bay was filling with water, starting at the space door and rising in toward the interior wall. Jessica was soon slapped back against the door.

Once the bay had filled, Keith spoke to her once more. "Okay, now turn around and drill a hole about ten centimeters in diameter in the outer docking-bay door. Hold the beam emitter right against the door; you don't want to boil the water around you."

"Will do," she said, her space suit now a diving suit. She stood on the space door and held the gray metal cone of her geological laser like a jackhammer. She then fired down between her feet. Soon, part of the space door was glowing cherry red, then white-hot, and then, and then . . .

*Starplex* spun like a top against the night, green starlight winking off its hull.

The five remaining Waldahud ships were approaching. Two of the ships were coming in from above and three from below, heading toward the ring of docking bays. Doubtless the ship was rotating too fast for any of the Waldahud pilots to notice the tiny incandescent spot in the middle of the door to bay sixteen, a spot that glowed, flared, and burned away. And suddenly—

Water began to spray out into space, flinging away from the rapidly rotating ship. And as it hit vacuum, it evaporated immediately into vapor, and then, once enough vapor had accumulated to make for considerable pressure, the water recondensed into liquid, the plankton, salt crystals, and oceanic detritus providing seeds for droplet formation, and then here, shaded from the green star by the intervening dark-matter field, it froze into ice—

Millions upon millions of ice pellets, flinging away from *Starplex* at high speed, propelled by the explosive force of all the water behind and by the centrifugal force of the rapidly rotating ship. Countless diamonds against the night, winking green in the light of the nearby star—

The first Waldahud ship was hit by a barrage of ice chunks, that ship's speed toward *Starplex* being added to the pellets' own velocity, making for a truly high-speed collision. The initial half-dozen chunks were deflected by the ship's force screens, shields designed for guarding against single microme-teoroid impacts, not a sustained onslaught. Then—

Ice pellets ripped through the Waldahud hull like teeth through flesh, tearing up the habitat, expelled air freezing and adding to the hailstorm in space.

On the bridge, Keith called out, "Now, Thor! Rock the ship!"

Thor complied. A new streamer of ice chunks angled off in a different direction, impacting a second Waldahud ship, ripping it open. Then a third ship exploded, a silent flower against the dark background, as frozen bullets ripped into the tanks containing its atmospheric-maneuvering fuel.

Thor rocked the ship the other way, and ice pellets were flung toward the fourth remaining ship. By this time, its pilot had come up with a counterstrategy. He rotated his own ship so that its fusion exhaust cone faced toward *Starplex,* and he fired his main engine, melting the ice into water drops, which immediately boiled into vapor before they could hit his ship. But the pilot of one of the other remaining ships had been unprepared for this maneuver, or too preoccupied with saving his own tail by heading toward the shortcut. His course took him in the path of his comrade's fusion exhaust, and the white-hot flames tore into his vessel. It exploded, leaving only two ships—one of which was Gawst's.

The expanding ring of water pellets deflected most of the ship debris away from *Starplex,* but the crew of the Waldahud craft that had tried the fusion-exhaust trick wasn't so lucky. A large, jagged piece of hull rammed into their ship. The impact set it spinning away, out of control— directly toward the field of dark matter. The pilot seemed almost to regain control when he was a few million kilometers away from the closest of the great gray balls of gas, but by then he was already caught in its gravity. It would take hours for the deadly trajectory to play out its course, but the ship was destined to crash into the darmat—

and, at that velocity, even the kind of soft impact that occurred when regular matter hit dark matter would be enough to pulverize the vessel.

Gawst's ship was still intact, holding station with a tractor beam beneath the central disk. There was no way Thor could aim the ice-pellet stream there. Still, *Starplex* could keep spinning until Gawst ran out of fuel, if need be . . .

"Uh-oh." PHANTOM's translation of the rippling lights on Rhombus.

Thor looked up. "God damn," he said.

Emerging from behind the limb of the green star were one . . . two . . . *five* more Waldahud fighters. Gawst had not been fool enough to use all his forces on the initial attack. One of the newcomers was a giant, ten times the size of the smaller probecraft.

*Starplex*'s five dolphin-piloted ships had backed off, avoiding the ice barrage. But now they were linking up in formation, and heading toward the approaching attack force, determined to get to it before it could get to their mothership.

And then . . .

"What the hell?" said Keith, gripping his armrests.

"Jesus . . ." said Thor. *"Je-sus!"*

The vast field of dark matter had begun to move, slowly at first, but now with gathering speed. It was spinning out into lumpy streamers, greenish on the side facing toward the rogue sun, inky black on the other. The streamers grew longer until they spread out over millions of kilometers, tubes of gravel with planet-sized spheres distributed along their length like knuckles on ethereal fingers.

The *Starplex* probeships dived above or below the streamers. The Waldahud pilots found their ships traveling in erratic courses, unable to compensate for the streamers' gravitational attraction. In the spherical hologram, Keith could see the attacking ships staggering in drunken, weaving lines, pulled off course by the hundreds of Jupiter-masses within each dark-matter ribbon.

The streamers were growing with surprising speed. Keith still had trouble with the concept of macrolife living freely in space, but of course most life-forms could move quickly when they wanted to . . .

The pilots of the incoming Waldahud ships were realizing that they were in trouble. One of them aborted what had clearly been an attack run toward *Starplex,* and was now veering off at a steep angle. Another fired its braking jets, the exhausts four ruby pinpricks against the blackness. But the darmats continued to reach for them, long, puffy fingers against the night.

If the ships had been able to use hyperdrive, they could have escaped. But the gravity well from the green star, and the shallower but still significant wells created by the darmats, prevented that.

The farthest of the new fighters was now only a few kilometers ahead of one of the dark-matter tendrils. Keith watched as the gap was closed, the ship disappearing within the fog of gravel.

Thor provided a schematic, showing the fighter's position within the streamer—a streamer that now was no longer reaching forward, but had started pulling back, its gravity dragging the Waldahud vessel with it . . .

Soon a second dark-matter tentacle had enveloped another Waldahud ship. A third fighter was trying desperately to get away; Keith could see the flash of explosive bolts as it jettisoned its weapons clusters in order to decrease its overall mass. But the dark matter was still gaining on it.

Meanwhile, the two tendrils that had already caught ships were still pulling back, and—that was curious—had begun curling in on themselves, arching away, like cobras made of ash.

The third small ship was finally caught, and its gray finger started pulling back, too. The giant Waldahud ship was also being approached from above and below by separate dark-matter tentacles. Only the fifth new ship seemed likely to get away, although Keith's heart was pounding as he saw that Rissa and Longbottle were now pursuing it. His son's face flashed in front of his eyes—still a kid at nineteen, the goatee notwithstanding. How would he break the news to him if his mother got killed?

The first two tentacles had arched back into semicircles, the cups of which were facing away from the green star. At the same moment as the large vessel was engulfed by the two converging streamers that had been pursuing it, the first of the dark-matter fingers snapped forward like a whip. The Waldahud fighter that had been embedded in it shot ahead, out of the tentacle, tumbling end over end. Keith saw the pinpoint lights of ACS jets firing, but the ship's wild rotation continued unabated as—

Keith's jaw fell open. *Good Christ—!*

—as the ship was flung directly toward the green star.

The vessel continued to rotate over and over as the distance between it and the star diminished rapidly. The pilot finally managed to gain control, but he was too close to the 1.5-million-kilometer-wide ball of fire. Prominences licked toward the incoming projectile—

—and the ship turned to vapor in the star's upper atmosphere.

Keith shouted, "Rhombus, hail our probeships!"

"Channel open."

"Return to *Starplex!*" said Keith. "All ships, return at once to *Starplex!*"

Four probeships acknowledged and changed course, but one was still pursuing its target.

"Rissa!" Keith shouted. "Turn back!"

Suddenly the second dark-matter whip cracked across the night, sending another Waldahud ship hurtling toward the green star. Keith's head kept snapping left and right between the twin horrors of Rissa's ship receding from *Starplex* and the fighter's head-over-heels rush toward destruction.

The *Rum Runner* was corkscrewing wildly as it approached the enemy vessel. Laser fire from the Waldahud's rear cannons kept missing the probeship, or glancing off its force screens. But, after a moment, the firing stopped as the Waldahudin aboard presumably became absorbed in the spectacle they, too, were no doubt monitoring.

The second ship the darmats had tossed toward the sun was rapidly reaching its destination. Lifeboats popped away from it, but their puny motors weren't strong enough to let them achieve orbit around the star. The last sight the dying Waldahudin probably saw on their monitor screens was the star's strange dumbbell-shaped sunspots, gray-black splotches against a hell of liquid jade.

The *PDQ* and the *Dakterth* were returning to *Starplex* now. Of course, they had to approach from above or below to avoid the torus of hail surrounding the ship. Rhombus was using tractor beams to pull them down onto the flat surface of the central disk. There was no way to get them into the docking bays—the ice prevented that—but there were emergency docking clamps on both faces of the disk.

*Rum Runner* was still giving chase. "Rissa!" shouted Keith into his mike. "For God's sake, Rissa—come home!"

Suddenly the *Rum Runner*'s laser erupted, PHANTOM dutifully drawing in its beam on the holographic display. It swept across the starscape. Rissa's aim was perfect, severing the ship's engine pod from the craft in one clean slice. The pod tumbled against the night, a puff of expelled gas around it shining like a halo of emeralds. And suddenly—

The pod flared brilliantly, brighter even than the nearby star, as it went up in a fusion explosion. Longbottle executed a crazed arcing maneuver to avoid the expanding ball of plasma, then began a laser-straight path for *Starplex*. The engineless Waldahud ship shot away at an oblique angle under momentum, unable to maneuver.

The third dark-matter whip cracked, sending another Waldahud fighter pinwheeling across the firmament. As this one passed by, Keith saw that several of its hull plates had been deliberately blown away; the crew had apparently preferred opening the ship to vacuum over cooking alive as they plunged into the sun.

Next the combined double finger that had enveloped the huge Waldahud ship began to rotate around its midpoint, playing out into a spiral design like a galaxy as it did so, turning faster and faster. PHANTOM showed the location of the ship buried within one arm of the spinning mass. The rotation became more and more rapid, until finally, like an athlete throwing a discus, the dark matter hurtled the giant ship away from it. The bigger ship managed to regain control before it impacted the sun, but as it started to alter its course, the white fusion flames of its exhaust stark

against the green inferno, a giant prominence arched upward
from the photosphere, engulfing it.

"Four of our five probeships are safely clamped to our
hull," reported Rhombus. "And the *Rum Runner* will be
back in eleven minutes."

Keith let out a heavy sigh. "Excellent. We must have
everyone out of the lower decks by now, right?"

"The final elevator is on its way up," said Lianne. "Give
it another thirty seconds."

"Okay. Keep the lower decks at zero-g so no more water
will flow down. Thor, stop spinning the ship."

"Will do."

"Director," said Rhombus, "Gawst's ship has attached
itself to the surface of our hull. He's holding in place with
a tractor beam."

Keith smiled. "Fancy that—a prisoner of war." He spoke
loudly. "Excellent work, everyone. Thor, Lianne, Rhombus—
excellent." He paused. "Thank God the darmats sided with us.
I guess it never hurts to be on speaking terms with the stuff that
makes up most of the universe, and—"

"*Jesus.*" Thor's voice.

Keith's head snapped up to face the pilot. He'd spoken too
soon. Tendrils of dark matter were now closing on *Starplex.*

"We're next," said Rhombus.

"But we're orders of magnitude bigger than the Waldahud
ships," said Thor. "Surely they can't toss us into the star?"

"Only a third of the dark matter participated in the attack
on the Waldahud forces," said Rhombus. "If it all comes
after us—PHANTOM, can they do it?"

"Yes."

"Hail Cat's Eye," said Keith. "I better talk to him."

"Locating vacant frequency," said Rhombus. "Transmitting . . . No response."

"Thor, get us out of here," said Keith.

"Course?"

Keith considered for half a second. "Toward the shortcut." But he immediately realized that dark-matter tendrils
had already started to intervene between *Starplex* and that
invisible point in space. "No, change that," he snapped.

"Bring us in close to the green star, in the opposite direction. And get Jag down here, PHANTOM."

"You ordered him barred from this room, sir," said the computer.

"I know that. I'm giving you new instructions. Get him down here right away."

There was a moment's silence while PHANTOM conferred with Jag. "He is on his way."

"What've you got in mind?" asked Rhombus. Dark matter was approaching *Starplex* on three sides, like a fist closing around a bug.

"Hopefully, a way to get out of here—if it doesn't kill us."

The starfield split open, and Jag walked in. For the first time, Keith saw a look of humility on the Waldahud's face. Jag had presumably been watching the space battle, and had seen his compatriots slammed into the emerald star. But still some of the old defiance was in his voice as he looked suspiciously at Keith. "What do you want?"

"I want," said Keith, his voice tightly controlled, "to slingshot *Starplex* around the green star, and hurtle it into the shortcut from the far side."

"Jesus God," said Thor.

Jag grunted a similar sentiment in his own language.

"Can it be done?" said Keith. "Will it work?"

"I—I don't know," said Jag. "I would normally like a few hours to do the calculations for something like that."

"You don't have hours—you've got minutes. Will it work?"

"I do not—yes. Maybe."

"Melondent," said Keith, "transfer control back to Jag's station."

"So doing," said the dolphin.

Jag slipped into his usual spot. "Central Computer," he barked, "put our trajectory on this monitor."

"You are barred from issuing nonhousekeeping commands," said PHANTOM.

"Override!" snapped Keith. "Jag's house arrest is suspended until further notice."

The requested schematic appeared. Jag squinted at it. "Magnor?"

"Yes?" said Thor.

"We have only perhaps ten minutes until we are engulfed. You will need to fire all our ventral thrusters. Copy my monitor six in touch-screen mode."

Thor pressed buttons. "Okay."

Jag ran a flat finger in an arc along the schematic. "Can you manage a course like that?"

"You mean on manual?"

"Yes, on manual. We have no time to program the run."

"I—yes, I can do it."

"Execute it. Execute it now!"

"Director?"

"How long until the *Rum Runner* is anchored to our hull?"

"Four minutes," said Rhombus.

"We don't have the time to wait for her," said Jag.

Keith turned to snap at Jag, but stopped himself. "Options?" he said generally to the people on bridge.

"I can put a tractor beam on the *Rum Runner*," said Rhombus. "I won't be able to haul her in before we hit the shortcut, but she should be dragged over to it with us and then hopefully Longbottle can pilot it through."

"Do that. Thor, get us out of here."

*Starplex* rushed toward the star at an oblique angle. "Thrusters on full," said Thor.

"There's another problem we still have to deal with," said Jag, turning to Keith. "There's a good chance that I can get us to the shortcut, but once there, we'll just plunge through it. We won't have any time to slow down and do a controlled approach at a specific angle, and with our deck-seventy hyperscope array damaged I can't even predict which exit we'll pop out of. It could be anywhere."

The dark-matter fingers were still stretching toward *Starplex*. "In a few minutes, anywhere will be preferable to this place," said Keith. "Just get us out of here."

The ship began to careen around the star. Half of the bridge hologram showed the green orb, its granular surface detail and dumbbell sunspots visible. Most of the rest of the view was cloudy, with dark-matter tendrils eclipsing the background stars. "Rhombus, do you have a solid lock on the *Rum Runner*?"

"It's still four hundred kilometers away, and dark matter is starting to intervene, but, yes, I've got it."

Keith breathed a sigh of relief. "Good work. Have you been able to contact Cat's Eye, or any darmat?"

"They're still ignoring our hails," said Rhombus.

"We can't go in as close to the star as I would like," said Jag. "There's not enough water left in the ocean deck to make an effective shield, and our force screens are still burned out. There's a thirty-percent chance that the darmats will ensnare us."

Keith felt his heart pounding in his chest. *Starplex* continued to swing around the star in a parabolic course, the tendrils still stretching toward it. The *Rum Runner* was indicated in the holo bubble as a tiny square, with an animated yellow tractor beam lancing out to it. The starfield wheeled—Thor was angling the ship as they grazed the star's atmosphere.

Finally, *Starplex* reached the cusp of the parabola and, picking up enormous velocity from slingshoting around the star, raced toward the shortcut. In the holo bubble, PHAN-TOM brightened the yellow tractor-beam animation, indicating that additional power was being pumped into it. *Starplex*'s course, four hundred kilometers closer to the star, was significantly different from the path the *Rum Runner* would have been following if it had been looping around the orb under its own momentum.

"Two minutes to contact with the shortcut, mark," said Rhombus.

"We've never gone through a shortcut this fast before—no one has," said Jag. "People should secure themselves, or at least hold on to something."

"Lianne, pass on that recommendation to all aboard," said Keith.

"All personnel," said Lianne's voice, reverberating over the speakers, "brace for possible turbulence."

Suddenly a large, irregular object eclipsed part of the view. "Gawst's ship," said Lianne. "He's pushed off our hull. Probably thinks we've all gone insane."

"I could grab him with another tractor," said Rhombus.

Keith smiled. "No, let him go. If he thinks his chances are better with the darmats, that's fine by me."

"Eighty seconds, mark," said Rhombus, orange clamps rising up from the invisible floor to hold on to his wheels.

"One-point-four degrees to port, Magnor," said Jag. "You're going to miss the shortcut."

"Adjusting course."

"Sixty seconds, mark."

"Everyone hold on," said Lianne. "It's—"

Blackness. Weightlessness.

*"God damn it!"* Thor's voice.

Barking—Jag speaking. No translation from PHANTOM.

Flickering lights—the only illumination in the room: Rhombus saying something.

"Power failure!" shouted Thor.

Red emergency lighting came on, as did emergency gravity—a priority because of the Ibs. There were loud splashing sounds from either side of the room: the water in the dolphin workstations had swelled up into great dome shapes under zero gravity, domes that had collapsed, splattering liquid everywhere as weight returned.

No holographic bubble surrounded the bridge; instead its blue-gray plastiform walls were visible. Keith was still in his chair, but Jag was on the floor, obviously having lost his balance during the brief period of zero-g.

The three consoles in the front row—InOps, Helm, and ExOps—flickered back into life. The back-row stations were less critical, and stayed off, conserving battery power.

"We've lost the *Rum Runner,*" said Rhombus. "It was cut loose when the tractor beam died."

"Abort the shortcut insertion!" snapped Keith.

"Way too late for that," said Thor. "We're going through under momentum."

Keith closed his eyes. "Which way did the *Rum Runner* go?"

"No way to tell until I get my scanners back on-line," said Rhombus, "but—well, we were hauling her in, meaning she would have been moving pretty much in a line back toward the green star . . ."

"The number-one generator blew," interjected Lianne, consulting readouts. "Battle damage. I'm switching over to standby generators."

PHANTOM's voice: "Re-in-ish-il-i-zing. On-line."

The holographic bubble re-formed, beginning as a burst of whiteness all around them, then settling down to the exterior view, dominated by the green star, the rest obscured by the pursuing tendrils of dark matter. Keith looked in vain for any sign of the *Rum Runner*.

Thor's voice: "Ten seconds to shortcut insertion, mark. Nine. Eight."

Lianne's voice, overtop, coming from the public-address speakers. "We should have full power back in sixty seconds. Prepare—"

"Two. One. Contact!" The red emergency lighting flickered. The shortcut appeared like a ring of violet arcing around them, visible above their heads and beneath their feet, as the infinitesimal point expanded to swallow the massive ship.

Everything to the stern of the ring was the now familiar sky of the green star and the pursuing dark matter. But in front of the ring was an almost completely black sky. The passage through the shortcut took only a few moments as *Starplex* hurtled through at breakneck speed.

Keith shuddered as he realized what had happened. Rhombus's lights swirled in patterns of astonishment. Lianne made a small sound in her throat. Jag was reflexively smoothing his fur.

All around was black emptiness, except for an indistinct white oval and three smaller white splotches high above their heads, and a handful of fainter white smudges tossed at random against the night.

They had emerged in the empty void of intergalactic space. The white splotches weren't stars; they were whole galaxies.

And not one of them looked like the Milky Way.

# XVIII

Rissa felt her throat constricting as the *Rum Runner* was flung away from *Starplex*.

"What happened?" she called.

But Longbottle was too busy to answer. He was twisting and turning in his tank, fighting to bring the ship under control. On her monitors, Rissa saw the green star swelling ahead of them, its surface a roiling ocean of fiery emerald, jade, and malachite.

She fought down a wave of panic, and tried to assess for herself what had gone wrong. There's no way Keith would have cut power to the tractor beam, so either Gawst had used some sort of interfering transmission to sever the tractor, or *Starplex* had suffered a power failure. Either way, they'd been hurled away from the mothership, and almost directly toward the star. Through the clear wall between her air-filled chamber and Longbottle's water-filled one, Rissa saw the dolphin sharply arching his body in what seemed to be a painful way, and bashing the side of his head against the opposite wall, as if by that sheer additional effort he could force the ship in the direction he wanted it to go.

Rissa looked at her monitors, and her heart skipped a beat. She saw *Starplex* disappear through the shortcut to—to wherever it had gone. The great ship's windows were dark, confirming that a power failure must have occurred. If the ship was truly without power, Rissa hoped it had come through the shortcut network at New Beijing or Flatland—where there would be other vessels to help it. Otherwise, it might not be able to return through whatever exit it emerged from—and a search of all the active exits might not be completed before *Starplex*'s batteries ran out, leaving it without life support.

But Rissa only had a few moments to think about the fate of her husband and colleagues; the *Rum Runner* was still heading toward the green star. The bow window had already darkened considerably, trying to filter out the inferno ahead of them. Longbottle was still struggling with the controls attached to his flukes and fins. Suddenly he flipped around in his tank, and Rissa saw the green star wheel away from view. Longbottle was bringing the main engines around to face the star, and firing them as brakes. The ship rattled; Rissa could see Longbottle disabling emergency cutoffs with presses of his snout.

"Sharks!" shrieked Longbottle. At first, Rissa thought it was just a swear word for the dolphin, but then she saw what he was referring to: tendrils of dark matter were now obscuring half the sky, the gray spheres within the miasma of luster-quark gravel like the knots on a cat-o'-nine-tails.

Longbottle twisted to his right, and the ship followed suit. But soon a much more sharply defined blackness obscured their view.

"Ship of Gawst," said Longbottle.

"Damn," said Rissa. She brought her hands down on the two grips that controlled the geological laser. She wasn't going to fire unless he did, but —

Ruby dots on Gawst's hull. Rissa moved her thumb over the laser's twin triggers.

Longbottle must have seen her do that. "ACS jets," he said. "Not lasers. He, too, tries to get away from darmats."

The view in the window changed again as Longbottle altered the *Rum Runner*'s course. Green star to the rear, enemy ship to port, darmats to starboard and coming in above and below. There was only one course possible. Longbottle jabbed controls with his snout. "To the shortcut!" he shouted in his high-pitched voice.

Rissa flipped keys, and one of her monitors showed the hyperspace map, the maelstrom of tachyons visible around the exit point.

"More maneuverable are we than *Starplex*," said Longbottle. "An exit we may choose."

Rissa thought for half a second. "Can you tell where Keith and the others went?"

"No. Shortcut rotates; I can match their angle of approach, but no time to work out if that will mean we exit at the same place."

"Then—then go for New Beijing," said Rissa. "*Starplex* will eventually end up there for repairs—if it can."

Longbottle squirmed in his tank, and the *Rum Runner* arched upward then down, coming at the shortcut from above and behind. "Insertion in seconds five," he said.

Rissa held her breath. There was nothing visible on her monitors. Nothing at all—

A flash of purple.

A different starfield.

A massive black starship.

A starship firing on a flotilla of United Nations vessels.

Four—no, five!—dead hulks pinwheeling against the night, surrounded by clouds of expelled atmosphere.

Everything was bathed in bloody light from the red dwarf that had recently emerged from this shortcut.

It flashed in front of Rissa's eyes, the words fully formed, like a chapter title on some future textbook screen—

*The Rout of Tau Ceti.*

Waldahud forces attacking the Earth colony, seizing the one shortcut that serviced human space, a giant battle cruiser easily dispatching the tiny diplomatic craft normally stationed there—

A giant battle cruiser that had all its force screens aimed forward, protecting it from the returning fire being launched by the UN ships—

A giant battle cruiser that the *Rum Runner* was directly behind.

Rissa had never killed before, had never even deliberately injured before, had—

*The Rout of Tau Ceti.*

She swung the handles that aimed the laser, and leaned on the triggers.

PHANTOM wasn't here to animate in the beam for her, and the Waldahudin battleship was too far away for her to see the red dot moving across its hull —

Moving across its thruster fuel storage tanks—

Ripping them open—

Igniting the fuel—

And then—

A ball of light, like a supernova—

The bow window going completely black—

Longbottle arching in his tank, moving the *Rum Runner* away from the expanding sphere of debris.

Rissa took her hands off the triggers. The window grew clear again. She was shaking from head to foot. How many Waldahudin had been aboard a ship that size? A hundred? A thousand? If they'd planned to actually move on to Sol system and storm Earth and Mars and Luna, perhaps as many as ten thousand soldiers—

All dead.

Dead.

There were other Waldahudin ships in the area, but they were tiny one-person fighter craft. The big black vessel must have been their mothership.

Rissa exhaled noisily.

"You acted well," said Longbottle gently. "You did what you had to."

She said nothing.

The UN ships were banking now—New Beijing was a

human-*dolphin* colony—and coming in to attack the small Waldahud fighters. The *Rum Runner* buffeted slightly as it passed through the cloud of expelled atmosphere from the destroyed battleship.

Rissa's console beeped. She looked at the glowing red indicator, like a drop of blood, but did not move. Longbottle eyed her for a moment, then nosed the similar control in his tank. A woman's voice came over the speakers. "This is Liv Amundsen, commander of the United Nations police forces at Tau Ceti, to *Starplex* auxiliary craft." Rissa glanced at her monitors. Amundsen's ship was still three light-minutes away; no point in trying a real-time conversation. "We have identified your transponder signal. Thank you for your timely arrival. Our casualties are heavy—over two hundred dead—but you've saved New Beijing. You can bet they'll pin a medal on your chest, whoever you are aboard that ship. Over."

A medal, thought Rissa. Jesus Christ, they give medals.

"Rissa?" said Longbottle. "Do you want me—?"

Rissa shook her head. "No. No, I'll do it." She tapped a key. "This is Dr. Clarissa Cervantes aboard the *Rum Runner;* I'm here with a dolphin pilot named Longbottle. *Starplex* was also attacked by Waldahud forces; it headed through the shortcut network to destination unknown, but may require emergency drydock facilities. Can you accommodate?"

She watched the stars drift by as she waited for her signal to reach Amundsen's ship, and the reply to make its way back. *The Waldahud forces were repelled at Tau Ceti,* said the history book in her mind. But what was the next chapter? Two hundred from Earth or its colonies were dead . . . Dolphins didn't believe in vengeance, but would the humans demand it? Would this be the one skirmish, or were we about to see all-out war?

"Negative, Dr. Cervantes," came Amundsen's voice, at last. "Our dock facilities were the first thing the Waldahudin fired on." Of course, thought Rissa. Pearl Harbor all over again. "Suggest *Starplex* try the Flatland drydocks—although it should be careful when moving through the shortcut to there. Remember, a G-class subgiant recently emerged from that shortcut. We can, however, offer repair services here for a small ship such as yours."

Rissa looked at her monitors. The battle wasn't quite over. Police ships were still engaging a few Waldahud craft, although some of the invaders seemed to have surrendered, jettisoning their own engine pods.

"We more fuel need," said Longbottle to Rissa. "And thrusters must be allowed to cool—I overworked them badly."

"Fine," said Rissa into her microphone. "We're coming in." She nodded to Longbottle, and he rotated in his tank, moving the ship. Rissa's heart was still pounding. She closed her eyes, and tried not to think of what she had done.

# XIX

"Lianne, damage report!" snapped Keith.

"I'm still tabulating everything from the battle, but there were no new problems caused by the high-speed shortcut passage."

"What about casualties?"

Lianne tilted her head, listening to reports over her audio implant. "No deaths. Lots of bone fractures, though. Couple of concussions. Nothing too serious. And Jessica Fong got out of docking bay sixteen all right, although she has a broken hip and arm, and a lot of bruising."

Keith nodded and breathed a sigh of relief. He looked around the holo bubble, trying to make out detail in the faint smudges of white against black infinity. "God," he said under his breath.

"All the gods," replied Jag, softly, "are a very, very long way from here."

Thor turned around and looked at Jag. "It *is* intergalactic space, isn't it?"

Jag lifted his upper shoulders in agreement.

"But—but I've never heard of any shortcut exit this far out," said Lianne.

"The shortcuts have only existed for a finite time," said Jag. "Even hyperspace signals from one in intergalactic space might not have reached any of the Commonwealth worlds yet."

"But how can there be a shortcut in intergalactic space?" asked Thor. "What's it anchored to?"

"That's a very good question," said Jag, bending his head down to look at his instruments. "Ah—there it is. Check your hyperspace scanner, Magnor. There's a large black hole about six light-hours from here."

Thor let out a low whistle. "Adjusting course. Let's give it a wide berth."

"Are we in any danger from it?" asked Keith.

"Not much, boss—unless I fall asleep at the wheel."

Jag touched some controls, and a framed-off area appeared in the holo bubble. But the space inside the frame was just as empty and black as the space outside it.

"Normally you can see the accretion disk around a black hole," said Jag, "but there's nothing out here to be pulled into it." He paused. "My guess is that it's an ancient black hole—it would have needed billions of years to get out here. I suspect it's the remains of a binary star system. When the larger component went supernova, it could have caused an asymmetric kick which propelled the resulting black hole out of its home galaxy."

"But what would have activated this shortcut?" asked Lianne.

Jag lifted all four shoulders. "The hole would pull in any matter that wanders by. Something that was being sucked in by it probably fell through the shortcut instead." Jag tried to sound jaunty, but it was clear even he was staggered by it all. "We're actually pretty lucky—shortcuts in intergalactic space are probably as rare as mud without footprints."

Keith turned to Thor. He made an effort to keep his voice

calm, controlled. He was the director; no matter how much *Starplex* usually behaved like a research lab rather than a sailing vessel, he knew all eyes would be on him, looking for strength. "How soon can we go back through the shortcut?" he asked. "How soon can we go get the *Rum Runner*?"

"We've still got major electrical problems," said Lianne. "I wouldn't want to move the ship until those are stabilized—and I'll need at least three hours for that."

"Three hours!" said Keith. "But—"

"I'll try to cut it down," said Lianne.

"What about sending a probeship through to help Rissa and Longbottle?" asked Keith.

The room was silent for a moment. Rhombus rolled over to the command workstation, and touched Keith's forearm lightly with one of his manipulator ropes. "My friend," he said, PHANTOM translating the low intensity of his lights as whispering, "you can't do that. You can't put another ship in danger."

I'm the director, thought Keith. I can do what I damn well please. He shook his head, trying to get control. If anything had happened to Rissa . . .

"You're right," he said at last. "Thanks." He turned to Jag, and felt his heart rate increasing. "I should put you back under house arrest, you . . ."

"'Pig,'" said Jag, his underlying bark an excellent mimicking of the English word. "Go ahead and say it."

"My wife is out there somewhere—possibly dying. Longbottle, too. What the hell were you trying to accomplish?"

"I admit nothing."

"The damage to this ship will cost billions to repair. The Commonwealth will bring charges against you, you can be sure of that—"

"You will never be able to prove that my request to move *Starplex* had anything to do with the subsequent events. You can revile me all you wish, human, but even your unenlightened courts require proof to substantiate a charge. The dark-matter being I wanted to examine did indeed have an unusual hyperspace footprint; any astronomer will verify that. And it was indeed invisible from *Starplex*'s vantage point before the move—"

"You said that darmat was about to reproduce. It hasn't done a thing."

"You are spoiled by being a sociologist, Lansing. In the hard sciences, we occasionally have to face the reality that some of our theories will actually be disproven."

"It was a ruse—"

"It was an experiment. Suggesting anything else is conjecture; persist publicly in it, and I shall bring defamation charges against you."

"You bastard. If Rissa dies—"

"If Dr. Cervantes dies, I will mourn. I wish her no ill. But for all we know, she and Longbottle have maneuvered through the shortcut to safety. It is *my* compatriots who have died today, not yours."

Lianne spoke softly from her console. "He's right, Keith. We've lost equipment, and we've got several people who are injured. But no one from *Starplex* is dead."

"Except possibly Rissa and Longbottle," snapped Keith. He took a deep breath, trying to calm himself. "It's all about money, isn't it, Jag? Of all the Commonwealth homeworlds, Rehbollo's economy took the biggest hit when interstellar commerce opened up. You guys never build two things the same—"

"To do so is an affront to the God of Artisans—"

"To do so is efficient, and your factories and workers were not. So you tried to goose the government coffers. Even disassembled for parts, *Starplex* would be worth trillions—lots of glory in that. And if war erupted over its seizure, well, nothing like a little war to give the economy a boost, eh?"

"No sane being wants war," said Jag.

"PHANTOM," snapped Keith, "Jag is again under house arrest."

"Acknowledged."

"It may please the punitive in you to do that," barked Jag. "But this is still a science vessel, and we are the first Commonwealth beings ever to be in intergalactic space. We

should determine our exact location—and I am the most
qualified person to undertake that task. Rescind the arrest
order, shut up and leave me alone, and I shall try to figure
out where we are."

"Boss," said Thor gently, "he's right, you know. Let him
help."

Keith fumed for a few moments longer, then nodded
curtly. But when he did nothing further, Thor spoke into the
air. "PHANTOM," he said. "Cancel house arrest on Jag."

"Cancellation requires authorization from Director Lansing."

Keith exhaled noisily. "Do it—but, PHANTOM, monitor
every command he issues. If any of them seem unrelated to
determining our location, notify me at once."

"Acknowledged. House arrest ended."

Keith looked at Thor. "What's our current heading?"

Thor consulted his instruments. "We're still on a modified version of the parabolic course we used to slingshot
around the green star. Obviously, the path changed when we
ceased to be under that star's gravitational influence, so—"

"Magnor," said Jag, interrupting. "I need you to rotate the
ship in a Gaf Wayfarer pattern; we are missing one hyperscope
array, but I need a parallactic full-sky hyperspace scan."

Thor tapped some keys. The holographic bubble around the
bridge began a complex series of rotations, but because the
bubble was empty save for a few indistinct smudges of white,
the tilting and turning didn't cause vertigo. The pilot looked at
Keith again. "As for getting home, the shortcut exit behind us
shows in hyperspace just like every other one I've ever seen,
complete with zero meridian. Assuming the damned things
still work the same way over millions of light-years, once
Lianne gets our full electrical system back on-line, I should be
able to put us back at any active shortcut you specify."

"Good," said Keith. "Lianne, how badly damaged were
we in the battle?"

"Decks fifty-four through seventy are flooded," she said,
into a hologram of Keith's head, "and everything from deck
forty-one down has some water damage. Also, all decks
below the central disk took a heavy hit of radiation as we

careened around the green star; I advise declaring the entire lower half uninhabitable." She paused. "The *Starplex 2* team is going to be pissed off with us—we've now fried both sets of lower-habitat modules."

"What about our shields?"

"Our forcefield emitters were all overloaded, but I've already got my engineers working on repairs; we should have minimal screens within an hour. In a way, it's good we came out in intergalactic space. The chances of running into a micrometeoroid out here are slim."

"What about the damage done when Gawst carved out our number-two generator?"

"My teams have put temporary bulkheads in place around the hole where it was removed," said Lianne. "That should hold until we get back to a spacedock."

"And the other generators?"

"Number three has had all its electrical connections severed. I've got a crew working on hooking it back up again, but I don't know if we've got enough wide-gauge fiber-optic cable in stock to do the job; we may have to manufacture some. Anyway, until we get it back on-line, we won't be able to use the main engines. One of the other Waldahud ships had started carving out the number-one generator, as well. That's the one that quit, causing the power failure. We should be able to repair that damage, though."

"And what about the docking bays?"

"Bay sixteen is filled with frozen water," said Lianne. "Also, three of the five probeships that were involved in the battle are in need of repairs."

"But we're still spaceworthy?" asked Keith.

"I want to schedule about three weeks in dock for repairs, but, yes, we're in no immediate danger."

Keith nodded. "In that case, Thor, as soon as Lianne says we're ready for powered flight, I'll want you to plot a course through the shortcut that will pop us out where we started, back near the green star."

Thor's orange eyebrows lifted. "I know you want to rescue the *Rum Runner*, Keith, but if they survived, Longbottle will have already taken them out of there through the shortcut."

"Probably so, but that's not why I want to go back." He looked over at Rhombus. "You were right a few minutes ago, my rolling friend. I've got to keep my priorities straight. Contact with other life is why *Starplex* was built in the first place. I'm not going to let the Commonwealth become like the Slammers, cutting off all communication because of a misunderstanding. I want to talk to the darmats again."

"They tried to kill us," said Thor.

Keith raised a hand. "I'm not fool enough to give them a second chance to toss us into the green star. Can you plot a course that will bring us out of the shortcut, whip us around that star, then bring us back to the shortcut, diving through on a vector that will take us out at the Flatland 368A exit?"

Thor considered for a moment. "I can do that, yes. But F368A? Not New Beijing?"

"For all we know, the attack on *Starplex* was not an isolated event. New Beijing may be under siege. I want to go to a neutral location." A pause. "Now, with the course I've described, will the darmats be able to grab us again?"

Thor shook his head. "Not at the speed we'll be going, unless they're all lying in wait for us just outside the exit."

"Rhombus," said Keith, "as soon as Lianne's got the appropriate systems back on-line, send a probe through to the green-star exit. Include a hyperspace scanner on it so you can locate the darmats by the dents they make in spacetime. Also, have it do a wide-spectrum radio scan, in case Waldahud reinforcements have arrived. And"—Keith tried to keep his voice calm—"have it check for the *Rum Runner*'s transponder code."

"It'll be at least thirty minutes before we can do that," said Lianne.

Keith pursed his lips, and thought about Rissa. If she were gone, it would take all the billions of years he had left to get over the loss. He looked at the smudges of galactic light against the abyss. He didn't even know which direction to look in, which way to concentrate his thoughts. He felt incredibly small, insignificant, and lonely beyond belief.

There was nothing to focus on in the holo bubble—nothing sharp, nothing well defined. Just an abyss—an ego-crushing emptiness.

Suddenly there was a strange sound like a dog's cough from his left; PHANTOM translated it as an expression of "absolute astonishment." Keith turned to face Jag, and his mouth hung open as he stared at the Waldahud. He'd never seen Jag's fur do *that* before. "What's wrong?"

"I—I know where we are," said Jag.

Keith looked at him. "Yes?"

"You're aware that the Milky Way and Andromeda have about forty smaller galaxies bound to them gravitationally, right?" said Jag.

"The Local Group," said Keith, irritated.

"Exactly," said Jag. "Well, I started off by trying to find some of the Local Group's distinctive features, such as superbright S Doradus in the Large Magellanic Cloud. But that didn't work. So I sorted the catalog of known extragalactic pulsars by distance—which corresponds to age, of course—and used their signature radio pulses to orient myself."

"Yes, yes," said Keith. "And?"

"And the closest galaxy to us right now is that one there." Jag pointed beneath his feet to a fuzzy spot in the hologram. "It's about five hundred thousand light-years from here. I have identified it as CGC 1008; it has several unique attributes."

"All right," said Keith, sharply. "We're half a million light-years from CGC 1008. Now, for us nonastrophysics types, how far is CGC 1008 from the Milky Way?"

Jag's barking was subdued, almost soft. "We are," said the translated voice, "six billion light-years from home."

"Six . . . *billion*?" asked Thor, turning to face Jag.

Jag lifted his upper shoulders. "That is correct," he said, his voice still soft.

"That's . . . staggering," said Keith.

Jag lifted his upper shoulders. "Six billion light-years. Sixty thousand times the Milky Way's own diameter. Twenty-seven hundred times the distance between the Milky Way and

Andromeda." He looked at Keith. "In terms you nonastrophysics types might use, one hell of a long way."

"Can we see the Milky Way from here?" asked Keith.

Jag made a gesture with his arms. "Oh, yes," he said, his barking still subdued. "Yes, indeed. Central Computer, magnify sector 112."

A border appeared around a portion of the holographic bubble. Jag left his workstation and walked toward it. He squinted for a moment, getting his bearings. "There," he said, pointing. "That one there. And that's Andromeda next to it. And this is M33, the third-largest member of the Local Group."

Rhombus's lights twinkled in confusion. "Boundless apologies, but that can't be right, good Jag. Those aren't spiral galaxies. They look more like disks."

"I'm not mistaken," said Jag. "That is the Milky Way. Since we are now six billion light-years from it, we are seeing it as it looked six billion years ago."

"Are you sure?" said Keith.

"I am positive. Once the pulsars had told me approximately where to look, it was easy enough to identify which galaxy was the Milky Way, which was Andromeda, and so on. The Magellanic Clouds are too young for any light from them to have reached this far out, but globular clusters contain almost exclusively ancient first-generation stars, and I've identified several specific globulars associated with both the Milky Way and Andromeda. I am sure of it—that simple disk of star is our home galaxy."

"But the Milky Way has spiral arms," said Lianne.

Jag turned to her. "Yes, without question, the Milky Way today has spiral arms. And, just as surely, I can now say that when it was six billion years younger, it did *not* have spiral arms."

"How can that be?" asked Thor.

"That," said Jag, "is a vexing question. I confess that I would have expected a Milky Way even half its present age to still have arms."

"Okay," said Keith. "So the Milky Way gains spiral arms sometime in the interim."

"No, it is *not* okay," said Jag, his bark returning to its usual sharpness. "In fact, it has *never* made any sense. We've never had a good model for galactic spiral-arm formation. Most models are based on differential rotation—the fact that stars near the galactic center make several orbits around the core in the time it takes for those farther out to complete just one. But any arms that resulted because of that should be temporary phenomena, enduring at most for a billion years. Oh, we should see *some* spiral galaxies, but there is no way that three out of every four large galaxies should be spirals—which is the ratio we actually observe. Ellipticals should far outnumber spirals, but they do not."

"Obviously, then, there's a flaw with the theory," said Keith.

Jag lifted his upper shoulders. "Indeed. We astrophysics types have been limping by for centuries with something called 'the density-wave model' for explaining the abundance of spiral galaxies. It proposes a spiral-shaped disturbance that moves through the medium of a galactic disk, with stars getting caught up in it—or even being formed by it—as the wave rotates. But it has *never* been a satisfactory theory. First, it fails to account for all the different types of spiral forms, and, second, we don't have a good answer as to what would cause these imagined density waves in the first place. Supernova explosions are sometimes cited, but it's just as easy to model such explosions canceling each other out as it is to get them to build up long-duration waves." He paused. "We've had other problems with our galaxy-formation models, too. Back in 1995, human astronomers discovered that distant galaxies, observed when they were only twenty percent of the current age of the universe, had rotational rates comparable to what the Milky Way has today—that's twice as fast as they should have been rotating at that age, according to theory."

Keith thought for a second. "But if what we're seeing right now is correct, then spiral galaxies like ours must somehow form from simple disks, right?"

Another lift of the Waldahud's upper shoulders. "Perhaps. Your Edwin Hubble proposed that galaxies each start as a simple sphere of stars, gradually spin out into a flat disk, then develop arms that open up more and more over time. But although we now have observational proof that that sort of evolution does indeed happen"—he gestured at the disk of stars in the glowing frame—"we still don't have an explanation for *why* the evolution takes place, or why the spiral structures persist."

"But you say three quarters of all large galaxies are spirals?" asked Lianne.

"Wellll," said Jag, PHANTOM translating a hissing bark as a protracted word, "actually, we don't know much directly about the ratio of elliptical to nonelliptical galaxies in the universe at large. It's hard to make out structure in dim objects that are billions of light-years away. Locally, we see that there are many more spirals than there are ellipticals, and that spirals contain a preponderance of young blue stars, whereas our local ellipticals contain mostly old red stars. We've assumed, therefore, that any vastly distant galaxy that showed lots of blue light—after correcting for redshift, of course—was a spiral, and any that showed mostly red was an elliptical, but we really don't know that for sure."

"It's incredible," said Lianne, looking at the image. "So—so if that's how it looked six billion years ago, then none of the Commonwealth homeworlds yet exists, right? Is there—do you suppose there's any life in the galaxy now?"

"Well, 'now' is still 'now,' of course," said Jag. "But if you're asking if there was any life in the Milky Way back when that light started its journey to us, I would say no. Galactic cores are very radioactive—even more so than we used to think. In a large elliptical galaxy, such as we're seeing here, the whole galaxy is essentially the core. With stars that close together, there would be so much hard radiation everywhere that stable genetic molecules wouldn't be able to form." He paused. "I guess that means it's only middle-aged galaxies that can give rise to life; young, armless ones will be sterile."

There was silence on the bridge for a time, broken only by the gentle hiss from the air-circulating equipment and the occasional soft beep from a control panel. Each person contemplated the small fuzzy blot of light that one day would give rise to all of them, contemplated the fact that they were farther out in space than anyone had ever been before, contemplated the vastly empty darkness all around them.

Six billion light-years.

Keith remembered reading about Borman, Lovell, and Anders, the *Apollo 8* astronauts who had circled the moon over Christmas of 1968, reading passages from *Genesis* back to the people on Earth. They had been the first human beings to get far enough from the homeworld so that they could cup it in an outstretched hand. Maybe more than any other single event, that view, that perspective, that image, had marked childhood's end for humanity—the realization that all their world was one tiny ball floating against the night.

And now, thought Keith, maybe—just maybe—*this* image was the one that marked the beginning of middle age: a still frame that would become the frontispiece of volume two of humanity's biography. It wasn't just Earth that was tiny, insignificant, and fragile. Keith lifted his hand and reached out toward the hologram, cupping the island of stars in his fingers. He sat silently for a long moment, then lowered his hand, and allowed his eyes to wander over the overwhelming dark emptiness that spread out in all directions. His gaze happened to pass over Jag—who was doing exactly what Keith had done a moment ago, using one of his hands to cup the Milky Way.

"Excuse me, Keith," said Lianne, the first words spoken by anyone on the bridge for several minutes. Her voice was soft, subdued, the way one would talk in a cathedral. "The electrical system is repaired. We can launch that probe anytime you like."

Keith nodded slowly. "Thank you," he said, his voice wistful. He looked once more at the young Milky Way floating in the darkness, and then said softly, "Rhombus, let's have a look at what's going on back home."

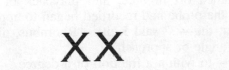

# XX

"Launching probe," said Rhombus.

In the holo bubble, Keith could see the silver-and-green cylinder moving away from the ship, illuminated by a tracking searchlight on *Starplex*'s hull. It looked out of place against the fuzzy splotches of distant galaxies. Soon the probe touched the shortcut and disappeared.

"The run should only take about five minutes," said Rhombus.

Keith nodded, trying to contain himself. He didn't know which he wanted more: to have the probe report that it had detected Rissa's transponder—meaning the *Rum Runner* was at least still intact—or for it to report nothing, meaning the probeship *might* have made it through the shortcut to safety.

Time passed, and Keith's nervousness grew. A watched pot never boils, but . . .

He looked up at the trio of clocks floating in space above the hidden port-side door. "How long has it been?"

"Seven minutes," said Rhombus.

"Shouldn't your probe be back by now?"

Lights moved up the Ib's web.

"Then where the hell—"

"Tachyon pulse!" announced Rhombus. "Here it comes."

"Don't wait until it's docked," said Keith. "Download the data by radio and display it."

"Doing so with delight," said Rhombus. "Here we go."

The probe's scan was low resolution, and video, rather than holographic. A part of the all-encompassing bubble was framed off in blue, and playback of the flatscreen images the probe had recorded began to appear.

"What the—?" said Keith. "Rhombus, did you use the correct angle of approach?"

"Yes—to within a fraction of a degree."

Jag said a Waldahudar swear word. By default, PHANTOM didn't translate profanity, but Keith felt like swearing himself. "That's not where we came from," he said.

Jag's fur was motionless. "No," he said. The image in the screen showed tightly packed red stars. "At a guess, I'd say it's not even anywhere in the Milky Way. That looks like the inside of a globular cluster. There are dozens associated with CGC 1008, so it might even be one of those."

"Which means—"

"Which means," said Thor, lifting his hands from the helm console, "that we can't go home. We don't have the correct address."

"The latitude/longitude coordinate system must not work the same way over such great distances," said Lianne.

Keith's voice was small. "Even at full hyperdrive—"

Jag snorted. "Even at full hyperdrive, to cover six billion light-years would take two hundred and seventy million years."

"All right," said Keith. "We'll try sending probes through in a search pattern. Rhombus, start by piercing the tachyon sphere around the shortcut at the north pole, then work your way down, trying again at every five degrees of latitude and five degrees of longitude. Maybe, if we're really lucky, we'll see something we recognize in the scans they bring back."

Rhombus began launching probes, but it soon became apparent that they were all going to either the globular cluster, or to another region of space where the sky was dominated by a ring-shaped nebula.

"From the point of view of this shortcut," said Rhombus, "there are only two other active shortcuts. I suppose that means we're lucky our initial probe came back to us—it only had a one-in-two chance of doing so."

"Not much of a choice, is it?" said Keith. "Here on the periphery of a black hole in intergalactic space; off in a globular cluster—presumably full of old, lifeless stars; or over to that ring nebula."

"No," said Jag.

"No what?"

"No, we cannot be limited to those choices."

Keith let out a sigh of relief. "Good. Why not?"

"Because the God of Alluvial Deposits is my patron," said the Waldahud. "She would not abandon me."

Keith felt his heart sink. He stopped himself before he snapped out something nasty.

"There *has* to be a way back," said Jag. "We came here, and therefore we must be able to return. If only we—"

"Speed!" shouted Lianne.

Keith looked at her.

"Speed!" she said. "We went through the shortcut at very high speed. Perhaps the velocity range at which you enter a shortcut selects which other family of shortcuts you have access to. We've always previously done it at very low relative velocities in order to avoid impacts. After all, one does go through a shortcut blind, not knowing for sure what's on the other side. But this time, we whipped into it at substantial fraction of light-speed. We may have keyed into another level of shortcuts by doing so."

Keith turned to Jag. He lifted all four shoulders. "It's as good an explanation as any."

"Rhombus, launch another probe," said Keith. "Put it on

a long trajectory that will let it accelerate to the same speed we were at when we passed through the shortcut, and aim for the exact latitude and longitude that corresponds to where we came from."

"Doing so with transcendent joy," said the Ib.

The probe was launched, built up speed, pierced the shortcut. They all held their breaths. Even Rhombus's pump, which operated without guidance from the pod, apparently sensed that something important was happening. Its central orifice temporarily halted its constant sequence of open, stretch, compress, and close.

And then the probe returned. Rhombus's ropes whipped his console, making loud slapping sounds as they did so, and the framed-off area filled with the probe's recorded images.

Thor was grinning from ear to ear. "I never thought I'd be glad to see that thing again," he said, jerking a thumb at the image of the green star.

Keith breathed a long sigh of relief. "Thank—thank the God of Alluvial Deposits."

"According to the probe's hyperscope, the darmats have moved well away from the exit point," said Rhombus.

"Excellent. Thor, take us home. Execute the course we discussed earlier. I want to have a word with Cat's Eye."

# XXI

*Starplex* moved through the intergalactic abyss toward the shortcut. The ship—seeming minuscule amidst all the emptiness—gathered speed as it approached, Thor revving up the thrusters. When it touched the shortcut, a ring of violet fire passed over the vessel as it traversed six billion light-years—60,000,000,000,000,000,000,000,000 kilometers—in the blink of an eye. There was a spontaneous cheer from those on the bridge as the holographic bubble was filled again with countless stars. Keith felt his eyes stinging, the way they had the last time he'd returned to Earth.

Thor immediately began making manual adjustments; they hadn't been monitoring the green star long enough to know its exact trajectory away from the shortcut, and his guess of where it would be was somewhat off. He soon had the ship settled into the parabolic course Keith wanted—a much wider parabola than their previous passing, avoiding any dangerous proximity to the green star, which now once again dominated the holo bubble.

"Scan for the *Rum Runner*'s transponder," said Keith.

"Doing so," said Lianne. But then, a moment later, "I'm sorry, Keith. There's nothing."

Keith closed his eyes. She *could* be safe, he told himself, she could have gone through to another exit, she could—

"Tachyon pulse!" said Rhombus in what PHANTOM translated as a shout.

Keith swiveled around to look at the shortcut, now swelling into a purple-limned shape—in the exact cross-sectional outline of a Commonwealth probeship.

"It's the *Rum Runner*!" crowed Thor.

"Incoming signal," said Lianne. She touched keys and a hologram of Rissa's beaming face appeared inside a floating frame.

"Hello, everyone," said Rissa. "Fancy meeting you here."

"Rissa!" said Keith, rising to his feet.

"Hello, darling," said Rissa, smiling radiantly.

"Rhombus," said Keith, "can they dock with us, given the course we're on?"

"They can if I give them a tow with a tractor beam."

Keith was grinning widely. "Please do so!"

"Okay, guys," said Rhombus, "prepare to be grabbed by a tractor."

Longbottle's gray face popped up next to Rissa's. "Prepared are we! Home we come!"

"Locking on," said Thor.

"Thor," said Keith, "do you have a fix on Cat's Eye?"

"Yes. He's about ten million klicks ahead, at about nine o'clock to the green star."

"I've located a vacant frequency in the darmat babble, in case you want to talk to him," said Lianne. "Somebody must have left the conversation recently."

"Excellent," said Keith. "Keep track of it. As soon as Rissa's back on board, I'll want to open communication."

"We'll have the *Rum Runner* in docking bay seven in about three minutes," said Rhombus.

Keith was anxious as hell. He tried to hide it by checking

status reports on his monitor screens, but his mind wasn't registering the words. At last, the starfield split and Rissa appeared, framed by the corridor beyond. Keith ran to her, and they hugged, then kissed. The rest of the bridge crew cheered as she entered. A moment later, Longbottle popped up in one of the two open pools. Rissa knelt down beside him and rubbed his bulging forehead. "Thanks for getting us home safe and sound, buddy," she said.

"We're doing a quick parabolic path," Keith said to them. "I don't think the darmats can grab us this time, but I want to communicate with them—find out why in the hell they attacked us."

Rissa nodded, stood up, kissed Keith once more, then moved over to her workstation. She pressed keys, calling up the translation program.

"Do we still have a vacant frequency?" asked Keith.

"Yes," said Lianne.

"All right. Let's jump into the conversation. Lianne, open a channel from my console with automatic translation, but put a five-second delay in before you send whatever I say." He looked at Rissa. "I'll speak directly to Cat's Eye, but if I say anything wrong or something that you don't think will translate properly, jump in, and we'll reword the message before it goes out."

Rissa nodded.

"Ready," said Lianne.

"*Starplex* to Cat's Eye," said Keith. "*Starplex* to Cat's Eye. We are friends. We are friends." Keith glanced at a counter. At light-speed, it would still be thirty-five seconds before the message reached Cat's Eye, and almost that long again before any reply would arrive.

But no reply came. Keith waited an extra full minute, then another. He touched a key and tried again. "We are friends."

Finally, after a forty-second delay in addition to the round-trip signal time, a reply came through. Just two words, in a curt French accent: "Not friends."

"Yes," said Keith. "We are friends."

"Friends not hurt," came the reply, with no delay beyond that caused by transmission times.

Keith was taken aback. Had they somehow hurt the darmats? It was almost inconceivable that they could injure such giant creatures. Still . . . perhaps the sampling probes had caused pain. Keith didn't have the slightest idea how to apologize; the vocabulary Rissa had built up didn't deal with such concepts.

"We did not mean to hurt you," said Keith.

"Not directly," said Cat's Eye.

Keith spread his hands and looked around the bridge. "Anybody understand that?"

"I think he means whatever injury we caused wasn't a direct injury," said Lianne. "We didn't hurt them, but hurt—or were going to hurt—something that was important to them."

Keith touched the transmit key. "We intend no injury to anything. But you—you deliberately tried to kill us."

"Make you. Not make you."

Keith keyed the mike off. "'Make you. Not make you,'" he repeated, shrugging helplessly. "Anybody?"

Lianne lifted her hands, palms up. Jag moved all four of his shoulders. Rhombus's web was dark.

Keith reactivated the mike. "We want to be friends again."

The response time was getting shorter as *Starplex*'s parabolic course brought the ship closer to Cat's Eye. "We want to be friends again, too," said the darmat.

Keith thought for a moment, then: "You say we injured you somehow. We did not intend any injury. So that we don't do it again, will you tell us what we did wrong?"

The delay time was nerve-racking. Finally: "Attacking each other."

"You were bothered by the battle?" asked Keith.

"Yes."

"Worried that explosions would hurt you?"

"No."

"But then why did you fling those ships into the star?"

"Afraid."

"Of what?"

"That your activities would destroy . . . destroy . . . point that is not a point."

"The shortcut? You were afraid that we would destroy the shortcut?"

"Yes."

"No explosion could damage the shortcut. It's not fragile."

"Did not know."

Jag barked softly. "Ask him why he cares."

Keith nodded. "Why do you care about the shortcut, anyway? Do you use it yourselves?"

"Use? No. Not use."

"Then why?"

"Spawn."

"They're important to your spawning practices?"

"No, one of our spawn," said the voice from the speaker.

It was frustrating—and probably as much so for the darmat as it was for Keith. Cat's Eye was used to being part of a community whose members had been talking among themselves for millennia. They understood the context of each other's remarks, the history. Explicating a thought in detail was not normal for them—and possibly even rude. "One of your spawn," Keith said again, helpfully.

"Yes. Touched the point that is not a point."

Oh, my God. "You mean one of your youngsters went through the shortcut?"

"Yes. Lost."

"Christ," said Thor, turning around. "That's what activated this shortcut—a darmat baby going through!"

Keith leaned back in his chair. "And if our fighting had accidentally destroyed the shortcut, your child would never have been able to find its way home again, right?"

"Rightness abounds. When you first arrived, we thought you had come to bring our spawn home."

"You never asked us about that."

"Wrong to ask."

"Darmat bad manners," said Rissa, eyebrows raised.

Keith spread his arms. "We didn't know about your child. How long ago did it go through the shortcut?"

"Time since you first arrived, doubled."

Keith turned to his left, looking at Jag. "The child couldn't have gone far from the exit point, then. Any way of knowing which shortcut it would have come out from?"

"Well," said Jag, "the child must have emerged through an already active exit. But, as we found when we went careening through this shortcut ourselves, there are more active exits than we were aware of—possibly trillions more, if they permeate intergalactic space and other galaxies. And, since the shortcuts rotate, without knowing to the second what time the child went through, even duplicating the approach angle wouldn't help us. The thing could be anywhere."

"But if we could find the child and bring it safely home," said Keith, "well, not only would that be the right thing to do, it would also help cement our relationships with the darmats." He looked around the bridge. "Anyone disagree?" He turned the mike back on. "Does the child have a name? A unique identifying word?"

"Yes. It is"—PHANTOM's own voice replaced the synthesized one coming through the speaker—"untranslated term."

Keith gestured at PHANTOM's eyes. "Call it—call it Junior," he said.

"Acknowledged."

Keith looked over at Rhombus, who could see Keith clearly, of course, even though his backside was to him. "Rhombus, what do you think?"

"It could be a very steep slope that ends in a cliff," he said—a wild-goose chase. "But, as you have said, establishing friendly relationships is what *Starplex* is all about. I say we at least try."

"Should we ask one of them to come with us?" asked Lianne.

"There is no way we could go through the shortcut together," said Thor, turning to face her. "Remember, even the smallest of those beings masses as much as Jupiter. And without precisely controlling its entrance angle, the darmat might end up coming out of a different shortcut, meaning we'd have two lost darmats, instead of one."

Keith reactivated the mike. "We will look for your child," he said. "Would you please call out to it? We will record that, and play it back at each possible place it might be. Call out to it, and ask it to come with us. Tell it that we will not hurt it, and that we only want to guide it home."

"Record?"

"Like an oral history; we will repeat it."

"Doing," said the voice from the speaker. Keith let the entreaties spill into PHANTOM's memory.

"We have it," said Keith, once Cat's Eye stopped transmitting.

"Find our child," said Cat's Eye. "I—words unavailable."

The translation exercises hadn't covered this topic. But Keith understood across species lines—across *matter* lines. He nodded.

# XXII

Keith was in his office, going over proposals for finding the darmat baby. It was the first of the month; the holo on his desk of Rissa had automatically changed to a pose of her in shorts and tank top, taken during a hike through the Grand Canyon. The Emily Carr painting had switched to an A. Y. Jackson view of Lake Superior.

"Jag Kandaro em-Pelsh is here," announced PHANTOM.

Keith spoke without looking up from the datapad he was reading. "Let him in."

Jag entered and helped himself to a chair. He had all four arms crossed in front of his massive chest. "I want to go get the darmat child," he barked.

Keith leaned back in his chair and looked at the Waldahud. "You?"

Jag's dental plates clicked together defiantly. "I."

Keith breathed out slowly, using the time it took to complete the exhalation to gather his thoughts. "This is a delicate mission."

"And you do not trust me anymore," said Jag. He moved his upper shoulders. "I realize that. But the attack on *Starplex* was not authorized by Queen Trath. And the attack on Tau Ceti that Rissa has told us about was repulsed. Matters are at an end right now—unless you humans wish to prolong them. Where do we go from here, Lansing? Is it over? Or do we go on fighting? I am prepared to act as if—"

"As if nothing had happened?"

"The alternative is war. I do not want that, and I had believed you did not want it, either."

"But—"

Jag's barks were sharp. "The choice is yours. I have volunteered a peaceful coexistence. If you want your—what is the human metaphor?—your pound of flesh, I refuse to grant it. But finding the child and getting it home will require the utmost skill in shortcut mechanics. Magnor is good at such matters, but I am better. Indeed, there is no one better in all the Commonwealth. You know this to be true; if it were not, I would not be assigned to this ship."

"Thor is trustworthy," said Keith simply.

The Waldahud's two right eyes were already locked on Lansing, and a moment later the two left ones converged on him as well. "The choice is yours. You have my report." He gestured at the datapad Keith was still holding. "I have suggested we send a probeship to find the child. I should be on that ship."

"All you want," said Keith, "is access to the darmats for your people. Bringing home their child would earn you much gratitude."

Jag moved his lower shoulders. "You do me a disservice, Lansing. Indeed, the darmats do not yet know that there are a thousand entities aboard this ship, let alone that they represent a quarter-sixteen of races."

Keith thought for a moment. Damn, he hated being pushed. But the bloody pi—but Jag was right. "Okay," he said. "Okay—you and Longbottle, if he's up to it. Is the *Rum Runner* in any condition for another mission?"

"Dr. Cervantes and Longbottle had it serviced at Grand

Central," said the Waldahud. "Rhombus has confirmed that it is spaceworthy."

Keith looked up. "Intercom: Keith to Thor."

A hologram of Thorald Magnor's head appeared floating above Keith's desk. "Yes, boss?"

"How are we for travel through the shortcut?"

"No probs," said Thor. "The green star is far enough from it now to allow just about any entrance angle. You want me to program a run?"

Keith shook his head. "Not for the whole ship. Just for the *Rum Runner* and a one-person travel pod. I'm going to have to return to Grand Central for a meeting with Premier Kenyatta." He looked back at the Waldahud. "Despite what you just said, Jag, there's going to be hell to pay."

It was the ultimate grand tour: around the galaxy in twenty shortcuts—a quick survey of all the active exit points. The *Rum Runner,* with Jag and Longbottle aboard, zoomed away from *Starplex*'s docks and, after Longbottle's requisite joyride, headed for the shortcut.

As always, the exit point expanded as the ship touched it. The purple discontinuity moved from bow to stern, and then the ship was zooming through a different sector of space. There were no spectacular sights to be seen at this first exit: just stars, somewhat less densely packed than they had been on the other side.

Jag was intent on his instruments. He was doing a hyperspace scan, looking for any large mass within a light-day of the exit. Finding the darmat child would be hard. Dark matter, by its very nature, was very difficult to detect—all but invisible, and the radio signals it put out where very weak indeed. But even a baby darmat was going to mass $10^{37}$ kilograms. It would make a dent in local spacetime that should be detectable in hyperspace.

"Anything?" asked Longbottle.

Jag moved his lower shoulders.

Longbottle arched in his tank, and the *Rum Runner* curved back toward the shortcut.

"Again we go," said the dolphin. The ship dived toward the point—

—and popped out near a beautiful binary star system, streamers of gas flowing from a bloated, oblate red giant toward a tiny blue companion.

Jag consulted his instruments. Nothing. The *Rum Runner* did a loop-the-loop and came down upon the shortcut from above, diving through, a burst of Soderstrom radiation washing over the ship, the spectacle of the binary pair being replaced by a new starscape, with a great yellow-and-pink nebula covering half the sky, a pulsar at its heart cycling dim and bright over a period of a few seconds.

"Nothing," said Jag.

Longbottle arched again, and plunged toward the shortcut.

An expanding point.

A ring of purple.

Mismatched starfields.

Another sector of space.

A sector dominated by another green star pulling away from the shortcut. Longbottle maneuvered furiously to avoid it.

Jag's scan took longer; the nearby star overwhelmed the hyperspace scanner. But, finally, he determined the darmat child was not there.

Longbottle rotated in his tank, and the *Rum Runner* did a corkscrew flight back into the shortcut. When they popped out this time, it was through Shortcut Prime, near the galactic core, the initial shortcut that had presumably been activated by the shortcut makers themselves. The sky blazed with the light of countless tightly packed red suns. Longbottle nosed a control, and the ship's shields increased to maximum. They were close enough to the heart of the galaxy to see the coruscating edge of the violet accretion disk surrounding the central black hole.

"Not here," said Jag.

Longbottle maneuvered the ship back to the shortcut in a simple straight line. They hadn't been close enough to be caught by the singularity's ravenous gravity, but he was taking no chances.

They next exited into another seemingly empty region of space, but Jag's hyperspace scanners indicated the presence of substantial concealed mass.

"Suppose not do you?" asked Longbottle.

Jag shrugged all four shoulders. "It couldn't hurt to check," he said, adjusting the shipboard radio to search near the twenty-one-centimeter band.

"Ninety-three separate frequencies currently in use," said Jag. "Another community of darmats."

They were tens of thousands of light-years from the first darmats they had encountered, but, then again, the darmat race was billions of years old. It was possible that they all spoke the same language. Jag scanned the cacophony, found the topmost frequency group, and, since there were no vacancies, transmitted just above it. "We are looking for one called Junior"—the ship's computer substituted the baby's real name.

There was silence for a lot longer than round-trip message time would require, but then, finally, a reply did come through.

"No one here by that name. Who are you?"

"No time to chat—but we'll be back," said Jag, and Longbottle turned the ship back toward the shortcut.

"Bet surprised them that did," said the dolphin as they passed through the gateway.

This time they emerged near a planet about the size of Mars, and just as dry, but yellow rather than red. Its sun, a blue-white star, was visible in the distance, about twice the apparent diameter of Sol as seen from Earth. "Nothing here," said Jag.

Longbottle allowed himself the luxury of moving the *Rum Runner* in such a way that the bulk of the yellow planet precisely eclipsed the star. The corona—mixing purple and navy and white—was gorgeous, and covered much more of the sky than the dolphin had expected. He and Jag basked in the sight for a moment, then they dived back through the shortcut.

This exit point had also recently had a star emerge from it, but it wasn't green. Rather, as at Tau Ceti, this one was a red dwarf, small and cool.

Jag consulted his scanners. "Nothing."

They dived through again, the shortcut opening like a purple-lipsticked mouth to accommodate them.

Pure blackness—no stars at all.

"A dust cloud," said Jag, his fur dancing in surprise. "Interesting—it wasn't here the last time anyone went through to this exit. Carbon grains mostly, although there are some complex molecules, too, including formaldehyde and even some amino acids, and—Cervantes will want to return here, I think. I'm picking up DNA."

"In the cloud?" asked Longbottle, incredulous.

"In the cloud," said Jag. "Self-replicating molecules floating free in space."

"But no darmat, correct?"

"Correct," said Jag.

"A wonder for another time," said Longbottle, and he spun the ship around, fired retros, and headed back through the shortcut.

A new sector of space—another one that had recently had a star erupt from it. This time the intruder was a blue type-O, with more purple sunspots than a fair-haired human had freckles in summer. The *Rum Runner* had emerged right on the edge of one of the Milky Way's spiral arms. To one side, the sky was thick with bright young stars; to the other, they were sparse. Overhead, a globular cluster was visible, a million ancient red suns packed together into a ball. And—

"Bingo," said Jag—or, at least, he barked something that would be translated as that in English. "There it is!"

"See do I," agreed Longbottle. "But . . ."

"Parched land!" swore Jag. "It's trapped."

"Agree—caught in the net."

And indeed it was. The baby darmat had obviously stumbled out of the shortcut only a few days before this blue star had arrived, and the star had been expelled from the exit in approximately the same direction as the darmat. As they'd all discovered to their shock, a darmat could move with surprising agility for a free-floating world, but the gravity of a star was enormous. The baby was only forty million kilometers from its surface—less than Mercury's distance from Sol.

"There is no way it can manage escape velocity," said Jag. "I'm not even sure it's managed to settle into orbit; it may be spiraling in. Either way, though, that darmat is not going anywhere."

"Will signal," said Longbottle—and he set the ship's transmitter to broadcast the prerecorded message on all the frequencies that the members of the darmat community had used.

They were about three hundred million kilometers from the star; the signals took over fifteen minutes to reach the darmat, and the quickest any reply could be received would be another fifteen minutes after that. They waited, Jag fidgeting, Longbottle amusing himself by painting a sonar caricature of Jag as he fidgeted. But no reply was received.

"Well," said the Waldahud, "there's so much radio noise coming from the star, we might not be able to pick up the darmat's transmission. Or it might not be able to hear us."

"Or," said Longbottle, "darmat may be dead."

Jag made a noise like bubble wrap being burst, his snout vibrating as he did so. That was the one possibility he didn't want to consider. But the heat that close to the star would be incredible. The side of the darmat facing it might be over 350 degrees Celsius, hot enough to melt lead. Neither Jag nor Delacorte had yet worked out all the particulars of luster-quark meta-chemistry, but many normal complex molecules broke down when heated that high.

Another thought occurred to Jag. What, if any, funereal customs would the darmats have? Would they want this world-sized corpse brought home? He glanced at Longbottle. Dolphins just let the body float away when one of their own died. Jag hoped the darmats would be equally sensible.

"Let's head back," said Jag. "There's nothing we can do on our own."

The *Rum Runner* zoomed toward the shortcut in one of Longbottle's patented sweeping curves, hitting the point at the precise angle required to exit where they'd started all those jumps ago. *Starplex* was there, floating against the night, tinged green by the light of the fourth-generation star. Beyond it were the dark-matter beings, tendrils of gas stretching between them. The question now was what to do next. For one brief moment, Jag sympathized with Lansing. He wouldn't want to swim the choppy waters of the river that now spread out before the human.

Keith was in his apartment, preparing to leave for his upcoming meeting with Premier Kenyatta at Grand Central Station.

An electric bleep sounded. "Rhombus would like to see

you," announced PHANTOM. "He requests seven minutes of your time."

Rhombus? Here? Keith really felt like being alone just now. He was marshaling his thoughts, trying to decide what to say in the meeting. Still, having an Ib disturb him at home was unusual enough to pique his curiosity. "The time is granted," said Keith—the appropriate answer dictated by Ibese manners.

PHANTOM again: "Since you are going to have an Ib visitor, may I dim the lights?"

Keith nodded. The ceiling panels decreased their intensity, and the glaring white glacier in the wall hologram of Lake Louise turned a muted gray. The double-pocket door slid aside and Rhombus rolled in. Lights flashed on his web. "Hello, Keith."

"Hello, Rhombus. What can I do for you?"

"Forgive me for intruding," said the pleasant British voice, "but you were quite angry on the bridge today."

Keith frowned. "Sorry if I was harsh," said Keith. "I'm furious with Jag—but I shouldn't have taken it out on anyone else."

"Oh, your anger seemed quite focused. I doubt you gave offense."

Keith lifted his eyebrows. "Then what's the problem?"

Rhombus was quiet for a moment, then: "Have you ever wondered about the apparent contradiction my race represents? We are obsessed, you humans say, with time. We hate to waste it. But we nonetheless spend time on being polite, and, as many humans have noted, we take pains not to hurt feelings."

Keith nodded. "I've wondered about that. Seems that wasting time on social niceties would take away from more important tasks."

"Precisely," said Rhombus. "Precisely the way a human would see it. But we do not perceive it that way at all. We see getting along as going—well, our metaphor is 'hub in wheel,' but you'd say 'hand in hand'—with a philosophy of not wasting time. A brief but unpleasant meeting ends up squandering more time than a longer but agreeable one."

"Why?"

"Because after an unpleasant encounter, one spends much time going over the meeting in one's mind, replaying it again and again, often seething over the things that were said or done." He paused. "You've seen with Boxcar that under Ibese jurisprudence, we punish direct wastings of time. If an Ib wastes ten minutes of my time, the courts may order that Ib's life shortened by ten minutes. But did you know that if an Ib upsets me through rudeness or ingratitude or deliberate maliciousness, the courts may impose a penalty of *sixteen* times the amount of time apparently wasted over the issue? We use a multiple of sixteen simply because, like the Waldahudin, that number is the base for our system of counting; there really is no way to quantify the time actually wasted mulling over an unpleasant experience. Years later, painful memories can—again, metaphors fail me. I would say 'roll up beside you'; you'd probably say 'rear their ugly head.' It is always better to leave a situation on pleasant terms, without rancor."

"You're saying we should really put the screws to the Waldahudin? Get back sixteen times what they did to us in damages?" Keith nodded. "That certainly makes sense."

"No, you miss my meaning—doubtless due to my lack of clarity in expressing it. I'm saying *forget* about what has transpired between you and Jag, and between Earth and Rehbollo. I despair over how much of your mental resources—how much of your *time*—you humans will waste over these issues. No matter how bumpy the terrain, smooth it in your mind." Rhombus paused for a moment, letting this sink in, then: "Well, I've used the seven minutes you granted me; I should leave now." The Ib began to roll away.

"People have died," said Keith, raising his voice. "It's not that easy to smooth it all out."

Rhombus stopped. "If it is difficult, it is only because you choose for it to be that way," he said. "Can you foresee any solution that will bring the dead back to life? Any reprisals that won't result in more people dead?" Lights played across his web. "Let it go."

# ETA DRACONIS

*Glass looked at Keith, and Keith looked at Glass. Something in the being's manner told Keith this would be their final conversation.*

*"You mentioned during your introductory speech that your Commonwealth currently consists of three home-worlds," said Glass.*

*Keith nodded. "That's right," he said. "Earth, Rehbollo, and Flatland."*

*Glass tipped his head. "There are, in fact, only seven thousand worlds with native life on them in this entire universe at your time—and those few worlds are spread out over all the billions of galaxies. The Milky Way has far more than its fair share: during your time, there are a total of thirteen intelligent races within it."*

*"I'll keep score," said Keith, smiling. "I won't give up until we've found them all."*

*Glass shook his head. "You will find them eventually, of*

*course—when they're ready to be found. The shortcuts'
facilitating of interstellar travel isn't just a side effect of
their shunting stars back to the past. Rather, it's an integral
part of the plan. But so is the safety valve that keeps sectors
of space isolated until their native inhabitants become
starfarers on their own. Of course, if you have the appropriate key, as I do, you can travel between any shortcuts,
even apparently dormant ones. That's important, too, because we shortcut makers will need to make extensive use of
them. But the way they work without the key is designed to
foster an interstellar community, to give rise to the kind of
peaceful and cooperative future that's in everyone's interest." Glass paused, and when he resumed speaking, his tone
was a little sad. "Still, you won't be able to keep score of
how many races you have yet to discover. When I send you
back, I will wipe your memories of the time you've spent
here."*

Keith's heart fluttered. "Don't do that."

"I'm afraid I must. We have an isolation policy."

"Do you—do you do this often? Grab people from the
past?"

"Not as a rule, no, but, well, you're a special case. I'm
a special case."

"In what way?"

"I was one of the first people to become immortal."

"Immortal . . ." Keith's voice trailed off.

"Didn't I mention that? Oh, yes. You're not just going to
live for a very long time—you're going to live forever."

"Immortal," said Keith again. He tried to think of a
better word, but couldn't, and so simply said, "Wow."

"But, as I said, you—I—we are a special case of
immortality."

"How so?"

"There are, in fact, only three older human beings than
me in the entire universe. Apparently, I had a—what do you
call it?—an 'in' that got me the immortality treatments
early on."

"Rissa was working on senescence research; I assume

*she ended up being codeveloper of the immortality tech-
nique."*

"Ah, that must have been it," said Glass.

"You don't remember?"

"No—and that's the whole problem. You see, when they
first invented immortality, it worked by allowing cells to
divide an infinite number of times, instead of succumbing to
preprogrammed cell death."

"The Hayflick limit," said Keith, having learned all
about it in conversations with Rissa.

"Pardon?"

"The Hayflick limit. The phenomenon that limits the
number of times a cell can divide."

"Ah, yes," said Glass. "Well, they overcame that. And
they overcame the old, natural limitation that said you were
born with a finite quantity of brain cells, and that those cells
were not normally replaced. One of the keys to immortality
was to let the brain constantly create new cells as the old
ones wore out, so—"

"So if the cells are replaced," said Keith, eyes growing
wide, "then the memories stored by the original cells get
lost."

Glass nodded his smooth head. "Precisely. Of course,
now we offload old memories into lepton matrices. We can
remember an infinite amount of material. I don't just have
access to millions of books, I actually remember the
contents of millions of books that I've read over the years.
But I became an immortal before such offloading existed.
My early memories—everything from my first couple of
centuries of life—is gone."

"One of my best friends," said Keith, "is an Ib named
Rhombus. Ibs die when their early memories get wiped
out—new memories overwrite their basic autonomous routines, killing them."

Glass nodded. "There's a certain elegance to that," he
said. "It's very difficult to live without knowing who one is,
without remembering one's own past."

"That's why you were disappointed that I'm only forty-
six."

*"Exactly. It means there's still a century and a half of my life that you can't tell me about. Perhaps someday, I'll locate another version of me, from—what would that be?—from about the year 2250 in your calendar." He paused. "Still, you remember the most crucial parts. You remember my physical childhood, you remember my parents. Until I spoke to you, I wasn't even sure that I'd had biological parents. You remember my first love. All of that has been gone from me for so incredibly long. And yet, those experiences shaped how I behave, set down the patterns of my personality, the core neural nets of my mind, the fundamentals of who I am." Glass paused. "I have wondered for millennia why I act the way I do, why I sometimes torture myself with unpleasant thoughts, why I interact with others as a bridge-builder or a peace maker, why I internalize my feelings. And you have told me: I was once, long ago, an unhappy child, a middle child, a stoic child. There had been a horizon in my past, a curve beyond which I could not see. You have taken that away. What you have given me is beyond price." Glass paused, then his tone grew lighter. "I thank you from the bottom of my infinitely regenerating heart."*

*Keith laughed, like a yelping seal, and the other Keith laughed too, like wind chimes, and then they both laughed at the sound the other had made.*

*"I'm afraid it's time for you to go home," said Glass.*

*Keith nodded.*

*Glass was silent for a moment, then: "I have refrained from giving you advice, Keith. It is not my place to do so, and, frankly, there are ten billion years between us. We are, in many ways, different people. What is right for me, now, at this stage of life, may not be right for you. But I owe you—for what you have given me, I owe you enormously, and I would like to repay you with a small suggestion."*

*Keith tilted his head, waited.*

*Glass spread his transparent arms. "I have seen the ebb and tide of human sexual morality over the eons, Keith. I've seen sex given as freely as a smile, and I've seen it guarded as though it were more precious than peace. I've known people who have been celibate for a billion years, and I've know others have had more than a million partners. I've seen sex between members of different species from the same world, and between those who evolved on different worlds. Some people I know have removed their genitals altogether to avoid the issue of sex. Others have become true hermaphrodites, capable of procreative sex with themselves. Others still have switched genders—I have a friend who changes from male to female every thousand years, like clockwork. There have been times when humans have embraced homosexuality, and heterosexuality, and incest, and multiple concurrent spouses, and prostitution, and bestiality, and sadomasochism, and there have been times when all of those have been abjured. I have seen marriage contracts with expiration dates, and I have seen marriages last five billion years. And you, my friend, will live long enough to see all these things, too. But through all of it, there is one constant for people of conscience, for people like you and me: if you hurt someone you care about, there is guilt."*

*Glass dipped his head. "I do not remember Clarissa. I do not remember her at all. I have no idea what happened to her. If she, too, became an immortal, then perhaps she still exists, and perhaps I can find her. I have loved a thousand other humans over the years; a paltry number by many people's standards, but sufficient for me. But there is no doubt that Rissa must have been very, very special to us; that's apparent in the way you speak of her."*

*Glass paused, and Keith had the eerie feeling that eyes—invisible in that smooth transparent egg of a head—were seeking out his own, seeking the truth behind them. "I can read you, Keith. When you told me earlier to move along, to pick another topic, it was obvious what you were hiding, what you have been contemplating." A beat of silence; even the forest simulacrum around them held its peace. "Don't hurt her, Keith. You will only hurt yourself."*

*"That's the advice?" asked Keith.*

*Glass lifted his shoulders slightly. "That's it."*

*Keith was quiet for a time. Then: "How will I remember*

*that? You said you were going to wipe my memories of this meeting."*

*"I will leave that thought intact. You will indeed have no memory of me, and you'll just think it came from yourself— which, of course, it did, in a way."*

*Keith thought for a time about what the appropriate reply was. Finally, he said, "Thank you."*

*Glass nodded. And then, sadly, he said, "It's time for you to go."*

*There was an awkward moment during which they stood and looked at each other. Keith started to extend his hand, but then let it drop to his side. Then, after a second of hesitation, he surged forward, and hugged Glass. To his astonishment, the transparent man felt soft and warm. The embrace lasted only a few seconds.*

*"Perhaps someday we'll meet again," said Keith, taking a step back now. "If you ever feel like popping through to the twenty-first century for a visit . . ."*

*"Perhaps I will. We are about to start something very, very big here. I told you at the outset that the fate of the universe is in question, and I—meaning you, too, of course—have a key role to play in that. I gave up being a sociologist ages ago. As you might guess, I've had thousands of careers over the millennia, and now I'm a—a physicist, you might call it. My new work will eventually necessitate a trip to the past."*

*"Just remember our full name, for God's sake," said Keith. "I'm listed in the Commonwealth directory, but you'll never find me again if you forget."*

*"No," said Glass. "This time I promise I will not forget you, or the parts of our past you have shared with me." He paused. "Good-bye, my friend."*

*The forest simulation, along with its motionless sun, daytime moon, and four-leaf lucky clovers, melted away, revealing the cubic interior of the docking bay. Keith started walking toward his travel pod.*

*Glass stood motionless in the bay as it opened to space. More magic; he needed no space suit. Keith touched a key, and his pod moved out into the night, the six-fingered pink nebula that had once been Sol staining the sky on his left, the robin's-egg-blue dragon receding behind him. He flew the pod toward the invisible point of the shortcut, and as he made contact, he felt a faint itching inside his skull. He had just been thinking about—about something . . .*

*It was gone now, whatever it had been.*

*Oh, well. The ring of Soderstrom radiation passed over the pod from bow to stern, and Keith's view was filled with the sky of Tau Ceti, Grand Central Station visible off to his right, looking odd in the dim red light from the newly arrived dwarf star.*

*As he always did when he came here, Keith amused himself for a few seconds finding Boötes, then locating Sol. He nodded once and smiled. Always good to know that the old girl hadn't gone nova . . .*

# XXIII

Keith had always thought Grand Central Station looked like four dinner plates arranged in a square, but today, for some reason, it reminded him of a four-leaf clover floating against the stars. Each of the leaves or plates was a kilometer in diameter and eighty meters thick, making the station the largest manufactured structure in Commonwealth space. Like *Starplex*'s own much-smaller central disk, the outward facing edges of the plates were studded with docking-bay doors, many of them bearing the logos of Earth-based trading corporations. The computer aboard Keith's travel pod received docking instructions from Grand Central's traffic controller, and flew him in toward a docking ring adjacent to a large corrugated space door bearing the yellow-script symbol of the Hudson's Bay Company, now in its fifth century of operation.

Keith looked around through the travel pod's transparent hull. Dead ships were floating across the sky. Tugs were arriving at the docking bays hauling wreckage. One of the station's four plates was completely dark, as if it had taken a major hit during the battle.

Once his pod was secured, Keith exited into the station. Unlike *Starplex,* which was a Commonwealth facility, Grand Central belong entirely to the peoples of Earth, and its common environment was kept precisely at terrestrial standard.

A governmental aide was waiting to greet Keith. He had a broken arm. It likely occurred during the battle with the Waldahudin, since the bone-knitting web he had on would normally only be worn for seventy-two hours after the injury. The aide took him to the opulent office of Petra Kenyatta, Human Government Premier of Tau Ceti province.

Kenyatta, an African woman of about fifty, rose to great Keith. "Hello, Dr. Lansing," she said, extending her right hand.

Keith shook it. Her grip was firm, almost painfully so. "Ma'am."

"Please, have a seat."

"Thank you." No sooner had Keith sat down in the chair— a regular, nonmorphing human chair—than the door slid open again and another woman came in, this one Nordic in appearance and a little younger than Kenyatta.

"Do you know Commissioner Amundsen?" said the premier. "She's in charge of the United Nations police forces here at Tau Ceti."

Keith half rose from his chair. "Commissioner."

"Of course," said Amundsen, taking a seat herself, "'police forces' is a euphemism. We call it that for alien ears."

Keith felt his stomach knotting.

"Reinforcements are already on their way from Sol and Epsilon Indi," said Amundsen. "We'll be ready to move on Rehbollo as soon as they arrive."

"Move on Rehbollo?" said Keith, shocked.

"That's right," said the commissioner. "We're going to kick those bloody pigs halfway to Andromeda."

Keith shook his head. "But surely it's over. A sneak attack only works once. They're not going to be coming back."

"This way we make sure of that," said Kenyatta.

"The United Nations can't have agreed to this," said Keith.

"Not the United Nations, of course," said Amundsen. "Dolphins don't have the spine for something like this. But we're sure the HuGo will vote for it."

Keith turned to Kenyatta. "It would be a mistake to let this escalate, Premier. The Waldahudin know how to destroy a shortcut."

Amundsen's sapphire eyes went wide. "Say that again."

"They could cut us off from the rest of the galaxy—and they only need to get one ship through to Tau Ceti to do that."

"What's the technique?"

"I—I have no idea. But I'm assured it works."

"All the more reason to destroy them," said Kenyatta.

"How did they sneak up on you?" asked Commissioner Amundsen. "Here at Tau Ceti, they sent one large mothership through, and it disgorged fighters as soon as it arrived. I understand from what Dr. Cervantes said while she was here that they sent individual craft after *Starplex*. How was it that you didn't notice when the first one arrived?"

"The newly emerged star was between us and the shortcut."

"Who ordered the ship to take that position?" asked Amundsen.

Keith paused. "I did. I give all the orders aboard *Starplex*. We were engaged in astronomical research, and had to move the ship away from the shortcut to facilitate that. I take full responsibility."

"No need to worry," said Amundsen, grinning like a skull. "We'll make the pigs pay."

"Don't call them that," said Keith, surprising himself.

"What?"

"Don't call them that name. They are Waldahudin." He managed to say the word as a bark, with perfect accent and asperity.

Amundsen was taken aback. "Do you know what they call us?" she asked.

Keith shook his head slightly.

*"Gargtelkin,"* she said. "'Ones who copulate out of season.'"

Keith suppressed a grin. But then he sobered. "We can't go to war with them."

"They started it."

He thought of his older sister and younger brother. He thought of an old black-and-white movie with dueling anthems, the *Marseillaise* drowning out *Wacht am Rhein.* And he thought most of all of the sight of the young Milky Way, cupped in his outstretched hand.

"No," said Keith simply.

"What do you mean, 'no'?" snapped Amundsen. "They did start it."

"I mean it doesn't make any difference. None of it does. There are beings out there made of dark matter. There are shortcuts in intergalactic space. There are stars coming back from the future. And you're worried about who started it? It doesn't matter. Let's end it. Let's end it here and now."

"That's exactly what we're talking about," said Premier Kenyatta. "Ending it once and for all. Knocking the pigs on their hairy asses."

Keith shook his head. Midlife crisis—for all of them, humans and Waldahudin. "Let me go to Rehbollo. Let me talk to Queen Pelsh. I'm supposed to be a diplomat. Let me go and talk peace. Let me build a bridge."

"People have died," said Amundsen. "Here at Tau Ceti, humans beings have died."

Keith thought of Saul Ben-Abraham. Not the horrid picture that usually came to mind, Saul's skull opening like a red flower in front of his eyes, but rather Saul alive, great wide grin splitting his dark beard, a home-brewed beer in hand. Saul Ben-Abraham had never wanted war. He'd gone to the alien ship looking for peace, for friendship.

And what about the other Saul? Saul Lansing-Cervantes— unable to carry a tune, sporting a silly goatee, shortstop on one of Harvard's campus baseball teams, a chocoholic—and a physics major, the kind they would draft to be a hyperdrive pilot if it came to war.

"Humans have died before, and we have not sought vengeance," said Keith. Rhombus had been right. Let it go, he'd said. Let it all go. Keith felt it leaving him, the unpleasant thing he'd carried around for eighteen years. He looked at the two women. "For the sake of those who have died—and for all those who *would* die in a war—we have to put out the fire before it's too late."

Keith reboarded his travel pod, left Grand Central, and headed back toward the shortcut.

He had spent hours arguing with Commissioner Amundsen and Premier Kenyatta. But he wouldn't give up. *This* was the windmill he'd been looking for. This was the battle worth fighting—the battle for peace.

An impossible dream?

He thought of his great-great-grandfather's wonder-filled life. Cars and airplanes, lasers and moon landings.

And his own wonder-filled life.

And all the wonders yet to come.

Nothing was impossible—not even peace. Any sufficiently advanced technology is indistinguishable from magic.

*Sufficiently advanced.* Races *did* grow up, did enter a state of maturity. He was ready for that. At last, he was ready.

Others must be, too.

Borman, Lovell, and Anders had cupped the Earth in their hands. Just a quarter of a century later, that same world had begun disarming itself. Einstein hadn't lived to see it, but his impossible dream of putting his nuclear genie back in the bottle *had* come to pass.

And now humans and Waldahudin had both cupped the galaxy in their hands. A galaxy that Keith, and surely others, would live to see rotate around its axis time and again.

There would be peace between the races. He would make sure of that. After all, what better job was there for a middle child with billions of years to spend?

Keith's travel pod touched the shortcut, the purple halo passed over the spherical hull, and he emerged back near the green star.

*Starplex* was up ahead, a giant silver-and-copper diamond against the starry backdrop. Keith could see that docking bay seven's space door was open, and the bronze wedge of the *Rum Runner* was in the process of landing— meaning Jag and Longbottle must be returning with news of their search for the darmat baby. Heart pounding, Keith activated his pod's preprogrammed docking sequence.

Keith hurried to the bridge. Although he'd only been gone a short time, he felt a need to hug Rissa, who happened to be there using her console even though it was delta shift. He held her tight for several seconds, feeling the warmth of her. Wineglass politely rolled away from the director's workstation in case Keith wished to use it, but Keith motioned for the Ib to return to it, and Keith took a chair in the seating gallery at the back of the room.

No sooner had he done so than the forward bridge door opened and Jag waddled in. "The baby is trapped," he barked as he made his way over to the physics station, which was currently unoccupied. "It's stuck in close orbit around a star that emerged from the same shortcut the baby did."

"Did you call out to by radio?" asked Rissa. "Any response?"

"None," said Jag, "but the star is a real noisemaker. Our message might have been lost going in, or the reply might have been lost coming out."

"It would be like trying to hear a whisper during a hurricane," said Keith, shaking his head. "All but impossible."

"Especially," said Longbottle, popping up in the starboard pool on the bridge, "if the darmat is dead."

Keith looked at the dolphin's face, then nodded. "That's a good point. How do we tell if something like that is still alive?"

Rissa frowned. "None of us would survive five seconds

close to a star without a lot of shielding or heavy-duty force screens. The baby is naked."

"It's worse than that," said Jag. "The thing is *black*. Although the luster-quark matter is transparent to electromagnetic radiation, the regular-matter dust that permeates it is not reflecting any appreciable amount of the star's light and heat. The child may be cooking itself."

"So what do we do?" asked Keith.

"First," said Jag, "we should get it into the shade—build a reflective foil parasol that could be jockeyed in between the darmat and the star."

"Can our nanotech lab do that here?" asked Keith. "Ordinarily, I'd have New Beijing build such a thing and shunt it through the Tau Ceti shortcut to us, but I saw the mess they were in when I popped back for my meeting."

There was a young Native American sitting at InOps. "I'd have to check with Lianne to be sure," he said, "but I suspect we can pull it off. It won't be easy, though. The parasol will have to be over a hundred thousand klicks wide. Even at just one molecule of thickness, that's still a lot of material."

"Get to work on it," said Keith. "How long?"

"Six hours if we're lucky," said the man. "Twelve if we're not."

"But even if we shield the baby, then what?" asked Rissa. "It's still trapped."

Keith looked at Jag. "Could we use the parasol as a solar sail, and let the solar wind blow it away from the star?"

Jag snorted. "Ten to the thirty-seventh kilos? Not a chance."

"Okay, okay—what about this?" said Keith. "What if we protect the baby with some sort of force shield, and then detonate the star, so that it goes nova, and—"

Jag was barking in a staccato pattern—Waldahud laughter. "Your imagination is unbridled, Lansing. Oh, there has been some theoretical work on controlled nova reactions—I've been exploring that area a bit myself—but there's no shield we could build that would protect the baby from a star going nova only forty million kilometers away."

Keith was not to be deterred. "Okay, try this: Suppose we force the new star back through the shortcut. When it passes through the shortcut, its gravitational pull will disappear, and the baby goes free."

"The star is moving *away* from the shortcut, not toward it," said Jag. "We cannot move the shortcut at all, and if we had the power to turn a star around, we would also have the power to skim a Jupiter-sized object out of a close orbit around the star. But we don't." Jag looked around the room. "Any more bright ideas?"

"Yes," said Keith, after a moment. He looked directly at Jag. "Yes, indeed!"

When Keith had finished talking, Jag's mouth hung open for a few moments, showing the two curving blue-white translucent dental plates within. Finally, he barked in a subdued fashion. "I—I know I said such things were possible, but it has never been tried on anything approaching this scale."

Keith nodded. "Understood. But unless you have a better suggestion—"

"Well," said Jag's Brooklynite voice, "we could leave the darmat baby in orbit around the star. Assuming it is still alive, once we put the parasol sun-shield in place, it could, in theory, live out the rest of its natural life—however long *that* is—in close orbit around that star. But if your plan does not work, the darmat child will be killed." Jag's voice became quieter. "I know, Lansing, that I am the one always looking for glory—and, since my role in what you propose is pivotal, I have no doubt that considerable glory would accrue to me were we able to pull this off. But it really is not our decision to make. Ordinarily, I'd say ask the—the *patient*—for permission before attempting something as risky as this, but that is not possible in this case, because of the radio noise. And so I suggest we do what both your race and mine would do in such circumstances: we should ask the next of kin."

Keith thought about that, then began to nod slowly. "You're right, of course. I keep seeing the macro-issue, that if we pull this off, it'll be great for our relationships with the darmats. Damn, sometimes I'm pretty pigheaded."

"That is all right," said Jag lightly, choosing not to take offense at Keith's unfortunate choice of words. "Rumor has it that you are going to have a very long time to acquire more wisdom."

Keith spoke into the mike. "*Starplex* to Cat's Eye. *Starplex* to Cat's Eye."

The incongruous French accent; Keith half expected the thing to say *bonjour.* "Hello, *Starplex.* It is wrong to ask, but . . ."

Keith smiled. "Yes, we have news of your child. We have located it. But it is in close orbit around a blue star. It is unable to get away under its own power."

"Bad," said Cat's Eye. "Bad."

Keith nodded. "But we have a plan that may—I repeat, may—allow us to rescue the child."

"Good," said Cat's eye.

"The plan involves much risk."

"Quantify."

Keith looked at Jag, who lifted all four shoulders. "I can't," said the human. "We've never done anything like this on this scale before. Indeed, I only recently learned that it was theoretically possible. It may work, or it may not—and I have no way of knowing the likelihood of either outcome."

"Better idea available?"

"No. No, in fact, this is our *only* idea."

"Describe plan."

Keith did so, at least as much as the limited vocabulary they had established allowed.

"Difficult," said Cat's Eye.

"Yes."

There was a long period of silence on the frequency used by Cat's Eye, but lots of traffic on the other channels—the darmat community discussing its options.

At last, Cat's Eye spoke again. "Try, but . . . but . . .

two hundred and eighteen minus one is much less than two hundred and seventeen."

Keith swallowed. "I know."

The *PDQ* (containing the cetacean physicist Melondent) and the *Rum Runner* (with Jag and Longbottle aboard) headed through the shortcut to the sector containing the darmat baby. Working in tandem, the two ships deployed the molecule-thick parasol. Reaction motors were mounted on the parasol's frame, firing away from the blue star to keep the solar wind from blowing it away. Once the baby was in the shade, its nearside surface temperature began to drop rapidly.

Next, 112 hastily constructed buoys, each consisting of a hollowed-out watson casing with special equipment mounted inside, were popped through the shortcut from *Starplex*. The two probeships used their tractor beams to array them in interlocking orbits around the baby.

On one of his tall, thin monitor screens aboard the *Rum Runner,* Jag displayed a hyperspatial map showing the steep local gravity well with the star at the bottom. The sides of the well were almost perpendicular this close to the star; they only began to flare out just before the orbiting darmat was encountered. The baby made a second, smaller well of its own.

Once the buoys were in place, the *PDQ* headed off, moving past the shortcut without going through it, and continuing on for half a day. Finally, they were all lined up in a neat row. At one end was the *Rum Runner*. Next to it was the darmat baby. Forty million kilometers beyond the baby was the fiery blue star. Three hundred million kilometers farther on was the shortcut, and a billion kilometers beyond that was the *PDQ*—Melondent was now a total of seventy-two light-minutes from the star, far enough away that her local space was now reasonably flat.

"Ready?" barked Jag to Longbottle, in the *Rum Runner*'s piloting tank.

"Ready," the dolphin barked back in Waldahudar.

Jag touched a control, and the lattice of buoys surrounding the darmat baby sprang to life. Each buoy contained an artificial-gravity generator, powered by solar energy stolen from the very star they were trying to fight. Slowly, in unison, the buoys increased their output, and just as slowly, a flattening pocket began to develop in one wall of the star's steep gravity well.

"Gently," said Jag, under his breath, watching his hyperspace map. "Gently."

The pocket continued to grow more and more flat. Great care had to be taken not to flatten out the darmat's own gravity well: if the effects of the baby's own mass were suppressed—which, after all, was what was holding it together—it would lose cohesion, and expand like a balloon.

The buoys' output continued to grow and the curvature of spacetime continued to diminish, until, until—

Flatness, like a plateau jutting from the side of the well. It was as if the darmat were in interstellar space, not spitting distance from a star.

"Isolation complete," said Jag. "Now let's get it out of there."

"Activating hyperdrives," said Longbottle.

The antigrav buoys made up points on a sphere around the baby, but now, as their individual hyperspace field generators came on, that whole sphere seemed to mirror over, as if it were a glob of mercury floating freely in space. In a matter of seconds, the glob shrank to nothingness and disappeared.

The buoys were preprogrammed to run the darmat baby away from the blue star as fast as possible. The *PDQ* was waiting near the point at which the darmat should emerge from hyperspace, far enough from the star that the hyperdrive field should collapse without difficulty.

The *Rum Runner* set out for the same location, traveling under thruster power. As they passed near the shortcut point, a radio message from Melondent came through, blueshifted because of the *Rum Runner*'s acceleration toward her ship.

"*PDQ* to Longbottle and Jag. Arrived has darmat baby; popped into normal space it did right in front of my eyes.

Hyperdrive field collapse uneventful was. But baby shows
still no signs of life, and responds does not to my hails."

Jag's fur moved pensively. No one had known for sure
whether the baby would survive unprotected during its brief
journey through hyperspace. Even if it had been alive
beforehand, that might have killed it. Maddeningly, there
was no way to tell.

The space-flattening technique *was* risky. Rather than use
it themselves so that Longbottle could engage the *Rum
Runner*'s hyperdrive, they flew out to their rendezvous with
the *PDQ* under thruster power. To fill the time, and to get his
mind off of the fate of the baby, Jag spoke with Longbottle,
who, to his credit, was piloting the ship in an absolutely
straight line.

"You dolphins," said Jag, "like the humans."

"Mostly," said Longbottle in high-pitched Waldahudar.
He let the piloting drones disengage from his fins, and put
the ship on automatic.

"Why?" barked Jag sharply. "I have read Earth history.
They polluted the oceans you swam in, captured you and put
you in tanks, caught you in fishing nets."

"No one of them has done any of that to me," said
Longbottle.

"No, but—"

"It is the difference: we generalize do not. Specific bad
humans did specific bad things; those humans do we not
like. But the rest of humanity we judge one by one."

"But surely once they discovered you were intelligent,
they should have treated you better."

"Humans discovered intelligent we were before we discovered that they were."

"What?" said Jag. "But surely it was obvious. They had
built cities and roads, and—"

"Saw none of that."

"No, I suppose not. But they sailed in boats, they built
nets, they wore clothes."

"None of those were meaningful to us. We had of such
things no concept; nothing to compare them to. Mollusk
grows a shell; humans have clothes of fabric. The mollusk's

covering is stronger. Should judged we have the mollusk more intelligent? You say humans built things. We had no concept of building. We knew not they made the boats. We thought perhaps boats alive were, or had once been alive. Some tasted like driftwood, others ejected chemicals into the water, just as living things do. An achievement, to ride on the back of boats? We thought humans were like remoras to the shark."

"But—"

"They our intelligence did not see. They looked right at us and see it did not. And we looked at them and did not see theirs."

"But after you discovered their intelligence, and they yours, you must have realized they had been mistreating you."

"Yes, some in the past mistreated us. Humans *do* generalize, they blamed themselves. Learned have I since that concept of ancestral guilt—original sin—is to many of their beliefs central. There were cases in human court to determine compensation due to dolphins. This made to us no sense."

"But you get along with humans now, which is something my people are having trouble managing. How do you do it?"

Longbottle barked, "Accept their weaknesses, welcome their strengths."

Jag was silent.

Finally, the *Rum Runner* reached its destination, 1.3 billion kilometers from the star, and a billion kilometers past the shortcut. Jag and Melondent consulted by radio about the exact trajectory they wanted to launch the darmat child on, then the gravitational buoys were activated again, pushing and pulling the world-sized being, which, as planned, started to fall in toward the star, sliding back down the gravity well it had earlier been whisked out of. But this time, the shortcut point was in between the darmat and the star; this time, if all went well, the child would touch the shortcut, its approach to it speeded somewhat by the attraction of the star's gravity beyond.

Even at full thrusters, it took more than a day for the buoys to bring the darmat back in to the vicinity of the shortcut. Melondent popped a watson through to *Starplex,* warning them that, if all went well, the baby was about to reemerge on their side.

When they did get close to the shortcut, the buoys fought to slow down the baby's speed so that it would pass slowly through the portal. The whole rescue effort would be for naught if the darmat ended up whipping in toward the green star near *Starplex.* Once it had been braked to a reasonable speed, they adjusted the baby's trajectory so that it would pass through the tachyon sphere on the precise course required.

First to pass through the shortcut where some of the gravity buoys, then, at last, the baby itself touched it. The point began to swell, widening, enveloping the darmat, lips of purple lightning surrounding, then engulfing, the giant black sphere. Jag wondered what was going through the darmat's mind during the passage, assuming it was still alive.

And if it was alive, and did at some point regain whatever passed for consciousness, then, Jag wondered, what if it panicked? What if it was unable to make sense out of being partly in one sector of space and partly in another? It might grind its own passage to a halt. If the beast were to expire there, halfway through the shortcut, there might be no way to dislodge it. The shortcut opening formed a tight seal around the passing body, so no coordination of the use of gravity generators on both sides would be possible. And that would mean that the *Rum Runner* and the *PDQ* might be trapped forever here, out on the edge of the Perseus arm, tens of thousands of light-years from any of the home-worlds.

The darmat was deforming a bit as it moved through the opening, the shortcut's periphery clamping down on it. Such clamping was normal, and the effect on rigid spaceships was negligible, but the darmat was mostly gas—exotic, luster-quark gas to be sure, but still gas. Jag feared the baby would be cleaved in two—similar to the normal birthing process, but possibly fatal when done unexpectedly. But it seemed the creature's core was sufficiently solid to prevent the shortcut from pinching all the way through.

At last, the darmat completed its passage. The shortcut collapsed down to its normal dimensionless existence. Jag wanted Longbottle to immediately dive through the shortcut so that they could see the result of all their efforts. But they, and Melondent aboard the *PDQ,* had to wait for hours to be sure the darmat had moved far enough from the shortcut so that a collision—or just tidal stress from its enormous gravity—wouldn't destroy their ships when they popped through to the other side.

At last, after a probe had indicated it was safe to go through, Longbottle programmed the computer to take them home. The *Rum Runner* moved forward. The shortcut swelled, and they passed through to the other side.

It took Jag a few moments to take in all that he was seeing. The baby was there, all right. And so was *Starplex.* But *Starplex* was surrounded on all sides by darmats, and the ship itself looked dead, all the lights in its windows dark.

# XXIV

The shortcut point began to expand, starting as a violet pinprick of Soderstrom radiation, and growing as an ever-expanding purple ring. First to pop through was one of *Starplex*'s hastily constructed antigravity buoys, and then another and another. They zoomed across the sky like bullets. They'd been tugging the darmat baby, but since they came through the portal before it did, they were severed from its mass and so shot ahead. Soon, though, the bulk of the darmat baby began its passage, bulging out through the ring of purple in the sky.

On *Starplex*'s bridge Thorald Magnor let loose a great cheer, and it was echoed by hundreds of others from all over the ship, as everyone watched the spectacle either through a window or on a viewscreen.

Cat's Eye and a dozen other adult darmats moved closer to the shortcut, calling out to the baby. Over the bridge speakers, PHANTOM played a translation of what Cat's

Eye was saying, but many of the words were missing; the leader of the darmats was not limiting his vocabulary to the few hundred words Rissa and Hek had learned. "Come forward . . . forward . . . toward . . . you are . . . we . . . come . . . hurry . . . do not . . . forward . . . forward . . . "

Rhombus was using the deck-one array to monitor the emerging baby, but so far it hadn't transmitted a word of its own, at least not on any frequency even close to the twenty-one-centimeter band.

Lianne Karendaughter was shaking her head. "It's not moving at all under its own volition," she said. "It must be dead."

Keith ground his teeth together. If it was dead, all this was for nothing— "It's possible," he said, at last, trying as much to convince himself as Lianne, "that a single darmat can't move on its own. They may need to play off each other's gravity and repulsion. The baby may not yet be far enough out for that."

"Forward," said Cat's Eye. "Forward . . . come . . . you . . . forward."

Keith had never heard of anyone trying so slow a passage through a shortcut before—there was an unspoken sense that one should hurry through, that to tarry would be tempting fate, lest the magic of the thing fail.

At last the baby completed its passage. The shortcut collapsed, although, moments later, it opened slightly several times as additional antigrav buoys popped through from the other side.

The darmat child was moving away from the shortcut, but only under momentum. It had not yet—

"Where . . . where . . . "

Still a French-accented voice, but, in a stroke of rare creativity, PHANTOM had chosen a child's tones for this translation.

"Home . . . back . . . "

Thor let loose another thunderous cheer. "It's alive!"

Keith found his eyes misting over. Lianne was openly crying.

"It's alive!" Thor shouted again.

The darmat baby did, finally, begin to move, heading toward Cat's Eye and the others.

The speakers changed back to the voice PHANTOM had assigned to Cat's Eye. "Cat's Eye to *Starplex*," it said.

Keith keyed his mike. "*Starplex* responding," he said.

Cat's Eye was quiet longer than the round-trip signal time would have required, as if he was searching for a way to express what he wanted to say using the limited vocabulary available. Finally, simply, he said, "We are friends."

Keith felt himself grinning from ear to ear. "Yes," he said. "We are friends."

"The child's vision is damaged," said Cat's Eye. "It will . . . become equal to one again, but time is required. Time, and absence of light. Green star is bright; not here when child left."

Keith nodded. "We can build another shield, to protect the baby from the green star's light."

"More," said Cat's Eye. "You."

Keith was momentarily puzzled. "Oh—of course. Lianne, kill all our running lights, and, after warning people, douse the lights in all rooms with windows. If people want to put their lights back on, tell them to draw the shades first."

Lianne's beautiful face was split by a wide smile. "Doing so."

*Starplex* went dark, and the darmat community moved toward the great ship and their newly returned child.

The *Rum Runner* popped through the shortcut, followed moments later by the *PDQ*. Radio communication soon assured their crews that *Starplex* was all right, and the ships curved in toward the docking bays. As soon as the *Rum Runner* was safely aboard, Jag headed for the bridge.

Keith was still talking to Cat's Eye when Jag entered the bridge. The director turned to the Waldahud. "Thank you, Jag. Thank you very much."

Jag nodded his head, accepting the comment.

The voice of Cat's Eye came over the speakers. "We to you an incorrect," he said.

A wrong, thought Keith. They did us wrong.

"You into point that is not a point had to move with high speed."

"Oh, it wasn't so bad," said Keith, ever the diplomat, into the mike. "Because of that we got to see our group of hundreds of millions of stars."

"We call such a group a"—PHANTOM translated the new signal—"*galaxy.*"

"You have a word for galaxy?" said Keith, surprised.

"Correct. Many stars, isolated."

"Right," said Keith. "Well, the shortcut put us six billion light-years from here. That meant we were seeing our galaxy as it looked six billion years ago."

"Understand looking back."

"You do?"

"Do."

Keith was impressed. "Well, it was fascinating. Six billion years ago, the Milky Way didn't have its current shape. Um, I guess you don't know this, but it's currently shaped like a spiral." A light flashed on Keith's console, PHANTOM notifying him that he'd just used a word for which there was as yet no darmat equivalent in the translation database. Keith nodded at PHANTOM's cameras. "A spiral," he said into the mike, "is . . . is . . . " He sought a metaphor that would be meaningful; terms such as "pinwheels" would convey no information to the darmat. "A spiral is . . ."

PHANTOM provided a definition on one of Keith's monitor screens. He read it into the mike. "A spiral is the path made by an object rotating around a central point while also receding from that point at a constant speed."

"Understand spiral."

"Well, the Milky Way is a spiral, with four major"—he wanted to say "arms," but again that was a useless word—"parts."

"Know this."

"You do?"

"Made."

Keith looked at Jag, who moved his lower shoulders up and down in a shrug. What did the darmat mean? That he'd been made to learn this fact in some dark-matter equivalent of grammar school?

"Made?" repeated Keith.

"Once plain, now . . . now . . . no word," said the darmat.

Lianne spoke up. "Now *pretty*," she said. "That's the word he's looking for, I bet."

"To look at it, one plus one greater than two?" asked Keith into the mike.

"Greater than. More than sum of its parts. Spiral is . . ."

"Is *pretty*," said Keith. "More than the sum of its parts, visually."

"Yes," said Cat's Eye. "Pretty. Spiral. Pretty."

Keith nodded. There was no doubt that spiral galaxies were more interesting to look at than elliptical ones. Keith was pleased that humans and darmats apparently shared some notion of aesthetics, too. Not too surprising, though, given that many artistic principles were based on mathematics.

"Yes," said Keith. "Spirals are very pretty."

"That why we make them," said the synthesized voice from the speaker.

Keith felt his heart jump, and he saw Jag do a reflexive splaying of all sixteen of his fingers, the Waldahud equivalent of a double take.

"You make them?" said Keith.

"Affirm. Move stars—small tugs, takes long time. Move stars into new patterns, work to hold them there."

"You turned our galaxy into a spiral?"

"Who else?"

Who else indeed . . .

"That's incredible," said Keith softly.

Jag was rising from his chair. "No, that makes sense," the Waldahud said. "By all the gods, that makes sense. I said there was no good theory for explaining why galaxies acquired or maintained spiral shapes. Being deliberately held in place by conscious dark matter—it's mind-boggling, but it *does* make sense."

Keith keyed off the mike. "But—but what about all the other galaxies? You said three quarters of all galaxies are spirals."

Jag did a four-armed Waldahud shrug. "Ask it."

"Did you make many galaxies into spirals?"

"Not us. Others."

"I mean, did others of your kind make many galaxies into spirals?"

"Yes."

"But why?"

"Have to look at them. Make pretty. Make—make—a thing for expressions not mathematic."

"Art," said Keith.

"Art, yes," said Cat's Eye.

Having left his chair, Jag now dropped down to all fours, the first time Keith had ever seen him do that. "Gods," he barked, his voice subdued. "Gods."

"Well, it certainly fills that theoretical hole you were talking about," said Keith. "It even explains that bit you mentioned about ancient galaxies seeming to rotate faster than theory suggests they should. They were being *made* to rotate, in order to spin out spiral arms."

"No, no, no," barked Jag. "No, don't you understand? Don't you see? It's not just an esoteric point of galaxy formation that's been explained. We owe them everything— everything!" The Waldahud took hold of one of the metal legs supporting Keith's console and hauled himself back onto two feet again. "I told you earlier: Stable genetic molecules would have an almost impossible time existing in a densely packed mass of stars, because of the radiation levels. It's *only* because our homeworlds exist far from the core, out in the spiral arms, that life was able to arise on them at all. We exist—all the life made out of what we arrogantly refer to as 'regular matter'—all of it exists simply because the dark-matter creatures were playing with stars, swirling them into pretty patterns."

Thor had turned around to face Jag. "But—but the

biggest galaxies in the universe are ellipticals, not spirals."

Jag lifted his upper shoulders. "True. But maybe shaping them is too much work, or too time-consuming. Even with faster-than-light communications—with 'radio-two'—it would still take tens of thousands of years for signals to pass from one side of a truly giant elliptical to the other. Maybe that's too much for a group effort. But for mid-sized galaxies like ours and Andromeda—well, every artist has a preferred scale, no? A favorite canvas size, or an affinity for either short stories or novels. Mid-sized galaxies are the medium . . . and . . . and *we* are the message."

Thor was nodding. "Jesus, he's right." He looked at Keith. "Remember what Cat's Eye said when you asked it why it tried to kill us? 'Make you. Not make you.' My father used to say that, too, when he was angry: 'I brought you into this world, boy, and I can take you out of it.' They *know*—the darmats know that their activity is what has made our kind of life possible."

Jag was losing his balance again. He finally gave up, and dropped back to his four hind legs, making him look like a chubby centaur. "Talk about an ego blow," he said. "This one is the biggest of them all. Early on, each of the Commonwealth races had thought its homeworld was the center of the universe. But, of course, they weren't. Then we reasoned that dark matter must exist—and, in a way, that was even more humbling. It meant that not only were we *not* the center of the universe, we're not even made out of what most of the universe is made from! We are like the scum on a pond's surface daring to think that we are more important than all the vast bulk of water that makes up the pond.

"And now this!" His fur was dancing. "Remember what Cat's Eye said when you asked it how long ago dark-matter life had first arisen? 'Since the beginning of all the stars combined,' he said. 'Since the beginning of the universe.'"

Keith nodded.

"He said they *had* to exist that far back—had to!" Jag's fur was rippling. "I thought it was just a philosophical position, but he's right, of course—life had to exist from the beginning of this universe, or as near to the beginning as physically possible."

Keith stared at Jag. "I don't understand."

"What arrogant fools we are!" said Jag. "Don't you see? To this day, despite all the humbling lessons the universe has already taught us, we still try to retain a central role in creation. We devise theories of cosmology that say the universe was destined to give rise to us, that it had to evolve life like us. Humans call it the anthropic principle, my people called it the *aj-Waldahudigralt* principle, but it's all the same thing: the desperate, deep-rooted need to believe that we are significant, that we're important.

"We talk in quantum physics about Schrödinger's cat or Teg's *kestoor*—the idea that everything is just potentialities, just wavefronts, unresolved, until one of us all-important qualified observers lumbers by, has a peek, and, by the process of looking, causes the wavefront to collapse. We actually allowed ourselves to believe that that is how the universe worked—even though we know full well that the universe is many billions of years old, and not one of our races is more than a million.

"Yes," barked Jag, "quantum physics demands qualified observers. Yes, intelligence is necessary to determine which possibility becomes reality. But in our arrogance we thought that the universe could work for fifteen billion years without us, and yet that it somehow was geared to give rise to us. Such hubris! The intelligent observers are not us—tiny beings, isolated on a handful of worlds in all the vastness of space. The intelligent observers are the dark-matter creatures. They have been spinning galaxies into spirals for billions upon billions of years. It is their intellect, their observations, their sentience that drives the universe, that gives quantum potentialities concrete reality. We are *nothing*— nothing!—but a recent, localized phenomenon—a spot of mold on a universe that doesn't need us, or care that we exist. Cat's Eye was absolutely right when he said we were insignificant. This is *their* universe—the darmats' universe. They made it, and they made us, too!"

# XXV

Keith sat in his office on deck fourteen, looking over the latest news from Tau Ceti. Reports were sketchy, but on Rehbollo, forces loyal to Queen Trath had put down the insurrection against her, and twenty-seven conspirators had been summarily executed in the traditional method of being drowned in boiling mud.

Keith set down the datapad. The report strained credulity— it was the first he'd heard of any political unrest on Rehbollo. Still, maybe it was true—although more likely it was just a government desperately trying to distance itself from a disastrous initiative.

A chime sounded, and PHANTOM's voice said, "Jag Kandaro em-Pelsh is here."

Keith exhaled. "Let him in."

Jag entered and found a polychair. His left eyes were on Keith, but the right pair were scanning the room in the instinctive fight-or-flight pattern. "I suppose at this juncture," he said, "I must fill out some of those forms you humans are so fond of."

"What forms?" said Keith.

"Forms for resigning my position aboard *Starplex,* of course. I can no longer serve here."

Keith rose to his feet, and permitted himself a stretch.

It had to begin somewhere—maturity, the stage after the midlife crisis, peace. It had to begin somewhere.

"Children play with toy soldiers," said Keith, looking now at Jag. "Child races play with real ones. Maybe it's time all of us grew up a bit."

The Waldahud was quiet for a long moment. "Maybe."

"We all have loyalties hardwired into our genes," said Keith. "I won't push for your resignation."

"Your comments assume that I am guilty of something. I reject that. But were it true, you still misunderstand. Perhaps . . . perhaps your people will always misunderstand mine." Jag paused. "And the converse, too, of course." Another pause. "No, it is time for me to return to Rehbollo."

"There's a lot of work left to be done here," said Keith.

"Doubtless so. But the job I set for myself has been completed."

"Oh," said Keith, understanding dawning. "You mean you've accrued sufficient glory to win Pelsh."

"Exactly. The discoveries I have been a part of involving the darmats will make me the most celebrated scientist on Rehbollo." A pause. "Pelsh will make her decision soon. I can tarry here no longer."

Keith thought for a moment. "No female Waldahud has ever worked aboard *Starplex.* When my term of office ends, it will be an Ib's turn to be director; I suspect Wineglass will get the job. But after the Ib, the position will then fall to a Waldahud—and I know the Waldahudin will demand a female leader. What if—what if you and Pelsh came to *Starplex* together? From what I've heard, she'd be a natural for the director's job."

Jag's fur rippled in surprise. "We can't do that. We will both still be part of a larger grouping. She will retain her entourage until she dies."

Keith's eyes widened a bit. "You mean the males that don't succeed with her don't get to try their luck elsewhere?"

"Of course not. We will remain a family. We have all been pledged to Pelsh since childhood."

"Perhaps you could all come to serve aboard *Starplex*—all six of you."

Jag moved his lower shoulders. "*Starplex* is for the best and brightest. I would never speak to a Waldahud in disparaging terms about other members of my lady's entourage, but I will tell you the truth. It has never a contest between me and four others. Never. It was between me and one individual. That was clear from the beginning. The others . . . lack distinction."

"But I thought Pelsh was related to the royal family. Forgive me, but why would she have less than the most qualified suitors?"

"An entourage must continue to function even after a mate is chosen. A skillfully selected entourage will contain several members who will be content with lesser stations. Indeed, an entourage composed entirely of what you humans call alpha males would be doomed."

Keith thought about this. "Well, if the only way we can get you is to take your whole family, then I will see to it that we do so."

"I—I do not think you will follow through on that."

Keith blinked. "I'm a man of my word."

"The real contest for Pelsh was between me and one other. That other, of course, has a name." Jag's four eyes locked on Keith's two. "That name is Gawst Dalayo em-Pelsh."

"Gawst!" said Keith. "Who led the attack on *Starplex*?"

"Yes. He escaped the darmats and is now back on Rehbollo."

Keith was still for ten seconds, then began to nod. "You had to help him, didn't you?"

"I have admitted nothing," said Jag.

"If you didn't help him, all the glory in bringing *Starplex* home to Rehbollo would have been his; he would have been chosen by Pelsh. By assisting him, you assured that the glory would be shared."

"There are two hundred and sixty Waldahudin aboard *Starplex*," said Jag.

The sentence floated between them for several moments. Keith nodded, understanding. "So if you hadn't helped him, doubtless he would have found someone else who would have," said Keith.

"Again," said Jag, "I admit nothing." He was quiet for a time. "Of course, Queen Trath's government may bring criminal charges against Gawst. He soon may not have his liberty—or even his life."

"My offer still stands," said Keith.

Jag bowed his head. "I—we—shall consider it." And then Jag did something Keith had never seen any Waldahud do before. He added the words, "Thank you."

It was evening; the corridor lighting was dimmed. As he always did just prior to dinner, Keith dropped by the bridge, and had a word with the gamma-shift director, a Waldahud named Stelt. Everything was running smoothly, Stelt said. Not a surprise; Keith would have been called at once had something been amiss. Keith wished everyone a pleasant night and left the bridge, heading toward the central shaft.

Lianne Karendaughter was there, sitting on a bench in the widened part of the corridor just before the elevators. She looked lithe and sexy in a skintight black jumpsuit.

Surely a coincidence, thought Keith. Surely she didn't know his routine—know that he passed this way every evening at this time. She must be waiting for somebody else.

Lianne had her hair down; Keith had never realized that it went halfway down her back. "Hello, Keith," she said, smiling warmly.

"Hello, Lianne. Did—did you have a good day?"

"Oh, yes. I mean, you saw alpha shift today—a breeze. And I got to do some swimming and fencing during beta shift. How about you?"

"Fine. Just fine."

"That's good," said Lianne. She paused for a moment, and looked down at the rubberized flooring. When she lifted her head again, she didn't quite meet Keith's eyes. "I, ah, understand Rissa is away today."

"That's right. She's taken a pod back to Grand Central. I

think she's trying to find a way not to have to accept a medal, or have a parade in her honor."

Lianne nodded. "So I was thinking," she said, after a moment, "that perhaps you'd be all alone for dinner."

Keith felt his pulse quickening. "I—I suppose I am," he said.

Lianne smiled at him. She had perfect white teeth, perfect alabaster skin, and the most beautiful dark, haunting, almond-shaped eyes. "I wondered if you'd like to join me. I've got a wok in my apartment; I could make that stir-fry I promised you."

Keith looked at . . . at the *girl,* he thought. Twenty-seven. Two decades younger than himself. He felt a slight shifting in his shorts. It was probably just an innocent invitation. She felt sorry for the old guy, or maybe was trying to ingratiate herself with the boss. Just some stir-fry, maybe some wine, maybe . . .

"You know, Lianne," said Keith, "you are a very beautiful woman." He held up a hand. "I know, I'm not supposed to say things like that, but we're both off duty. You're a very beautiful woman." She lowered her eyes. He paused and chewed on his bottom lip. And a thought welled up in his brain.

Don't hurt Rissa.

You'll only hurt yourself.

"But," he said at last, "I think it's better if I just admire you from afar."

She met his eyes for a moment, then dropped hers again. "Rissa is a very lucky woman," Lianne said.

"No," said Keith, "I'm a very lucky man. See you tomorrow, Lianne."

She nodded. "Good night, Keith."

He went home, made himself a sandwich, read a few chapters in an old Robertson Davies novel, then went to bed early.

And slept like a log, absolutely at peace with himself.

Alpha shift the next day started uneventfully. Rhombus had arrived precisely on time, of course; Thor came in, put his feet up on the helm console, and started dictating instructions into the navigational computer; Lianne was hard at work briefing little holographic heads of her engineers on the day's proposed work. In the back row, Keith was talking quietly to Rissa, who had just returned from Grand Central.

But then the starscape split, and Jag came in, moving with more of a run than a waddle.

"I've got it!" he said—although from the excited waving of his fur, perhaps "Eureka!" would have been a more appropriate translation.

Keith and Rissa turned to look at Jag. He didn't go to his workstation; instead, he moved to the front of the room, standing about two meters ahead of Thor's console.

"What have you got?" asked Keith, resisting the potential straight line.

"The answer!" barked Jag excitedly. "The answer!" He caught his breath. "Bear with me for a moment; this will take some explaining. But I'll tell you one thing up front—we *do* matter! We do make a difference. Gods of the mountains, rivers, valleys, and plains—we make *all* the difference!" His eyes diverged, one falling on Lianne, a second on Rhombus, a third on Rissa, and the fourth on Thor and Keith, who were lined up one behind the other from Jag's point of view.

"We know now that time travel from the future into the past is possible," he said. "We've seen it happen with the fourth-generation stars, and with the time capsule Hek and Azmi built. But consider the implications of that. Suppose that at noon tomorrow, I used a time machine to send myself back in time to today. What would we have then?"

Keith said, "Well, there'd be two of you, right? The Jag from today, and the Jag from tomorrow."

"That's right. Now think about that: if you have two of me, you've doubled the mass. I mass one hundred and twenty-three kilograms, but if there were two of me here, then there'd be two hundred and forty-six kilos of Jag-mass aboard this ship."

"But I thought that was impossible," said Rissa, "because of the law of conservation of mass and energy. Where did the extra hundred and twenty-three kilos come from?"

Jag looked triumphant. "From the future! Don't you

see? Time travel is the only conceivable way to overcome
that law. It's the only way to increase the total mass in
the system." His fur continued to dance. "And what about
the stars from the future? As each arrives, the mass of the
present-day universe is increased. After all, even fourth-
generation stars are made up of preexisting recycled sub-
atomic particles. Pushing them back in time means that
those particles have essentially been duplicated, doubling
their total mass."

"An interesting side effect no doubt," said Rhombus. "But it
still doesn't explain why the stars are being sent back."

"Oh, yes it does. The doubling of mass is not just a side
effect—not at all! Rather, it's the *whole point* of the
operation."

"Operation?" said Keith.

"Yes! The operation to save the universe! These stars are
being pushed back in time to increase the mass of the entire
universe."

Keith felt his jaw dropping. "Good God."

All four of the Waldahud's eyes converged on Keith.
"Exactly!" barked Jag. "We've known for over a century that
the visible matter in the universe accounts for less than ten
percent of the total that must be present. The rest is neutrinos
and dark matter, like our giant friends outside the ship. We now
know *what* all the matter in the universe is, but we don't know
*how much* there is in total. And the fate of the universe
depends on how much mass it has, on whether the total is
above, below, or precisely at the so-called critical density."

"Critical density?" asked Rissa.

"That's right. The universe is expanding—and has been
ever since the big bang. But will that expansion go on forever?
That depends on gravity. And how much gravity there is, of
course, depends on how much mass there is. If there isn't
enough—if the mass of the universe is less than the critical
density—gravity will never overpower the original explosion,
and the universe will continue to expand forever, all the matter
in it spreading out farther and farther. Everything will grow
cold and empty, with light-years separating individual atoms."

Rissa shuddered.

"And if the opposite is true—if the mass of the universe exceeds the critical density—then gravity *will* overcome the force of the big bang, slowing down and eventually reversing the universe's expansion. Everything will fall in on itself, collapsing in a big crunch into a single block of matter. If conditions are right, that block might eventually expand again in another big bang, creating a new, and probably radically different, universe—but everything that had been part of this universe would be destroyed."

"That hardly sounds much better," said Rissa.

"True," said Jag. "But if—if!—the universe has *precisely* the critical density of matter then, and only then, can our universe go on in a viable state forever. The expansion caused by the big bang will be slowed to a virtual halt by gravitation—the expansion will asymptotically approach a zero rate. The universe will not die a cold, empty death, and it will not collapse back in on itself. Instead, it will exist in a stable configuration for trillions upon trillions upon trillions of years. For all practical purposes, this universe will be immortal."

"And which is it?" asked Rissa. "Is the universe above or below the critical density?"

"Our best current estimates are that the mass in the entire universe of all that we can see, plus the mass of all we cannot, including all dark mater, falls five percent short of the critical density."

"Meaning the universe will expand forever, right?" said Lianne.

"Exactly. Everything will continue to fling away from everything else. The cosmos will die with all of creation ending up the merest fraction of a degree above absolute zero."

Rissa shook her head.

"But it doesn't have to happen," said Jag. "Not if they can pull it off."

"Not if who can pull it off?" asked Keith.

"The beings in the future—the descendants of the Commonwealth races. You said it yourself, Lansing: you are going to become vastly old, live for billions of years. In other words, immortal. Well, truly immortal beings would eventually have to deal with the death of the universe; it's the one thing that could indeed end their lives."

"But what about entropy?" asked Lianne.

"Well, yes, the second law of thermodynamics does predict an eventual heat-death for any closed system. But the universe may not be entirely closed; there are, after all, good theoretical reasons to believe our universe is only one of an infinite number. It may be possible to pull in energy from another continuum, or to simply conserve energy here, producing minimal entropy, so that this continuum will be viable virtually forever. In any event, they would have untold trillions of years before that issue would have to be faced—trillions of years to come up with an answer."

"But—but—it's an inconceivable project," said Keith. "I mean, if we're currently five percent below the critical density, how many stars would have to be pumped back? Even one from every shortcut wouldn't be enough, would it?"

"No," said Jag. "Our best estimate is that there are four billion shortcuts in our galaxy. Let's assume that that's typical—that they've built one shortcut for every hundred stars not just in the Milky Way, but in every galaxy in the universe. Stars account for roughly ten percent of the mass of the universe; the other ninety percent is dark matter. So, if you pumped one average star through each shortcut, you'd increase the mass of the universe by one one-thousandth of its current total. To increase the mass by one-twentieth—which is five percent—you'd need to pump fifty stars through each shortcut."

"But—but surely if you have time travel, you don't need to save the universe," said Keith. "You could live for ten billion years, then time travel back to the beginning, live another ten billion, travel back again, and so on, forever."

"Oh, indeed—and who knows how many cycles of that our descendants might go through before they work up the nerve and the technology to undertake this project? The endless time-jumping method gives a pseudo-immortality— it's clearly inferior to actually making the universe last forever. Not only does it mean no building or other structure can have a lifespan longer than ten billion years, but it limits immortality to those beings who actually have time travel."

"I suppose," said Keith. "But what a project!"

"Indeed," said Jag. "And it might be even greater in scope than it first seems. Tell me: How old is this universe right now?"

"Fifteen billion years," Keith said. "Earth years, that is."

Jag moved his lower shoulders. "Actually, although that is the most commonly cited figure, no astrophysicist believes it. Fifteen is a compromise, halfway between the ages of the universe suggested by two different lines of reasoning. The universe is either as young as ten billion years, or as old as twenty. Since the mid-1990s, the accepted value of the Hubble constant—which measures the rate of expansion of the universe—has been about eighty-five kilometers per second per megaparsec. That means the universe is still flinging apart at a great rate from the original big bang—that gravity has done little to slow the expansion so far—and therefore it can't be much more than about ten billion years old.

"But spectral studies of extreme first-generation stars, especially those in globular clusters, suggest that such stars have been undergoing fusion for almost twice that length of time. We've long assumed that one calculation or the other must be wrong. But perhaps neither is. Perhaps what we're seeing now is merely the most recent phase of a multistage project. Perhaps I was premature in rejecting Magnor's suggestion earlier about pushing globular clusters through shortcuts. Perhaps such clusters, each containing tens of thousands of stars, have already been shoved back from the future. It's possible that originally this universe contained far, far less than ninety-five percent of the critical density of matter, and that the current phase of the project is just some fine-tuning."

"But—but surely the mass doubling is only temporary," said Lianne. "To go back to your original example, if you traveled back from tomorrow to today, there'd be two of you today—but tomorrow, one of them would presumably disappear back into the past."

"Perhaps so," said Jag. "But for the entire span between the departure point in the future and the arrival point in the present, you *have* doubled the mass. And if those two points were separated by ten billion years, then you've doubled the mass for a very long time indeed—long enough for its effects to put the brakes on the universe's expansion. If you calculate with great care, you don't need to permanently increase the mass of the universe. You only need to do it long enough for gravitational attraction to halt the rate of expansion of the original explosion. If you do it just right, even without a permanent increase in mass, you could end up with a universe in the far future that is indeed precisely balanced—a universe that will live forever."

Jag paused for breath. "It's the most massive engineering project ever undertaken," he said. "But it sure beats the alternative—which was to let the universe die." He beamed at the members of the bridge staff. "*We* did it. Regular-matter creatures—creatures with *hands*! In the end—correction, to *prevent* the end— the universe needed us!"

The ceremony, held in their favorite Waldahud restaurant, was short. The audience was much bigger than their original family-only wedding in Madrid; any sort of celebration was welcomed aboard *Starplex*.

Thorald Magnor had been promoted to acting director for the day so that he could perform the service. "Do you, Gilbert Keith," he said, "again take Clarissa Maria, to love, honor, and cherish, in sickness and in health, for richer or poorer?"

Keith turned to face his wife. He remembered the day twenty years ago, the day they had first gone through this ritual, a wonderful, happy day. It had been a good marriage—stimulating intellectually, emotionally, and physically. And she was, if anything, more beautiful, more challenging today than then. He looked into her large brown eyes, and said, "I do." Thor turned to face her, but before he could speak, Keith squeezed his wife's hand and added, loudly, for all to hear, "For as long as we both shall live."

Rissa smiled at him radiantly.

Hell, thought Keith, twenty years was just scratching the surface . . .

# EPILOGUE

Keith Lansing had been sleeping well for weeks now. He lay in bed, next to his beautiful wife, drifting off to sleep. So what if he and Rissa and Jag and Longbottle and Rhombus and all the other billions of Commonwealth citizens didn't yet amount to a hill of beans in this crazy universe? So what if they were a cosmic afterthought, an unexpected by-product of dark-matter art? Someday they *would* make a difference—they would make *all* the difference . . .

Keith woke with a start. He pulled back the little card covering his clock face; it was 0143. He sat up in bed and listened to the white noise PHANTOM was playing through the room's sound system.

Christ, he thought. Good Christ.

Pushing billions of stars from the future back in time would change the past—change it radically, change it chaotically. There's no way the time line would unfold the same way as it had originally—no way this past would end

up giving rise to the same future. You couldn't avoid a
paradox—unless . . . unless . . .

Unless you were going to come back in time yourself—
back to a time *before* the first matter from the future
appeared. Keith felt his heart racing. All the beings from the
far future must be here already, somewhere in the present.

He recalled the pictures he'd seen of that smooth ball of
metal—metal that had once been the boomerang sent from
Tau Ceti to the Tejat Posterior shortcut, metal altered by
fantastically advanced science.

The Slammers had indeed closed the door on the Commonwealth . . . closed the door on their own past. They'd made
it very clear that they wanted to—*needed to*—remain isolated
from the earlier versions of themselves.

Using that shortcut—and doubtless countless others—
were people from the future. And among those people
would be the version of himself that had signed the message
on the time capsule, the version who was apparently a leader
of the project to save the universe—a multibillion-year-old
Keith Lansing, a Keith Lansing who had become, quite
literally, the grand old man of physics. How he would love
to meet that other self . . .

Keith looked at Rissa in the dim light. She was still fast
asleep, but his movements in the bed had pulled the sheet
off her. He gingerly replaced it, then lay back against the
pillow, and slowly fell into unconsciousness, dreaming of a
glass man.

# ABOUT THE AUTHOR

Nebula Award winner Robert J. Sawyer is Canada's only native-born full-time SF writer. He lives in Thornhill, Ontario, with his wife Carolyn Clink, with whom he is co-editing the Canadian SF anthology *Tesseracts 6*. Rob's "On Writing" column appears in each issue of *On Spec*, Canada's principal SF magazine.

Orson Scott Card, reviewer for *The Magazine of Fantasy & Science Fiction,* chose Rob's first book, *Golden Fleece,* as the best SF novel of 1990. Rob has been a finalist for the Hugo Award and has also won two Aurora Awards (Canada's top honor in SF writing) and an Arthur Ellis Award from the Crime Writers of Canada. Four times in a row, he won the Homer Award for best novel of the year voted on by the 30,000 members of the Science Fiction and Fantasy Literature Forum on CompuServe. Rob's novels have also twice been finalists for the Japanese Seiun Award.

An avid stargazer, Rob has written for *Sky & Telescope* magazine and *'Scope,* the newsletter of the Toronto Centre of the Royal Astronomical Society of Canada. In 1980, one of his short stories was produced as a dramatic starshow by the Strasenburgh Planetarium in Rochester, New York.

To find out more about Rob's fiction, visit his World Wide Web home page at: http://www.greyware.com/authors/sawyer